All the characters in this book have no existence outside the imagination of the author, and have no relation whatsoever to anyone bearing the same name or names. They are not even distantly inspired by any individual known or unknown to the author, and all the incidents are pure invention.

First published in Great Britain 2010
Harlequin Mills & Boon Limited,
Eton House, 18-24 Paradise Road, Richmond, Surrey TW9 1SR

© Jennifer Ann Ryan 2010

ISBN: 978 0 263 87673 4

Harlequin Mills & Boon policy is to use papers that are natural, renewable and recyclable products and made from wood grown in sustainable forests. The logging and manufacturing process conform to the legal environmental regulations of the country of origin.

Printed and bound in Spain
by Litografia Rosés, S.A., Barcelona

WHAT'S A HOUSEKEEPER TO DO?

BY
JENNIE ADAMS

MILLS & BOON®

Australian author **Jennie Adams** grew up in a rambling farmhouse surrounded by books, and by people who loved reading them. She decided at a young age to be a writer, but it took many years and a lot of scenic detours before she sat down to pen her first romance novel. Jennie has worked in a number of careers and voluntary positions, including transcription typist and pre-school assistant. She is the proud mother of three fabulous adult children and makes her home in a small inland city in New South Wales. In her leisure time Jennie loves long, rambling walks, discovering new music, starting knitting projects that she rarely finishes, chatting with friends, trips to the movies, and new dining experiences.

Jennie loves to hear from her readers, and can be contacted via her website at www.jennieadams.net

For the girls in my bunker.
For cheeky lunch-time topics and midnight IMs.
For the Toby addiction (yes, you L), for the Rwoooarhhh!
(yes, you C). For talking me down on the phone (yes, you
V). For hugs in person and hugs long distance. For being
my cheer squad. For sharing the path with me with grace.
For understanding about the boots.

For my editor Joanne Grant, and my senior editor
Kim Young. I am blessed. Thank you.

For my precious ones, and for you.

CHAPTER ONE

'I REALISE it's a little unusual, conducting this kind of business in the middle of a lake.' Cameron Travers' mouth turned up with a hint of self-directed humour before he shrugged broad shoulders in the misty Adelaide morning air. 'When I started wondering about this scene idea, and I knew I'd need a second pair of hands to test it out, I decided to combine our interview with some research. I hope you don't mind too much.'

'It's a nice setting for a job interview, Mr Travers, even if it is unusual. I'm more than happy to oblige.' If the man needed to row a boat around a lake at dawn to research for his crime-thriller writing, then Lally Douglas could work with that. She offered what she hoped appeared to be a completely relaxed smile because, yes, she did have a little bout of nerves going on. After all, she'd never had a 'real' job-interview before, let alone with a millionaire property-developer and world-famous crime-thriller author!

Cameron's attractive mouth curved. 'I appreciate your willing attitude. I could really do with some help for a while with the basics of day to day life so I can focus my energy on the property development I'm undertaking here in Adelaide, and to crack the challenges I'm having with writing my current book.'

The words somehow let her in. His smile let her in further. How could a simple, wry grin all but stop a girl's breath? Lally searched for the answer in deep-green eyes fringed with curly black lashes, in a lean face that was all interesting angles and planes in the early-morning light. In the charming sense of welcome and acceptance that seemed to radiate from him.

She'd sensed he was a nice man when they'd spoken on the phone to arrange this interview. They'd both approached a local job-agency and got an almost immediate match. And now again when they met up here in this leafy Adelaide suburban park to conduct his research experiment, and her job interview.

He was quiet, thoughtful even, and, from the depths Lally discerned in his eyes, he seemed to be a man who kept his share of things to himself. He also had a lovely way of making others feel somehow welcomed by him. 'I'd love to be able to help you so you could concentrate more of your efforts on your work.'

'Having someone to handle housekeeping and some general secretarial work for me—very basic stuff—will free up enough of my time so I can really do that.' Cameron Travers continued to row their small boat out towards the middle of the lake.

Not with muscle-bound arms, Lally. You're not even noticing the muscles in his arms. You're focused on this interview.

Eight weeks of employment as his temporary housekeeper with a little secretarial work thrown in as and when needed: that was what was on offer if she landed the job. Such a period of time in her life would be a mere blip, really.

'Did the agency explain what I'd want from you?' Cameron asked the question as he rowed. 'I gave them a list of specifics when I lodged my request.'

'I'd have the option of living in or arriving each morning. I'd cook, clean, take phone messages, maybe do a little clerical work, and generally keep things in order for you.'

Lally had no trouble parroting the work conditions. And, feeling that openness was the best policy from the start, she said, 'I would prefer to live in. It would be cheaper than staying with Mum and Dad and travelling across the city each day to get to work.' Well, if she had to take a job outside the family, the least she could do was choose something she felt would be interesting and make herself comfortable in it.

'You have a good understanding of my requirements. I've always done everything for myself.' His brows drew together. 'But time is ticking away. My agent is getting twitchy. I need to hone my focus on the book and the property development and nothing else. I'm sure taking this step will be all I need to get past the writer's block that's been plaguing me.'

Lally didn't know how long it took to write a top-selling novel in a crime-thriller series, but she imagined it would be quite stressful not to be able to get the story moving while the days rushed by towards a deadline.

And, for Lally, she needed to work to put some money in the coffers. When the job ended she would dig back into her usual place among her relatives and continue to look after them through a variety of gainful employment opportunities.

For their sake. Lally worked for their sake. And it didn't mean there was anything wrong just because she'd been obliged to get out into the real workforce at this time either. No one in the entire mix-and-match brood happened to need her just at the moment. That was all.

Lally tipped her chin up into the air, drew a

deep breath and forced her attention to their surroundings; South Australia in November. It was cool and misty over the lake this morning, but that was only because the park was shaded, leafy, the lake substantial and the hour still early. Later it would get quite warm.

'It is certainly mood-inducing weather,' Lally said. 'For this kind of research.'

'Yes, and the burst of rain last night has resulted in a nice mist effect here this morning.' He glanced about them.

Lally was too interested in the man, not the scenery. She admitted this, though she rather wished she hadn't noticed him quite so particularly. She usually worked very hard to avoid noticing men. She'd been there and made a mess of it. She still carried the guilt of the fallout. What had happened had been so awful—

Lally pushed the thoughts away and turned her attention to the dip of the oars through the water, turned her attention back to Cameron Travers, which was where it needed to be. Just not with quite so much consciousness of him as a man. She trailed her fingers through the water for a moment and quickly withdrew them.

'You said on the phone yesterday that you have plenty of experience in housekeeping?' The corners of Cameron's eyes crinkled as he studied her.

Lally nodded. 'I've worked in a housekeeping role more than once. I'm a confident cook, and I know how to efficiently organise my time and my surroundings. I'm a quick learner, and used to being thrown in the deep end to deal with an array of tasks. I see new challenges as fun.'

'That sounds like what I need.' His voice held approval, and for some silly reason her heart pattered once again as she registered this fact.

'I hope so.' Lally glanced away and blabbed out the first thing that came to her mind. 'Well, it may be November, but trailing my fingers through that water made it clear it's still quite chilly. I wouldn't want to fall in.'

'Or dip your hand into water that might be hiding a submerged crocodile.' Cameron eased back on the oars a little. 'Wrong end of Australia for that, of course.'

'I've spent time in the Northern Territory and the Torres Strait islands. I have relatives up that way, on my mother's side of the family, but I've never seen a crocodile close up.' Lally suppressed a shudder. 'I don't want to.'

Lally didn't want to fall into awareness of her potential new boss, either—not that she was comparing him to a dangerous crocodile. And not that she was falling into awareness.

Cameron gave a thoughtful look as he continued to ply the oars until they reached the centre of the lake. Once there, he let the boat drift. 'It looks quite deep out here. I suspect the water would stay cold even in mid-summer.'

In keeping with the cool of the morning, he wore a cream sweater and blue jeans. The casual clothes accentuated his musculature and highlighted the green of his eyes.

Lally glanced at her own clothing of tan trousers and black turtleneck top. She needed to take a leaf out of her dress-mode book and be sensible about this interview, instead of being distracted by the instigator of it. She drew a steadying breath and gestured to the package in the bottom of the boat. 'You said we'd be tossing that overboard?'

He'd told her that much about his morning's mission when they'd met where the boat had been moored, at a very small-scale jetty at the edge of the lake.

'Yes. It's only a bundle of sand in a bio-friendly wrapping. I'll be using my imagination for the rest.' His gaze narrowed as he took careful note of their surroundings. 'I need to get the combination of atmosphere and mechanics properly balanced in my mind. How much of a splash would there be? How much sound? How far out would the water ripple? The dumping would need to build tension without the reader figuring out what's going on, so I'm after atmosphere as well.'

'Ooh. You could throw a body over.' Lally paused to think. 'Well, no, the sand isn't heavy enough for that. What are you throwing in the story—a weapon? Part of a body?'

'Do I detect a hint of blood-thirsty imagination there?' He laughed, perhaps at the caught-out expression that must have crossed her face.

'Oh, no. Well, I guess maybe I was being blood-thirsty…a little.' Lally drew a breath and returned his smile. 'You must have a lot of fun writing your stories.'

'Usually I do.' His gaze stilled on her mouth and he appeared arrested for a very brief moment before he blinked. Whatever expression she'd glimpsed in his eyes disappeared.

'If you take me on as your housekeeper, I'll do everything I can to help you.' When she'd applied for this job Lally had only had two criteria in her mind: it had to be temporary, and she had to feel she could do the required work. Now she realised this truly could be interesting as well, even perhaps a little exciting; there was also plenty of room for a sense of achievement and to know that she had truly helped someone.

She might only be the housekeeper, but she'd be housekeeping for a crime writer on a deadline!

If it occurred to Lally that she had been a little short on excitement for a while, she immediately pushed that thought aside.

Lally shifted on her bench seat and quickly stilled the motion. She didn't want to rock the boat—literally. 'I haven't read anything suspenseful for a while. I usually save that for watching movies, but a good crime novel, curled up on a sofa…' She drew a breath. 'I'll try not to badger you with questions while you're plotting and writing. Well, that is, if you end up employing me.'

'I doubt it would bother me if you asked questions.' He smiled. 'Provided they don't start or end with the words "How many pages have you written today?"'

'I think I could manage not to ask that.' That would be like her mum painting, or Auntie Edie working with her pottery, and Lally demanding an account of the time they'd spent.

Lally cast another glance at Cameron Travers. He shared her dark hair, though his was short and didn't grow in waves, unlike her own corkscrew curls that flowed halfway down her back.

He had lightly tanned skin, and 'come lose yourself in me' eyes; now that she looked closely she saw very permanent-looking smudges beneath those beautiful eyes.

So, the man had a flaw in his appeal. He wasn't totally stunning and irresistible to look at.

If you could call looking weary a flaw. 'Will I be helping you to get more rest?' That hadn't exactly come out as she'd intended. 'That is, I don't mean to suggest I'll be boring you to sleep at the dinner table or something.' He probably had a girlfriend to fuss over him anyway. Or maybe one tucked in every port, just like Sam had.

Well, Sam had had a wife.

And Lally.

She was not going there.

Sam was a topic Lally rarely allowed to climb all the way to the surface of her thoughts. It annoyed her that it had happened now—twice, really, if she counted that earlier memory of the mess she'd made of her life, and several others in the process.

Lally stiffened her spine and firmed her full lips into what she hoped was a very businesslike expression. 'I'll help you in any way that I can. It's just that you look a bit exhausted. That's why I asked the question.'

'Your help would allow me to focus my energy where I need to.' His gaze searched hers. 'That would be as good as helping me to get more rest. I don't sleep much.

'Now, are you ready to toss the sand-bundle overboard for me? It's quite a few kilos in weight. I do need a woman to throw it, as the "passenger" in the boat, but I hadn't stopped to think…' He hesitated and his gaze took in Lally's slender frame.

'I can manage it.' Lally flicked her hair over her shoulder where it wouldn't get in her way.

She might be slender but she was five-foot seven inches in height and she had plenty of strength. If she could lift her nieces, nephews and little cousins of various sizes and ages, she could toss a packet of sand. 'Any time you're ready. Shall I stand and drop it like a bomb—hurl it from a sitting position? Do you want a plop or a splash, water spraying back into the boat?'

'Hurling would be fine, thank you. Preferably far enough out that we don't get drenched in the process.' Did Cameron's lips go from a twitch to a half-concealed grin? 'I think you should be able to throw the packet from a standing position, if we're careful. I do want to try that.'

He clasped her hand to help her come upright, and there went her resolve not to notice him in the slide of warm, dry skin over her palm, in the clasp of strong fingers curled around her hand.

Lally braced her feet and gave a slight cough. 'I'm, eh, I'm fine now, thanks. I have my balance. You can let go.'

He did so and she stifled a reaction that felt as much like disappointment as relief. It was neither, of course, because she wasn't fazed one way or the other by his touch.

Really, how could the clasp of a hand for a couple of seconds, a down-bent gaze as he helped her up, a curve of a male cheek and the view of a dark-haired head, make her heart beat faster?

How could his gaze looking right into her eyes, and his expression focusing with utter totality on her for one brief blink in time, make her feel attractive to him, for Pete's sake?

Trust me, Lally, you are not necessary to his very ability to breathe. You're looking like a solid possibility as a temporary employee, maybe, but the rest?

'Ready?' Cameron met her gaze with raised brows.

Lally uttered, 'Yes.'

He put the packet into her hands. It was heavy, but she invested all her effort into tossing it.

It landed several feet away with a satisfying splash and she eased back into her seat while Cameron's eyes narrowed. He mentally catalogued the impact—the upward splash of water droplets, water rippling out, the way the mist seemed to swallow everything just moments after it happened.

Lally watched Cameron, then realised what she was doing and abruptly looked away.

'Thank you. At least I know now that with two in the boat, even if he's otherwise occupied, she can toss the package over without drawing too much attention.' He stopped and smiled. 'Now that we've taken care of my research, tell me

about your previous work-experience.' Cameron's
words drew her gaze back to his face.

And put everything back in to perspective as
an interview, which was of course exactly what
Lally wanted.

'You don't need to make notes?' Well, obviously he didn't, or he would be doing so. She
waved away the silly question. 'I've worked for
the past six years for my extended family, doing
all kinds of things: housekeeping, bookkeeping
and cooking. I've been a waitress at my father's
restaurant, *Due per*. It's small, but the place is
always packed with diners.

'I've worked at my uncle's fresh-produce store,
and another relative's fishing-tackle shop. My
mother, several of her sisters and a couple of
brothers are all Aboriginal and Torres Strait artists
of one description or another. I've helped them at
times, too, plus I've done nanny duties for my
three sisters, and my brother and his wife.'

Lally drew a breath. 'I've travelled with Mum
on painting expeditions. Anything the family's
needed from me, I've done.' Except she had
avoided Mum and Auntie Edie's attempts to get
her to paint. Lally somehow hadn't felt ready
for that, but that wasn't the point.

She fished in the deep orange, crushed-velour
shoulder-bag she'd tucked beneath her seat and
pulled out her references. Lally fingered the three-

inch thick wad of assorted papers. 'I gave the employment agency three, but these are the rest. I have everything here that you might want to see in relation to my work experience.'

A hint of warmth crept into Lally's high cheeks. 'I probably didn't need to bring all of them.' But how could she have cut it down to just a few, chosen just some of them over the others?

'Better too many than not enough. May I see?' He held out one lean hand and Lally placed the papers into it.

Their fingers brushed as they made the exchange. One part of her wanted to prolong the contact, another worried that he'd know the impact his touch had on her. The same thing had happened when he'd helped her into the boat this morning.

Cameron flicked through the pages, stopping here and there to read right through. Aunt Judith had written her reference on an indigenous-art letterhead and added a postscript: *Latitia needs to pursue art in her personal time before she gets a lot older.* At least Aunt Judith hadn't labelled the reference with 'B-'. That was what Lally got for having an aunt who'd been a schoolteacher before she left work to paint full-time.

Cameron's mouth definitely quirked at one corner as he read Aunt Judith's admonishment.

Her uncle's reference was on a fruit-shop order form. Well, it was the content that counted.

'I don't know how you manage with so many relatives.' The concept seemed utterly alien to Cameron.

'Is your family…?' *Small? Non-existent?* Lally cut off the question; not her business, not her place to ask.

And just because she needed her family the way she did didn't mean everyone felt like that.

'There's only ever been my mother.' His gaze lifted to her face and he gave her a thoughtful look. He cleared his throat and returned his attention to the references. As his expression eased into repose, the sense of weariness about him returned.

How did he survive in life with only one relative? His expression had been hard to read when he'd mentioned his mother. Lally imagined they must be extremely close.

'I'm more than happy with the references.' Cameron said this decisively as he watched a grey-teal duck glide across the water beside them. 'Do you have computer skills?'

'I can type at about fifty words a minute in a basic word-processing programme, and I've spent plenty of time on the Internet.' Lally would do her best. She always gave one-hundred-and-fifty percent. 'You said on the phone that you're refurbishing the old Keisling building. I looked it up on Google. The place looks quite large; it must be a substantial project to undertake.'

Adelaide had a lot of old buildings. Lally loved the atmosphere of the city; it combined a big, flat sprawliness with all mod cons.

'The Keisling building was initially a huge home. I'll be converting it to apartments.' He nodded. 'Once the work is done, I'll either sell it or put tenants in.'

'There are a lot of old buildings in Adelaide that I haven't seen.' Lally made the comment as he began to row them back towards shore. 'I've seen a reasonable amount of Australia generally, though.' She paused as she realised the interview appeared to be over. 'Am I rambling?'

'Slightly, but I don't mind. You have a soothing voice.' Cameron continued to row. 'I've travelled a lot myself. Sydney is where I keep a permanent apartment, and I'm in the same boat with that.' He glanced at the oars in his hands and humour warmed his eyes. 'I know a lot of Australia, but there are parts of Sydney that I don't know at all. There's a tendency to stick to what you need to know on local turf sometimes, isn't there?'

'Indeed there is.' Now Lally could add 'empathy' and 'able to laugh at himself' to his list of attributes. Employer's attributes. 'Do you often travel and incorporate your writing research or settings with your property-development projects?'

'Yes. I work long hours and need to keep

occupied, so I actively seek ways to keep my mind fresh and to keep busy.' A slight sound that could have been a sigh escaped him before he returned his attention to his rowing. 'Property development came first for me. I got into that straight out of school, and was fortunate enough to make money and be able to expand and make a strong, successful business of it. When I needed more to keep me occupied, I hit on the idea of writing a book. I mostly started that for my own amusement because I enjoyed reading. I was quite surprised when my first book was picked up by an agent, and from there a publisher. Making a second career out of writing was an unexpected bonus.'

And now he entertained and fascinated readers around the world.

I'm not fascinated by him, Lally told herself.

But her other side wanted to know why she couldn't be a little fascinated within reason, provided the fascination was focused on his work. 'And you became a famous author.'

'An author with a looming deadline and an unwelcome bout of writer's block.' Cameron brushed off her reference to his fame.

But he was famous. His series had gained a lot of popularity over the past few years. He had become at least somewhat a household name.

Cameron seemed to hesitate before he went on. 'Usually I'd thrive on my deadlines, but lately?

There's the development of this property to get in motion, the rest of the business to keep an eye on via remote control and I'm more tired than usual—maybe because I've been pushing harder with the writing, trying to get somewhere with it.'

He didn't just want an assistant, he *needed* one.

The knowledge went straight to the part of Lally that had given herself to her family so exclusively for the past six years. The part that yes, had felt just a little threatened when they hadn't needed her at the end of her last job. Even her sisters had said no to child minding, and they were always asking if Lally could find blocks of time for that.

'Oh, no thanks, Lally. I've put them all into after-school care and a sports programme for the next few months.'

'Actually, Ray's parents are going to have the girls after school for a while.'

And so it had gone on.

Who'd heard of Douglas children going to after-school care? The family did that! And Ray's parents never had them.

It had felt like a conspiracy, but that thought was silly. Lally shoved it aside accordingly.

'You need to be looked after a little, to have someone to take the stress off you so you can focus on what you most need to get done.' Lally could care for this man for two months, and then she would go back to where she wanted and needed to be—to the heart of the family who had all been there for her through thick and thin. 'I'll be the best housekeeper and assistant I possibly can, Mr Travers, if you choose to employ me.'

Cameron eased the boat in towards the makeshift dock. 'I do want to employ you.' He named a generous salary. 'We'll need to figure out what days you'll be having off, that sort of thing.'

'I have the job? Oh, thank you!' The wash of happiness Lally experienced had to be relief that she would be financially secure for the next two months, she decided. Her family would have helped her out, of course, they'd all offered that. But she couldn't accept that kind of support and then just sit around and twiddle her thumbs.

So this was good. Very good. 'Thank you, Mr Travers. I'll do everything I can to be a valuable employee to you.'

For some reason he looked quite taken aback for a moment. Cameron let the small craft bump into the dock. 'How soon can you start?'

'Later today, or first thing tomorrow. Which would suit you best?' Lally said—judiciously, she hoped, though excitement was bubbling all through her.

'Let's go with first thing tomorrow.' Cameron left the boat with an agility that made it look easy. He extended his hand and offered a smile that seemed to wash right through her. 'It will be nice to have someone else in charge of some of these things while I try…'

He didn't complete the sentence, but Lally assured herself that that was not because he was distracted by the touch of her hand in his.

More likely he had to focus on not letting her plop into the water like that packet of sand, because she wasn't paying as much attention to proceedings as she should have been as she wobbled her way out of the boat and onto the dock.

Pay attention, Lally, to getting your feet on solid ground—or planks as the case may be—not to the feel of warm skin against your hand!

'Um, thank you.' Lally detached her hand from where it had somehow managed to wrap very securely around his. She could feel the pink tingeing her cheeks again; yes, it was possible to *feel* pink.

'You were about to say, while you try…?'

'To manage two key areas of my life so they both get, and stay, under control.' Cameron pushed his hands into the pockets of his trousers.

He appeared quite unaware of the way that the action shifted the cream jumper across his chest so Lally could enjoy an unimpeded view of the movement of the muscles that ran beneath the layer of cloth.

She was not noticing!

To make up for her consciousness, Lally gifted Cameron Travers with a full-wattage, 'thank you for employing me' smile. 'Your property work and your writing. I understand. So, seven tomorrow morning at your development site, bags packed and ready to leap straight in to whatever is on your agenda for the day? Me, not the bags, I mean.'

Cameron blinked once, and the dark green of his eyes darkened further. 'Yes. That will be fine. We'll eat breakfast while I give you a list of duties to start you off.'

'Excellent.' Lally considered shaking his hand again, and rejected the idea.

Better to keep her hands to herself. Instead, she tucked a long brown curl behind her ear and turned towards the exit of the park. 'I'll see you tomorrow, Mr Travers.'

'Cam,' he offered mildly, and took her elbow in a gentle grip. 'Cameron, if you really must. I'll walk you back to your car.'

'And I'm Latitia. Well, you'd have seen that on my job application and some of the references. But I prefer Lally. Um, will your boat be safe?' Lally's words ran together in a breathless rush.

'I hired the boat. The owner should be along to collect it soon.' Cameron didn't seem worried one way or the other.

He could probably simply buy a replacement. The man no doubt had the money to do that if he wanted.

Lally hot-footed it at his side to the exit as quickly as she could, where she immediately made her way to her elderly, fuel-inefficient station wagon, and bade him an equally swift farewell. The car seated six people, and that was important when a girl had a really big family. She needed to regroup and get her thoughts sorted between now and tomorrow, so she could approach this new work from the right perspective. From a completely efficient, professionally detached, businesslike perspective.

'See you tomorrow.' He turned to walk towards his own car, parked some distance beyond them.

The last thing Lally saw as she drove away was Cameron getting into a sky-blue convertible and putting the top down.

Her final thought was of how much she would love a drive through the countryside in that vehicle with him.

Even if it would only fit the two of them.

Not that she was thinking of them as 'two'.

That would be just plain silly, and dangerous into the bargain.

Lally hadn't protected her emotions and avoided men for the past six years to now get herself into trouble again in that respect!

CHAPTER TWO

'HERE I am, suitcases in tow as promised.' Lally spoke the words in a tone that was determinedly cheerful and didn't quite cover a hint of nerves.

She pulled the suitcases in question behind her along the courtyard pathway. 'I have more things in my car, but I can get those later. I pretty much take my whole world with me to every new job among the family; it's a habit I've formed over the years. I like to surround myself with my belongings. That way I can feel at "home" wherever I am. I'm sure I'll feel at home here, too, once I've settled in.'

Perhaps she'd formed the habit of chattering sometimes to try to hide things such as nerves.

Cam felt an odd need, that seemed to start in the middle of his chest, to reassure her and set her at her ease. He rose from where he'd been seated at the outdoor dining-table, and started towards her. 'I take a few regular things along when I travel.'

Those things were mostly to do with both aspects of his work commitments: laptops, business files, his coffee machine and research materials for his writing. The coffee machine was definitely work related! 'Let me help you with that lot; your load looks ten times heavier than you. And I'm looking forward to you getting settled here too.'

It was ages since he'd spent any significant amount of time in close company with a woman. The last effort had been a disaster, but this was different, a working relationship. Cam wanted his housekeeper to feel welcome and comfortable.

She drew in a deep breath and let it out slowly, and he watched much of the tension ease out of her.

Lally Douglas was a beautiful woman. It would be a very novel experience for him, to have a woman living in as his housekeeper, and to have this woman specifically. He'd anticipated some-one older, perhaps in semi-retirement.

Maybe he would learn some things through contact with Lally Douglas that would help him to pin down the quirks and foibles of the female character for his book.

He did wonder why his new housekeeper carried that edge of reserve that seemed contrary to the vibrancy of her imagination, and the sparkle in her deep-brown eyes when something inter-ested her. Cam put this curiosity down to his writer's mind, and studied Lally for a moment from beneath lowered lashes.

She was a slender girl with skin the colour of milky coffee, and curly almost-black hair; she had thick lashes, high cheekbones and a heart-melting smile that revealed perfect white teeth when it broke over her face. Today she wore a tan skirt that reached to her knees, sandals with a low heel, a simple white blouse and a light camel-coloured cardigan thrown over her shoulders.

'I can manage the suitcases.' Lally gestured behind her. 'As you can see, they stack, and the whole lot is on wheels.'

'Yes, I can see.' But he took the handle from her anyway. Their hands brushed and he tried, really tried, not to notice the smoothness of her skin or the long, slender fingers with perfectly trimmed, unadorned nails. Cam wanted to stroke that soft skin, wrap those fingers in his.

And do what? Bring her hand to his lips and kiss her fingertips? *Not happening, Travers.* He'd had this same reaction to her yesterday, and had done his utmost then to stifle it. Mixing business with awareness to a woman really wasn't a smart idea.

Cam didn't have time to worry about an attraction anyway right now. He saved that for when he felt like socialising, and chose companions who were not looking for a long-term involvement. Past experiences in his life hadn't exactly helped him to trust in the concept of women in deeper, personal relationships, between the way his mother had raised him and the one relationship he'd tried to build in his early twenties that had failed abysmally.

Cam towed the load of suitcases to the doorway of the complex's large apartment and pushed them inside before he turned back to Lally.

She had dropped her hand to her side almost awkwardly. Now she gave a small smile. 'Thank you for that.'

'You're welcome.' He gestured behind him. 'That's the apartment we'll share while you're with me. It's the only one in the building that's been kept in half-decent order and fully furnished, as caretakers have come and gone prior to my purchase of the place. I've claimed one of the bedrooms for office space, but there are two more, as well as all the other necessary amenities.'

'That will be fine. Dad checked with the agency and confirmed your character references.' She bit her lip.

'It's best to feel certain that you're safe.' Cam led the way to the outdoor-dining setting and indicated she should take her seat. It was a large table, with half a dozen wrought-iron chairs padded with cushions facing each other around it. Lally and Cam sat at one end.

'Thank you; I appreciate that you understand.' Lally's gaze went to the covered food-dishes and settled on the silver coffee-pot. 'If all that's as good as it smells, I think I'm being very spoiled on my first morning at work.'

Cam shrugged, though her words had pleased him. 'It took less than half an hour to put together. I cooked while I tried to brainstorm some more ideas for my story.' 'Tried' being the operative word.

'I'll make sure I have a good breakfast ready for you each morning from now on.' As Lally spoke the words, the noise level at the far end of the site increased as two of the workers began to throw tiles off the roof into a steel transport-bin below.

Lally tipped her head to one side and her big, brown eyes filled with good-natured awareness. 'Has the noise been interfering with your writing?'

'No. I can usually work through any amount of noise.' He wished he *could* blame his lack of productivity on that. Cam didn't know what to blame it on, or how to fix it, other than sticking at the writing until he got a breakthrough with this tricky character, and using Lally's help to allow him to really hone his focus on that. 'But they only actually started the work this morning. I've been here less than a week myself, and most of that time's been spent organising a work crew, working with the site boss to get our orders in for materials, that sort of thing.'

Cam liked a good work challenge. He just wasn't enjoying it quite as much as usual this time, thanks to his problems with the book. He'd always managed both aspects of his life—the property development and the writing—and kept both in order. He didn't like feeling out of control at one end of the spectrum.

'It's good that noise isn't a problem to you.' Lally glanced around her, taking in the large pool that looked more like a duck pond at the moment. 'Oh, look at the swimming pool. It's a nice shape, isn't it? A kind of curvy-edged, squished-in-the-middle rectangle. Very mellow.' Her gaze moved around the large courtyard area, and encompassed the building that surrounded it in a U-shape on three sides, before returning to meet his eyes.

'I can see why you wanted this place. It will be wonderful when the work is done.' An expression that seemed to combine interest in her new job and a measure of banked-down hurt came over her face. 'At least I'll have plenty to do here while my family don't need me.' She drew a breath.

'Ah—your family?'

'I'll be back in the thick of it with them straight after this.' She rushed the words out as though maybe she needed to do so, to fully believe in them herself. 'I help out in all sorts of ways.'

'I'm lucky to have you to look after me for a while.' It was true. His body was exhausted, pushed by even more hard work beyond the usual state of tolerable weariness induced by him being an insomniac-workaholic. 'It'll be nice to have someone to take care of some of the very ordinary everyday tasks.'

Heaven knew, he could afford to pay for the help; he'd just never sought it before. Doing the cooking and cleaning for himself burned up time, and time was something he usually had oodles of on his hands. He still had lots of time, but, thanks to a female character who simply refused to come to life on the page for him, that time wasn't productive enough.

Cam lifted the coffee pot, glanced at the cup in front of Lally and raised his eyebrows in a silent question.

'Yes please.' The colour of her eyes changed from dark brown to clear sherry and a dimple broke out in her cheek. 'I'm ready for my first dose of caffeine for the day.'

They sipped in silence for a moment. Cam let the rich brew hit the back of his throat and give his body a boost. He'd tried leaving coffee out of his diet for a while, hoping it might have a positive impact on his sleep issues, but it hadn't made any difference.

Lally laced her fingers together in front of her on the table and looked about her again. 'This property would make a great base for a character in your book.'

She cast a sheepish glance his way. 'I bought the first book in your series yesterday after our interview. It said in the back that you sometimes use your development projects as settings for your stories.'

'I hope you're enjoying the read.' It made Cam happy to know he was providing entertainment for readers, but Lally had said she didn't usually read crime novels. 'My kind of books aren't to everyone's taste.'

Lally said earnestly, 'Oh, I finished it! I was on the edge of my seat the whole time. I'm looking forward to reading the rest of the books in the series so far. The only thing that could have made the story better would have been a love interest for your hero.' She clapped a hand over her mouth. 'I'm so sorry. What would I know about it?'

Cam gave a wry grimace. 'The need for a love interest is an opinion shared by my editor and agent. I'm quite prepared to add her in, but I'm having trouble cracking her characterisation.

'Let's eat, anyway.' Cam lifted the covers off the hot food and invited her to help herself. He'd prepared bacon, eggs, sausages and grilled tomatoes, and had added fresh bread-rolls from the small bakery two blocks away. 'I hope there's something here that's to your taste, but if not I have cereal, fruit and yoghurt inside as well.'

'This will be fine. Thank you.' She helped herself to an egg, two grilled tomatoes and a warmed bread roll. 'I'm truly sorry for what I said about your book. It's none of my business.' Lally still looked stricken. 'I shouldn't have told you that I wished there was a female counterpart in that book.'

Cam said gently, 'It's all right. My ego can take some constructive criticism of my work. Who knows? I might bounce some of my ideas off you. In fact, I'll almost certainly ask you to help with research, as you know your way around a computer and the Internet.' That was a bonus Cam hadn't expected to get in his temporary house-keeper.

'Ooh. Helping will be fun.' Lally's eyes gleamed. 'I can look up all sorts of interesting things for you.'

Cam smiled. 'Perhaps I should just be grateful that my editor and agent waited until my sixth book to talk to me about the need to include this new character.'

'Yes. You escaped it until now.' Her grin started in the depths of chocolate eyes, crinkled the skin at their corners and spread across her lips like sunshine.

Teasing; she was teasing him.

And Cam was enjoying being teased. A corresponding smile spread across his face and they stared at each other; the atmosphere changed and suddenly he was looking deep into her eyes and the humour was gone. His hand lifted towards her.

He dropped it back to his side. They broke eye contact at the same time.

Cam reminded himself that this awareness he felt towards her, and that she perhaps felt towards him, wasn't a good thing. Cam lived a chronically busy lifestyle. It had been that way for years. He pushed himself to survive, survived to push himself more. By doing both, he filled the endless hours in which he could never manage to sleep properly.

There was no breaking that cycle. He had to live with it. It was the only way he could live. It certainly wasn't a cycle that lent itself to him getting into any kind of meaningful relationship with a woman. He'd proved that fact in the past.

Yet, you're thirty-two now. What if you get hit with one of those biological urges and need to settle down, produce children or something?

Like his mother had produced and settled. Well, she'd produced.

Cam shoved the conjecture aside. It was quite pointless.

Lally took another sip of coffee and looked at him over the rim of the cup. 'This is very nice. Thank you. I have to admit, I hang out for my first dose of coffee each morning.' She gestured towards the far side of the building. 'The work crew seem to know what they're doing. If they keep on at that cracking pace, the work will be done quickly.'

'That's my goal.' Cam glanced towards the crew and then let his gaze trail slowly back over the courtyard area; a small frown formed between his brows. 'I'm not quite sure what to do out here. It needs something.' He didn't know what; surely getting the place organised into apartments was enough anyway?

He was only going to rent or sell them, so what did it matter if he thought the courtyard lacked soul? 'I want to have the pool converted so it's heated for year-round use. The courtyard and surrounding gardens need to be brought up to scratch as well.'

'The place will be a hive of activity for the next while.'

They ate in silence for a few moments. Cam watched Lally's delicate movements, observed the straightness of her back in the wrought-iron chair.

Her fingers were lovely. If Cam had to create a

female love-interest for his book, she would have hands like Lally's, he decided. They'd look good wrapped around a gun, a champagne glass or an assassin's throat while his heroine resisted the threat with all her worth, or the woman could even be an assassin.

Cam had lots of ideas. He just couldn't seem to hone them into something coherent. He cleared his throat. 'The duties list…'

'Do you have a written list for me?' Lally asked her question at the same time.

They stopped and each took a sip of their coffee. Lally drew a breath that lifted her small breasts beneath the cowl-neck top. Her hair was loose about her shoulders, as it had been yesterday.

Her top was sleeveless, and Cam wanted to stroke his fingers over the soft smoothness of her skin. She had strength in those slender arms, despite her small size. So much for deciding he wasn't going to notice her appeal.

While Lally nibbled on a bite of tomato, Cam fished a piece of paper from his shirt pocket. 'I've jotted down a few basics for now.' He handed it across the table to her.

While she read, he got on with his meal.

Lally finished the last of her tomato and egg while she read through the duties list. Though his gaze wasn't on her, she felt his consciousness of her, and had to force herself to concentrate on the words in front of her.

The list included taking care of his laundry, cleaning the apartment, meals and changing the linens. She would be in charge of his mobile phone during the hours he was writing, take messages and make the decision as to whether to interrupt him or not depending on what messages came through from his Sydney business.

There were a few lines about how to deal with the work crew, but he mostly wanted to handle that for himself.

'That all seems very reasonable.' Lally glanced up.

'I may ask for other duties as time progresses. Once the crew begins to get the apartments up to speed, I may send you in to clean them ready for occupation.'

'I'll be glad to do that.' Lally wanted to work hard for him. 'I like to keep busy. The task doesn't matter, just so long as I'm occupied.'

Had she made herself sound boring?

Why would it matter if you had, Latitia? You're his housekeeper. You don't have to be interesting, just productive and helpful.

'I'm good at multi-tasking through phone calls.' Lally's phone usually ran hot with calls and text messages. Yet, in the beaded bag at her feet, her phone was still and silent. The contact from her family had all but stopped since Lally had realised she was going to have to go outside normal channels to look for a job.

A man in a hard hat strode across the courtyard towards them. He stopped just short of their table. 'Morning, Mr Travers. Sorry to interrupt, but I'm ready to discuss these plans any time you are.' He gestured to the clipboard in his other hand. 'The crew should be in this morning to start the work to get that swimming pool up to speed too. They'll have to drain it, to do the work to turn it into a heated pool, but the water's too far gone to fix by shocking it with chlorine and balancing agents, so you're not losing anything on that score.'

Cam glanced towards the building. 'What other plans are on for today?'

'Makes the most sense to strip all the apartments at once, so that's what we'll be doing.' The man's gaze shifted to Lally and lingered. 'We, eh, you don't need any of the other apartments until all the work is done, so this'll streamline the process.'

'Thank you.' The words emerged in a deeper than usual cadence. Cam frowned and then said, 'Let me introduce you. Jordan Hayes, this is my housekeeper, Lally Douglas. Lally, meet my site manager.'

The man stuck out a hand. 'Nice to meet you.'

Lally shook his hand, reclaimed her own, and

got to her feet. 'I'll leave you both to your discussion. I'd like to get started on my workload.' Her gaze shifted to the breakfast table. 'I'll clear this away once I've settled my belongings inside.'

Lally slipped away before Cam could think of anything to say in response, and then the site manager spoke and Cam forced his thoughts onto the work here.

Cam didn't want to examine the tight feeling that had invaded his chest when Lally had slipped her hand into the other man's grip. If that reaction had been possessive, Cam had no right to it. His mouth tightened. He did his best to relax his expression as he spoke to the manager. 'We'll go into my office and talk there. It will be a bit quieter.'

Perhaps if he tucked himself away in there after this talk—focused on the property development, checked in with his Sydney office for the morning and then attacked his writing—he would get his thoughts off fixating on a certain brand-new, temporarily employed housekeeper.

For the truth was she had looked far too good when she'd arrived this morning, pulling a bunch of suitcases along behind her while her hips swayed and her legs ate up the ground beneath her feet in long strides. Cam had noticed how good she looked, far too much.

It was one thing to do such minor and insignificant things as notice the shape of her hands, he told himself, but that noticing had to stop.

Cam led the way into his office, the site manager behind him.

He would put Lally Douglas right out of his mind and not think about her again until lunchtime.

It wasn't as though he couldn't control his mild attraction to her. How ridiculous would that be?

CHAPTER THREE

'YOU'RE quite sure you're okay, Aunt Edie?' Lally had her mobile phone jammed between her shoulder and her ear. It felt right there, and so it should. Usually she spent a lot of her day with a phone in that exact position, talking with one relative or another while she went about her work and various family members checked in with her.

Today she'd had to phone Auntie herself; she had only received a couple of text messages all morning, mostly from two of her teenage cousins who'd recently got their first-ever mobile phones.

Of course, she'd been kept busy with calls and a few text messages coming in to Cam's mobile. It felt a little intimate to take all his calls and messages. What if a woman phoned?

And what if the phone he gave her was purely for business and he had another one for his social life? Lots of people did that.

Right. Why was Lally fixating on Cam's social

life, anyway? She should be fixating on her family's silence. Lally had kept so close to all her family in the past. It felt unsettling now not to hear from them much.

'You're working an outside job,' she muttered. 'They probably don't want to call and disturb that.'

'Beg pardon, dear?'

'Oh, sorry, Auntie. It was nothing; I was just talking to myself.' She was talking to Auntie, who seemed quite happy to talk, so what was Lally worrying about anyway?

Lally whisked eggs in a bowl and quickly poured the results over a selection of cooked vegetables in a heated pan on the stove. 'Promise me you're well, Auntie. You're taking all your meds? You've got Nova coming over to sort them out for you for the start of each day? Because I could drive over at night during my time off.'

'I'm fine, Lally. Nova comes every day, but even if she didn't I could cope. You just enjoy your work out there in the world where you might meet—' Her aunt coughed. 'We all think you'll do a very good job, just as you always do, dear.'

'Thank you. I appreciate that.' And Lally did. She was being quite silly to feel displaced. For heaven's sake, she'd only been at the new job for half a day. By the end of the week she might be getting so many calls and messages from her family that her new boss would be quite angry with her, if he didn't see that she always kept working throughout those calls and messages, hard and at speed.

And, of course, she would put answering his mobile first.

Lally had learned a long time ago to multi-task. Cameron seemed to live that way too. It was something they had in common.

What you have in common is that he's the boss and you're the employee, Lally. Try to remember that!

'Shouldn't you be focusing on your new job this morning, Lally?' Auntie asked the words into the silence, almost as though she'd read Lally's mind.

'I am.' Lally glanced around the kitchen. Cam had left no mess, so it had been easy to give the whole area a deep clean. Now Lally sprinkled fresh, chopped herbs into the frittata and turned it down to heat through.

With a light salad, that would take care of their lunch, and this afternoon she'd see about their dinner. So far she'd cleaned most of the rooms, settled her things into the room across the small hall from Cameron's bedroom, looked over the pantry supplies, made a list of things she would need to buy soon and organised this meal.

And had taken Cameron's messages. None of

them had sounded unbearably urgent, though the content of many of them from his Sydney office had brought it home to Lally that Cameron truly dealt in big dollars.

Lally prepared the salad with cherry tomatoes, lettuce, mushroom slices and slivers of avocado mixed with a tangy dressing; that job was done. She checked on the frittata; it was almost cooked.

Sam had liked tangy dressing on his salad.

The thought slid sideways into Lally's mind; it wasn't welcome. She so rarely thought about Sam. If getting out and working with a man would make that a common occurrence, Lally was not going to be pleased. 'I'm working and talking at once, Auntie. I can talk. Tell everyone else they can call me too. Even if just early in the mornings, or in the evenings, if they're worried that much about my job. I'm sure I can fit in some calls—'

But her aunt had already rushed out a, 'Love you,' and disconnected the call at her end.

Well!

Lally drew a deep breath. 'It might have been nice to get to say "I love you" back—'

'Whatever that is, it smells wonderful.' The deep words sounded over the top of hers and cut them off abruptly. 'Sorry, were you on the phone?'

'Oh. I didn't realise you were there.' She'd been talking out loud like a loon. 'Um, no, I'm all finished with my phone call. It was my phone that time, but I have a heap of messages from yours.'

'On the phone to the boyfriend?' Cam's words were unruffled, and yet something in his tone made Lally seek his gaze.

His eyes were shielded by those long, silky lashes.

'I should have brought this up at our interview. I apologise that I didn't, but I'll cover it now.' She did feel guilty, even though there was no need. 'I like to speak with family members when I have a moment. I'll do it discreetly, I won't disrupt you in any way, and I always keep working. I can assure you I don't lose any work time or concentration over the calls I make, and of course I'll always use my own phone.'

'Family.' Cameron's expression was complex. He ran his fingers through his short hair. 'Of course that's not a problem. You're welcome to keep whatever contact you need.'

'Thank you.' Lally considered telling him there was no boyfriend, but he'd probably figured that out anyway. In any case, it wasn't important. 'I appreciate you being understanding about my need for contact with my family.'

Now, if Lally could just get her *family* to come back on board with that contact.

'I can see you've been busy.' Cameron's glance

roved the kitchen, dining room and lounge areas, before it came back to rest on her, and his expression softened. 'Thank you for what you've done already to help make me comfortable.'

'That's what I'm here for.' But his praise and appreciation wrapped around her just the same.

Being needed: it was an issue for Lally. She knew it; she would even admit it. Until now she'd thought it was all just about family relationships for her.

And it was. This just felt sort of similar because she was helping him, too, and that was what she did for them. Her happiness certainly had nothing to do with that softening of his expression when his gaze rested on her. She wasn't looking for tenderness from him, for goodness' sake; that would be ridiculous.

Lally was too wary to consider something like that with a man again anyway. And she was still young, she justified to herself. She had plenty of time to think about getting back into the dating game. And she'd been really busy with family commitments.

Busy enough that they might have pushed her out so she'd find time for a social life again?

Her family had been known to stick their noses into each other's lives at times. Lally had been guilty of it too. In a big, loving family that would always happen, and she'd had her share of them hinting that she could do with getting out more.

But they wouldn't take it this far, would they? Of course they wouldn't…

'Lunch is almost ready now, if you want to take a seat in the dining room.' Lally would far rather eat lunch than go on thinking about that topic. She gestured to the freshly polished dining-table. 'Or we can eat outside, if you'd prefer? It's frittata. I hope that's okay.'

'Inside will be fine, and I eat most things.' He paused and the hint of a smile lifted the edges of his mouth. 'No artichoke. Other than that, I'm very agreeable about food.'

'That will make cooking for you a dream. I'd like to take advantage of the fresh markets for produce for a lot of our meals.' She wanted to feed him on the freshest items available, because she thought it might help with whatever had been exhausting him—lack of sleep, long hours, book stress, whatever the problem. Even if it didn't, it would put his body in a good place, health-wise.

Yes, fine, she was acting like a little mother. Why not, when she'd had a hundred or so relatives to practice those skills on? They all deserved to be loved to bits and looked after as much as possible, especially considering how much they'd had to put up with from her.

Not that she felt the need to earn their love. Well, that would be just silly, wouldn't it? And she didn't feel like a little mother; she felt like a determined housekeeper.

Lally turned the frittata onto a serving plate, carried it and the salad to the table she'd set, and took her seat. 'I hope you'll eat while the food is hot and at its best, and have as much as you want. I made plenty. I do have a bunch of messages from your phone, but I think they can all wait until after you've eaten.'

Now she sounded as though she was very generously allowing him to eat his own food, and making his work-related choices for him while she was at it. 'What if your editor rings?' Lally asked suddenly. 'Or your agent?'

'You'll be able to tell if they need to speak to me urgently, otherwise they can wait.' He gave a wry smile. 'I'm too professional to ask you to dodge them on my behalf if they phone and then ask for a progress update—though there might be certain days when I'll be tempted to do that if things keep going the way they have for the past few weeks.'

'You can't help it if you're in the middle of a sticky patch with your muse,' Lally declared. 'These things happen. It must be quite amazing to be internationally famous too. You probably have fans chasing after you and everything. Lots of women—'

The words burst out of her and Lally's face flooded with heat.

'I can't say I've been particularly *chased*, at least not to my knowledge.' Cam drawled the words. He felt far too pleased that Lally's words—when she'd got to the 'women' part of her statement—had sounded as though she was quite jealous at the thought of such a thing happening.

Two seconds later he realised that wasn't exactly the response he should have to her. And he didn't *want* women chasing him; he'd rather go and find them when he felt the need.

Cam helped himself to a piece of the frittata and some salad and took a first bite. The frittata was perfect, the accompanying salad the exact counterpoint for it; the zing of tangy dressing hit Cam's tongue, completing the experience. 'Did you make the dressing yourself? Where did you learn your cooking skills?'

'I did make the dressing. I learned to cook from two parents who both love it, and do it very differently but equally as well.' Lally's smile softened at whatever memories were in her head. 'What they didn't actively teach me, I guess I've learned by observation anyway.'

She seemed to take her skill level as nothing out of the ordinary.

'Your father runs a restaurant; I momentarily forgot that.' She'd told him that at their interview, and Cam had spent a few moments piecing together her family history in his mind. Torres-Strait Aboriginal mother, Italian father; the surname of 'Douglas' suggested that her father might not be fully Italian.

'Dad's mother married a Scotsman, just to keep things interesting.' Lally's lovely smile lit her face again.

'You have a diverse family tree.' Cam returned the smile, and gestured to his plate. 'The food is delicious, thank you. I think I've struck it lucky with you, Lally, if this meal and the work you've got through already are any indication.'

'You're welcome for all of it.' Her skin didn't show a blush. Yet somehow he suspected one had just happened—by the change to the sparkle in her eyes, perhaps?

What would she be like in the middle of passion?

Cam cut the thought off. The answer to that question was that it was not his business to wonder.

'I've done as much work as I could this morning.' Lally seemed flustered as she pulled the duties list from her pocket and flattened it on the table beside her plate. She glanced at it and raised her gaze to his face. 'I'll do all that I can to look after you, help you start to feel more rested and focus on what you need to do with your time.'

'I appreciate that.' Surely in another week or

two he would get back to sleeping at least the four to four-and-a-half hours a night he usually got? Cam didn't expect Lally to be able to do a thing about that. Why would she? All the experts had failed to give him any long-term solutions that didn't involve knocking himself out at night with medications he didn't want to let become a habit in his life.

'I haven't forgotten about book research.' Her finger rested on a point on the list. 'I'm ready to help you with that in any way required.'

'I have a research project for you for after lunch, actually.' Cam went on to explain what he needed. 'I have two laptop computers. What I'd like you to do is use the second laptop and get the prohibition laws about using these substances in this state…' He jotted the names of several chemical compounds onto the bottom of her list.

'I'll do the rest of the research myself. Some of it has to be handled carefully; I don't want you dealing with anything that could be potentially dangerous to you.' He paused. 'At least I can still make forward progress with my lead character's investigations and activities to some degree, even if other aspects of the story are being difficult.'

Lally's eyes widened and her soft lips parted. '*You* take care with your research? You keep yourself safe?' Her words were so genuine, filled with concern for him.

Cam got that strange feeling in his chest again. 'Always. I always take care.' He was even more determined to take care of *her* in this admittedly small way.

As their gazes met and held, Cam was very conscious of her.

She was conscious of him. It was there in her guarded expression, the rejection and the self-protectiveness in every line of her body, and didn't fully manage to conceal the interest beneath.

They threw sparks off each other, and Lally didn't want to feel those sparks.

Were they for him? Or for any man at the moment?

And, either way, *why?*

But he didn't need to know why; Cam told himself this. He needed to develop a three-dimensional book character, not know every aspect of his new housekeeper's make-up.

They both dropped their gazes at the same time and Cam rubbed his face wearily.

'Are you okay, Cam? You mentioned you don't sleep well—I assumed that was due to stress or work pressures.' Lally's soft words impinged on his thoughts. 'If there's anything else I need to know…'

'I'm a long-term insomniac. It's annoying sometimes but it's nothing to worry about.'

Though he didn't care who knew about it one way or another, this wasn't something he discussed often. Cam wouldn't have held the answer back from her, though, not when her face had filled with such concern.

Lally gave a nod of acknowledgement. 'It's no wonder you felt like being spoiled a little. Maybe you can enjoy some more rest than usual, even if it doesn't come in the form of sleep.'

'Maybe I will. I've got my eye on the pool.' He shrugged his shoulders. 'A swim now and then would be relaxing.' He hesitated. 'If you hear me up and about in the middle of the night...'

'Do you like company at those times, or to be by yourself?' Lally's expression had softened so much, it was almost as though she needed to find a chink in his armour and felt somehow reassured by finding it. 'I'd be happy to heat you some warm milk or sit up and talk.'

Cam pictured them sitting at this table at midnight. Somehow he doubted that drinking milk or talking would be the first things on his mind. He'd be thinking about kissing his way up the slender column of her neck until he reached those luscious lips and closed his own over them.

The urge to kiss her now, right in this blink of time, silenced him for a moment. It was one thing to imagine, even to want, but this urge felt somehow to be more than that.

Maybe you should just ask her if she'd curl up on the sofa with you, with your head in her lap, and stroke your face with her fingers until you fall asleep, you big baby.

Or you could admit you find her more than a little intriguing and that you're not doing a very good job of pushing back that interest.

All right, he did find her intriguing, but he wasn't about to act on it. Theirs was a working relationship and that was exactly how Cam wanted it to be.

And that left how he wanted to deal with the rest of the day. And the next.

Cam cleared his throat and side-stepped the question. 'I'll take you to the market tomorrow morning and we can buy fresh produce together. I'll be awake anyway, so it makes sense that I go with you the first time at least.'

He could tell her what foods he liked the most, could carry her basket for her.

Or throw down his cloak for her to step on if she came across a puddle in her path!

'Excuse me.' He got to his feet and assured himself the only thought on his mind was getting back to business.

He was not running; he was planning and retreating so he could focus on his book. A totally different thing.

Cam took Lally's written list of phone messages

and the phone itself from the table. 'I'll see to these and drop the phone out to you before I start writing, if that's okay?'

'Thanks.' Lally glanced down at the notes he'd written for her to research. 'And I'll bring my research results to you as soon as I have them.'

Cam looked at the sweep of her long black lashes. 'Other than that, perhaps you can just keep going with your housekeeping jobs.' If Cam stayed clear for a few hours, maybe he would get these strange reactions to her sorted out a little better.

Lally rose and started to gather dishes into capable hands. 'Good luck with the writing.'

'Thanks.'

Cam nodded and left.

CHAPTER FOUR

'I MEANT to unpack all this as soon as we got home.' It was the next afternoon. Lally reached into one of the string bags sitting on the kitchen counter in the apartment and pulled out several canned goods.

Her voice was raised a little to be heard over the outside noise of the refurbishing crew. Cam had to admit that right now they sounded more like a destruction mob. 'Are you okay with that noise? It's not driving you crazy?'

'Oh, no,' she said. 'I'm fine with it. If anything would get to me, I think it would be too much quiet.'

Cam understood that only too well. Maybe noise was what he needed at night.

You've tried that, remember? You've tried every trick there is. Noise or no noise; light or dark; quiet or loud; whatever, you don't sleep beyond what your body has to have to survive. That's all there is to it.

He returned his gaze to his housekeeper. 'You got busy when we got back here.' Lally had called it 'home' and hadn't seemed to notice the word. But in truth where did Lally Douglas call 'home'? She'd told him she had a room at her parents' home; was that it? At twenty-four, didn't she want her freedom at some point?

And why did it even matter to Cam? 'Home,' he'd never had. A faceless, nameless apartment in the centre of Sydney that he visited now and then hardly counted.

Yet wouldn't it be nice to have a home? A real one? With a permanent housekeeper like Lally to look after him?

Dumb thought, Travers. This was a temporary measure, nothing more. Cam drew a breath. 'There's nothing in the foodstuffs that will have spoiled.'

'No. I put the perishables away straight off, at least.' Lally removed the remaining articles from the bags and started to pack them into the larder.

Cam resisted the urge to help. He'd crossed the line enough by insisting they shop together at the market first thing this morning. When they'd got back, he'd eaten breakfast with her—then had taken himself off to his office and proceeded to give his hero's love-interest so many of Lally Douglas's traits and characteristics that he'd had to delete half the work he'd written.

So he'd deleted, and he'd wrestled with his story some more, and he'd come up with what he knew was a great scene-idea—but then he couldn't get that to work either. Without realising he did it, Cam heaved a sigh.

'Is the writing not going well?' Lally's words were empathetic.

He shook his head. 'I've got a scene planned in my mind, but when I try to write it I can't visualise it properly. I can't "see" the heroine in my mind's eye. I'm not sure how to use their surroundings. It's a scene that I know will work, but I can't seem to *get* it to work. I think as long as the heroine remains shadowy in my mind, this problem is going to continue.'

'What would bring her to life for you?' Lally's eyebrows drew together as she considered the matter. 'Could you "interview" her? Ask her questions to get to know her?'

'Stream-of-consciousness interviewing? I did try that about a week ago, but I didn't get anywhere with it.' Cam forced himself not to scowl his irritation over this. 'I feel as though I need to somehow throw her into the middle of this scene, really get in deep there with her. Once I see how she reacts, the pieces will all come together. Maybe.'

'Hmm.' Lally was silent for a long moment. She tipped her head to the side and tapped her finger on her chin before her eyes lit up. 'When Mum gets stuck on a painting, she tells my aunt the concept. Auntie takes a sheet of paper and whips out her interpretation of how she'd do the painting. Mum invariably says that's *not* how the idea should be executed! Rejecting one idea helps Mum to figure out how *she* wants to execute it.'

'That's an interesting concept.' It was Cam's turn to frown. 'I'd try that, if there was a chance it would rattle loose *my* interpretation. But how?'

'You need a "volunteer from the audience".' The smile deepened on Lally's lovely mouth. 'Someone, or more than one person, to act out the scene for you. You don't have to like how they do it, but it might help you figure out what you *do* want for the scene.'

Cam gave a surprised laugh. 'That could just work. I'd have to find an acting society or a theatre group willing to act it.'

'Or you and I could do it.' The words came out in a little rush and she immediately bit her lip. 'Not if you didn't want us to, but if you didn't want the hassle of trying to find real actors—if you only needed to play-act it to help you figure it out—we could do that, couldn't we?'

'We could.' Her enthusiasm started to spread through him too. 'My idea is a wheels-within-wheels kind of situation, where he's pretending interest in her but he suspects her of being a double agent or spy or assassin. He thinks if he disarms her with food, wine and attention he'll figure out what she's up to.' He went on. 'She's got an equal number of suspicions about him. She pretends to be "buyable" for the night, to gain access to his hotel room to search it later, and then she's going to disappear—but he lures her to the roof top of the building after dinner when he suspects her motives are as duplicitous as his are.'

Cam drew a breath. 'Before dinner he spends money on her, buying her a dress and other gifts.'

'It really is wheels within wheels.' Lally's eyes were like stars. 'Oh, but that sounds so exciting. We could role-play the whole evening from beginning to end. It wouldn't have to be an exact match, but it could be a lot of fun!'

'Let's do it.' Cam's smile spread until it was as wide as hers. 'It'll have to be late in the day. If we're going to do this I want the right atmosphere, time of night, all of it.'

Happiness filled her face. 'Tonight?'

Cam couldn't seem to look away from that happiness. 'Yes, we'll do it tonight. We'll leave here at seven p.m. I'd better get on the computer and figure out where we can go that will provide the kind of backdrop I want.' He started to turn away; he *had* to turn away. 'Can you manage that?'

'Of course.' She did a little bounce on the balls

of her feet. 'I'll go on with other work until you're ready for us to leave.'

He looked at her and tried not to think about the curve of the side of her face, her cheek, her chin and her lush lips that looked soft and kissable. 'We'll be out until around midnight, so feel free to take some time off this afternoon before we leave. I don't want to over-tire you.'

'I'll take a nap for an hour if I can get to sleep,' Lally conceded, but with a glow of anticipation still all over her face.

Somehow Cam doubted she would relax into sleep in this mood, but he wasn't a good one to gauge her chances. Just because he wouldn't have been able to sleep in the afternoon didn't mean she might not be able to nod off any time she decided she wanted to.

'I'll see you at seven.' He glanced at her clothes. 'You can come dressed as you are now, or in something similar; it doesn't really matter. Choosing clothes in the same way the female character would do that tonight will be part of our role-play. I'll need to locate a big hotel that has boutique stores. We'll shop there, enact the time in the dining room, and then go up on the rooftop for that part.'

Her eyes widened. 'It—it won't cost you a lot, will it? I didn't mean to suggest…'

'Something that might get my writing back on

track after weeks of it driving me crazy because I haven't been able to get there?' He felt lighter than he had in all those weeks. 'If it costs me a little to organise this evening and I get a result, I will be more than happy, so don't give that another thought. Whatever I spend I'll be able to tax-deduct, anyway.'

'Well, I guess.' Lally frowned. 'Make sure it's a hotel that does clothing hire, or has cheap stores. We can go through the motions, buy or hire what we have to, I guess, but keep the expense right down.'

Cam smiled at the earnest face looking at him. 'You need to think of it as a cross between Cinderella and—I don't know—winning a shopping spree or something.'

'Oh, well, okay. I guess.'

'Good.' Cam turned away. 'I'll see you when it's time to go.'

'This is it. The boutique shops inside should provide what we need.' Cam spoke to Lally as he handed his car keys to a parking valet. He paused on the footpath that led into the hotel itself.

Lally drew a big breath. 'So we're all set for our night's acting. Oh, I hope it'll be fun, and you'll go back later and your story will just pour out of your fingertips because your imagination will have worked out what you want to do. The hotel looks awfully fancy.'

Her anticipation was so sweet that Cam just had to smile. Lally might enjoy wearing some different clothes, too, he thought with a hint of fondness that crept up on him. She dressed nicely already, but sometimes he felt she dressed to try not to be noticed. 'I haven't fully explained the final part of the evening when we'll go up on the rooftop: you'll be entirely safe, but I need an unanticipated reaction out of you. If you don't mind.'

'Your mysteriousness is making my imagination run wild.' Lally admitted this with a smile as she met Cam's gaze. 'I don't mind. You can surprise me. That can be part of the fun too.'

Cam cleared his throat. 'Thanks for being a good sport about it. You truly won't mind being dressed up and having your hair and make-up done?'

'Hair and make-up too?' Her eyes widened. 'I imagine I'll feel as though I'm being thoroughly spoiled.'

Lally gave her answer to Cameron and tried to gather her concentration. Cinderella; he'd said to think of it as that.

Her boss in a dinner suit; that was a big part of the reason for her distraction. In truth, Lally did feel like Cinderella—well, Cinderella with a slightly weary but anticipation-filled prince at her side.

A prince who looked divine clothed this way, and wore his exhaustion more attractively than should be legal.

When she'd first emerged from her room and seen Cameron waiting for her, Lally's pulse had raced.

'Thank you for agreeing to this,' he'd said, and clasped her hand briefly before leading the way outside to his car. Beautiful car, gorgeous driver. Cameron had relaxed her with easy conversation during the trip, and even now as they walked through the hotel he somehow made her feel special whether he was looking all about him to research his book or not.

A night out of time, that was what this would be for Lally. She could do it, of course she could, and have a whole lot of fun in the process!

Cam led her straight to the grouping of boutique clothing-stores with fashionably sparse window-displays. Lally glanced around the opulent hotel's interior; that opulence tied in with what she saw here. A qualm struck; she leaned towards Cam and whispered urgently, 'That looks like a *designer original* dress in the window.'

'It is, but from my research there are plenty of non-designer dresses in the shop as well.' Cam stepped inside without giving Lally a chance to argue it one way or another. 'And here's our shop assistant ready to help us.'

'But the money,' Lally whispered, and tugged on his arm. 'It *all* looks expensive. You can't…'

He turned and gave a reassuring smile. 'These purchases are a legitimate business expense. I'll claim them against tax, and I get to give a great housekeeper the gift of a few things after we've used them for my research—if you'd like them. You'll let me do that rather than throwing them out, won't you?'

'Throw?' Lally bit back a gasp. He wanted her to let him buy the things and then give them to her, but she'd thought if that happened it would be in a very inexpensive way.

'It's not hurting anything, Lally.' He said it in such a businesslike way. 'I need this kind of setting. You understand?'

Lally calmed down a little. This was just work, when all was said and done. Unusual, maybe, but still work.

If her awareness of him suggested differently, well, she would get that sorted out. She would. She'd just watch very carefully to make sure they didn't end up buying a dress that cost a ridiculous amount of money.

'Good evening. How may I help you?' The saleswoman was already sizing Lally up.

'We need a dress. Something bright, flattering and elegant; a handbag; earrings, and I think…' Cam's gaze shifted to Lally's neck and lingered there. 'Yes, a necklace. I'll know what I want for that once we choose the dress. Hmm…' He turned to the saleswoman.

'I don't know much about this, but something that will suit her colouring, bring out the brown of her eyes and make the most of her hair. That's what I want.'

You should be in colours, Latitia. You were born for them on all sides of your family tree!

Mum had said that to her—recently, actually, now Lally thought of it. She had given Lally an almost disappointed look when Lally had shrugged her shoulders and said she preferred plain colours, and shades that blended rather than stood out. Mum had looked away and muttered something about 'long-term hibernation behaviour.'

A week later Lally had finished working at the fishing-tackle-and-bait store, and she'd no longer been needed in the next job she'd had lined up in the family. The whole family had been just fine getting along without her, and she'd ended up with Cam.

Now they were shopping, and he had his arm loosely against her shoulders; when had that happened?

Lally looked away in case she was gaping over the list he'd just given the saleswoman. Lally's glance fell on a mirror on the shop-wall that showed their reflections. Cam had a spark of enjoyment in his eyes.

Worse was the corresponding sparkle in her eyes.

More dangerous still was how much she liked the look of those two reflections; side by side.

Lally could count on one hand the number of times she'd been out on a date since the disaster of Sam six years ago. The last time must have been over a year ago. Those dates had been pleasant enough, she supposed, but in a very controlled way for her, and she'd never looked for a repeat.

Her reaction just now hadn't felt controlled. Plus, this was *not* a date!

'Nothing designer,' Lally said with about as much spine in her tone as an overcooked noodle. She cleared her throat and tried again. 'Maybe you have a sale rack?'

'Perish *that* thought.' The sales lady said it with good humour, disappeared for a moment and returned with a garment over her arm. 'Perhaps you'd like to try this? It's middle range, though it's an odd thing to be told *not* to include designer choices!' She held up a flow of deep-red silk.

'Oh, it's…gorgeous.' The words poured out of Lally's mouth before she could stop them; to her credit she tried to back-pedal as soon as it happened. 'That is, I'm not sure. It's awfully noticeable—the colour and style…' Lally broke off and turned to Cam. 'I guess that doesn't matter. It's only to help you to figure out what you want.'

'That's right. It seems…as good a choice as any.' He nodded. 'I'm having fun, Lally, and that's got to be good for my muse. So, go and try the dress on, please.'

'It will make you look absolutely radiant, dear.' Somehow the woman had her hustled through the store and into a changing room with the dress pushed into her hands before Lally quite realised what had happened. Her last glimpse before the dressing room door closed was of Cam turning to examine a shelf of evening bags with a purposeful and cheerful glint in his eyes.

Lally locked the dressing-room door, turned to the mirror, and saw a bright-eyed girl with red silk clutched in her hands.

'It won't fit,' she muttered, not sure if she was being hopeful, practical, hedging her bets or trying to talk herself out of a love affair that had already taken wings the moment the saleswoman held up the dress.

'You're such a predictable female, Lally.' She muttered the words beneath her breath. 'The first time someone throws a pretty dress at you, and all your past decisions about fashion choices and colours go out the window.'

Oh, but this was different. This wasn't for *her,*

not really. This was for research so Cam could look at Lally and choose a whole different look for his book character.

It was reverse psychology, and it would work; Lally just knew it would. Lally was just the human mannequin for the evening, as cardboard and one-dimensional as could be.

She was filled with a lot of excitement for someone who was one dimensional, though.

'Are you done?' Cam's voice sounded from outside the cubicle. 'May I see the dress on you?'

Lally was done. She'd simply been standing there staring mutely at the transformation that had appeared in the mirror. She didn't feel much like a mannequin; she felt like a girl in a gorgeous dress.

'I'm not sure if this…' Lally put her hand on the door latch, unlocked it and pulled it open.

'You…' The single word trailed away as Cam's gaze slowly travelled from her head to her toes and back again.

'It seems to be the right size.' Lally resisted the urge to fidget with the hem or twitch the fabric over her hips. The dress fitted like a glove and flowed over her curves in all the right ways.

'It's perf— That is, I'm sure it'll be fine for our purpose, to help me figure out what the heroine in the story would wear.' Cam gave one slow blink and his voice deepened as he held out his hand. 'Put these on with it, please.'

A drop-necklace and set of dangling earrings were settled into the palm of her hand, and her fingers were curled closed over them. 'I slipped out to the jewellery store beside this one while you changed into the dress.'

'Okay, well, I'll put them on.' Their fingers brushed as Lally made sure she had a proper grip on the items.

Her heart was pounding. It was so stupid, but she fell silent as she withdrew her hand. Had Cam's hand moved away quite slowly, as though he might have been almost reluctant to lose the contact?

'There's a bag too.' His voice was deep and he cleared his throat before he went on. 'I'll give that to you when you come out.'

Lally could have put the necklace and earrings on in front of him, but she was rather glad for a moment to herself. She had to pull herself together.

The earrings were simple gold with a pearl drop that bumped against her neck when she moved her head. The matching pearl-drop necklace nestled between her breasts. It would have been difficult to find a set to create a better foil for the dress.

No, Lally, it suits you and *the dress perfectly.*

Lally tucked her hair behind her ears to showcase the earrings. They really needed an upswept hairstyle; so did the dress. Lally took another proper look in the mirror.

The dress was deep red with a crossover V-neckline that cupped her breasts. It was deceptively simple, clinging in beautifully cut lines until it fell in loose folds to just below her knees. The hem was handkerchief-cut and swirled as she moved.

Cameron had dressed her the way she would have dressed herself six years ago. No; he'd dressed her the way that eighteen-year-old would have dressed six years on if she hadn't hidden herself in bland colours.

She hadn't *hidden* herself. She'd outgrown colours.

Have you, Lally? Because you look great in this, vibrant and alive and ready to take on the world. Ready to participate *in the world, not avoid it from within the heart of your family.*

Oh, this was silly! Lally was helping Cam; they were doing research. She wanted to get on with that and leave these other thoughts behind her. He'd look at all this, and it might look good on her, but it would help him see how he wanted to dress his heroine. He might put his character in faux fur, or shiny pink plastic, or dress her in blue velvet.

Lally gathered her other clothes into her hands, flung the door open and stepped out. She joined Cam at the service counter where he'd just finished paying for his transaction. 'I'm ready to get on with the rest of our research.'

And *that* was what this was truly all about.

CHAPTER FIVE

'THE hairdresser is next.' Cam made this announcement and led Lally towards the hotel salon. He pressed a small sparkly bag into her hands as they walked. His other hand held a bag the saleswoman had kindly supplied for Lally's day clothes. 'In the scene, the female character would make out that she wanted to be showered with as much "spoiling" as she could get.'

'And your male lead would be determined to do that, to keep her suspicions at bay about his real motives. They'll be deep in their false roles.' Lally took the small bag; she couldn't take her eyes from his face. The grooves at the sides of his mouth were deep. His face had the kind of stillness that concealed attraction and awareness.

Though she knew she shouldn't, though there were a thousand reasons why it would be better if she failed to react to this at all, Lally's gaze locked with his. Her fingers closed about the short strap of the bag, she drew a deep, deep breath and admitted, to herself at least, that she was equally attracted to Cam. That had to stop right now. They had to get the fun back and avoid these other inappropriate responses to each other. It was probably just the atmosphere getting to both of them, anyway.

Somehow Lally got through the appointment with the hair stylist. It helped that Cam sat on a lounge in the waiting area and buried his nose in a magazine.

Half an hour later Lally got up from the chair with her curls artfully drawn away from her face in a high pony-tail with just a few tendrils trailing down her back.

'Shoes.' Cameron murmured the single word as his gaze tracked over her hair and the vulnerable nape of her neck.

'You'll have to decide about your heroine's hair,' Lally said, and hoped the desperate edge couldn't be heard in her tone. 'It's probably ice-blonde, straight and swept up in a bun away from her model-gorgeous face.'

'Uh, yes. Perhaps.' Cam drew her to a shoe shop.

Lally's transformation to Cinderella-dressed-for-the-ball reached its final moment as they stepped through the door. She spotted the sandals immediately. They were third row down on an elegant stand, they had their own name—Grace After Midnight—and she had to have them.

Six inch stiletto gold-and-black heels; tiny criss-cross gold-and-black strips across the instep. Elegant ankle straps. All of Lally's sensible thoughts and cautions disintegrated for that moment of time. She forgot the purpose of the night, forgot everything—well, not Cam, but he did take second place to the shoes for a minute.

'I'll pay for these myself.' They were in her hands before she finished speaking the words, on her feet moments later. They fit like a dream; these shoes were meant to be.

Lally had her credit card and there were fifty dollars in the pocket of the skirt that had gone into the dress shop bag with her other clothes. She held her hand out to Cam. He came back into focus, and so did his grin that held outright amusement—was that a hint of enchantment?

Of course it isn't, Lally. It so totally isn't! 'I need the bag, please.'

'No. I've got this.' Cam paid for the shoes and hustled her out of the store.

'You don't understand. I had to have them, you see.' How did she explain the compulsion that took a pair of shoes from stage prop to girl's best friend? And how that meant she couldn't let him pay for her pure indulgence.

'And I'd have paid that much or more for any

choice that you made.' With those few words, Cam dismissed the matter.

And he truly did dismiss it. The glint in his eyes was a good-humoured one, but it also warned her that arguing would be futile. He tucked her arm through his and led her towards the hotel's restaurant. 'You look great, Lally. You're made for bright colours.'

'That's what Mum says.' *Business, Lally!* She must remember tonight was about his work, no matter how he'd been looking at her or how it felt to walk at his side and feel as though she were made to belong there.

'Over dinner we'll discuss where this has put you in terms of figuring out your heroine,' Lally declared, and led the way with determination towards their dining table.

Lally looked amazing; the thought washed through Cam yet again as he escorted his housekeeper into the restaurant. She looked amazing, was dressed amazingly and walked incredibly in heels that would have stopped a lot of women in their tracks.

He'd told Lally she was made for colours. What he hadn't said was that she was made for all of this—the dress, the shoes, the lovely hair, the sparkle in her eyes…

Yes, he had needed this research for his story.

Seeing Lally in the clothes had somehow made her more vibrant and real to him, and that had, indeed, already helped him to start seeing his book's heroine.

Not an ice-blonde, but a woman in her late thirties with elegant looks and straight brunette hair in a cap-cut to her head. A woman who wore classic black. Lally's reverse-psychology theory was working. Her quirky approach to the problem had got him well on the way to resolving it.

He'd thought that to fix his writer's block he needed a housekeeper to free up his time so he could concentrate better.

What he'd needed was tonight's insights.

'This way, please.' The waiter seated them with a flourish at the table Cam had booked earlier. The man's gaze rested for a long moment on Lally's beauty.

Cam could only silently agree.

'I feel quite transformed.' Lally's fingers toyed with the clasp of the small bag in her lap after the waiter walked away. 'Cinderella ready for the ball, except the shoes aren't glass.' Her lips pressed together. 'Well, this isn't about me. What would your book character be wearing? What would she have bought in the shop?'

'The shoes are better than glass.' They revealed the beauty of Lally's calf muscles, the delicate shape of her feet, the slender ankles. But that wasn't something Cam should tell his house-keeper. 'My heroine would be in a black dress. Full length and fitted. She's in black stiletto-shoes with a closed toe and heel—what do you call those?'

'Pumps?'

'Yes.' Cam nodded. 'She's wearing diamonds, a choker around her throat, a thick tennis-bracelet style of cuff on her right wrist. Earrings that are a carat apiece.'

'You're working her out! That's great.' Lally glanced down at the bag in her lap. 'The diamanté on this is amazing. It looks so real.'

Cam thought about avoiding her gaze when she raised it, but in the end he simply returned it and hoped he didn't look too guilty. Or too sheepish. 'They are real, but there aren't many, and they're very small. The bags with fake stones cost nearly as much.'

He added somewhat craftily, 'It's the perfect size for a small ladies' handgun.'

'Ooh.' Lally's eyes lit up and she leaned forward in her chair, her whole face alight with interest and excitement. 'Is she an assassin? A double agent?'

'Close to that.' He knew he was being mysteri-ous, but the desire to tease her just a little had got hold of him. Cam's gaze tracked over her hair and the sweep of her neck, the soft nape, and he forgot about his characters.

Instead, Cam wanted to kiss Lally right there at the base of her neck, to inhale the scent of her skin and brush his lips over the side of her neck and across her face. He felt ridiculously proud that he'd been able to distract her about the cost of the bag. 'Don't tell anyone what ideas I have in mind for the heroine.' He winked. 'I have to keep the book's secrets until it hits the shelves, otherwise my career as a writer is over.'

'I won't tell a soul.' She crossed her heart with her fingers, joining in the fun. 'I guess it's all right to confess I'm enjoying the dress, and I love the shoes. I had a pair that were similar when I was fresh out of high school.' Lally made this admission almost guiltily. 'They were cheaper, and not quite as pretty, but they made me feel…'

'Beautiful? You are.'

Maybe he shouldn't have said it—*probably* he shouldn't have said it—but the words were out.

'Thank you.' Lally registered Cam's words and tried not to let her feelings melt. If she simply felt complimented, that would be okay, still manageable. The charming man tells the girl she looks great, the girl appreciates his words of admiration and takes them for what they are: a compliment. The same as he might give to any other woman while they were working on an unusual project together.

But she didn't feel only complimented; she felt

Cam's awareness of her, and hers of him. She felt the consciousness that flowed back and forth between them that had been beneath the surface from the start of the night, but hidden under the excitement and fun factor of their research and role-playing.

That consciousness *was* there. Even now as they sat here, Cam's upper body leaned forward as though he'd like to close the distance of the table that separated them and press a soft kiss to her lips.

Lally's body leaned in too, until she forcibly stopped herself and straightened her spine.

She had to remember that Cameron Travers was her employer, not a man she would like to melt into, to kiss and be kissed by.

'We should choose something to eat.' Lally dropped her gaze to the menu; she flipped it open and stared blindly at the *entrées*. 'Do you need us to choose anything specific for research purposes?'

'No. Just choose what you'd like to eat.' Cam, too, turned his attention to his menu.

You see? They were being perfectly sensible.

Eventually the list of dishes unscrambled itself enough that Lally could read it: tuscan prawns; artichoke and sweet-potato soup—Cam would avoid that one—lamb, leek and bread broth; baked cheese bites in puff pastry with a dark-plum dipping sauce.

'I think I'll have the broth.' Lally rejected the appeal of spicy prawns, of sensually melted cheese in pastry. 'Yes, the broth. Something healthy and ordinary. It seems exactly what I'd like.'

She was a sensible, ordinary girl, after all, even if she had allowed herself to be swept up in the purchase of a lovely dress and a pair of stunning shoes.

Over all, Lally had progressed past being influenced by emotions, sudden whims or anything else uncontrolled.

Sam had taught her that lesson—well, in truth, the pain she had caused out of knowing him had taught her. Lally's good cheer wobbled.

In that moment Cam glanced at her, smiled and said softly, 'Thank you, Lally, for being such a good sport tonight. I've really enjoyed myself, enjoyed the research. I've got ideas coming into focus in my mind. You've helped me to get the muse back on track.'

'You're welcome. It's been my pleasure to help you.' Lally pushed those other unhappy thoughts far away.

Cameron's eyes moved over his menu, but a smile lingered on his face. After that he led the conversation onto the topic of his property development; maybe he knew she needed that easing of tension.

He talked about the challenge of obtaining good workers in locations all around Australia wherever he purchased properties to develop, and the properties themselves. Lally relaxed and her happiness came back.

'You've certainly developed some interesting projects over the years. Several of my family members might be interested in the art gallery you mentioned in the tourist township on the Queensland coast.' Some of them might like to have work exhibited there, if the gallery manager was interested.

Their *entrées* arrived and Lally dipped her spoon into the broth. It was thick with chunks of lamb, loaded with fresh colourful vegetables, and the aroma was spicy. She took the first taste onto her tongue and closed her eyes while the flavours exploded on her palate.

Cameron cut a piece from a Tuscan prawn, popped it into his mouth and chewed. He gestured towards her soup bowl. 'How is it?'

'Fabulously interesting and totally yummy.' Lally smiled in wry acceptance. She was wearing a beautiful red dress and killer heels—would it really hurt for her to eat exciting food too?

They talked about nothing much. It should have been totally unthreatening; instead, a rising consciousness seemed to fill the air between them once again until every breath she took held the essence of that consciousness, whether Lally felt ready to feel like that or not.

When Cam picked up his fork and knife, Lally realised they'd both been sitting there staring at each other in unmoving silence.

At what point had they put down their implements and simply sat in quiet stillness?

Almost…like lovers.

The way you used to stare at Sam across a dinner table, totally besotted, and with no thought for anything beyond the smooth words, smoother smiles and the looks he used to send your way?

'How, um, how would your heroine behave at this point of the evening?' They'd finished the *entrées;* Lally sipped her water and told herself she had to do better than this.

'Here we are.' A waiter deftly reordered their table setting and offered Cam a choice of wines to go with their main course. Cam had chosen flame-grilled steak; Lally, Barramundi fillets with a creamy herbed-lemon dressing.

'I'd like Chardonnay, please.' Lally felt pleased that her voice sounded normal. They'd opted out of the wine to start with, and she'd appreciated that too.

Cameron examined the labels of the wines the waiter had brought and approved a Chardonnay for Lally and a red for himself. The waiter poured and left, and they started their meals.

Cam answered her question then. 'The heroine would be doing her best to distract the hero and keep his mind jumping so he doesn't have time to wonder what she's up to.' He glanced at his plate and then hers. 'For us, for now, I'd like descriptions of the food so I can use the dishes in the book, I think. I can see the characters eating these meals.'

'Oh—okay. The fish is moist and flaky; the sauce is tart enough to balance the creaminess.' Lally did her best to describe the combination of textures and tastes.

She could see Cam making mental notes, and she tried to feel that they'd left behind their consciousness of each other, but it felt as though it still simmered beneath the surface.

There had to be some way to stop that simmering. It was inappropriate for her to simmer in this setting.

And if your boss is simmering?

Well, Lally didn't know—and what were they anyway, a matching set of human saucepans?

'Do you think you'll take on other property-development projects in Adelaide?' Yes, that was the way to express an everyday, businesslike interest and nothing more—ask a question that made her sound as though she wanted to be assured he wouldn't be leaving after a few short weeks!

'Tell me about your family. You mentioned art and restaurants.'

Cam spoke at the same time. They both stopped. He brushed his hand over the back of his neck.

If Lally got started on family, they would still be here when the place closed for the night. And she did want to know what his future plans might be, even if that made her nosy.

'I may take on further projects here.' Cam didn't seem to make too much of her question. He started to talk about other buildings in various parts of Adelaide. 'There's a block of apartments, dilapidated but in an area that I know would resell really well. I put an offer in on those earlier today.'

As though there was nothing exciting or fascinating about buying up another building; perhaps to him there wasn't. He bought and sold in dollar figures she could only dream about. She found his ability to write stories fascinating, too, his imagination and his interest in hands-on research. The dimple in his chin, the groove on his forehead…

Are not fascinating, Lally!

All right, fine; as a person, Cameron Travers was interesting—complex, busy, bordering on workaholic. And an insomniac. And, for whatever reason, Lally found all of this a little too intriguing for her own calm and controlled state of mind.

They made their way through the remainder of the meal. Cameron occasionally jotted notes on a small note-pad he drew from his trouser pocket, but Lally felt as though his attention never left her, never left *them*. Which was quite silly, because this wasn't about her or *them*.

Finally, they finished the last sip of their coffee. Lally pushed away her half-eaten dessert of a profiterole filled with *crème* custard and coated in crunchy strands of caramelised sugar. 'That's delicious, but I can't fit it all in.'

Cam patted his flat stomach and pushed the platter of cheese and crackers into the middle of the table. 'I'm done there too.' He glanced at his watch and met her gaze with eyes that were piercing and interested, weary, alert and conscious of her all at once. 'It's after eleven. Will you come and do the final step of tonight's adventure with me now?'

Deep tone. Words meant to be about his work. Expression that was somewhat about that. Yet…

'That's what we're here for.' Lally agreed while her senses were in a muddle reacting to him.

She agreed before her brain engaged at all, really. That was dangerous, as was the feel of his arm holding her fingers tucked against his side as they left the restaurant after he paid for their meal. She could feel the muscles over his ribs moving as he walked; his skin beneath his shirt was warm against the back of her fingers.

He felt lean and fit—he *was* lean and fit—and gorgeous and appealing into the bargain. Lally shouldn't be feeling these responses to him because she needed to protect herself. She was not ready to tackle another relationship with a man, and, even if she was, that man wasn't going to be a millionaire, incredibly focused, fabulous and famous temporary boss: Cam was way out of her league.

So, what was she about, leaning against his side this way?

They climbed into a service lift that took them to the top of the hotel.

'It's only five storeys high, but I do want to go all the way to the roof for this.' Cameron said it almost as though he felt he should apologise for this fact.

'Whatever works best for your story.' Lally told herself she had overcome her momentary lapse, that she had herself well in hand now.

That theory lasted until she looked into Cameron's eyes and her pulse started to throb at her wrists and at the base of her neck. And—oh, it was silly—she suddenly she felt a bit…nervous too.

'That's exactly what I wanted to see, Lally— the edge of caution, even though at this stage you don't believe you're in any true danger.' His words were a glide of consonants and cadence that crossed her senses like the brush of velvet over her skin. 'That's a look I can describe for my heroine to good effect in the book.'

The lift stopped and they stepped out onto the flat rooftop area of the building. Cam glanced around and led her towards the edge with a firm grip on her arm. 'You don't suffer from vertigo or anything like that?'

'No. I don't.' Even so, Lally made no bones about leaning into his firm hold now; it was a long drop to ground level. Too bad if that made her look clingy just at the moment. 'What?'

'Look at the drop for me. Then we're going to act out...' He led her close enough that she could look over.

As Lally truly registered that they stood five storeys up on a deserted rooftop late at night, her imagination kicked in. What did Cam plan to write about this setting? What did he want her to do?

Lally glanced at her boss, and adrenalin and excitement coursed through her veins. It seemed necessary to speak in a hushed tone, and she whispered, 'This is going to be a real rush, isn't it? Like skydiving or something. My instincts are telling me it will be exciting. My heart's in my throat already and I don't even know yet.'

'I don't know what you'll think.' His fingers tightened their hold around her arm. 'But we're going to find out.'

CHAPTER SIX

'YOU'LL be completely safe, Lally, but you may not feel safe for a moment or two.' Cam's gaze searched her face.

'Whatever it is, I'm ready.' Lally ignored the breathless edge to her voice and the nervous tension that went with it.

Cam clasped his fingers loosely about her elbows. 'This would all happen very fast. She wouldn't have time to think, but for the point of this exercise I'll talk you through some of it. I want your thoughts on what her reactions would be.'

It was automatic for Lally's hands to come up and splay against his chest through the cloth of his dinner jacket. The evening bag was over one of her wrists. 'I think your heroine would feel her heart-rate speed up, and she would tell herself to be careful. Be very careful.'

Cameron's glance rested briefly on her mouth.

'She doesn't know whether he intends to kiss her, attack her, accuse her, hold her at gunpoint, try to overpower her or throw her over the edge. Is he on to her secrets?'

'And is she on to his?'

No sooner had Lally got the question out than Cam drew her back a little from the edge. He swept her up in his arms in a lightning-fast move. One hand came under the back of her thighs, the other cupped behind her shoulders. Her handbag was jammed between their bodies. His face was inches from hers.

They were a safe distance from the edge but, oh, it didn't feel safe in those first moments. Lally caught her breath and a soft gasp of sound left her parted lips. Her free hand locked around the back of his neck.

'Easy.' Cam felt Lally's arm lock around the muscles in his neck, and he took two long steps, not towards the edge but parallel to it. 'Sorry. I need to know how my male lead would feel carrying her.'

'If he's doing it to get closer to the edge, she'd be fighting him.' Lally's words brushed against his temple and cheek. 'She'd struggle to get free.'

Lally was tense, but not struggling.

Cam had to think about his characters. The research. He could see the characters clearly in his mind.

That was great; his instincts told him he would be able to write this scene. He had his female character fixed now, defined, he knew who she was and that she would work well for his story. That issue was resolved for Cam.

What wasn't resolved was his desire for the woman in his arms. That had been getting further and further away from his control since they'd first schemed this idea up earlier today. Maybe the excitement of it, the sheer fun of planning and executing it, was why Cam hadn't controlled his other responses to Lally very well.

'Yes, she would struggle to get free, but I'll deal with working that out for myself or we can role-play it elsewhere. Even though we're away from the edge, I don't want to risk losing my balance or anything while we're up here.' He tried to sound focused and interested in the research. Not distracted...

'If he does intend to throw her, the best thing she could do is refuse to release her hold on him, unless he was prepared to go over with her.' Lally made this observation with what judiciousness she could find in the face of her distraction. Being held this way, held close to Cam's broad chest, made thinking difficult. 'Or unless he had the capacity to subdue her some other way before he tossed her over.'

In tandem with her words, Lally's hand locked harder about his neck.

Cam moved his body enough to allow her to get her other hand free. 'In the scene, she would struggle to get that hand loose.'

Lally added it to her hold about his neck. 'So she'd hold on like this?'

'At this stage, yes.' God, his voice was way too deep, and his entire body seemed utterly focused on what he held.

And what he held was Lally Douglas in a flowing, beautiful dress that made her look both sultry and alluring. He felt the brush of the soft fabric over his hand where he held her in his arms; the hem wrapped around his trouser legs. He held Lally, her face upturned towards his, excitement and an edge of uncertainty stamped on that face.

It was not because she didn't feel safe with him. There was apprehension of another kind, the sort a person felt when they entered uncharted territory with someone they found attractive.

Are you cataloguing her reactions now, Travers, or your reactions to her?

Cam stopped walking and murmured, 'She would quite probably try to reach for the gun in her purse.'

'Yes.' Her words whispered into the stillness. She didn't move.

Cam's focus was on her face, his gaze touching on each feature—eyes, cheeks, nose, finally lingering on her mouth. His look, filled with want, desire and something perhaps deeper than both of those things, drew Lally's gaze to his eyes and locked it there. Her breath stilled all over again. All around them was darkness and city silence, which was no silence at all, but it still shrouded them in isolation here while the world went by below.

Darkness and aloneness and consciousness.

Cam's gaze met hers once more in the dimness, and everything slid into a different place for Lally. The evening; the slow meal and their talk about his writing and work projects; her determination not to look too deeply into herself: it had all mixed in together and blurred into this one moment that was so much more than the compilation of those parts. That really had nothing at all to do with those parts.

'I shouldn't have picked you up like this.' He murmured the words, but he didn't let her go.

Instead his hand wrapped more firmly behind her shoulders and he shifted to stand with his legs splayed apart.

His head lowered towards her. 'Tell me not to…'

'Not to…?' But Lally knew. She looked into his eyes and she couldn't say the words. How could she say those words to Cam when his gaze was on her this way, desire stamped across his cheekbones, burned into the shadows beneath his eyes, etched over lips that softened and dipped towards hers?

She should say no. She needed to protect her emotions and not take risks, but Lally could only wait while her lips softened in anticipation.

And then he was there. The kiss she had secretly longed for was happening.

His lips tasted faintly of coffee, and were both firm and gentle as he softly kissed her, oh, so softly, as though they had all the time in the world and all he wanted to do was this.

She'd thought she was holding her own, that she had control over this evening with him. That she had at least held on to a little of what it was all about, remembered they were doing this for his research and no other reason.

Well, this didn't feel like research. Her lips softened beneath his and when he slid her slowly down his body until her feet touched concrete it felt natural and right to let his arms close around her, to step fully into his embrace and let the kiss take them where it would.

Cam made a soft sound in the back of his throat. He deepened their kiss, his lips caressing hers, moulding to hers, tasting and giving and taking. One hand splayed against the small of her back; the long, lean fingers of the other wrapped around her jaw.

Lally responded with a deepening of desire for

him, but she also softened for him. Her emotions melted into a puddle inside her; if he'd wanted, he could have walked straight in and…

Well, she wasn't sure. Taken whatever he wanted? Hurt her because she wasn't ready to trust a man again, wasn't sure she could ever do that again? She wasn't sure she could trust herself.

Lally became conscious of just how intimately they were pressed together; their bodies were flush against each other from chest to knee. Cam's fingers were stroking up and down her bare shoulders and back. Hers—were in his hair, clasping his shoulder while her entire body seemed to strain for closeness with his.

Oh, Lally. What are you thinking?

Lally forced her mouth to leave his, her body to draw back. Each action felt as though it took an aeon to execute. She shouldn't feel *anything* towards Cam, not in this way. He was her boss; she was his employee. Lally felt panicked.

Think how Cam kissed you, Lally. How he drew a response from you so easily and so thoroughly, made you feel as though you were receiving your first ever real kiss.

Sam had made her feel that way. With Sam, it *had* been her first ever kiss. First kiss, first everything.

That was hardly the point here.

Well, what was the point? She couldn't let

herself be affected by what they had shared in these moments. She couldn't let herself care again—

Lally forced herself to meet Cam's gaze and opened her mouth to speak, to play this down, to say something about work or characterisation or research.

Anything.

But her lips still tingled from the press of his. Even now her body begged her to step back into his embrace, to take their kiss even further, prolong the closeness and connection.

Finally Lally found words. 'I'm not looking for an involvement. Not that I'm suggesting you are. This… We forgot ourselves for a moment. There's no need to make a fuss about it, but it mustn't happen again; it's not wise. You're a busy man with loads on your plate, and your struggle to sleep to deal with, let alone a recalcitrant muse and a highly demanding business in Sydney. And I work for you!'

'I know.' He swallowed hard. Regret etched lines into his face that hadn't been there before. 'I understand all of that, Lally. It was wrong of me to kiss you. I'm not looking for a relationship. I don't—that's not in my agenda, and it's not smart to mix work with that anyway. And you're quite right. You wouldn't want…'

Whatever he'd been about to say, he cut the

words off, but the message was there anyway. He agreed with her. This kiss shouldn't have happened. They had to respect the boundaries of their working relationship. He didn't want her, not really. Not like that.

Lally drew a breath and blurted, 'I didn't mean to set up this night to lead to this.'

'I know.' His words were deep and genuine. 'I had a problem with my writing, you thought of a great solution. We both got excited about it and in that excitement, for a few moments, we forgot ourselves.'

His summary of events left out a few things— such as the way they'd both become more aware of each other as the evening had worn on—but Lally nodded. 'That's right. I'm glad we got that sorted out.' She forced a relieved smile. 'Phew. Well, are we finished here? Do you have what you need for your research? Maybe we should head home—I mean, back to your property development.'

'I have everything I need.' Cam watched emotions flit across Lally's face and felt them churn inside him. Kissing her had been amazing. Yes, he'd made all sorts of comments on how that had come about and why it shouldn't have and everything else. Those comments were real and true; they just weren't all of it. And they didn't even begin to touch on how he'd felt inside himself as a result of these shared moments. Cam didn't want to examine those feelings, but the thoughts came anyway.

He'd kissed her softly in a way he had never kissed any other woman. He'd kissed Lally after trying to ignore the need to do it all night. He'd kissed her to pay homage to her beauty and how lovely she looked in that dress. He'd done it because something inside him had needed to.

He couldn't tell her any of that. Because Lally didn't want this. She'd made that clear and she'd looked scared when she said it. Scared from somewhere inside that Cam shouldn't mess with because she could end up getting hurt, and the last thing he wanted was to hurt her.

He wanted to know *what* had hurt her, but he mustn't mess with that either. He had no right, no claim on her, aside from being her very temporary employer, nor would he ever seek to change that. Cam didn't want this either; he couldn't pursue it. He'd only end up disappointing her, not being what she needed. He'd proved that about himself already.

He was an insomniac, workaholic, novel-writing businessman who couldn't stay in one place, couldn't rest, had no idea how to be a family. He and his mother might have been linked during his childhood but she hadn't wanted him. And Cam had learned not to be wanted.

He'd tried to break out of that once, in his mid-twenties. Gillian…

Cam had built up Gillian's expectations, and when she'd realised just how much of him would never be hers, when she had come to understand just how much his past history and his insomnia impacted on his daily life, she'd been let down, disappointed and ultimately hurt. She'd wanted and needed more than he'd been able to give her. She'd been right to want that, and right to walk away.

They'd gone their separate ways and Cam had learned a lesson. He didn't want to hurt a woman like that again. He didn't want to set himself up for that kind of loss again either. He knew what he could and couldn't have.

Yet tonight Cam had forgotten all that past history, that painful learning-curve that he'd sworn not to repeat. He'd kissed a slip of a girl on a rooftop, had found all this tenderness and all these other responses to her inside him. He hadn't simply wanted to give them to her, he'd felt *driven* to bring them to her. That wasn't something he'd experienced with Gillian; it wasn't something he'd ever experienced with any woman.

That fact perhaps had driven him to kiss Lally. It had certainly made his reactions to her even more dangerous. He forced his arms to drop away from her, forced himself to take a step back. Every fibre of his body and mind seemed to object at once. If he drew her close again, he knew he wouldn't want to let go at all. He'd take her hand, lead her back through this hotel, take her home and make her his completely.

Not happening, Travers.

'We should go.' He led Lally back the way they had come and ushered her into the service lift.

As the doors closed, Lally turned to him and said quietly, 'Your book—did we achieve what you needed?'

It was a ploy to get the focus off them and back to the reason for this evening. Cam acknowledged this and did his best to further it. 'I've decided the female character will be an undercover special-services officer, but she's a double agent with marksman skills and a history as a hired assassin as well…' Cam talked about his story until he had Lally out of the hotel and safely ensconced beside him in the car.

In the car's dim interior, Cam could hear every breath Lally took, smell the soft scent of her skin and whatever lotion she'd rubbed into it after her shower tonight. He tried not to notice any of it.

'I'm glad the research was successful and that you have a good understanding of this new character you're bringing into your story.' Her fingers fidgeted with the small bag in her lap. 'You know, I really shouldn't keep any of these things.'

'Please. Maybe you'll wear them some place again one day.' *And think of me.* Was that what Cam wanted? His eyebrows drew together.

As they passed beneath a streetlight, Cam glanced towards her. The breeze had whipped at her hair, dishevelled it just enough to make him want to bury his hands in it, caress his fingers over her scalp and use that touch to tilt her head so he could kiss her neck, kiss her chin and find his way back to soft lips.

You're not thinking about kissing her, remember?

They'd researched; that research had led to a kiss that shouldn't have happened. A kiss that had blown him away, because she'd been so giving and he'd loved that and had wanted to give back in equal measure. Cam drew the convertible to a halt in an allotted space inside the property-development site. No matter how tempting, no matter how much she soothed him—no matter anything—he had to take due care that nothing like this happened again.

A woman like Lally deserved better than an insomniac workaholic who had no sense of family or ability to meet a woman's deep needs.

There was no other way for Cam. No other way that he knew.

CHAPTER SEVEN

'HE PUSHES himself so hard, Auntie. I really want to help him find a way to get more sleep. It's the one thing I think I might be able to do for him, beyond the work I'm already doing.'

A week had passed since the night Lally and Cam had role-played, when he had tried to 'toss her over' the top of the hotel.

Lally had revisited those moments more often than she wanted to admit—not the pretend tossing, but the kissing that hadn't been about role-playing at all.

Cam had placed his lips over hers and it had felt like the sweetest kiss of all time, sweet and gentle and tender, and Lally needed to forget it. She must have built it way up in her mind, anyway, mustn't she? For how could she feel such a depth of reaction and response to something that, for him, must only have been the result of place, time and circumstance, nothing more?

She couldn't start to have feelings about Cam, or towards Cam, not like those.

Lally bit back a sigh. 'He's my *employer.*' She put a certain emphasis on the word 'employer'; yes, that drew even more attention to her need to hold him to that role in her thinking.

If she thought of him in that light, spoke of him in that light, then eventually she would accept he *was* only in that light for her.

Lally glanced about her. It was only just past dawn, but already the markets were teeming with life. Mum stood with her arm linked through Aunt Edie's. Well, that was family; you all looked after each other.

Lally felt a sudden tug of emotion as she acknowledged that thought. For six years she'd built her life around looking after everyone as best she could, and then they hadn't needed her.

'I've missed everyone. You didn't mention how Jodie is getting along. How could I not ask about one of my sisters? Thanks for meeting me here this morning for coffee and talking about so many of them.' She'd asked them to come and had used wanting to help her boss as her reason. And that *had* been the reason. Mostly.

They'd talked. Mum and Auntie had brought her up to speed on all the gossip about the family—well, almost all. Lally reiterated that she could take calls and text messages at work, that her boss wouldn't mind.

Mum and Auntie seemed fine about that, but Lally still came away from that part of the conversation wondering if there was more under the surface. Maybe she should have just asked, but a part of her was scared of the possible answer.

Perhaps the issues with her employer were behind her general sense of unease. He'd done an exemplary job of avoiding her in the past week, aside from meal times, handing over work-lists and asking her to do various specific jobs for him. Another research trip had needed two sets of hands, not one.

He hasn't avoided you at all, Latitia. You've seen loads of him.

Lally frowned. That was right, she had seen loads of him, so why did she almost feel as though she was missing him?

'Jodie's fine,' Mum said.

Lally bit her lip. 'Good. I'm glad.' She was. And, if the answer to her other question was that she wanted Cam all over her with gentle feelings, and maybe the need to kiss her again, then she needed to stop longing for things that were completely out of the question. She was better off without them, because she really wasn't ready to face that kind of emotional gymnastics again.

You don't deserve ever to have a meaningful fulfilling relationship. Not after all the harm you've caused in the past.

The thought sent a shaft of pain through Lally's chest. 'What were we talking about?'

'You were telling us about your hunky new employer,' Auntie declared, and a grin split her weathered brown face.

'My boss has insomnia,' Lally said primly, and in a depressing tone focused on stopping Auntie's speculations. 'I woke three times last night, and every time I could see a strip of light beneath his office door and knew he was in there, working.'

Lally had been restless; she'd been restless ever since the night he'd kissed her, to be honest. 'I wanted to know about bush foods and remedies for Cam in case there might be something that would help him sleep better.'

Her voice softened when she said his name; it went completely to mush just like that. And, because that was such a give away, Lally felt a blush build beneath her skin. She needed to put Auntie and Mum off the scent, not encourage more speculation.

'Fresh food is a good start, of course.' Auntie spoke as she examined Lally's face.

'For Cam, yes.' Mum chipped in with her opinion, and a gleam in her eyes that definitely seemed to hold a hint of satisfaction.

Could the family have conspired to get Lally out into the world, as she'd wondered, with a view to her meeting a man, maybe?

Lally glanced at her watch and found a sudden need to become highly time-efficient. 'I should get on with my shopping while we finish this talk.' Lally strode to the nearest fruit stall and lifted a ripe pawpaw. If this also happened to mean that she wasn't quite so obviously the centre of their speculation, well, that was purely happenstance.

Mum and Auntie quickly caught up with her, and Lally decided, if they were talking, she might as well spit out something else that she'd avoided once already this morning. It was bothering her. She was better off dealing with it so it could stop doing so.

Lally turned. 'This job is the first one I've had where I wasn't working for family. I want to do well at this, but I also need to know I'll be coming back to the family the minute my work is done for Cameron Travers. Someone will need me, won't they?'

'Oh, well, I'm sure they will, but haven't you found spreading your wings to be fun? It sounds as though it has been.' Mum went on, 'You say your employer bought you a dress and a handbag, and you helped him with research on the roof of a hotel at midnight?'

Well, not at midnight, but Lally supposed that was near enough. And, yes, it had been exciting. It just had also become somewhat complicated by the end of the night. 'Yes, we did some research for his current book.' Lally paid for the pawpaw and set it gently into the bottom of her shopping basket. 'But, truly, the only reason I brought up his name this morning is because I want to try to help him sleep better. He looks so exhausted.' She turned to her aunt. 'Do you have any ideas?'

Auntie's wrinkled face creased into even deeper lines. 'There *are* bush foods and remedies; it depends on why he's that way in the first place. Has he seen a doctor?'

'I asked him about that the other day. He's visited doctors and sleep specialists, done all the sleep studies. I think he's tried everything he's been told to try and come to the end of the line with no real solutions.' Lally hesitated. 'It's not that he's not alert, because he always is—he's sharp as a whip—it's just that…'

'He's sharp while he's pushing himself, can't relax, only sleeps until the edge is off his exhaustion, then he wakes and it's on again for another day for him.' Auntie nodded.

She transferred her hold from Mum's arm to Lally's and they made their way through the remaining market-stalls. Lally worked through her shopping list while Auntie talked.

'You remember the tribal elder I took you to visit when you were a girl?' Auntie named the elder. 'He has a store. He and his wife know just about all there is to know about this kind of thing. It might be worth giving them a call.'

Lally did remember, and wished she'd thought of this earlier. 'Thanks. That's exactly what I need.'

They completed the shopping. 'Thanks for meeting me this morning. I should get back to work.'

Mum laid her hand on Lally's arm. 'If you're interested in your boss…'

Yes, there was definitely a gleam in Mum's eyes that said 'the plan is working.' Auntie's too.

Lally's mouth formed words before she could stop them. 'You all ganged together to say there was no work so I'd get out more, didn't you?'

She wanted to be angry, to say 'how could you?'

But Mum gave a sheepish nod and came right out and admitted it. 'We wanted you to have some fun, Lally. Maybe this boss…'

'He kissed me and I kissed him back, but it was a bad idea on both our parts and neither of us wants it.' Lally drew a breath. Apparently her mother still possessed the ability to get her to confess, even when it should have been Mum doing the confessing. 'I just care about his insomnia issues. It's in my nature to care. I've always cared about the family.'

Lally gave Mum a stern stare. 'Even when

they've tossed me out on some made-up pretext without so much as a by your leave.'

'The family cares about you, Lally.' Mum sighed. 'Please don't be angry. Maybe we shouldn't have done that, but it's only for two months. We wanted to help, to see you enjoy yourself, maybe just make some nice friends.'

'Or meet a man friend?' Lally shook her head. 'I wish you hadn't. You don't understand.' But she wasn't mad, and she gave Mum a hug to make that clear. 'It's too late to change anything now, but I'd appreciate it if you all didn't do this again.'

'We interfered too much. I'm sorry, Lally.' Mum looked guilt-ridden.

Lally let it go. 'It's okay.' She gave a wry smile. 'In a family the size of ours, interfering happens. I know that.' Lally couldn't explain why she didn't want a man in her life again. She bit her lip.

Auntie had wandered a little distance while Lally and Mum talked. She returned now and glanced at her watch. 'Are you ready to go, Susan?'

'Indeed I am.' Mum gave Lally another hug.

Auntie gave Lally a hug.

Lally hugged both of them back, and then there were more quick words and waves. There was no need to say anything to Auntie about the rest of it.

They disappeared, and Lally walked towards

the exit of the market. It was only a few blocks back to her boss's development; maybe the walk would help her to clear her mind. At least she knew what her family had been up to now. They'd better all start contacting her again, or she *would* have something to say about that!

Lally glanced into her basket, checked the contents one last time and realised she'd forgotten the baby-spinach leaves she'd wanted to use in a warm chicken salad for lunch. She turned around and strode back into the heart of the market again.

'Lally, wait up, I'll carry the basket for you.' It was Cam's voice, morning-roughened and deep.

He'd called from behind her; Lally turned her head and looked over her shoulder and there he was, his gaze fixed on her as he strode forward through the crowd.

Her heart did a ridiculous lift. The world seemed suddenly brighter simply because she'd caught a glance of his face, a glimpse of a smile and softened expression directed her way.

Oh, Lally, can't you do better than that at resisting how he makes you feel? Do you want *to end up out of your depth again? He's already made it clear he isn't interested.*

Lally just couldn't trust again. The risks were too big. So she had to focus on the ways she could be a good employee to him.

As he joined her, Lally examined his face for

signs of weariness—she found them. 'You couldn't sleep again this morning?'

'No, and I'm sorry if I disturbed you last night.' He scrubbed a hand over his jaw; it bore a day's beard-growth. That combined with a pair of jeans, black T-shirt, and shades pushed up on his head, looked just a little disreputable. Appealingly so.

Not noticing, Lally!

She said quickly, 'You didn't disturb me. I was already awake. I'm just sorry you haven't been managing to sleep more.'

'That's how it is.' He took her arm and raised his eyebrows. 'Where are you headed? When I first spotted you, I thought you'd finished and were ready to go home.'

He'd walked here just to meet her, to carry the basket for her; Lally handed it over and Cam held it easily in one hand.

She drew a breath. 'I forgot to get baby spinach. I want it for our lunch.' Healthy foods, healthy ingredients; she would try to help Cam eat well and sleep better. She had to try. 'Have you had a check-up lately for your insomnia? There might be new treatments. I meant to ask that when we discussed this the other day.'

'I have check-ups a couple of times a year.' He shrugged his shoulders. 'So far, permanently fixing it for me hasn't worked out. I know it's not something people can put up with.'

Now, what did he mean by that?

'Let's get the spinach. Over there?' He waited while she made her purchase, and then walked with her back to the exit. They walked through and started back home along the suburban streets.

Lally had to stop thinking of it as home. It wasn't even particularly home-like; the project was going to be full of rental apartments, for goodness' sake, and Cam wouldn't even be staying here once the work was done. Just because she'd become used to thinking of all sorts of places among her family as home didn't mean she could add Cam's property-development project to that list.

Lally didn't know what he'd meant about people not putting up with his insomnia, but was the answer all that relevant? She could try to help him, that was all.

'I met my mother and aunt here this morning and asked Auntie about folklore. Changes in diet and some bush remedies may help—they won't harm you, and I'd like to try.'

'You're welcome to do that.' It was clear he meant it. 'It's thoughtful of you.'

Lally's heart did an odd little stutter. 'I'm happy to do that.' *Don't let yourself be too happy with him, Lally. It's dangerous.*

But she turned her face up to the sun and felt

happiness get her anyway. 'I think it's going to be quite hot later today.'

'Yes, help yourself to a swim in the pool if you want to. It's safe to swim in now.' He led her around a child's tricycle that had been left abandoned on the footpath. 'I swam in it myself this morning before I came out to find you. The water's the perfect temperature, thanks to the pool's heating.'

'I brought a swimsuit; I might take a dip some time. We could—I mean *I*...' Lally cut herself off quickly before she could say more. What she definitely must not do was let her mind wander to swimming in that pool with her employer.

At midnight, when it was quiet and silent and they had complete privacy to bathe by moonlight, or at least by city light. Either way would be quite romantic.

Which ruled the idea out entirely!

As for her happiness, that stemmed from no longer feeling uneasy about her work future, or her family.

Yes. It was all about that.

Cameron watched the changes of expression cross Lally's face, watched interest and attraction to him war with good sense.

Lally had met with her mother and aunt at least in some part for his sake. Cam couldn't remember the last time anyone had done something to try to care for him. He couldn't remember that ever happening. His mother hadn't exactly been the type, and he'd gone out on his own the first chance he'd got anyway.

Nowadays his mother just gave in to her wandering gene completely and went wherever the mood took her without ever making even a half-hearted effort to convince herself to try to settle anywhere.

Most of the time he wouldn't have been able to track her down if he'd wanted to. The thing was he pretty much didn't want to any more.

Whatever missing gene his mother lacked when it came to family had passed squarely down to Cam. He'd got over trying to connect with her.

Yet he would have liked to meet some of Lally's family.

'I'm sorry I missed meeting your mother and aunt.' Cam tucked her hand more securely against his side. 'And thank you for wanting to help with my sleep issues. Having you around to do some of the day-to-day things is a help all by itself, whether I'm sleeping more as a result or not.'

He turned his head to smile down into her upturned face. Had he gone about with blinkers on until now to stop himself from truly noticing loveliness? Because Lally was lovely in ways he hadn't seen before in anyone else. Beautiful, oh yes, she was that—but her beauty came from inside her as well as from her looks. He'd wanted—no, needed—to dress her in that vibrant outfit last week to pay homage to that beauty, to see it shine, and let all the world see it shine.

The night might have started out as an attempt at trying to rattle his muse loose, and Cam was grateful that that had indeed happened and he'd made good progress with his book since then. But he'd taken pleasure in Lally from the outset that evening. He forced himself to admit this.

Lally had shone. Her eyes had glowed, and she'd chosen the sexiest pair of high heels and worn them as though she'd been made to wear such things. Cam had wanted to sweep her up and kiss her senseless.

He'd done exactly that, and come out of it feeling as if he'd been the one swept off his feet at the top of that building. He hadn't been able to get their kiss out of his mind since. For the first time in his life, Cam was faced with a particular dilemma that he hadn't faced before: he wanted something that he knew he couldn't have, and he couldn't seem to get past the depth of that wanting. He wanted that closeness with Lally again, wanted to be able to take it forward, but he wasn't capable of successfully doing that, and he knew it.

'Auntie knows a lot of bush lore, remedies from

our people that might help you.' Lally's eyes had softened and mellowed into warm, sherry pools.

Cam noted that, noted the sting of deeper colour across her cheekbones, and felt the skin of his face tighten in response. Did she know he could see her awareness, her interest, even as she did all she could to fight it? She was trying to stick to the topic of helping him somehow, and even that was way too sweet of her. But her expression also gave away other feelings.

Cam shouldn't want to see that…

Lally's gaze locked with Cam's and for a long moment she didn't breathe. Her body distilled into consciousness of Cam even as they walked the final stretch of footpath and began to hear the sounds of construction, men calling to each other, hammers, drills and pieces of timber being lifted and dropped.

Her gaze shifted to a point just below Cam's chin. 'I won't try any quack remedies on you, in case you're worried. Auntie would never recommend anything dangerous, or suggest I consult with anyone who would. I know I can trust her judgement with that.'

'What does your aunt do for a living? Or is she retirement age?' Cam asked the question to force his thoughts away from wanting to take her into his arms, but he realised he was truly interested. In fact, he admitted he had been intrigued and interested in Lally's history from the day they'd met. He'd put that down to the curiosity of his writer's mind, but he had to admit this felt more personal. He wanted to *know* Lally, know her deeply, understand what made her tick.

Cam had needed to figure out the female character for his book. Lally had helped him with that.

But the need to know *Lally*, to understand her, that was something that still burned in Cam.

'My aunt is an artist and a potter.' A hint of pride crept into Lally's voice. 'Her pottery and clay sculptures are truly unique and very beautiful. She's fifty-five but I don't think she has any plans to stop working on her art any time soon.'

'Your family seems to have a lot of talent between them.' Cam's words held admiration.

'I think so. I'm very proud of them.' Lally waited while Cam walked them through the courtyard area and into his apartment.

And then she did what she needed to do, and had to keep doing until it became her habit, her 'this is how it is and will go on being' self.

'Thank you for carrying the produce for me. If you have anything new for my duties list, please jot it down and leave it on the kitchen bench for me. I'm going to start some laundry and then I'll be back to prepare breakfast. I'm sure you'll be very busy, so I'll make sure I keep out of your way.'

Without looking at Cam's face, Lally removed

herself to the laundry and buried her thoughts in the process of sorting the fluffies from the non-fluffies.

That was what housekeepers did—and her work was *all* Lally should focus on doing!

CHAPTER EIGHT

'I WISH I could figure out what's missing from the courtyard area.' Cam had just come from a phone call that Lally had asked him to take and had walked into the kitchen to return the mobile phone to her.

The call had been about an issue happening at his Sydney firm, and he'd resolved it easily enough. When he rejoined Lally in the kitchen, his gaze had shifted to the courtyard, and he'd again been struck by the thought that something was missing out there. 'I've already discussed with the site boss making the courtyard a feature area in the complex. He's advised against it. He feels that smaller, separate outdoor-areas would be the way to go. But people might want to be able to mingle.'

'It could turn into a real little community, almost like a family,' Lally said.

'Can you spare a minute, Mr Travers?' The site boss spoke as he knocked on the open apartment-door. 'Those door panels we ordered have arrived. I think they'll do as a substitute for the ones you originally wanted that were out of stock, but I figured you'd want to see for yourself.'

Cam did want to see. Lally was already turning away to start her lunch preparations.

'I'll come now.' Cam stepped outside and told himself it was perhaps best that they'd been interrupted. What was the point of plying Lally with personal questions that couldn't make any difference to their relationship anyway?

That would be the relationship you're not having with her—the one that involves not thinking about kissing her, not wanting to kiss her again and not needing to know everything about her and understand her even more?

Lally Douglas was his housekeeper and assistant. He didn't need to know her past and her history and what made her tick. *He didn't.*

Cam's mobile phone beeped in his pocket and he made a mental note to check his text messages straight after this. Somehow, multitasking every moment of his day didn't feel quite as appealing any more.

When had that happened to him?

'Right. Let's look at these panels.' He strode purposefully forward with the site boss. At least his writing and the development were going well.

* * *

Two evenings later, Cam and Lally stood in the swimming pool with their arms resting on the edge. It was Friday, around eight p.m. The day had been unseasonably hot, and they'd both made their way to the pool to cool off. Cam had already been in the water doing laps when Lally had joined him.

They'd swum, and Cam had told himself not to think about long, bare limbs and a flow of wet hair down the graceful curve of her back. Now they were side by side in the water at the edge of the pool, looking out over the courtyard. Lally wore a one-piece teal swimsuit. It was modest, not that Cam should be giving more than a cursory glance anyway.

'I'd put a pebble mosaic there.' Lally raised one wet arm to point her finger at the centre of the courtyard. 'One with a water feature in the middle so it made the area feel cool and restful all year round. I'd do it in earth tones and use a style similar to a dot-work motif.'

'Symbolic of a traditional Aboriginal painting?' Cam forced his thoughts to that idea. 'That would look good. The colours would work with the existing pavers. The fact that they're weathered would work really well with it. Do you know much about that kind of work?'

Cam turned his head to look at her, and came very close to totally losing his train of thought.

Lally was in the process of wringing the excess

water out of her hair. The swimsuit *was* modest—one-piece, cut to her thighs, criss-crossing over her breasts and coming up into a halter tie at the back of her neck—but the outfit also left rather a lot of her back bare to his gaze. Her shoulders were gently sloped, fine-boned and sun-kissed. Cam wanted to follow where the sun had been, kissing his way to where she'd lifted her hair to wring it out and tie it in a loose knot at the back of her head.

Sleek, touchable hair that looked different with some of the curl soaked out of it.

No touching, no thinking about touching, and definitely no memory of kissing or wanting to do it again.

'I've done mosaics myself.' Lally uttered the words in a voice that held an edge of breathlessness, but not because of the topic of conversation. Her gaze dipped to his bare chest and skittered away again. That simply, that easily, they were back to where they'd been all those nights ago when he'd held her in his arms at the top of that building.

Cam had tried not to let his thoughts return there. He tried now, but he couldn't tear his eyes from her—from every feature, every curve and dip, and all the loveliness from her soft, brown eyes to the lips that he had tasted and dreamed of tasting again. 'Lally?'

'I'd make a circular theme for the mosaic.'

Lally pushed the words out as Cam leaned towards her, and she leaned towards him.

'That sounds good.' It did, but looking into her eyes felt better. Stupid, maybe, but better.

'With…' Lally stopped and drew a deep breath. 'With a pathway leading to the water feature and leading away from it. The feature itself would be at the centre of the circles.'

Cam's hand rose; his fingers just brushed across her damp shoulder. He wanted to pull her against his chest and kiss her until he was satisfied by the taste of her, the velvet of her mouth, the press of her softness against him. Instead, he nodded. 'With the right colours and design, that could be really striking. Restful and interesting at the same time.'

Cam cleared his throat and discovered his hand had come to rest on the pool-edging beside her. Though he wasn't touching her at all, his body formed a half-cradle around hers. She could shift away in an instant, or she could take that one movement forward, all the way into his arms.

'That's what I thought.' Her words were as distracted and breathless as his had been deep. She seemed to force herself to stick to the topic. 'There's a lot of garden edging the courtyard area—predominantly green most of the year, I'm guessing, with a few assorted colours of flowers? I think a mosaic in traditional colours from white sand through to ochre and dark browns would work really well.'

'Yes.' Cam inhaled and didn't think about her mouth. Not at all. 'And the mosaic itself could tell a story, couldn't it?'

'It could. The stones in the centre, surrounding the water feature, could represent a lake or the sea.' She drew a shaky breath. 'Coming in and going out of the feature could be rivers surrounded by their sandy banks.'

'Right.' Cam's mind worked through the idea slowly at first, but he liked it. 'Will you do it for me, Lally?'

Before she lowered her gaze, he thought that she had murmured she would do anything for him.

When she lifted her head, her shoulders were thrown back and she had a glint of determination in her eyes, a businesslike determination. 'You should know I've only done a couple of smaller mosaics in the past, but I do have confidence that—with the help of the site boss to guide me with the water-feature part of it—I could do a good job of this.'

If Lally said she could do it, she could do it. 'We'd need to make some trips to beaches to gather the colours of pebbles you want.'

'I'd thought to perhaps source the pebbles industrially, but gathering them straight off beaches would mean more interesting stones.' Lally nodded. 'They would definitely give the mosaic a more natural look and feel.'

'You didn't tell me you're an artist like some of the others in your family.' One of her referees had noted that Lally should be painting—was she capable of that too?

Lally moved away from him finally and made her way to the steps. She grasped the railing with one hand and looked at him over her shoulder. He could almost believe that those earlier moments hadn't happened. Almost.

'I haven't done much painting.' Lally went on. 'More than one family member has encouraged me to really take it on, and I would like to learn. It's a privilege to be handed down painting traditions and stories within the family. I don't know why I've put it off.' Yet shadows filled her eyes as she admitted she'd stalled on pursuing this part of her life.

'What's in your past, Lally Douglas?' What was there to make her feel she couldn't let herself have that privilege she'd just described? Had she held herself back from painting, just as she'd held back from allowing herself to bloom with all the vibrancy and colour she should embrace in other ways? What would make her feel that way?

'Nothing. There's nothing,' she uttered.

Cam wrapped a towel around his waist while

she dried off in jerky movements and tied her towel sarong-style with a knot between her breasts. The words had come out too quickly, too defensively.

Their eyes met and locked, and Cam sensed so much hurt.

'I didn't mean to pry.' His gaze softened on her taut face, the tight shoulders and defensive posture. He wanted to cuddle her, to pull her gently into his arms, to wrap his hold right around her and encourage her to feel completely safe, unthreatened and secure.

Cam wanted to protect Lally, because there *was* something. That fact was now abundantly clear. Cam thought it might have been a man.

The thought of some nameless male hurting Lally was hard for Cam to take. He didn't want to think of anyone doing that to her.

So don't you mess with her, Travers. You can't give her those gentle, kind things you just thought about. You might have had a random thought about them, but they're not for you to give to her. Don't hurt her by pulling her into anything when you can't follow it through.

If Cam drew Lally close, he would end up hurting her.

So he looked away, and Lally looked away.

She said with a great attempt at brightness, 'The garden would play its part to make a pebble mosaic look great. The two things would complement each other. There's already potential in the garden; it's overgrown and untended but the basics are there.'

She stepped across the courtyard to the nearest part of the garden and tugged a leaf from a mint plant. When she rubbed the leaf between her fingers, the pungent smell of the mint released into the air. 'The mosaic would boost the garden, and the garden would enhance the mosaic.'

'You're completely right. I wanted a solution for this area, and what you've suggested works.'

Lally had said it would make the area feel welcoming, and she'd mentioned giving a sense of community, like a family. If Cam wanted that…

He wanted it for his prospective tenants, even if the site boss recommended otherwise.

And when it came to his responses to Lally, his consciousness of her, yes, Cam still felt the tug of desire, the war of emotions he didn't understand. He also felt the ongoing impact of gut-deep weariness.

He didn't notice that as often when he was in her company. And he felt Lally's secrets, whatever they were. He had his, too, and these facts just underlined the importance of keeping an employer-employee line in the metaphorical sand between them.

For both their sakes, for so many reasons.

'My mother asked me to travel to a place on the coast to see her.' Cam's text messages had told him this; now he put it together with the thought of Lally creating this mosaic. 'She's going to be there tomorrow and invited me to have dinner with her. The town she'll be in is out of the way, slow roads for some of it, but there are a lot of good beaches around that area.'

Cam kept his mother informed of his where-abouts. She usually failed to respond to any of that information, but now and again they managed a meeting. It was usually Cam who went looking for those, though he didn't look all that often.

'That'll be nice for you, but perhaps a bit of a strain with the trip itself.' Lally made this comment as she absorbed her employer's state-ment that he planned to see his mother. 'You'll take care on the roads? Not drive if you're too tired?'

Lally wanted the meeting to be great for Cam. She'd thought he and his mum would be close, but he'd said they didn't see each other often. And his tone of voice as he'd said that…?

'Would you like to make a combined trip of it? We can scour up and down some beaches in that area for pebbles.' Cam's words interrupted her thoughts. 'I wouldn't anticipate us being with my mother for more than a couple of hours. We could squeeze in scouring one beach, maybe, before we meet her tomorrow. Stay overnight somewhere, look at some more beaches the following day, early, then head back here? I'd really like you to do this work, Lally. If you're willing.'

'I would like to do it.' Oh, Lally would like it very much. But an overnight stay away with him?

She told herself this was about practicalities, about getting materials, and it *was* about that. He'd asked about her past, but that wasn't relevant to this. It didn't come into making a mosaic, or attending dinner with he and his mother. Or anything.

'I think I'd really like you to meet my mother.' Cam murmured the words and then seemed surprised by them.

Lally was, too, and then it hit her that she would be meeting her boss's only relative. Whether it turned out they were close or not, what would his mother think of her? Lally wanted to make a good impression.

'I have to figure out what to wear,' she blurted, and blushed with fiery heat beneath her skin. Yes, she needed to make a good impression, but only as his employee. 'Um, I mean, I'd like to know where we'll be meeting her. Will it be a casual sort of place, or more formal? Because I can do either, but not in that dress we bought for your research. That would be way too much.'

As was her mega-blabbing!

Lally closed her teeth together with a snap so no other words could rush out.

But Cam just smiled. 'If I know my mother, it won't be a formal style of restaurant. Whatever we wear for wandering around on the beach will do.'

Lally appreciated the way he said 'we', as though both of them had been stressing over this topic. Cameron Travers truly was a kind and generous man, one whose smile disappeared when his mother's name was mentioned. That knowledge made Lally concerned, and a little sad, because she didn't think she was imagining this.

Cam said quietly, 'It will be nice to have company while I visit Mum.'

And just like that, he made Lally feel wanted, needed and let in; the idea of going away with him seemed totally appropriate despite anything she'd just been thinking, even while they were standing here in their bathing suits discussing it. Yes, they were covered in beach towels, too, but that was hardly the point.

Lally wasn't sure if she wanted to understand the point any more, to be honest. Because she had a suspicion it would end up being something to do with still being way too aware of her gorgeous boss, and now having far too many emotional connections towards him as well.

A genuine interest in him had developed—an

appreciation for his cleverness and imagination, a need to look after him. Concern about his relationship with his mother.

But she didn't want to let him into her personal life. Not the history part of it, anyway. *Do you, Lally?*

Cameron touched her arm with his fingers, the lightest of touches. 'So, do we have a plan? Leave first thing tomorrow morning with a couple of days' clothes, some buckets and strong plastic bags for the pebbles?'

'Yes. We have a plan.' Lally's skin tingled where his fingers rested against her.

Well, tomorrow she would be stronger.

Tomorrow she would be totally strong.

'I'd best go see about what I need to pack.' She excused herself and went inside. She wasn't removing herself from the way of temptation— that wasn't necessary, because Lally Douglas had her world, her attitudes, her thoughts and her feelings completely under control.

Oh, yes, she did!

CHAPTER NINE

'I MEANT to check the forecast for the next two days for this area.' Cam made the statement as they climbed from his convertible onto an isolated stretch of beach. It was mid-afternoon.

After the long trip, it was good to step out into such beautiful surrounds. The beach was not ideal for swimming; the sea looked too rough for that, but there was sand, the smell of salt water, gorgeous sky and sea extending until they melded their shades of blue together on the horizon.

Lally seemed happy, anyway. She breathed in a deep breath as they got out of the car and her face had relaxed into an expression of pleasure.

Cam told himself not to dwell too much on that look, to think rather about the business end of this trip, such as making sure it would work for Lally. For that reason he couldn't quite keep the self-directed disapproval from his tone as he went on, 'I usually think of those sorts of things, but, even though I spent hours working on business and writing and that should have meant I was totally focused on all the different things on my agenda, I didn't consider the weather.'

He'd focused on his business matters, had prepared instructions to leave for the site boss in case he and Lally weren't back to speak to the guy by mid-afternoon Monday and had worked on his writing. He was well on track for his deadline now.

Perhaps Cam had overlooked the weather because he'd been trying to avoid some of his thoughts. Thoughts that had to do with whether it was wise to take Lally on this trip. He'd touched her arm after they'd been swimming last night, just touched her, and all of his senses had gone on alert again. Cam couldn't—one hundred percent could not—allow himself to be so overwhelmed by her. He had to resist desiring her.

Cam needed to focus on professionalism where Lally was concerned. Wanting to understand her, know all about her, know her secrets—he couldn't pursue that.

'The weather looks fine. I don't think we'll have any problems in that respect.' Lally spoke after casting a brief glance at the sky.

'Here's hoping you're right. But I'm leaving the top up on the car anyway. I don't trust coastal weather, it can change very quickly.' Cam took two buckets from the trunk, lined them with thick plastic bags and led the way onto the beach. If he treated this time as perfectly ordinary, that was what it would become eventually—wouldn't it?

And he might do better if he didn't touch her. At all. 'Let's see if we can find some nice, coloured pebbles and stones for your mosaic. I'm not sure if I'll be able to help or just be the "carry person" for you. I guess that'll depend on how specific you need your choices to be.'

'At first I'll only know what I want when I spot it, but, once I know, I don't see why you won't be able to find similar pebbles and stones and help gather them.'

Lally wanted to create the mosaic for Cam, and perhaps a little for herself. Maybe her relatives were right and it was past time for her to explore her artistic ability. She shouldn't feel that. She had no right to feel that.

She did feel happy and full of anticipation. About the work; it had nothing to do with the idea of strolling along beaches with a gorgeous man. A man who had the ability to turn her senses and her emotions to mush just by letting her see into the depths of his eyes.

Oh, Lally. That's not a helpful thought to have!

'You're quite sure you're happy with the style and design I want to use for the mosaic?' She'd been up later than she should have been last night working on the fine-tuning of that design. Cam had been restless too. Lally had heard that, but only because she'd been awake anyway. He always tried hard not to disturb her sleep.

With ideas buzzing in her mind, Lally had sketched out her plan for the mosaic and had noted what colours she'd use for the various parts of it. She'd shown those plans to Cam this morning before they'd left the apartment. She thought about them again now to try to help her control her wayward thoughts.

'I'm totally fine with it. You're the artist at work in this situation, Lally. What you say about it goes.'

Cam had been very supportive of her ideas earlier too.

Lally rubbed her hands together. 'Let's see if we can find some suitable pebbles.'

Lally strolled the first part of the beach. She looked at pebbles scattered here and there, bent to examine a shiny, flat rock weathered into smoothness by time and tide. Truly she didn't think once about how good Cam looked in his jeans-shorts that reached just below his knees, running shoes and T-shirt. Not once.

Lally wore white capri-pants, runners and a red, short-sleeved blouse. Lately she'd been reaching more often for the few brighter clothes she had in her wardrobe.

You've been reaching for bright clothes, like the dress Cam purchased for you that night.

Well, it wasn't as though she couldn't give herself permission to wear whatever colours she wanted to wear.

Really? You don't think that's just one indication that you're attracted to Cam and you want to attract his attention right back the same way you worked to attract Sam's attention six years ago?

What did one have to do with the other? Lally suppressed a frown.

'Is that stone a yes as a keeper, or a no?' Cam held the two empty pails in his hands. He gestured to the stone she was turning over and over in her hand.

'Oh, um...' Lally glanced at the stone blankly and back up into Cam's face. He hadn't shaved this morning, and her fingers itched to run through the light covering of beard growth. The texture would be prickly and silky at once.

If he kissed her, she would feel that silky prickliness against her mouth, brushing over the sensitive nerve-endings beneath her lower lip. It might not be smart, but Lally wanted Cam to give her that kiss. She glanced into his eyes and caught an equally aware, desire-filled expression there.

So why not just give in and kiss him, get a second taste of something that had felt rather like paradise?

How could one girl, who didn't even want to be involved in such a way, miss a man's kiss after having it just once? How could she miss it enough to think such thoughts when they were dangerous to her emotional well-being? She searched Cam's eyes for the answer. But she wasn't sure if she wanted to find it.

Then she remembered a different question. 'The stone is smooth, beautifully rounded and a good colour. It's definitely a keeper.' She dropped it into the pail. She was supposed to be shopping for mosaic materials, not wishing she could kiss her boss.

Cam steered her in the direction of a ridge of pebbles that had been thrown up by the tide.

Lally bent to look and forced her mind to focus on the task of examining them and picking up the ones she thought had the best colours. She didn't want to think about any of the rest of it.

For the first while, Lally was uneasy as they gathered their pebbles. But Cam was a good help, standing patiently while she chose stones, picking out others that complemented the colours and shapes she'd chosen, and eventually she began to relax.

'Did you have any painting lessons at all? Non-traditional ones, I mean?' Cam asked as she sifted a handful of pebbles through her fingers.

'I painted a little during high school. Art

classes, how to paint fruit in a bowl, that sort of thing. But I stopped after that.' Lally dropped a few pebbles into the bucket and bent to scoop up more.

Cam reached down at the same time and their fingers brushed. The sound of the sea ebbing and flowing on the shoreline seemed louder as Lally's breath stopped. Her gaze turned to Cam's face and got caught in the deep green of his eyes.

'Sorry. I wasn't looking.'

'I should let you check them first.'

They both went to get up, and Lally's sneaker sank into the damp sand. It made a squishing sound, and she couldn't hold back a slight smile. 'Do you know? I wish I could feel the sand beneath my toes. I haven't walked barefoot on a beach in ages.'

'So take your shoes off and get the full experience.' Cam said it in a teasing tone. His lips quirked and he bent to remove first one shoe, then the other.

His encouragement could have stabbed right through her. For wasn't that exactly what she'd done to get herself in trouble in the past—been a hedonist? Indulged in what she wanted while blindly ignoring all warning signs that she might be headed for trouble?

That wasn't the same, Lally. You're just walking on the beach. Lally removed her shoes.

They abandoned both pairs right there, just like that. Well, Cam seemed more than comfortable. And what was the harm, really?

'No one will take them.' Cam glanced about. 'It's totally deserted here.'

He was right about that. When he set the bucket down and held out his hand to her, a little thrill went through Lally before she placed her hand in his and let him lead her to the water's edge.

Cool sea-foam washed over her feet and splashed against her ankles. Cam's hand felt warm and firm in comparison with the skin of her palm. As the water rolled out again, the sand sucked away beneath Lally's feet.

'I do love that sensation.' She glanced up at Cam and smiled. 'It's sort of icky and wonderfully good all at once.'

Cam laughed and his gaze softened as he looked into her eyes. There was such tenderness in that one glimpse of time. His hand tightened on hers; Lally realised they were still holding hands and told herself that should stop—but she didn't want to stop it. Particularly not when he looked at her this way.

Oh, but she needed to stop it, most of all because of that look; Lally broke away. 'We'd better get back to looking for pebbles. It's what we're here for—the mosaic. I want to do a good job of it for you.'

So they searched for pebbles and gathered quite a few. Lally loved the texture, the smoothness rounded into the stones by the constant movement, time smoothing off the edges. She glanced at Cam and thought, if only life could be that simple. Her six-year-old edges were still way too sharp.

Cam crouched down to sift through some pale-white stones. He played them through his fingers. From where she stood nearby, Lally had a view of the top of his head, the way his hair grew, the strength of the back and side of his neck and all of his face in profile.

'What do you think of these ones?' He looked up, caught her gaze on him and the green of his eyes darkened.

Lally's breath caught as her pulse sped up and her emotions responded to the expression in his eyes. He smiled then, and his smile was everything a woman could dream about. She wanted to melt into a puddle at his feet. She could have done that easily.

'The pebbles look good. Yes, I'd like to keep those ones, and I have some more.' Her fist closed about the ones she had gathered. She stepped forward and dropped them into the bucket beside him. 'I, um, I'll look further afield. Over there.' She gestured randomly and forced herself to strike out away from him.

He let her go. That was good because they couldn't be like this. *She* couldn't be like this. When had she become emotionally involved to the degree that she couldn't look at him in profile without wanting to step forward, wrap her arms around him, hold him and not let go?

'We'd better think about going if we're to meet my mother at the allotted time,' Cam said decisively as he stepped across the beach towards her about an hour later. He'd kept her supplied with buckets, but otherwise had left her alone.

Lally glanced up and her heart did it again— leapt, opened up, melted. She came forward with her current bucket brimming with stones; a mantra played in her head that she should play this cool, not let him see how he impacted on her.

'That was good timing. I think I have enough of any colours I can get from this beach.' She glanced down at her bucket and as she did failed to look where she was putting her foot. 'Ouch!'

A sharp sensation spread through her heel.

'Let me see.' Cam set his bucket down in the sand and had his fingers shackled firmly about her upper arm before she could even think.

It was natural to wrap her fingers around his strong forearm and use him for balance while she held her foot off the ground.

Cam looked at her foot, gently taking it in his other hand and turning it until he could see the bottom. Then he looked down into the sand. 'You've cut it on a rock. It doesn't look too deep, but it should be cleaned and dressed. Let's get you to the car so we can take care of it properly.'

'I might need your arm so I can hop along—' Lally got that much out before he swept her up into his arms and her thoughts fractured.

Consciousness of the sting in her foot faded as Cam's warm chest pressed against her arm and shoulder and his arms held her securely.

She'd been held by him like this before, at night at the top of the small, Adelaide-style skyscraper.

The whimsical thought brushed through her mind as her hands tightened together behind his neck. Lally told herself under no circumstances was she to stroke that neck, or in any other way reveal how being held by him made her feel.

You don't think that melting into him like a boneless blob might give him a hint?

'Okay. Let's sit you here and I'll take a proper look.' Cam eased her into the passenger seat of the convertible and seemed to release his hold on her reluctantly. He knelt at her feet and checked the wound. 'I've got a first aid kit. I think I can take care of this with cleaning solution and a couple of butterfly strips.'

'It probably only needs a plaster. Really, most of the sting has gone already.' Lally felt silly with her foot clasped in his hand and with him fussing over her. Silly and conscious of him all at once. 'It's just a cut. I'm sure if we clean it…' She leaned forward to try to take a look.

Cam tightened his fingers on her foot. '*I'll* clean it. You just sit tight and look beautiful.' He reached past her to open the glove compartment and pulled out the first-aid kit. He rummaged through it for the items he wanted. 'I've got a bandage too, so I can wrap that around it to make sure it all stays together when you put your shoe back on over the top.'

Lally sat back and let him take care of her, and he did, handling her foot gently and making sure he cleaned the wound thoroughly before he put on the steri-strips and covered it all in a bandage. He jogged back to the beach and retrieved both their pairs of shoes and the collection of stones, and helped her put her shoes on.

He was once again on his knees at her feet, a strong man who seemed completely comfortable kneeling before her, looking after her.

When he glanced up and caught her studying him, his gaze darkened as it had back on the beach—except now there was nowhere for Lally to go, nothing to do but acknowledge the way he made her feel.

His hands bracketed the seat on either side of her legs as he leaned closer. 'I don't like that you got hurt.' His gaze was locked on her lips.

'It wasn't hurt badly, and you looked after me.' He'd told her to sit back and look beautiful. His eyes had taken in the wildness of her hair and Lally had *felt* beautiful, lovely, appealing and desirable. She realised she hadn't let herself feel that way for a long time.

His expression made her feel that way now. Lally caught her breath and a reserve inside her that had held together for six years frayed rather noticeably around its edges.

'Lally.' He murmured her name and leaned closer.

Lally heard her name and the warning in his tone as he spoke it.

Don't let me, his tone seemed to say.

But she was too busy reacting, and that reaction was to lean towards him while he leaned towards her until they were almost nose-to-nose. She could smell the blunted, woodsy scent of his aftershave lotion where it had blended with his skin.

He smelled good. Lally wanted to press her nose to his neck and just inhale him.

'God, Lally, when you look like that…' Cam broke off and closed the remaining distance between them.

CHAPTER TEN

CAM's lips drew closer. Every pore of Lally's being wanted and needed his kiss. He kissed the side of her face in the shallow spot beneath her cheekbone. He kissed where her cheek creased when she smiled.

He kissed the edge of her lips with a teasing press; Lally turned her head and blindly sought the second full press of his lips to hers. She got it, and her eyelids felt way too heavy to hold open, so she let them flutter closed as he pressed more soft kisses to her lips, and she kissed him back just as softly.

The ocean rolled against the beach down on the shore. A seagull cried; Lally breathed Cam deep into her lungs and held him there.

His hands came up to clasp her shoulders, to brush gently over them and rub against her back. His fingertips worshipped the softness of her skin, and he made a sighing sound as though he'd found exactly what he'd been looking for and just wanted to enjoy it.

That slow, detailed attention swept Lally away more effectively than anything else would have. It was as though Cam took time in his hands and stilled it so they could have this, indulge in it and experience it in its fullest measure.

His lips pressed to hers.

Her mouth opened to him because he made what they were sharing feel so completely safe, so utterly right.

Lally forced her eyes open to seek his; slumberous green looked at her. He seemed so at ease, restful to the point almost of being sleepy. Lally didn't know why that response in him made her feel powerful, but it did.

'Lally.' His fingers sifted through her hair, caught the long strands and played with them, before he pressed those fingers with just the right amount of pressure against the base of her skull and drew her forward so he could deepen their kiss.

Their tongues met, stroked.

Lally didn't know how he did it, but somehow in his gentleness and focus Cam encouraged her to take whatever she wanted of him. He offered his tongue. She drew it into her mouth and explored the taste and texture. She felt her back arch as he gave a soft sound of pleasure and his arms drew her closer still.

His fingers pressed against her shoulders until their bodies were chest to chest. It felt good, it felt right, and Lally relaxed even more.

She didn't know when the kiss changed, when slow became deep, when sultry became focused, when restful became hungry and desperate became need-filled; it just happened. Cam was kissing her utterly then, his mouth locked over hers. All of his focus and all of hers was fixed on this exchange, these sensations.

Even as her hands rose to his chest, to his shoulders, Lally knew this kiss was different. This kiss was not Sam kissing her, relying on his charm to lead her to do whatever he wanted, to overwhelm her so she didn't think about his motives, so she didn't suspect them.

This kiss wasn't like Cam's last kiss either. That had been wonderful. This was more, so much more that Lally could not remember why she shouldn't do this. She needed this, *had* to do this. Lally *liked* Cam, admired him, was attracted to him not only physically but to his thought processes, his creativity, his business acumen, drive, ambition, attention to detail, enthusiasm for his work, imagination…

How could she fight this kind of attraction? It was more than she had ever felt for any other man, Sam included.

That fact got through to Lally as nothing else

had. If she let herself follow this path, where would it end? How capable would she be of getting hurt? How could anything be *more* than Sam had been in her life? Sam had irrevocably changed it.

Lally had to stop this. Even now her instincts fought her mind. Her lips remained right where they were, pressed to Cam's. Her hands slid to Cam's upper arms, a precursor to letting go, but her fingers clasped those arms. Lally dropped her hands but they slid away from him slowly.

It was Cam who broke the kiss itself, his gaze already searching hers. What Lally imagined he saw there was echoed in his own expression.

Desire and caution, want and the need to stop.

'Lally, we have to—'

'We have to stop—' Lally lost the words in the depths of his eyes, found them again in the drive inside her that insisted she keep herself safe, that she not get hurt again, not yield to feelings for a man who wouldn't value them, not make a mess, create guilt—oh, so many things.

Cam was her boss, he was wealthy, famous and amazing, and Lally was the temporary house-keeper and assistant. Cam was very much out of her league. In the end he was as much out of her reach, as Sam *should* have been, if for other reasons. And Sam was part of Lally's reason now, that tainted history.

The resignation in Cam's eyes told her he felt the same way about this, at least to the extent that he knew this had to stop, that it wouldn't be wise for them. What were his reasons?

'We should get going. Your foot's okay? It's not hurting you?' Cam put his shoes on while she settled herself properly in her seat.

'It's fine now that it's cleaned and wrapped. And we don't want to be late for dinner with your mother.' Lally spoke the words through kiss-swollen lips, over the taste of him that was still on her tongue, trying to make sense when she couldn't think straight.

Cam searched her eyes for a moment before he closed her car door, crossed in front and got into the driver's seat. Just a few moments with those broad shoulders in motion, his long legs eating up the ground until he slid behind the wheel, and Lally couldn't concentrate again.

'Would you like the top down again?' Cam glanced her way.

Lally quickly nodded. 'The breeze is nice.'

She didn't care about her hair getting whipped about; that could be fixed when they arrived. Maybe the wind would blow this lapse of control away.

Cam got things organised. Then he sat there with the engine idling and finally turned his gaze her way. 'Lally...'

'Don't.' She shook her head. 'Please. We have to see your mother. Can we just…do that?'

So they went.

'Here we are.' Cam drew the car to a halt in a restaurant's small parking-lot. 'Hopefully Mum will be here and won't have changed her plans without letting me know.'

'Does she do that often?' Lally asked as they made the short walk to the restaurant's entrance.

'It happens.' Cam's mother did a lot of things he didn't always like. 'How's the foot? If it's hurting, I can help you.'

'Oh, no, it's okay—and I wouldn't want your mother to think—' Lally broke off.

But not before Cam saw the memory of their kisses cross her face. Lally might have set out to say she didn't want his mother to think she was anything other than able to look after herself, or something like that, but her words had quickly led her thoughts elsewhere.

Cam could identify with that, because all his thoughts seemed to lead elsewhere at the moment.

And all those 'elsewhere' roads led to one place: the kissing Lally place. His lack of control around her was substantial, it seemed. Cam wasn't exactly proud of that and yet he couldn't regret what they'd shared.

'Then I guess I won't carry you inside.' He said

it with a smile that took effort at first. But he thought his mother might actually do a double take if she saw him walk into the restaurant carrying Lally clutched to his chest like a prize, and his smile became more natural.

He turned to her as they made their way inside. 'There's about an eighty-percent chance we'll be meeting someone else as well as my mother for dinner.'

'I'm not sure what you mean.' Lally seemed to be just on the edge of nervous.

Or maybe that was left over from what had passed between them back at the beach. Cam glanced at her. Even hobbling a little, she still managed to look graceful. He looked again. He realised his mother might be likely to bring 'a friend' yet again to meet him, but Cam wanted to show Lally off to his mother. That was very much a first.

As your employee. You want to show her off as your employee.

Yeah.

Right. That was what he wanted. That was no doubt what had driven him to kiss her again back there at the beach, lose complete sight of where they were. It was what he'd told himself he would and wouldn't do when it came to Lally.

Cam wasn't sure he wanted to think about his motives for that. Somehow they appeared to be linked to something far too deep inside him that he'd thought he had worked out. He *did* have it all worked out!

'I guess you'd say Mum's a free spirit. She's not someone who will pin down to anything for long, but when it comes to relationships that's not a lesson she's been able to acknowledge within herself. She keeps leaping in and backing out again just as quickly.'

'Oh.' Lally gave a calm nod. 'I have an older cousin who's like that—revolving-door relationships. I don't know how she deals with the stress, although, now that I think about it, she manages to walk away apparently unscathed each time. I couldn't do it.' She fell abruptly silent.

Cam had a feeling it had occurred to both of them at once that they weren't really in the best position to discuss this as uninvolved observers. 'We can't be—'

'Well, there you are. Cameron, come and meet Tom; he's such a darling. I don't know where I'd be without him.' His mother stepped forward as she spoke the flow of words, hugged him quickly and stepped back.

The obligatory hug was over for another year, and it had happened so quickly that Cam had almost missed it.

Men weren't supposed to feel the lack of that kind of thing, were they? Yet it occurred to Cam in this moment that he'd missed a lot of real, genuine hugs in his lifetime. Lally would never hug half-heartedly like that. Cam just knew this.

He'd felt it for himself when she'd held him, and everything inside him had relaxed and felt as though it could rest and be still.

That stillness wasn't something Cam understood, and he hadn't truly thought about it in relation to Lally until now. But she gave him that feeling. It was as though somehow being around her helped him to find peace or something.

And what are you now, Travers? Some kind of tortured soul? For crying out loud!

Cam turned his gaze to his mother. 'Hello, Mum. This is Lally. Lally, meet my mother, Dana.' He shook hands with—*John? No, that was the last one.* 'Hello, Tom.'

'What have you been doing, Cameron? Dull old business things, I suppose, with a bit of writing thrown in on the side?' His mother picked up her menu and started to scan it. 'You should rest more. Weariness isn't attractive, you know.'

'Insomnia isn't quite the same as weariness, Mum. And I always do try to rest.' Cam said it gently; he didn't expect Dana to really listen. He drew a breath to turn the conversation elsewhere.

'I think Cam deals really well with his insomnia.' Lally's words came softly into the conversation. 'It can't be easy to have all those long hours to get through, knowing you can't rest as much as you'd like to be able to.'

Cam hadn't expected her to speak. The support behind the words touched him. He stared into liquid brown eyes and felt much of the tension over seeing his mother again ease out of him.

With a few soft words, Lally had him in a better place with things. Cam needed to make sure his housekeeper and assistant was in a good place too, because beneath the surface of her cheerful attitude he could see a hint of unhappiness that he suspected might have been for his sake. His mother had turned her head to speak quietly to Tom for a moment.

Cam touched Lally's hand beneath the table. 'Thank you,' he murmured so only she could hear him. 'Mum doesn't mean any harm. We're not very close, you know? But I still like to see her occasionally. She's the only relative I've got.'

Could those words reassure a woman whose life to a large degree seemed to revolve around her love for her big extended family? It wasn't a topic Cam could cover further now, at any rate.

'You should just take sleeping pills, Cameron.' His mother tossed these words out. They were an easy solution, a fast solution; Dana was good at offering those and then forgetting all about whatever issue had arisen in the first place.

She just wasn't good at seeing that some things

didn't *have* fast, easy solutions. 'I'm sure after a few days of those your body would retrain and you'd be fine.'

'Lally's trying some bush-food remedies to see if they'll help,' Cam offered with a determined smile. 'And I have felt more relaxed in the past while.' That was down to Lally herself, in Cam's opinion, but he kept that thought to himself.

And now he really wanted to change the topic.

'I see.' His mother looked back at her menu then glanced at her watch. 'We should make our selections. I'm sure the waiter will be along at any moment.'

Lally blinked just once before she lowered her gaze to her menu.

Cam had the odd urge to take her hand again beneath the table and this time keep it in his clasp.

Instead, he turned his attention to choosing a meal.

Tom spoke, bringing up an interest in fishing and four-wheel-driving. 'What do you drive, Cameron?'

Cam gave the older man the make and model of his convertible. 'I like—'

'The fresh air.' Lally glanced at him and smiled. 'It was nice this morning, wasn't it? Coastal roads, warm weather and a sea breeze.'

'What exactly is your relationship to Cameron, Lally?' his mother suddenly asked nosily.

Cam opened his mouth to answer, somewhat protectively. His mum's tendency to stomp all over people's privacy with her questions was something Cam hadn't taken into account when he'd invited Lally along for this. He should have thought about it.

But Lally beat him to it. 'I'm working as a temporary housekeeper to Cam while he's in Adelaide.' She smiled. 'And building him a pebble mosaic for the courtyard of his property development there, while he creates his latest crime story to keep readers on the edges of their seats.'

'Oh.' Mum seemed to be somewhat at a loss. 'So, you're a bit of a Jill of all trades? Stone masonry is an unusual career choice for a woman.'

'Well, pebble mosaics are a little different to stone masonry.' Lally quickly outlined her vision for the mosaic. 'I'm looking forward to doing the work, anyway.'

'And I'm looking forward to seeing the end result.' Cam closed his menu. Because he didn't want his mum cross-questioning Lally for the rest of the meal, he really did change the subject now. 'Catch of the day for me. You can't beat fresh fish, isn't that right, Tom?'

They discussed fishing and real estate through the main course. When he'd first got enough

money to do it, Cam had bought his mother a
home in Sydney and had invited her to settle there.
He'd hoped to have her nearer, to be able to see
her more.

That had been a vain hope. His mother had
taken the property, immediately rented it out, and
gone on her way travelling, content so long as no
one asked her to put down roots.

'Remember, the house is always there for you,
Mum.' He didn't know what made him say it.

Dana gave him an uncomprehending look.
'Well, and so it should be. It was a pay-off for the
years I sacrificed to raise you. I deserve that rental
income to allow me to travel in my motor home
wherever I want to go.'

'You could change for the right man—settle
down in a real home,' Tom muttered beneath his
breath. He followed it up with a teasing smile, but
he frowned and pushed his dinner plate away at the
same time.

Cam glanced at his watch. Only a little over
half an hour had passed since they'd sat down; it
felt like much longer.

'I have family in Queensland and the Torres
Strait islands,' Lally said as she pushed a fat,
golden chip around her plate with her fork. 'My
mother tries to get up that way every couple of
years. I've enjoyed making the trips with her a
few times.'

Lally glanced briefly towards him.

Ah, Lally. Don't care about this. It just isn't worth it.

The conversation segued to a discussion of bush foods and other cuisine. That took them through the rest of the meal. When it ended and Cam's mother mentioned coffee, Cam shook his head and stood.

'We need to push on, find a suitable place to stay this evening. It was…good to see you.' He nodded to Tom. He didn't bother trying to kiss Dana's cheek or hug her. She hadn't got up and clearly didn't intend to.

Instead, Cam took Lally's arm in a gentle clasp, nodded to his mum and Tom once again and led Lally out of the restaurant.

'Your mother seems very…autonomous,' Lally said as diplomatically as she could.

Cam saw her effort to avoid saying so much else, and he appreciated it for what it was. He shook off his mood because there was no point and he didn't want to spoil the rest of their evening. 'She always has been. I try.'

Cam *did* try. He kept a one-way stream of communication with Dana throughout the year, using whatever medium of contact she made available to him. The contact just didn't come back his way very often.

'Did your mother look into your insomnia

when you were younger?' Lally asked with a frown.

'She didn't acknowledge it as anything more than a child being annoying about not wanting to sleep.' There'd been a lot of nights spent lying awake. The settings had changed all the time, but the end results had been the same.

Lally seemed to fight with herself for a moment before the need for expression finally got the better of her. 'Your insomnia probably started as a result of you being picked up and moved around all the time. If you'd received the right kind of attention back then...'

'That's a long way back. I don't think it was that.' Yet Cam had developed that problem as a child. He'd just assumed he got it from the gene pool of whoever had fathered him, that it was a genetic issue, not one that might have developed from his circumstances. 'I've lived away from that environment for a long time now.'

'And kept moving around, the way your mother always has.' Lally searched his eyes. 'I'm not saying you shouldn't travel if that's what keeps you happy, but maybe you haven't had a decent chance at finding that kind of peace to allow you to properly rest?'

Cam opened his mouth to say that moving around was as necessary to him as it was to his mother. Then he closed it again, because he wasn't quite sure if it *was* as necessary as he had always thought.

Yet, if it wasn't, why did he keep on the move all the time, constantly searching, looking for the next challenge, the next brick in the road, the next great book idea and property-development idea? 'I guess travelling has been a way to fill all the time that yawns in front of me.'

Cam just didn't know what else it meant. And he felt oddly uncertain about the whole topic. 'Let's go find a nice bed and breakfast for the night.'

'Yes. Let's.' Lally didn't push the topic. Instead, she drew a deep breath and smiled as they reached his car and climbed in.

They got on the road, and Cam slowly forgot about the visit with his mother.

Instead he took the opportunity to gently grill Lally about her family situation. Lally seemed to need them so much, and Cam wanted to try to understand where she stood in relation to all that.

He wanted to understand the why of her needs, and whether that somehow related to the occasional sadness he saw in her eyes.

'I'm looking forward to getting back to my usual work among the family after this assignment is over.' Lally glanced his way. 'I'm happy with you as well. I just need to do that for my family. It's safe—' Lally cut the words off and frowned.

They passed through one small place, but the accommodation didn't look particularly inviting. Cam chose to move on. He'd researched a bed and breakfast on-line in the next town that had looked good in the photos.

Lally leaned her head back against the seat and became silent. A few minutes later, she fell asleep.

CHAPTER ELEVEN

CAM reached into the car, lifted his slumbering housekeeper into his arms, carried her inside the bed and breakfast, up the staircase and into the only room they had free.

The rain had just stopped. It had pelted down for the last hour as he made the slow trip here. Cam had sat the last few minutes out in the parked car, right outside the B&B, with Lally gently sleeping in the seat beside him. She slept so peacefully—Cam could envy that!

She must have been exhausted, and Cam felt at least partly to blame for that. He'd been disturbing her sleep since she'd first moved in with him. He knew it, even though he'd tried to be quiet at night when he moved around in their apartment.

He should put her out into one of the other apartments. How long would it take to gather up enough furniture to make her comfortable? He could order the lot over the phone in about twenty minutes.

Cam's arms tightened about his burden that felt like no burden at all. He'd be quieter, make sure he didn't disturb her in future. He didn't want to move her out.

'Are we there already?' Lally murmured in a sleepy voice and then seemed to realise she wasn't on her feet. Confusion filled her gaze and she blinked at him with wide eyes that quickly changed from slumberous to conscious and softened as they locked on his face.

One look from her, one glimpse into those unguarded eyes, and all Cam wanted…

Well, he couldn't have what he wanted. If he'd let himself wonder otherwise, spending time with his mother today had concreted the fact that he just couldn't go there with Lally.

She deserved more than someone who'd pack up and move around all the time, who would not want to settle down somewhere with her, not want babies and a picket fence. Not know how to give that even if he had wanted it.

You could have babies and a courtyard and a big, old family home that you're converting into apartments right now. You already know it would work quite well as a home.

Since when had Cam started to think about that big, old place as a potential home, rather than a sound business-investment? Let alone think about settling down. It was out of the question; totally and utterly out of the question for him.

Cam set Lally down in the small living area of the room and backed away. 'Eh, you fell asleep in the car. There's been a storm, so I drove us to this B&B. All they had was this room, and they told me all the other accommodation in the area is booked out. The bad weather took a few travellers by surprise, apparently.'

He rammed his hand through his hair upwards from the base at the back. 'So, eh, I can sleep in the car.'

'Oh.' Lally blinked, blinked again and glanced around them, taking in the surroundings, the double bed beside the bank of windows. 'Well, um…'

'Yeah. I'll go get our things. At least I can have a hot shower.' Cam swung about and left the room.

As Cam left, Lally drew a deep breath and tried to calm herself. She wasn't nervous, though maybe that feeling would catch up in a minute. She was just trying to come to terms with waking up in his arms like that. Had she melted into him before she woke up? What if she'd talked in her sleep? Snored? Kissed him? Dribbled?

Oh, for heaven's sake; she was just snoozing.

Snoozing right through a fierce storm, apparently. And Cam had sat with her in the car then carried her inside. He must have a lot of patience.

Well, the man couldn't sleep himself. He was

probably used to needing a lot of patience to get through all those hours when he wanted to be asleep but wasn't. Maybe he'd got some vicarious satisfaction out of knowing she was sleeping.

And maybe Lally was letting her imagination run away with her so she wouldn't have to think about sharing a room with her boss tonight.

'Room service,' Cam quipped as he stepped into the room and dumped their bags. He glanced at her face, and shoved his hands in his pockets. 'I said it already, Lally—I'll sleep in the car.'

'Yes, well, you see, that's the problem—I can't let you do that. You'd be so uncomfortable. It's a great car, but it's not made for sleeping in.' She couldn't let him do that. 'There's really nowhere else we could go for the night?'

He was shaking his head before she even finished speaking. 'There's nowhere nearby, and they seem to think there'll be a second storm-front.'

'I don't know why I did that. Slept, I mean. It must have been all the fresh air and wandering on the beach earlier.'

'Fresh air and exercise has that effect on a lot of people.' He set their bags against the wall out of the way. 'They're offering winter warmers in the dining room: would you like to come down, have a hot drink, at least?'

Lally nodded. 'That would be nice. I'd better tidy up.'

At least they had their own bathroom tucked behind a door. Lally picked up her handbag that Cam had kindly brought in for her, stepped into the bathroom, shut the door and splashed water over her face. Her hair was springy from the weather. She knew better than to brush it. If she did, it would just get springier.

So she twisted and tied it in a loose knot to keep it half under control, applied some lipstick and a spritz of perfume and called the job done. 'I'm ready.'

'You look lovely,' Cam murmured, then took her arm and led her from the room. 'Let's go see what's on offer.'

Lally hadn't been alert enough to think about the intimacy of the room. Now she tried to absorb his compliment and felt a glow come over her, because being told by a man that she looked great would naturally give her a glow, wouldn't it?

It was nothing to do with this specific man. Any man saying that would have had the same impact.

Oh, she really wished her thoughts wouldn't step in and question her like that. Sometimes ignorance, or at the very least letting herself think whatever suited best, truly could be bliss. It was better than delving too deeply into the truth.

Like the truth of knowing you need to share a room with him tonight?

Maybe she should offer to sleep in the car.

But he wouldn't allow it, and Lally knew that.

'It looks like that table is free.' Cam led the way to a small table in the corner and they took their seats. The table was beside a window and outside streaks of drizzling rain ran down the pane of glass.

'I'd thought we might have to sit at one large, long table and share our company with everyone else,' Lally observed.

Since when did you become a hermit, Lally Douglas? Usually you love big dinners with lots of people around.

That was when she was with her family. This was different. She didn't want to admit that she wanted Cam all to herself.

She must be still sleepy, not thinking straight. 'Not that I'd have minded,' Lally declared a little too loudly and with a little too much emphasis, and felt telling heat creep into her face. 'I'd have been quite happy to share. I'd have been quite happy to share news with the other guests, have a bit of a chat. Well, the table setting is nice, don't you think?'

Lally gestured at it and told herself the fat red candle in its old-fashioned brass holder didn't look at all romantic, nor did her boss look equally so with candlelight playing across the angles and shadows of his face.

He was grinning, just the slightest bit—as one was wont to do when a woman blabbered, Lally pointed out to herself with an inner frown.

The guesthouse manager came to their table and gave a friendly nod. 'We're not overly fancy here, but we've got a really nice soup on offer, cake or dessert, plus tea, coffee and hot chocolate.' He rattled off a description of each choice.

Lally was surprised to discover she actually felt a little hungry. 'I'd love to try the soup.'

They both opted for that to start off.

Lingering over the supper would use up some of the time until they could go to bed and hope to sleep.

Well, Lally would hope to sleep. Cam didn't at the best of times; she doubted he'd do better when he didn't even have the bed to himself.

Thinking about getting into bed with him was really not a good idea when she was sitting across a romantic table-setting from him.

'It's *not* a romantic table-setting,' she muttered, and fell silent.

'Water?' Cam judiciously ignored her comment and poured water for both of them from a carafe on the table. He passed her drink to her before taking a sip of his own.

Lally watched him drink and thought he even did that appealingly.

Do not let your thoughts start wandering where

he's concerned. He's your boss. The boss and the housekeeper—got that? Good!

Maybe they could put a line of pillows down the middle of the bed or something. Or one of them could sleep rolled into a blanket so there was no chance that their bodies would touch. What did they call that in the old days—buffering? Bundling?

The soup arrived and Lally stirred her spoon through it. 'Mmm, I think it has some mushroom in it, beef and tomato, and I suspect some brown lentils. Basil, carrot; definitely parsnip. I'm not sure what else.'

Very good, Lally. Perhaps you could rabbit on about the soup some more, totally bore him under the table in the first five minutes.

'And some pasta whirls and green peas.' Cam dug his spoon around in his soup and glanced up at her through his lashes. 'There's also either sweet-potato or pumpkin. There's a reason they call some soups a meal in a bowl.'

In this case they were small, shallow bowls. Lally took the first mouth-watering sip of the soup and her respect for this tucked-out-of-the-way B&B rose even more. 'I wish I knew how they made this.'

'Would you like me to try to get the recipe for you?'

Lally wouldn't be surprised if he managed to

charm the recipe out of the manager's chef or wife, or whoever did the cooking. 'Well, only if the opportunity comes up. My sister Tammy would love to cook this.'

They fell silent for a few minutes, simply enjoying the warming fare.

Lally thought about something else that was on her mind and said, 'I'm trying to imagine what it would be like to only have one relative and not see her very often.'

The manager removed the empty soup bowls and offered them a selection of desserts off a trolley. After they'd chosen, he left again with a murmur. Outside, the rain started to come down in thick sheets. It spattered against the window and made Lally glad to be inside. The memory of Cam's kiss earlier today rose in her mind, and she tried very hard to push it back out again. She was too vulnerable right now to let herself remember.

Cam glanced at the window and returned his gaze to her. The green of his eyes seemed particularly deep in the candlelight as he met her gaze. 'I see my mother when she's prepared to fit me into her schedule. Usually that's a couple of times a year. To be honest, though, I do try to keep a flow of text messages and things going her way; that amount of contact is enough for me.'

Because his mother didn't take much notice of him when they *did* meet. She didn't listen to the things he told her; she was a lot more interested in herself than she was in him. Lally suspected that Dana Travers might not bother even to respond to many of her son's communications at all.

The woman had acted as though having a home given to her as a reward for putting up with him as a child was more than her due. 'Was your mother always…?'

'Like what you saw today?' He shrugged his shoulders. 'I came up knowing she hadn't really wanted the responsibility of a child, but she did keep me with her. She just did it her way, I guess.'

'By travelling all the time.' Lally's eyebrows drew together. She was trying hard not to judge the other woman too harshly but it wasn't easy. 'You must have been very good academically to survive that kind of existence and still do well.'

'Books helped.' Cam took a spoonful of fluffy lemon mousse, let it slide over his tongue and swallowed it. 'Every town we went to, I read as many library books as I could before we moved on again. I guess that helped a lot with keeping me where I needed to be with schoolwork. That and a few understanding teachers here and there along the way. I spent a lot of time by myself while Mum…'

'Wasn't there?'

'Yeah. We lived and travelled in a camper van.

I thought being left by myself was what happened to every kid.' He said it in a matter-of-fact tone, yet Lally felt certain he rarely if ever talked about this.

This amazing man had been more ignored into adulthood than raised. His mother had let him know he was an inconvenience to her. That was unkind, cruel, to a little boy. What had Dana been thinking?

She'd been thinking of herself, and not the impact that her attitude would have on her son.

And who are you to judge, Lally? You sent not one but three young boys away from their mother!

'You must have had a lot of nights when you went to sleep wondering where you'd be the next day.' Lally swallowed back her guilt.

'I did, but on the upside I got to see a lot of gum trees, caravan parks and bush campsites,' Cam quipped, and then fell silent. His eyebrows drew down and a thoughtful expression crossed his face before he sighed and shook his head. 'How's your dessert?'

'It's nice. I'm glad I chose the mousse too.' She dug her spoon into the dish and gave thanks that he hadn't discerned the tone of her thoughts. 'This tastes so good, I'm guessing there's got to be a gazillion calories in it. And that's just the portion I have on my spoon.'

Cam laughed, as she had hoped he would. They

fell silent, finished their desserts, lingered over coffee and ended up talking about football teams, current affairs and whether it made sense to invest in gold bullion in today's economy.

It was relaxing and interesting. Relieved, Lally found herself looking into his eyes for the sheer pleasure of seeing the almost sleepy expression there.

But it was the slumberous look of a big, contented cat. There was leashed power behind it, an interest in her that was also leashed. Lally knew that, and sensual awareness built gently between them as they shared that exchange of glances, long, silent looks and casual conversation that was a cover for all that wasn't being said.

The dining room began to empty out, and Cam gestured to her cup. 'Would you like me to try to rustle up another drink for you?'

'I've had enough, I think. I hope that I'll get at least *some* sleep tonight.' She stopped and bit her lip, because even mentioning that made this intimacy feel even more intimate.

'We'll go up.' Did his voice hold the slightest hint of inevitability?

Or was that all inside her?

He rose from the table and took her arm to guide her out of the room.

They trod the staircase in silence. As they moved upstairs, the sound of the rain became louder. It sounded so lovely, the water hitting the corrugated-iron roof of the old building, sluicing into the gutters and running down the drainpipes.

'I'll enjoy listening to that tonight for however long it lasts,' Cam commented as he unlocked the door to their room.

Their room. For the whole night. With Cam awake while she slept. 'I, um, I hope I don't snore or talk in my sleep.' Or cuddle up to him without realising it…

'I think any of that will be the least of our worries,' Cam murmured. He closed his eyes for a moment and opened them with a question on his lips. 'Would you like to use the bathroom first, Lally, or will I go?'

He asked it so gently.

'I'll go first, if you don't mind.' She got her things, slipped into the bathroom and used the time under the shower to try to pull herself together.

When she came out in her nightwear—boy's shorts and a matching camisole top covered with the longer shirt she'd had on today—Cam glanced at her.

His gaze dropped to her bare legs for a split second and slid away again, and he scooped up his things and closed himself in the bathroom.

That hadn't been too bad. Really, she'd been worrying about nothing. Lally shrugged out of the shirt, lifted the covers of the bed on the side closest to the window and scooched under.

Cam stayed in the shower until he couldn't put off getting out any longer. He dried off, used his deodorant, tried not to think about the scent of Lally in the bathroom that had been tantalising him since he stepped in here and pulled on his boxers.

Though he considered getting back into his T-shirt, he pushed the thought away. Sleep was difficult enough, and he never slept in a shirt. Lally would already be in bed anyway, probably with the light out if his guess was on the mark. So it wasn't as though she'd be looking at him, and she'd seen him dressed in as little when they'd been in the swimming pool anyway.

Cam pushed the bathroom door open, oriented himself, clicked the light off and made his way to the bed.

The room was quite dark; that was probably a good thing. Cam lifted the covers, got into the bed, drew a slow, single breath and held it.

He could smell the sweet scent of Lally's deodorant, and the body gel she'd used in the shower. He could smell her, warm and soft and very, very close to him. Close enough that he could feel her body heat beside him in the bed.

'Goodnight, Cam. I hope you sleep at least a

little. I don't want my presence to add to your trouble with that.'

She sounded concerned, and a little breathless.

Cam wanted to pull her into his arms and kiss her until she was breathless for other reasons.

Yeah, that would work well. He'd get her in his arms, not want to let her go and it would go way beyond kissing.

Don't think about kissing her. Think of standing outside in that driving rain getting soaked and cold.

'Goodnight, Lally.' He doubted he would sleep a wink, but there was no need to tell her that. 'The main thing is for you to relax and sleep as much as you can. I'll be happy lying here listening to the rain. I can spend some time plotting the next part of my story in my head. I might write a scene where they stay in a B&B during a wild storm.'

'Story writing must be great that way.' She said it sleepily. 'You can utilise all your experiences.'

'I guess so, though I'm not about to claim that I've experienced any of the gory stuff I write in my books.' He accompanied his soft chuckle with a nod, and realised he could see the outline of her face and the soft glow of her eyes.

His vision had adjusted to the dark. The crack of light coming in beneath the door from the hallway was enough to allow him that much. That meant Lally had been able to see him from the moment he'd stepped out of the bathroom because she'd already been lying there, warm and soft.

Enough thinking about that!

'More pebble-collecting tomorrow? We've done well so far, don't you think?' It was an odd version of pillow talk, but it was better than wrapping his arms around her and kissing her until he went mad with need.

Need? Or desire, want? Well, of course it could only be desire and want. He wasn't capable of anything else.

'We have done well with the pebble collecting. I hope the rain stops before we get up tomorrow, otherwise we might not get anywhere with the rest of our search.' She yawned into her hand and tucked the covers more snugly about her chin. Beneath the blankets, her knee brushed against his leg as she shifted position.

'Oh, sorry.' She whipped her leg away and said breathlessly, 'It's not a very big bed for a double.'

'Standard size, I think.' But he knew what she meant. All he'd need to do was reach for her, tangle his legs with hers…

'Goodnight.' He uttered that single word and rolled over so he was facing away from her. Amazing just how much a man could want to resist making that one, small move.

Cam lay in the darkness and kept his breathing deep and even. Lally first lay very still and barely breathed at all, then wriggled this way and that before finally relaxing until her breathing evened out to something close to the pace and cadence of his.

She was asleep about two minutes later, fully immersed in it within half an hour.

The rain continued to fall outside the window. Cam rolled over again and gave himself a moment of looking at her face in repose in the dimness. He drew a deep breath and yawned.

His body did a weird thing; it sort of relaxed, even though he was still utterly aware of her. Well, he was a man, they were in bed, she was beautiful, he liked her and he already knew what she tasted like.

Cam sent his thoughts outside into the driving rain again to get them off that particular trail. Obviously he wasn't going to be totally relaxed in these circumstances, but even so he felt calm. Content. He felt like he did when he finally got exhausted enough to sleep, but also different. He wasn't about to pass out but he felt like he could drift away on a cloud or something.

Maybe he would think about his story a bit later. He yawned again and all his muscles relaxed.

For now, he really was tempted to just close his eyes for a bit.

He did that…and slept.

CHAPTER TWELVE

LALLY woke to the sound of a cloudburst. In the moment that she opened her eyes, she realised it was pre-dawn—dim but not entirely dark; maybe about four in the morning.

Then Lally became aware of so much else: the press of a man's warm body against her soft curves. Cam. The scent of him mixed with her scent in the warmth of the bed they shared. A heartbeat registered through the tips of her fingers where they lay against his bare chest. Strong arms wrapped around her, skin on skin where the camisole top left so much of her back, arms and chest bare.

And a chin tucked over the top of her head so that she was cuddled into him, as though he'd reached for her, put her there and hadn't wanted to let go.

Lally's breath caught and her senses exploded with a surge of desire and need while her emotions clamoured with the torn feelings that came from being in his arms. So many conflicted feelings; she hadn't anticipated any of them, yet they washed all through her.

Lally tried to blame her rioting feelings on suddenly finding herself in this position. What if she'd ended up here because *she* had rolled into his arms, cuddled up to him quite shamelessly? What if she'd done that while he was wide awake and he'd put up with it rather than waking her? She wouldn't have said Sam's name in her sleep, would she?

But Lally knew she would not have done that, because it wasn't Sam who'd filled her thoughts since the day she'd met Cameron. Sam hadn't filled her thoughts for a long time, other than with guilt.

Cam made a contented, sensual sound in his sleep and his arms tightened their hold about her. Lally's worries gave way to more immediate responses, and not all of those responses came out of the fact of their physical closeness.

That set it all off. She wanted his kisses and to be loved by him; she wanted his body—but she also wanted him to want her soul. Lally wanted Cameron far too much to be safe in that wanting.

'Easy, Lally.' Cam stroked the backs of his knuckles gently over her back. His words were slurred and relaxed, more asleep than awake. 'It's just rain. We're safe. We know where we are.'

The mumbled words said so much about Cam's attitude to feeling misplaced.

'I wasn't…' *Worried about that.* She heaved in a breath. Given that brought them even more chest-to-chest, that didn't exactly help. His voice had been all raspy, as though he'd been in a deep, deep sleep. 'I know we're safe. We're at the B&B after our pebble collecting and dinner with your mother.'

She threw that in just in case he needed to be reminded, so he could completely orient himself.

Lally cleared her throat and whispered into the night, 'Did you sleep like that for long?'

There was a beat of silence and then a slow, surprised, 'Out like a light, and I must have slept for about six hours. I fell asleep listening to you sleeping. I'd still have been asleep if you hadn't started to wake.' His voice deepened again. 'Not that I minded.'

There was a great deal of 'not minding' along with the surprise that he'd slept so well in those few words, maybe more than he'd meant to let slip.

Lally felt thrilled because she'd helped him sleep. How silly was that? He'd probably slept due to some totally different reason. Maybe rain falling helped him to sleep. Didn't people listen to recordings of water falling and things like that, for that reason?

But he'd have tried that and be doing it all the time, if it worked for him. Cam's hand curved against her shoulder. He barely moved it, and yet all of Lally's body responded with a deep and demanding command to arch into his touch.

Was it the early hour of the morning and the dimmed intimacy of the room that made his words sound like the most sensual thing she had heard? His touch an invitation, a hope and a promise?

Lally tried desperately to pull herself together, but all that came out was, 'If I snored I'm going to die.' Her body arched into his despite herself. She stretched like a cat, right there in his arms. Lally stiffened with embarrassment and wished her emotions and responses would stop fritzing out on her.

Until Cam drew a deep, unsteady breath and went very, very still against her. 'You breathe like a kitten. You make purring sounds in your sleep. It's very…sexy.'

The words wrapped around her, made her feel desirable, gorgeous and lovely.

When had she stopped letting herself feel like that? Why had she stopped? The thoughts washed away as Lally registered the craving in his strong body, the desire mixed with gentleness in the fingers that stroked over her shoulder blades. They slowed as her body melted despite her, stroked to the back of her neck and oh, so softly drew her forward until his lips were a breath away from hers. 'May I?'

Kiss her? Love her? Do whatever he wanted with her and never, ever stop?

Her whispered, 'Yes,' ended in a sigh as his lips covered hers. Lally justified that it was only a kiss, one kiss, while rain fell on the roof above them. Cam tugged the sheet and blanket with his fist until it was wrapped around them, then she was snuggled hard against his chest while his mouth explored hers and their bodies pressed against each other.

There was always a point when the choice was made, a cut-off point, a chance to draw back; Lally and Cam pushed straight through that barrier with this one single kiss. He opened his mouth and offered her his tongue. She claimed him, exploring his mouth, letting their tongues brush, and to that claim she yielded herself.

'You're so beautiful.' Cam's hands skimmed over her upper arms. His fingers splayed over the side of her neck and speared into her hair. He buried his nose against her scalp, closed his eyes and inhaled, and his body tightened.

He pressed fully against her, tangled his legs with hers, and his muscles locked. 'I don't want to hurt you, Lally—emotionally. There are things I can't give you. In my past, I've proved that. This can't be…'

'I know.' And she did know. If Lally had thought about anything, it was that neither of them wanted to get twisted up in something that they couldn't walk away from.

If her heart hurt a little at that thought, it was probably because she'd once had a lot more faith in her ability in relationships.

But that was then, and this was now, and she liked to think that she and Cam were friends; in some ways, wasn't that far steadier and more special than a lot of other things might be? If they both had histories that held them back emotionally now, well, maybe that meant this was okay for her with him: no false expectations, no surprises.

Just this. Now.

'I don't want it to be anything other than this.' Not more than right now; she didn't want the complication. Lally told herself this and tried not to notice the thoughts in the back of her mind that clamoured for so much more. 'We're just two people reaching for each other out of friendship and mutual desire. That's all it is. And it's allowed to be that.'

It was safe to take that, and to give it. It wasn't the same as thinking she'd fallen deeply in love, only to discover the man of her dreams had deceived her and that a marriage had failed as a result of their association.

She'd thought she was in love back then, but it had got a lot worse than even that marriage failure.

Cam searched her eyes in the dimness. She searched his too, though she didn't know what she was looking for and didn't know what he would find.

After a long moment, he stroked his fingers over her jaw.

Then she didn't think any more because he was kissing her with slow kisses and touching her oh, so gently.

Lally eased into those kisses and touches. She couldn't have said when they built to need, and when need became more need, until it consumed her and her emotions flared and rushed through her, even though she'd thought she knew what they were all about; now she didn't.

Sensation crowded through her too. Her mouth melted beneath his, yielded parts of her that she hadn't known were shut inside, hadn't imagined she would give to him because this shouldn't have been about that.

In a few short words, they'd laid down their rules. Tangled feelings, overwhelming feelings, were not part of this, yet she felt them pushing from inside to try to come out.

Lally could have panicked then but she didn't get a chance. Cam brushed her hair away from her face. Their clothes had disappeared; now he brought her to a place of desperate neediness. He eased her closer still and kissed her mouth.

Though he smiled and his eyes were calm, they were also full of heat, and his heart was thundering against her chest. His body quaked against hers and his fingers trembled as he stroked her face and slowly entered her. 'Lally.' His mouth closed over hers, worshipping her lips with the sweetest of kisses.

Lally's eyes fell slowly shut, and opened again as her body adjusted to his presence. How could she explain the sense of rightness, the feeling that their bodies had been made for each other, for this moment together? She looked into his eyes and didn't know why she needed this the way she did. How could she think about that question when all she could do was feel with her body, her senses and her emotions?

'Are you all right?' He kissed her lips. His body rested against hers, stilled within hers, as he waited for her answer.

'Yes.' She drew a breath. 'Yes.' And she was. Lally just knew that; she accepted it and let her worries go.

He loved her gently, loved her thoroughly, until every sense and nerve ending was tuned to him and only him. With whispered encouragement he helped her climb towards completion. His gaze locked with hers and he gave her all his pleasure and tenderness.

At the last moment he splayed his hand across her shoulder blades and pressed them heart to heart; he kissed her as she shattered in his arms, and he shattered with her.

When Lally thought it was over, he kissed her neck and shoulders, and used his hands to massage the muscles in her back, waist and over her hips until her body arched. He whispered her name and they made love a second time.

Dawn came and went as she lay in his arms, drifting between contentment, completion, half-consciousness and sleep. Thoughts didn't exist. How could they when all she could feel was the soft stroke of his fingers on her skin? When all she could hear was the even tenor of his breath against her ear? Lally let go and allowed herself to sleep once again.

Cam held Lally while she drifted on the edges of consciousness, and eventually as he gentled her with his touch she drifted all the way over and gave way to sleep. He kissed the top of her head and let himself tuck her close, then come to terms with feeling as though he held the most incredible treasure in his hands, treasure that he didn't want to let go of.

Had he done the wrong thing by her with this? When he'd woken with her in his arms, it had been too easy to reach for what he'd known deep down they both wanted.

But had that been best for her? And for him? Cam sighed and tucked a strand of her hair behind her ear. He pressed his lips to her temple and gave her the softest butterfly kiss. Where did all this tenderness in him for her come from? Cam hadn't been tender in his life like this. He hadn't wanted to wrap a woman up gently in his arms, hold her softly, cuddle her for as long as she needed, and then cuddle her some more because *he* needed it.

He didn't understand such feelings and he couldn't begin to imagine where he should try to go with them. There was no place he could go with them. Lally was his employee, his temporary housekeeper. Even that wasn't going to last. And Cam wouldn't last in an ongoing relationship with her, would never be able to settle, stick with it and focus on it, be committed to it.

He spent most of his time warring with his inability to sleep, filling his life and his world with way too much work to make the long hours pass. Yes, he'd slept in Lally's arms, but that wasn't normal for him. It had probably happened for some random reason, or because he'd become so totally exhausted that his body had finally allowed him to take that rest that he'd so desperately needed.

Cam knew his limits. He shouldn't have

allowed this to happen, but he had, and how would they deal with this now?

Cam sighed, forced himself to let her go, and then he climbed out of bed. He'd take a shower and get dressed, and maybe then he would think about all of this more clearly.

She'd said she didn't expect more than what they had shared. Cam had ended up feeling that they had shared a great deal more than he had expected. But exactly *what* had they shared? What made him feel this experience was different, deeper, so much more? And what did he do about any of that?

He had no answers.

CHAPTER THIRTEEN

'LALLY. About last night.'

'It was special; a gift. I'm choosing to see it as a gift and think of it as that.' Lally's rounded chin tipped up and her eyes glittered with determination.

She didn't quite meet Cam's eyes, not fully.

He couldn't blame her. Instead, he admired her so much for this show of strength when they both felt awkward and uncertain. Cam felt uncertain, and Lally *looked* uncertain beneath the façade of control and wilful good-cheer.

Cam should be thanking Lally for the gift. Nothing he'd experienced in his life had come close to what they'd shared last night. She'd brought him peace, sleep, rest and then the most moving intimacy he had ever experienced. 'I don't know what to say to you. It was—I've never; I can't explain.'

'You don't have to, Cam. You don't have to

explain anything.' She kept her head facing forward.

They were in the convertible, headed for the first beach on their list for the day. A part of Cam had wanted to call the rest of their pebble-searching off and head straight back to Adelaide. But what would that solve? Nothing.

Yet Cam couldn't find the words to explain what was inside him. So he brought up one thing that should have been discussed last night—*before* they'd made love. 'Is there a chance you could end up…?'

'No.' She shook her head and warm heat flooded her face beneath the tan of her skin. 'I'm on the Pill—irregular periods.'

Right, well, that was good, then. No chance of a baby. Cam blew out a breath that had to be relief. He couldn't explain why the relief made his chest feel tight. His hands clenched around the steering wheel and he tried to relax them. 'Uh, this is the beach, just here.'

After stating the abundantly obvious, he pulled the car to a stop and they both climbed out.

It went like that all morning. They picked up pebbles, moved on to the next beach, picked up more pebbles. They were uncomfortable together, completely conscious of what had passed between them last night, silent about it, while unspoken further words screamed between them.

They finally finished finding pebbles and drove to the next town. They bought gourmet deli-sandwiches filled with prawns and other seafood on long rolls; they could eat them straight away, and they did, because it seemed the thing to do.

'We'll make good time back to Adelaide.' Lally got up from the park bench where they'd been sitting and brushed crumbs from her skirt.

Cam stood too, and his brow furrowed as he noted the shadows beneath her eyes. Those could have come from unhappiness or strain as easily as they could come from tiredness.

Lally stared at him as though willing him to just get them into the car so they could go. He returned her stare and dredged for words to say; he fought the need to hold her, and a wave of emotion rolled through him.

'Yes, we'll make good time,' Cam acknowledged, and Lally drew a shaky breath and headed for the car with such relief that he couldn't say another word. Not now. Not when she seemed so fragile.

And not when he didn't know what to say.

Cam just…didn't know.

'I'll let the supplier know we won't take the pavers, then.' Jordan, the site boss, shrugged his shoulders. 'My opinion stands. I'm sure the pebble mosaic will look great, and I'll help out with anything that's needed for it. But I think for the commercial plans you have for this place leaving the existing pavers down is going to make it look a little too comfy—like a big home, rather than a newly refurbished apartment-complex, albeit one created within an old building. Over all I don't think that's going to best serve the place.'

'And I respect your opinion, but I'll stick with the plans that I have for the mosaic and the existing paving of the courtyard area.' Cam shoved a hand through his hair. 'I have to go with my instinct on this. It feels right to do the area this way.'

Lally stood at Cam's side. It was afternoon. They'd arrived back, stepped out of the car and Jordan had asked for a few minutes to go over various matters. The courtyard area and a chance to get new pavers for it at a bargain price had topped the list.

Cam went on now. 'Lally's going to put in her mosaic, and you'll go ahead with the plans to get the garden surrounds into good order, but that's all that needs doing.'

'Okay. It's your call.'

The two men ended their discussion and the site boss walked away with no hard feelings.

That left Lally, Cam, a car full of pebbles, a few things that had been said and some that hadn't. Such as all the thoughts inside her head that Lally wasn't sure she wanted to examine. And the emotions that wrapped around the time she had spent in Cam's arms, how special that had been for her.

She wanted to walk away and never come back, to run and not stop running. At the same time, she wanted to step forward into Cam's arms, hold him, be held tight by him and never, ever let go. She hadn't been able to talk any more about it.

Lally had done what she'd promised herself she wouldn't do: she had let her feelings get involved. Now she had to un-involve them—somehow. She didn't know how.

Lally didn't know how she would get through the rest of her time with him at all. There were things inside her, deep, emotional things to do with them making love and the surrender to him that had somehow happened deep within her. Lally couldn't let herself think about those things, not if she wanted to get through this. Not with her past. With Cam, she'd taken something she had no right to. That was what kept coming to her.

'Lally.' Cam cleared his throat.

'There's nothing to say, Cam. Please, can we just forget it?'

'I'm not sure if I can forget.' He hesitated, then said on a short burst, 'I fell asleep with you. I didn't believe I was capable of doing that. Maybe it was a one-off…' Doubt filled his words. 'I can't be settled. I'm a man who will never be able to stop in one place. I don't know how to be in a normal, loving relationship. I tried; I made a total wreck of it. And my mother…'

'It's not your fault that your mother can't settle down.' Lally did *not* believe that Cam was the same as his mother. 'And if you can't sleep, you can't sleep. Any person who knows you and love—*cares* about you, shouldn't ever feel anything about that other than empathy with your difficulties with that.'

Lally managed to stop her flow of words, but she couldn't stop what she'd almost said pouring through her heart. It rolled over her and consumed her.

She'd fallen in love with Cam. The knowledge was deep down inside her, true, total and absolute. She'd fallen for him before she'd ever made love with him, and of course she should have known that that was so.

Why else would she have needed that intimacy so much, if not to put into expression what was inside her heart for him?

Oh, Lally. How could you fall in love with him? How can you protect yourself now that you've done that?

She had never felt this way about another person. Not Sam, and that shocked her, because she thought she'd loved Sam so much. Only Cam had said he'd tried to love once before and failed. That was his past, his secret—that he'd loved.

And don't expect him to love you, Lally. Don't expect it.

'I just want to do the mosaic for you.' For him, for her, to leave her mark here on this piece of property that would make a great family home, for a very large family to come and go. But not for Cam, who had almost no family and didn't want one of his own, and had only bought this place to develop it.

But he could be happy as part of a family. He wouldn't have to settle into one place to do that. If he needed to travel, couldn't he do that with someone at his side?

Oh yes, Lally? And would he choose you to be that someone? A woman who broke up a marriage? Had an affair with a married man? Sent a woman into a care facility and her children into foster care?

Lally hadn't been able to do anything to help them. Sam should have done that but instead he'd walked away. Lally's thoughts put an end to any dream she might have had. She'd lost her right to dream, and all she could see that she had left to lean on in that moment was her professionalism. If she returned her focus to her work, maybe she would manage to get through this without Cam realising that she had discovered she loved him.

She didn't want him to know. It wouldn't

change anything, would it? 'It shouldn't take me long to do the mosaic and have the water-feature put in. I'm happy to work with Jordan.'

'You're here for eight weeks.' Cam spoke as though he felt he needed to be assured of that.

It was her chance to say, no, the moment she finished the mosaic she would leave. Or turn around right now and walk away.

Lally couldn't do it.

She couldn't find it inside herself to lose any of the time she had left here, no matter what. Even though that probably made her a masochist. 'Yes. I'm here to take care of housekeeping duties, build the pebble mosaic and anything else that's required for your book research or your phone messages. You don't need to sacrifice time to help me with the mosaic. I'll be fine on my own.' She forced the words out. They had to be said. She would finish here, leave her gift, but that was all. 'It will be…better if I just do it.'

Cam's deep green gaze sought her eyes and locked. Oh, she wanted simply to let all the emotions inside herself loose, throw herself into his arms and hope for some miracle to make it all somehow work out.

But life wasn't that simple. Cam didn't want her with the kind of feelings she had for him, and if he did she'd have to explain her past—and Lally couldn't face seeing his reaction to that.

'Then I'll spend some time in my office now,' Cam said. 'Do some writing and catch up on my Sydney business interests.'

'That sounds like a good idea.' They'd had one special night. They'd made love. Lally had fallen *in* love with her boss, but that didn't mean he'd suddenly developed the same feelings towards her. Nothing had changed between them other than there was now the awkwardness of knowing what they had shared.

Well, Lally could finish out her time here without letting that history or her current feelings get in the way of doing a good job as his employee.

She could. She *would!* 'I need to get working too. I want to prepare a good meal for tonight, as well as do some preliminary work on the mosaic.' No matter how hard she wanted to work on the mosaic, or how quickly she hoped to get it finished, she did have to make sure that taking care of her boss still came first.

Because Lally was the housekeeper, with a side order of helping him with his book research if required.

And Cameron was the boss. He was a little unconventional in his requirements at times, perhaps, because of his career as an author, but still the boss.

There couldn't be more between them. He

hadn't offered more, and she needed to convince herself she didn't want or need more. Life had limits. In the case of 'Lally and Cam,' the limits were that there couldn't *be* a 'them' outside working together for a very temporary amount of time.

Lally wasn't sure she could lose that much, not yet. She didn't know how she would at all. So for the next five days she focused solely on doing her work on the mosaic and on looking after Cam. Her boss spent long hours in his office in the apartment, working. Sometimes at night she heard him out swimming laps in the pool. She swam, too, but never again at the same time as him.

Lally pushed her emotions down inside her and worked. And, despite doing that, or maybe because of it, the mosaic came together beautifully. When Lally stood back from the work on Friday night and dusted her hands down her legs over the denim cut-offs, she tried to give the mosaic an objective examination. Was it truly good? Or did she just want it to be, and so that was what she saw?

Lally admitted she not only wanted this work to be good, but she *needed* that, as her gift to Cameron. This was the part of herself that she could give to him and that he was prepared to keep. That was how Lally felt.

Oh, God. How could she walk away and leave him? Lally's heart filled with so much love for him in that moment that she hurt.

'It's brilliant.' Cam's quiet words sounded from a few steps behind her, deep words in the most gentle tone of voice, and then he was there. Lally had to do what she could to seem normal to him, while she felt her heart must truly be breaking in two, because she loved him so much. Yes, she could give him this, but she felt as though her one true opportunity to deeply give her love to him had been and gone too quickly.

Words rushed around inside her, came from her heart, filled her mind and had to be stopped before they crossed her tongue.

I don't want to leave you.

I don't know if I can stop loving you.

Can't there be a chance for us? Can't I be someone that you want enough that you overcome your hesitations about commitment? Can I hide my past from you, keep that secret and love you?

Of course that couldn't happen.

Oh, she hated this!

Lally turned slowly and tried simply to appear happy about his compliment, and about a job that he seemed to feel was well done. 'Thank you. I only finished it minutes ago. I was looking at it, trying to be objective. You're truly satisfied with it?'

His gaze shifted from the mosaic to her face. 'You've done an amazing job. You have true artistic talent, Lally. I think, if you wanted, you could do mosaics for a living.'

'Thank you.' Lally prayed that all her feelings weren't written across her face and tried to give him a simple, ordinary smile. If it was a little wobbly around its edges, she couldn't help that. 'I think the results work. The water feature is great; your site boss really came through with sourcing that.'

Cam's face relaxed into something close to a smile. 'He's a good site boss. I'd use him again any time. I didn't have the successful bid on the other property here in the city, but if anything else came up…'

'I imagine he'd be very happy to hear you'd use him again.' What if Cam told her that was enough now and let her go?

Suddenly Lally had her family on her mind. All the aunts, uncles, cousins, her sisters, brothers and parents. She'd missed them, and had worried, had wanted to get back to working with them. Yet now…

'It's a weird thing to ask, but I'm hoping I can talk you into going out for a fast-food meal instead of making dinner tonight.' He hesitated. 'You've worked really hard. We could go to a res- taurant, of course, it's just—would you come out for a hamburger? If you're in the mood for that kind of food.'

'You don't have to reward me.' She didn't want him to feel that he needed to do that. 'I loved doing the mosaic. It made me happy to do that for you.'

Cam's face softened.

She wanted to believe it softened with love towards her, but he was just showing appreciation.

And yet, he pushed his hands into the pockets of his jeans and came close to shuffling his feet before he glanced up at her through the screen of his lashes. 'Will you come and eat salty junk-food with me— hamburger and fries? And maybe a completely nu- trition-empty fizzy drink to go with them? Just…do that?' Not for a reward, just to do it.

'I will.' The words escaped her before she had any chance of recalling them.

Lally admitted she didn't want to take the words back.

If Cam wanted her company for an hour to go and eat fast food, she decided she would give herself that. There wouldn't be many more memories; maybe she should take them where she could find them.

'Good. That's good.' Cam took his hands out of his pockets and half-turned before he swung back to her. 'Half an hour? Time for you to shower off the dirt?'

'Yes.' She started towards their apartment.

His apartment, she corrected, in which she was a temporary, employed guest.

CHAPTER FOURTEEN

CAM stood in the centre of the living room, waiting for Lally. He didn't fully understand his edginess. No; that wasn't right. Cam knew the source of his inner upheaval. He'd been this way since he and Lally had returned from their trip to collect pebbles. He'd been edgy since they'd made love.

They'd both acknowledged they couldn't go there again, and Cam didn't need to know Lally's reasons for that. Yet in other things she was such an open girl. And Cam felt the need to understand her depths, even if his own weren't making a lot of sense to him right now.

Did he feel so affected by their love-making because it had followed *sleeping* beside her, sleeping whilst holding her? He'd never *slept* with a woman in his life. Sleep for him, solo, hadn't been a possibility for more than a certain amount of time. Sleeping with a *woman* in his bed? Yet with Lally he had slept, slept longer and better. He'd relaxed with her even in the face of wanting to make love to her.

Then he had made love to her. And now Cam had this urge to make sure she couldn't leave his employment, to find some way to keep her with him. Yet they couldn't remain lovers; it had been a mistake to let things go that way. If she stayed longer than the agreed time frame, was it even possible that they could relax into each other's company in a purely platonic way and be happy simply as boss and employee? As property developer–thriller writer and housekeeper?

Cam's mind told him that when the work on this complex was done—which would only be a few weeks away now—he had to let Lally go, say goodbye, move on with his life and forget her. That would be the smart thing to do.

So why ask her to go out to eat with him?

Because you've been here, and she's been here, and days have passed while you've both tried hard to get on with things, but you've missed her.

'I hope I didn't keep you waiting too long.' Lally spoke in a carefully neutral tone from behind him.

He turned and took her in. For an hour or so there'd be nothing to do but concentrate on each other, and Cam wanted to concentrate on her, and somehow without putting them in a worse place than they were now. He resisted the urge to jam his hand through his hair. Did he truly know what he wanted about anything any more? 'I really do like you in red.' His voice deepened despite himself. 'It's vibrant. It suits you.'

She'd dressed casually in a black skirt with splashes of tiny red flowers over it. The skirt flowed to mid-calf and swirled about her legs when she walked; sandals left her feet beautifully revealed. Her hair was up in a pony-tail, she had gold, dangly earrings in her ears, and she wore a fire-engine red, clingy, sleeveless blouse that showed her slender curves to perfection and accentuated the long lines of her arms and the narrowness of her waist.

Cam's body noted all these things, but it was something a lot deeper than awareness that locked his eyes to hers and made it impossible to look away. Something that came from way deep down inside him and gave him pleasure to see her dressing in a way that allowed all of her vibrancy to shine out.

'You look beautiful.' The words escaped without his control.

Lally's face glowed beneath her tan and she dropped her gaze. 'Thank you. I bought the blouse at a stall at the market a few days ago; I guess it just caught my eye.' She seemed almost surprised by this, or perhaps a little discomfited.

'Bright colours suit you.' He'd told her so before, but this time her gaze rose to his and there were a thousand questions in her eyes.

But she only said, 'Thank you,' and suggested they get going.

Cam took his cue from her and hustled her to his car, and they drove the twenty minutes' drive to the restaurant. 'One of the workers mentioned this place and said the food's good, a cut above the ordinary.' Cam told her the name of the restaurant. Yes, he was making small-talk, but that was a start. If they could relax…

'I've heard of it, but I haven't been there. I think it's a little more ritzy than an average fast-food outlet.' Lally seemed to be trying hard, too, and Cam hoped that she might want this time with him as much as he wanted it with her.

'So long as the food is salty, hot and at least a little bit fatty, I'll be happy.' He forced the words out and worked hard to produce a natural smile. 'There are just days—'

'When you want that kind of food.' Lally smiled a little, and then her smile became genuine.

Cam knew his had too.

Lally glanced again at Cam's face and some of her tension eased away. She didn't understand how she could relax in his company when her heart was aching so much. But she would rather be here with him than anywhere else in the world, and if she could have this, and they could enjoy themselves, well, she wanted it. She was glad he'd asked for this time.

Cam found a parking space and they walked the better part of a block to get to the restaurant.

The place was busy with a good cross-section of patrons; families, singles, people in business wear and tourists were all represented. Lally looked around and acknowledged she was happier in this moment than she'd been for days.

Just a little focused time with him, and she felt this way. Later she might feel twice as bad, but for now Lally was going to take what she could get.

A woman around Lally's age appeared and led them to a table tucked into a corner. She stared at Cam as they were seated, and then said, 'Oh, my God—aren't you Cameron Travers, the crime-thriller writer? I love your books. Oh, would you sign something for me?'

Cam signed the back of one of the paper menus for the woman and smiled her away. The back of his neck was red, and once they were alone he looked at Lally with a slightly trapped expression.

Delight washed through her, and she laughed. 'How often does that happen?'

'Not often, thankfully,' he growled. He lifted the other paper menu from the table and buried his nose in it. 'And we're short a menu now.' Cam lowered the one he held and laid it on the table so they could both look at it.

And, in the face of his discomfort at being recognised as a 'star', Lally relaxed the rest of the way into his company and just let herself enjoy their time together for what it was.

She was tired of trying to work things out in her head and heart. She loved this man with all her heart; that was fact. She couldn't avoid it or do anything about it, and there would be pain when she left him, but she wanted to try to enjoy her time with him until she had to leave. Was that so dangerous or foolish or silly? *Probably.*

They ordered the house special of a gourmet hamburger on a sour-dough bread roll baked on the premises and toasted to perfection, and a basket of fresh-cut chips. Lally gave up any pretence at being ladylike, picked up her hamburger in both hands and took a bite.

The tastes exploded on her tongue: the most divine, melt-in-your-mouth meat patty, crisp, fresh salad greens, spiced beetroot, succulent tomato, a barbecue sauce and mayonnaise that were both to die for. She watched Cam's face across the table as he, too, tried the hamburger.

His smile started in his beautiful green eyes and spread until it turned up the corners of his mouth. 'Do you think the trip was worth it?'

'Yes.' She'd have said so anyway for other reasons, but Lally simply smiled and went on, 'And we haven't even tried the chips yet.' She reached for the bowl in the centre of the table at the same time Cam did. Their fingers brushed, and his stilled where they touched hers.

He lifted his lashes and looked at her, and just for a brief moment his fingers stroked over hers before he took a chip, she took one too and they both ate.

'The, um, the chips are great too.' They were a perfect counter-balance for the delicious hamburger.

Cam reached for another one. 'The menu says they're oven baked, but they're so good I've decided to forgive the lack of excess fat.'

Lally licked the taste of salt from her lips and laughed, and a little silence fell as they paid attention to their food. It wasn't a bad silence but rather a comfortable one. Lally soaked it up with all her heart, studied each nuance of expression as it crossed his face and refused to think about any moment but right now.

The end of their meal coincided with the people at the table beside theirs receiving their desserts. Lally cast one longing glance in that direction before she shook her head.

Her boss gestured to the menu. 'We can take a selection of desserts home for later, if you'd like?'

It was a small thing, but that thoughtfulness made Lally feel treasured. Or was it the soft expression in his eyes as he waited for her response? Oh, why couldn't they?

'I'm tempted, but I don't think I'll be able to eat a thing until tomorrow.' She pushed the thoughts away. 'Thanks for the offer, though.'

Cam settled their bill and minutes later they stepped out onto the busy street and strolled back towards his parked car.

He turned to her as they reached it. 'Thank you for doing that with me tonight.'

'Thank you for asking me to come along.' Lally sought for something light to say. 'Maybe you'll be able to use that in your book somehow too.'

Her boss thought for a moment. 'There are possibilities: the scent of fries leads my super sleuth to his answers…'

They were still laughing about it when Cam unlocked the car. Lally stepped towards the kerb and glanced up as a woman's voice penetrated her thoughts.

'We'll go to look at the sports store, Danny. We just don't want to walk that far. Going in the car will be best.'

A man's voice joined in. 'I'll buy us all an ice cream after the sports store, so don't hassle your mum, okay?'

'Sorry, Mum.' A teenaged voice went on with

a hint of cheeky cheerfulness, 'You know I love ya, even when I whinge.'

General laughter followed this comment.

Lally knew that female voice. It wasn't one she would ever be able to forget. Memories and guilt, so many things, hit her at once; at the depths of them was remorse. She didn't want to look, but she had to see. Her head turned, and her gaze shifted over the small group of people preparing to get into the car behind Cam's convertible.

The man looked about forty. There were three boys ranging in age; Lally didn't know the exact ages, but the youngest had been under two years old back then. They all looked a lot like Sam; Lally noted that as she searched their young faces, searched all over each of them for signs.

And the woman was Julie Delahunty. Here. Right now. With all three of her sons. The group looked like a family, comfortable with each other. Happy.

In that moment, Julie looked up, recognised Lally, and her mouth pinched into a tight line while her face leached of every bit of colour. Her hands reached for the boys nearest to her, as though she needed to physically stop them from being taken from her side.

I am so sorry.

The thoughts were trapped inside Lally's mind, trapped deep in her heart. She'd written them to

Julie long ago; her counsellor had helped her to get them sent to Julie at the care residence. There'd never been a reply; Lally hadn't expected one. But something in the expression on Julie's face now told her she'd received and read the words. So at least she did know of Lally's regret.

It doesn't change anything, Lally!

And it didn't.

Lally's hand rose, palm up, in a silent expression of supplication. Her mouth worked, though no words came out. Guilt and remorse ached in her heart.

Cam's voice impinged. 'Lally? Sweetheart? What is it?'

She felt the touch of his hand on her arm, his fingers closing around her wrist in a gentle clasp as his body turned to hers, as though he would shield her from whatever harm was trying to befall her.

In all that had happened between Lally and Cam, she'd managed to push this part of her history mostly away. She hadn't let herself look at this, admit this, acknowledge how it stood between her and certain possibilities in life. Happiness; she didn't deserve happiness. Lally didn't see how that could ever change.

The woman hustled her sons into the car. The man spoke to her in a low voice, glanced in Lally's direction, and his mouth tightened too.

Lally wanted to turn, hide her face in Cam's chest and just will it all away. Shame stopped that thought before it fully formed. Lally had longed to be able to love Cam and have him love her back—oh, she admitted this—but how could she ever have hoped for that?

If Cam knew.

The family drove off into traffic. At least they were gone. There were other impressions from these moments trying to register, but Lally couldn't see past Julie's stricken face, her hands reaching for her sons.

Lally let Cam put her into the passenger seat and they too headed into traffic in the other direction, heading for…

Not home. Heading for Cam's property development.

'Who were they, Lally?' Cam's words were stern in a way she'd never heard from him before. 'It's clear that seeing those people has hugely upset you. I want—I *need* to know why. If you're in trouble, I'll help you, protect you.'

'Her name is Julie Delahunty.' Lally did not want to speak of this, but she couldn't leave Cam worrying for her sake.

She would tell him the same part of this that she had told her family. Lally's voice was a flat monotone as she said, 'I had an affair with her husband six years ago. Julie's three sons were smaller then, still very dependent on their parents, obviously.'

Dependent. 'When Julie found out about the affair and became...unwell over it, Sam, he walked away. He didn't care about her or his sons.' Sam hadn't cared about Lally, either, but that paled in comparison. Lally clamped her lips together. She'd already said more than she had wanted to.

She'd put the words to Cam more revealingly than the cold, minimal facts she had told her family six years ago.

Cam's hands remained relaxed on the steering wheel and his gaze was clear and steady as he cast a quick glance her way before turning his attention back to the road.

Lally saw his compassion, but he took care not to show pity or judgement.

He asked quietly, 'And the gentlemen with her just now wasn't her husband?'

'No. I don't know who he was.' Lally dredged her mind for a way to end this conversation. 'Please, Cam.'

What did he think of her, now that he knew she'd had an affair?

It didn't matter to Lally. There was no hope for her with him. This had just underlined that fact for her. The rest was irrelevant.

'I love my family.' The words were jerky; they

exposed her, came out as long-buried guilt and pain forced their way past her control and reserve. Past six years of silence. 'I've been trying—'

'Ever since to make it up to them?'

Somehow they were inside the apartment, and with the door closed behind them Cam threw his car keys onto the entry table and led her to sit on the sofa in the living room. He clasped her hand in his. Lally didn't deserve his comfort but they were here and he wasn't letting go.

She wanted to run, but a part of her wanted to confess things she'd not confessed, except to that counsellor who hadn't been able to accept, or judge, or punish, or forgive, who had only been able to acknowledge and try to guide Lally so she could fix this for herself.

Fix a guilt and heartbreak that was unfixable. So Lally had buried it deep, and, yes, she had hidden out in her family. She had needed to feel safe.

'Won't you tell me? Maybe I can help somehow.' Cam looked into Lally's beautiful brown eyes, and thoughts and emotions he'd stifled in the days since he'd made love to her bubbled to the surface inside him. 'You've done so much to try to help me.'

This beautiful girl had been punishing herself for so long. That was so clear now. He had half known, had half guessed that already from her silent determination not to get involved with him. He'd guessed it was because of a man somehow, but he hadn't guessed all this guilt.

She'd punished herself by wearing dull coloured clothes. She'd sown herself into serving her family and hadn't wanted to step outside of working among them. Lally had hidden herself because of guilt.

Within her family, she had maybe even tried to work off what she perceived as her sin by giving, giving and giving to them. Was Lally seeing her past in a genuine light? Or was it coloured, *mis*-coloured, by a young girl's memories and guilt that had never been resolved?

'How old are you now, Lally?' He asked the question in a calm tone while his fingers stroked over the back of her hand.

She'd relaxed that hand into his clasp, though he wasn't sure if she realised she had done that, trusting him with that much of herself. Cam wanted to help her, but he also wanted her to trust him with so much more. The thought drew his eyebrows together but he didn't get a chance to examine it before Lally answered his question.

'I'm twenty-four.' Her brown eyes shimmered with regrets and hurt. 'It was in my CV.'

'Yes. So you're twenty-four now.' Cam pressed on, 'That means you were eighteen when you were seeing that woman's husband—Julie, was it? And how old was he?'

'He was ten years older.' Lally bit her lip. 'I knew it wasn't a good idea to see someone that much older.'

A part of Cam wanted to go and find the other man and make *him* take responsibility for hurting the young girl Lally must have been then. He bit back that impulse and went on, 'Did you know he was married?'

Brown eyes met his gaze. 'No. I didn't know he was married.' She bit her lip.

And Cam said softly, 'What happened?'

She drew a deep breath and the words slowly came out. 'He swept me off my feet. He flattered me, said he loved the way I dressed in my bright colours, loved my vibrancy. Sometimes, when I've thought about it…' She stopped and swallowed hard, shook her head.

'You were very young, and you were preyed on by a man who must have known better.'

That's not your fault, Lally. Let yourself accept these facts and find the forgiveness you've been dodging all this time.

Lally's fingers gripped his as she went on. 'My family said it wasn't my fault. But they didn't know—I talked to a counsellor after it happened. I didn't need to say more to the family. It wasn't necessary.' Lally fell abruptly silent.

'It wasn't your fault, Lally.' He squeezed her hand. 'I'm guessing you've blamed yourself, perhaps, for his marriage breaking down?' It wasn't hard to work that out. 'You shouldn't. It was *his* behaviour that caused the breakdown of his marriage.'

'You don't understand.' Lally shook her head. Her tone became tortured. 'When she found out, his wife had a breakdown. Sam just walked away from all of it. Julie got put into a care facility and her sons were placed into foster care.'

She drew a shaky breath. 'I couldn't help. I broke up an entire family, harmed innocent children, made Julie so unhappy that she lost her grip on…'

And there it was; all of Lally's guilt was finally out there. Cam felt absolutely ferocious in that moment, ferocious in his need to protect her, to reverse time, to take this pain away for her. He needed to heal her as she had tried so hard to help him heal his insomnia, and help him in so many other ways.

Tenderness welled up with that protectiveness, soft emotions he couldn't name but had to act on.

'She was with her sons today,' he said carefully. 'That looked like a permanent arrangement. They looked like well-adjusted, typical boys for their ages, and she looked happy in her role as their mother, with a man who appeared to be her current partner.'

'Yes.' Lally frowned. 'She looked well and happy…at least, until she noticed me.'

'You can't change the past.' Cam said it in acknowledgement. 'But you're not to blame for it, Lally. So be glad that you saw her today, that you know she is well now and has her children with her. Let it go now so you can move on with your life.'

Lally searched Cam's eyes and couldn't believe that she had told him all of this. She felt lighter, somehow. Not suddenly all better, but Cam had accepted it. He hadn't judged her. 'How can you not think badly of me?' That was what Lally couldn't understand. She was happy that Julie's life seemed better now, but that still didn't change the past.

And, whatever Cam thought about this, it didn't change the fact that he didn't *love* her. He was kind, thoughtful, accepting. But he didn't love her. So what had changed, really?

'I need to get an early night.' Lally hit the end of her ability to cope, to think. To do anything. She just needed to get away. 'Thank—thank you for tonight, for the meal and for…this. But will you excuse me?'

Somehow she was on her feet and her hand was back in her possession, and Lally didn't wait to see what would happen after that. There was nothing that could happen. Because she and Cam didn't exist. They just didn't, and that was that.

CHAPTER FIFTEEN

'THANK you again for meeting me here. I realise I'm stepping over a line, but I hope you can understand why. You need to talk to your daughter, help her get this out so she can stop punishing herself.' Cameron's voice came to Lally clearly as she stepped around a corner stall at the market.

Two days had passed since they'd come across Sam's ex-wife and her new family, since Lally had admitted her guilt to Cam. She'd been silent, withdrawn, thinking about his words. But what difference did it make in the end?

'I should have guessed there might be more to this.' Mum's voice choked up. 'I feel just awful. We all thought Lally just needed a little push to get her to trust in life again, so we pretended no one needed her help right now.' Mum drew a sharp breath. 'All we did was take away the sense of safety that she needed. When that affair happened, wc wished we'd understood things sooner so we could have protected her from Sam Delahunty. We all felt we'd let her down. We didn't know about…the rest.'

Shock drove Lally forward. She stepped into their path. There was Cam, and there was Mum; Mum saw her and handed a bag of something to Cam. Lally was in Mum's arms, throttling back emotion because she didn't want to cry in front of him.

'Oh, Lally, I'm so sorry.' Mum's touch went straight into Lally's heart to wrap around a part of her that she hadn't realised was so broken. It didn't matter then that Cam appeared to have sought Mum out, or that they'd been discussing personal things about her.

Lally buried her face in Mum's neck and breathed in deep, and they stayed like that for a long minute.

Finally Mum stepped back and held her at arm's length so she could look deep into her eyes, brown eyes to brown eyes, filled with so much love. 'I should have talked to you about it more, Lally. I didn't realise…'

'I shouldn't have held onto the guilt the way I did.' Lally finally accepted that now. She hadn't meant any of Julie's hurt or the hurt of her sons. She had been tricked and she had made mistakes, but she hadn't done anything out of malice, lack of care or anything else like that. She could never have guessed what would happen.

'I can't regret that I spoke about this, Lally.' Cam's words were low and careful. 'I thought your mother needed to know.'

And she did. Lally's gaze shifted from Mum's face to Cam's, where he stood silently beside them.

Cam gripped the bag Mum had given him in tight fingers and used his other hand to rub at the back of his neck. 'Me meeting your Mum this morning—I got her phone number out of the book. She brought painting materials. One of your aunts is being pushy about you painting again, apparently.'

He shook his head. 'What am I talking about? That can wait.' Cam seemed at a loss as to how to go on.

Lally's heart melted all over the place because, whatever else there was, his care was so clear.

Lally looked deep into Cam's eyes and he looked just as deeply back. How did she respond to his kindness, to this thing he had done for her sake? How did she deal with all the feelings and emotions whirling about inside her right now? Feelings about Sam, Julie and the three boys, yes—but even more deeply about Cameron. Somehow, it was a big tangle. Lally had to figure out how to unravel it, if she could, or perhaps how to weave it together within herself. To weave her past in, and let it be part of her, but the right kind of part.

That wouldn't make a difference with Cameron; of course it couldn't. He didn't love her the way she loved him. He was wonderful and special, but she mustn't kid herself that his kindness meant he had very special feelings towards her.

But if she could convince him that he could commit? That his insomnia didn't need to get in the way of a relationship for him? That his past failure in a relationship didn't have to mean his next attempt would fail, that he, too, could address his past? That it was okay to acknowledge that his mother hadn't cared well for him and he wasn't obliged to feel close to her? If only Lally could help Cam see all his value purely for who he was. What was she thinking? None of it made any difference to *her* limitations.

'Lally, darling.' Mum touched her arm gently and released her. 'We do need to talk, but I'm guessing maybe that needs to wait a little.' Though she didn't glance in Cam's direction, Mum's eyes were full of far too much understanding, *Love* and understanding, that had always been there.

Mum started to turn away, and Lally uttered, 'We *will* talk, Mum. I'd like that. And I want to be taught painting.'

'I'm so glad, Lally. It's your tradition. It will be good for you to try it. I love you, Lally.' Emotion filled Mum's face. She gave a nod and a wobbly smile and disappeared, and Lally turned back to Cam. There were a thousand things she wanted to say; Lally couldn't find the words for any of them, and she said lamely, 'I saw your note that said you'd come to the market and would take care of the shopping.'

Lally had come to join him on the very thin pretext of helping. Even though she'd been withdrawn and hadn't wanted to talk about her past any further with him for the last couple of days, she had longed to be close to him, just *be* with him, in his company. Or something.

'I took care of the shopping.' He indicated the bag at his feet, and as he did so placed the bag her mother had handed to him inside it as well. 'Are you angry, Lally?' His gaze searched hers. 'That I interfered? After we talked, I...didn't feel that I'd fully helped you to let go of all that blame you'd been carrying. I thought maybe your mother could.'

Cam searched Lally's dear face as he waited for her answer, and he finally understood.

He had fallen in love with Lally. It was so simple, really; he didn't know how he could have missed it. He couldn't miss it now because it consumed him. He had a need that was all about her, all about needing to love her, care for her, help her resolve her problems and hurts, be there for her, protect her, encourage her.

Where could he go with these feelings?

'I'm not upset, not really. You wanted to help me.' Lally started to turn. In a moment she'd walk back to the property development.

'Please.' Cam didn't want to lose these quiet moments with her, not yet. He didn't know what he wanted to do, or say… 'Would you come to the park with me? It's not far from here, not far out of our way.'

'I guess that would be okay.' Lally didn't understand Cam's motivation.

She should give him her resignation and leave before this got any more complicated.

The smart, sensible, take-care-of-yourself part of her suggested that would be the thing to do.

But Lally had been running and backing away and not addressing things for long enough. If Cam wanted to go to the park, they would go to the park.

She walked silently at his side until they entered the park. Cam kept walking and Lally wondered if he would ever speak, and if he did what he would want to say. Lally had things to say. 'You said you'd had a failed relationship— in your past. That sounds as though *you* feel to blame for *that*.'

'I did. I'll explain.' Cam took Lally to the make-shift jetty. There was no little boat this morning, just the lake and quietness. He set down the bag. He'd taken the time during their walk here to try to marshal his thoughts into some kind of order; he wasn't sure if he'd achieved that. 'I'll come back to that.'

All he knew was he needed to express these feelings that were inside him. He needed Lally so much that he couldn't make himself step aside, not if there was any chance that they could find a way.

'I remember you interviewing me on the water. I was nervous that morning.'

'I'm nervous now.' He held her arm while she sat on the edge of the jetty. The jetty stuck out far enough over the water at the end that they could sit without their feet touching the water. Cam sat beside her and turned to face her. So much love welled up inside him. He didn't know what to do with all the feelings.

'Why would you be nervous?' Lally asked and shook her head. 'I'm the one with the horrible past and six years of going around with my head in the sand not dealing with it. I'm glad Mum knows it all now. Somehow that's a weight off my mind. I didn't want to hide it from my family, but I did, and then it felt too hard to try to tell them.'

Lally loved him for his admission of nerves. 'When I talk to Mum, maybe she might be able to help me work out a…healing process.' She dipped her head before she forced it up again. 'You might think it's silly, but there are spiritual things Mum could help me do.'

'I think that's a great idea.' Cam didn't even blink, simply gave his support.

Her expression softened as she searched his gaze. '*Your* mother might be still on the face of the earth, but she doesn't keep contact and closeness with you the way she should. I'm sorry you've missed out on that all your life.'

'You said something a while back about us moving around so much that I must have not known where I'd wake up half the time.' Cam had pushed the comment aside at the time. Maybe it had been easier to go on blaming his insomnia just being how it was.

'It's so long ago, but I developed a fear of sleeping back then. I used to be afraid that I'd wake up and Mum would have abandoned me somewhere and gone on without me.' He shook his head. 'It sounds stupid now. I've been a grown man and in charge of myself for a long time. I never thought about it until after that night that I…slept with you.'

'You trained yourself into a habit of not sleeping, and until you figured that out about yourself…'

'I had no hope at all of sleeping and feeling relaxed unless I felt deeply happy and secure.' As he had felt the night he'd held Lally in his arms and had drifted to sleep to the kittenlike sounds she'd made while she slept. Was it any wonder he'd woken and needed to express all his feelings to her the way he had? 'You gave me that feeling, and so much more.'

The sleep didn't even matter, and Cam needed to tell her that. 'I'm not doing a very good job of expressing myself. I don't need to get some instant or fabulous fix for my sleep issues. If I can go back for some further professional guidance about that, get in a better place with that now that I've realised that childhood fears have most likely contributed to the problem, that will be great—but if not...'

He drew a breath. 'I don't think I have to let that issue, or the hours that I work, or the way I was raised and my lack of closeness with my mother, stop me from trying to make a success of a relationship that matters to me.' He swallowed. 'Where there's a deep enough love, can't most things be figured out?'

He searched her eyes, and he wasn't sure what he saw there. Was it kindness that made her eyes shine in that way? Cam wanted her to let him in to her heart.

He took Lally's hands in his and gently squeezed her fingers. 'I thought I couldn't be in a relationship. I blamed that on the insomnia, my workaholic tendencies. What would I have to offer a woman? That's what I asked myself. I failed once, but I've realised now that I didn't love Gillian.' He drew a breath. 'I doubt she really loved me.' That didn't matter anyway, now.

'I've fallen in love with you, Lally. You're so deep in my heart and I can't bear the thought of you leaving me. I'd been wracking my brains for ways to keep you with me. I thought of asking you to be my travelling housekeeper, to go everywhere with me. But I don't want only that. I want *all* of you.' That was Cam's admission, and what he needed to say.

'I don't understand.' Lally wanted to comprehend this—her heart begged for that—but how? 'You know about my past.'

'And you know about mine. I want a chance for both of us to reach out and be happy. Past histories—they are *in* the past, Lally. They can make us stronger and better. They don't have to hold us down or hold us back.'

Cam had realised this; he needed Lally to see it too.

Lally looked at Cam. He wanted her to be happy with him? He'd said he loved her? Lally took the wondrous thought deep inside herself. Could it be true? It could, because Cam wouldn't say that if he didn't mean it.

The knowledge finally penetrated all the way to Lally's heart. Hope rose there. She looked into

Cam's eyes and knew she had to fully open her heart. 'I'm in love with you too. It happened the night we made love. I didn't understand then, but I realised later, and I didn't know how to deal with my feelings. I was certain you wouldn't be able to feel the same way towards me.'

'You love me?' Cam uttered, and his hands tightened, one around her hand, the other over her shoulder. The next moment she was snatched against his chest and his arms were against her back, his hands pressing into her shoulder blades before he reached very, very gently and raised her face so he could look into her eyes. 'Say that again.'

'I love you.' Lally did, and it felt so good to admit it and to realise that he loved her too.

'Do you truly believe we can have a future?' Dared she ask?

But, yes, Lally did dare ask because she longed for, wanted and *needed* a future with Cam. If there was any chance of that, she wanted to grasp it. For the first time in six years, she felt hope.

'Yes. Yes, Lally,' he uttered in the deepest, most sincere voice Lally had ever heard. 'I want for ever with you, and we can have it if we both try.'

Lally slowly nodded. 'If we love and accept. I would understand about your wakefulness, Cam, even if it never got any better. And your need to focus on your writing while your muse is willing to talk.'

Cam laughed and shook his head. 'I still have a deadline, but I must admit writing hasn't been my first priority since the night we made love. I've kept working, but all I've really wanted to think about is you.'

He drew a breath. 'Because that old relationship fell apart, and Gillian said she couldn't cope with my work focus and sleeplessness, I thought I didn't have enough to give. And I'm *not* close to Mum. You have a big family. I don't know if I could fit in.'

Lally searched Cam's face once more and knew his concerns were genuine. She smiled gently. 'You seem to get along okay with Mum.'

He nodded. 'Your mother is a kind, giving, lovely person…just like you.'

Oh, his words went straight to Lally's heart and found their way deep inside it. She let a teasing edge touch her smile as she responded, 'So just multiply Mum by about a hundred and you have my family. Since you're a rather great person to get along with yourself, I think you would be fine fitting in.'

It hit her then just how deep this conversation had gone. They were talking about 'for ever' kinds of things. Did Cam want…?

'I'd like to be part of your big family.' Cam's expression sobered into a deep, open love, into hope and need. 'And I would like to have babies with you, make our own special family, when we're ready for that step.'

In that moment, Lally gave herself utterly to this man who had been her boss, her lover, a friend and would now become everything to her. The thought of having his child overwhelmed her, filled her heart with a love she couldn't begin to comprehend.

Lally buried her face against Cam's chest and let her fingers rest over his heart. The brush of his mouth against her forehead made her lift her face, and he kissed her lips softly and drew back to look into her eyes.

'Will you marry me, Lally? Let me hold you in my arms at night, love you, be with you whether I sleep at your side or stay awake, and be happy because I'm with you?' He hesitated. 'I don't know if I can settle in one place. It's not something I've tried, but this property development— I thought from the day I met you that it would make a good family home, so maybe we could try…'

'Yes.' Yes to all of it, including trying. 'We can work those things out. We'll both need to adapt and understand what we want out of life together.' Lally would go anywhere with him. In her heart, she knew that, though it would be nice to be close to her family when possible.

'I won't take you from them, Lally.' He said it

gently and she knew he'd read her emotions on her face.

Lally was just fine with Cam knowing her feelings so well. 'If we travel, we can still come home here to the family, if you don't need to be based in Sydney for your business.'

'I've become quite adroit at running that business from afar. There's no reason why I can't continue to do so.' Cam smiled and hugged her. 'I will love your family, but I'll love you most of all. We can have this, Lally. We can go forward.'

She nodded. 'Let our pasts be what have formed us to this point, but we'll form our futures with each other.'

'Yes.' Cam's voice deepened. 'Yes, Lally.'

And there, on a makeshift jetty at the edge of a small lake in a suburban park, Cam proceeded to tell Lally about all the hope that was in his heart for their 'for ever.'

And Lally soaked up every word while the sun rose over the lake and sent vibrant sparkles of colour shining through the mist.

After a long moment, Cam said, 'I can't wait to marry you, to see you walk towards me on that special day and know you're going to be truly and completely mine to love and care for always.'

'Oh, I can't wait for that either.' Lally's heart filled with love for him.

His arms closed about her, and he turned her

face up and kissed her mouth gently. 'Our future starts right now. I want you in all of my life, Lally. Everything. I want you to learn to paint from your mother, or whoever else in your family will teach you. And I want to encourage you with more mosaic work.'

Lally's heart filled all over again with love for this wonderful man. 'We can travel all over Australia for a while leaving a trail of property developments with pebble mosaics in their courtyards if we want to.'

Cam's gaze met hers, with all his heart right there for her to see. 'So long as we keep coming home to *this* property, and settle here eventually. There'll be room for visits from all your relatives, and my mum, if I can ever convince her to stop by.'

'Maybe one day we will convince her.' In this moment, Lally believed that anything might be possible.

Home, happiness, family and a future. And, though they did travel, that was exactly how it turned out to be.

FREE BOOKS OFFER

To get you started, we'll send you
2 FREE books and a FREE gift

There's no catch, everything is **FREE**

Accepting your 2 **FREE** books and **FREE** mystery gift
places you under no obligation to buy anything.

Be part of the Mills & Boon® Book Club™ and receive your favourite
Series books up to 2 months before they are in the shops and delivered
straight to your door. Plus, enjoy a wide range of **EXCLUSIVE** benefits!

- Best new women's fiction – delivered right to
  your door with FREE P&P

- Avoid disappointment – get your books up to
  2 months before they are in the shops

- No contract – no obligation to buy

We hope that after receiving your free books you'll
want to remain a member. But the choice is yours.
So why not give us a go? You'll be glad you did!

Visit **millsandboon.co.uk** to stay up to date
with offers and to sign-up for our newsletter

2 **FREE** books
and a
FREE gift

NOFIA

Mrs/Miss/Ms/Mr   Initials

BLOCK CAPITALS PLEASE

Surname

Address

                                   Postcode

Email

MILLS & BOON®
Book Club

FREE BOOK OFFER
FREEPOST NAT 10298
RICHMOND
TW9 1BR

NO STAMP
NECESSARY
IF POSTED IN
THE U.K. OR N.I.

TIPPING THE WAITRESS WITH DIAMONDS

BY
NINA HARRINGTON

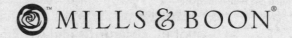

MILLS & BOON

First published in Great Britain 2010
Harlequin Mills & Boon Limited,
Eton House, 18-24 Paradise Road, Richmond, Surrey TW9 1SR

© Nina Harrington 2010

ISBN: 978 0 263 87673 4

Harlequin Mills & Boon policy is to use papers that are natural, renewable and recyclable products and made from wood grown in sustainable forests. The logging and manufacturing process conform to the legal environmental regulations of the country of origin.

Printed and bound in Spain
by Litografia Rosés, S.A., Barcelona

Dear Reader

Most people remember their first crush, and perhaps their first kiss. The angst and pain of unrequited teenage love never quite leaves us!

On occasional wistful moments we might wonder what happened to that person we imagined was so amazing and whom we longed to be with all those years ago!

What if you met them again by chance today? Would there still be a spark of attraction? And how much would you both have changed?

As a gawky, plump sixteen-year-old, Sienna Rossi was completely smitten by the intense and passionate trainee chef working in her family's Italian restaurant—except Brett Cameron seemed to be oblivious to her presence. Twelve years later Sienna discovers that, if anything, chef Brett is even more attractive when they agree to work together to save her aunt's trattoria from disaster.

I do hope that you enjoy Sienna and Brett's journey to love—where the waitress will be tipped with diamonds she will wear for the rest of her life, with her first and only true love by her side.

I would be thrilled to know how you feel about my idea for the perfect recipe for Valentine's Day, so please get in touch via my website at: www.NinaHarrington.com

Every best wish

Nina

Nina Harrington grew up in rural Northumberland, England, and decided at the age of eleven that she was going to be a librarian—because then she could read *all* of the books in the public library whenever she wanted! Since then she has been a shop assistant, community pharmacist, technical writer, university lecturer, volcano walker and industrial scientist, before taking a career break to realise her dream of being a fiction writer. When she is not creating stories which make her readers smile, her hobbies are cooking, eating, enjoying good wine—and talking, for which she has had specialist training.

'Complex characters with terrific chemistry enhance Harrington's simple plot. It's a delightful effort from a new author to watch.'
—*RT Book Reviews* on ALWAYS THE BRIDESMAID

Special Recipe for the Perfect Romance:

Step 1
Take One Single Italian Girl
Step 2
Add One Handsome Chef in a Kilt
Step 3
Throw in Two Teaspoons of Shock and Uncertainty
Step 4
Whisk Everything Together in a Tiny Bistro
Step 5
Add a Couple of Big Decisions...
Step 6
A Valentine Wish...
Step 7
Two Sparkling Brown Eyes...
Step 8
And a Pair of Pink Pyjamas
Step 9
Sprinkle with Pink Flamingos

Step 10

Add Hot Pink Psychedelic Flowers

Step 11

And a Box of Warm Memories

Step 12

Add a Platter of Sweet Dreams

Step 13

And Three Wedding Cakes…

Step 14

Eight Spinning Designer Rainbow Pizzas…

Step 15

And Two Glasses of Red Wine

Step 16

Smother in Wild Mushroom and Cream Sauce

Step 17

Mix with Three Heaped Spoonfuls of Tears

Step 18

And Two Pink Cupcakes

Step 19

Add One American Chef Without a Kilt

Step 20

Beat Vigorously

Step 21

Finish with One Portion of Chocolate Tiramisu

Step 22

Keep the Mixture Warm Until Valentine's Day; Top with a Red Rose Before Serving with a Kiss.

CHAPTER ONE

Step 1: Take One Single Italian Girl

ONCE UPON A time, Sienna Rossi thought as she sat back in a creaky staffroom chair, *restaurants were filled with wonderful guests who loved your food and drink and smiled sweetly to the waiting staff.*

Then she grimaced at the memory of the businessman who had snapped his fingers at her not once but *twice* within ten minutes, because first there had been too much ice in his drink and then his starter had arrived with a garnish of salad leaves which had clearly been added specifically to poison him. No leaves. *Those days were gone.*

I could have decorated the shoulders of his expensive business suit with the salad leaves and poured the dressing over his shiny head, Sienna thought.

But she wouldn't have done it, of course.

There was far too little dressing on the salad to

do any serious damage. Also, successful head
waiters did not do things like that in exclusive
country house hotels—especially head waiters
who wanted desperately to be promoted to restaurant managers.

*Now, if he had ordered Chef André's signature
Hollandaise sauce...* That might have been a different story.

Sienna yawned widely before reaching down to
pull off her stylish high-heeled shoes and massag-
ing her feet with a satisfied sigh of relief. She
should be used to swollen hot feet and crushed
toes after ten years in the restaurant trade but it
never got easier—especially in luxury hotels
which excelled in fine dining.

Greystone Manor had become famous for
fabulous food and its glorious English country
house setting, and business lunches were booked
weeks in advance. She should be delighted that
they had a full house every lunch and dinner service. Only it was *her* job, as head waiter and
sommelier, to make sure that every single one of
the sixty diners enjoyed some of the best food and
wine in England, excellent service, and came away
feeling that they had shared in the aristocratic lifestyle that living in a stately home could bring.

Unashamed award-winning luxury was tricky
to pull off day after day.

It was like being an actress in a top London

show, who had signed up to perform at both the matinee and the evening performances six days a week. In full make-up and tight costume, combined with even less comfortable shoes.

Singing and dancing on tables optional.

Sienna glanced at the huge antique wall clock as she rubbed the life back into her toes. Fifteen minutes to go. The new management team had called a special meeting to announce who they had decided to appoint to two crucial posts in their award-winning restaurant.

In a few minutes she would know the name of the new head chef. *And* find out who was going to be the restaurant manager who would be running front of house. That magical combination of wonderful food and excellent service which would take the Manor to the very top!

A shiver of anxiety ran across her shoulders and down her back, and she quickly checked that the staffroom was still empty. Of course she was nervous. But nobody else could know how scared she truly was.

Scared? Who was she kidding? Make that terrified.

On the glossy surface she was 'Miss Rossi'. The elegant and professional head waiter who was always immaculately turned out and who presented the perfect formal image the Manor aspired to in their fine-dining restaurant.

They would probably be horrified and totally amazed to know that the real Sienna Rossi was quaking inside the designer suit and shoes.

It had taken her four years of hard work to rebuild her shattered confidence to the point where she could even *think* about applying for the role of restaurant manager, in which she would be responsible for running her own projects and team.

This was going to be her dream job.

After so much sacrifice and hard work it was time to prove that she was capable of coming through heartbreak and rebuilding a career for herself.

A career in which she would never have to trust and rely on another person to make her dreams come true.

She *needed* this job so badly.

'You were a total star today. Did anyone tell you that? If I had an Oscar I would hand it over in an instant!'

Sienna blinked up from her reverie as her best friend Carla burst through the swing doors with a characteristic gush of black suited hotel receptionist elegance and single city-girl attitude.

'Thanks. You're cutting it fine today,' Sienna replied with a smile. 'I thought the staff meeting was at four.'

Carla grabbed what was left of Sienna's coffee and swigged it down in one gulp before sighing out loud as the espresso cup hit the saucer.

'It is. Two of the guests managed to get lost in the maze. I know, I know.' Carla waved both hands in the air. 'That is supposed to be the point of having a proper maze in the first place. But in February? I'm freezing! It has taken me twenty minutes, using cellphones and a whistle, but they are now sitting all comfy and warm by the fire with hot tea and crumpets. *Unlike* the rest of us.'

Carla shivered inside her smart suit and shoved her hands deep under her armpits as Sienna poured her a fresh hot coffee.

'"Chefs in Kilts"!' Carla suddenly squealed, reaching forward to snatch up the colour supplement of the *Hotel Catering* magazine. 'Why didn't you tell me? I've been waiting all week for this! Who have they got as Hunk of the Month this time? Maybe we'll be working with one of these hot young celebrity chefs in a few weeks. Wouldn't that be totally cool?'

Not if I have anything to do with it, we won't, Sienna thought in silence. *Never again! Been there and do not want to go back, even for a visit. And it would not be cool.*

Carla shook her head before passing Sienna her precious magazine. 'See you in five minutes. And best of luck with the job, sweetie—not that you need it. Every confidence!' And with a small finger wave she was gone.

Sienna chuckled and started gathering together the coffee cups, but as she did so the magazine flipped open and the breath froze in her lungs at the sight of a studio photograph of a tall, muscular man in a white T-shirt and tartan kilt.

Hunk of the Month: Brett Cameron.

In an instant she was transported back twelve years, to the cramped and crowded kitchen of Trattoria Rossi. And her first passing glimpse of Aunt Maria's new trainee chef.

She'd been sixteen and had wandered straight from school into the kitchen, where her father and older brother, Frankie, had been prepping for the evening service. Training places at Rossi's were fought over at the catering college, and only the best students made the grade.

Dominating the kitchen had been a skinny teenager with fire in his eyes who'd had the cheek to argue with her brother, Frankie, over the best way to divide fresh basil.

And she had been smitten.

Completely. Absolutely. Without hesitation or rational thought.

Smitten.

Just one look. That was all it took.

She closed her eyes and revisited the vivid

image that had been burnt into her memory all of those years ago.

Under a striped bandana, his long blond hair had been tied back in a ponytail which had highlighted the hard lines of a face so intense with suppressed fire and energy it that seemed to vibrate out and fill the air around him.

Every ounce of his concentration had been focused on the fresh green basil leaves in front of him, which he was tearing with long delicate fingers, while Frankie had shredded more fragrant leaves with a curved blade into thin strips.

Each of them had sprinkled sea salt and a little extra virgin olive oil onto their own stack of basil.

She had watched, entranced, as Frankie and then the blond had tasted each of the leaves in turn, with bread, then cheese and plum tomatoes, going back and forth between the two chopping boards until the blond had smiled up at Frankie and nodded.

Her brother had slapped the blond on the shoulder—which she had never seen him do to another chef in his life—and they'd turned around, smiling, to face her.

And for just one fraction of a second the skinny teenager had glanced up in her direction with such power and intense focus that it had felt as if a pair of pale blue lasers were boring holes through her skull.

Oh, boy...

Of course Frankie had broken off from the work to introduce his little sister to their new trainee, Brett, but by then she'd been a gibbering wreck.

No wonder he had responded to her squeaky hello with a low grunt. To Brett she must have seemed like just another idiot teenage girl—an interloper in this special world of edible sorcery where chefs were the magicians.

The fact that she'd been plump, awkward, clumsy and painfully shy when boys were around probably hadn't helped much, either.

For the next six weeks, which Brett had spent learning the trade in the Trattoria Rossi kitchen, it had been amazing how many excuses Sienna had found to be in the kitchen at the same time.

Desperate for the chance to be close to Brett for a few seconds.

To smell him.

To feel the frisson of energy that seemed to spark in the very air around him as he worked feverishly. To hear his voice respond with 'Chef!' when her father passed an order for a salad or cold starter.

To run to the dining table on Sunday afternoons so that she could have the chair facing Brett at the family and crew communal meals.

No other boy at school or in her life had come close to the great Brett Cameron.

She had spent her schooldays in a dreamy daze, in anticipation of those precious few moments when she could see him again, in the evening and at weekends.

Even if she *had* been so shy back then that she'd been totally incapable of speaking to him. That would have been far too terrifying even to consider.

Brett Cameron had been her first crush.

For a fleeting second Sienna succumbed to a ripple of those same teenage fears and intense shyness. She wasn't the first schoolgirl who had ever felt like a total outsider and fraud, and no doubt she would not be the last, but merely thinking back to those sad days was enough to take her to a dark place.

She shook off the memory and blinked hard to clear her head.

They had both come a long way since then.

Sienna smiled down at the magazine article and chuckled to herself for the first time that day. Hunk of the Month, indeed!

He was still the best-looking chef she had ever seen!

Back then, the nineteen-year-old Brett had been a tall, skinny teenager with a total obsession for food. His only clothing had been chef's trousers and two identical off-white T-shirts that had become increasingly less fragrant as each week went on.

Now he looked as if a team of professional stylists had spent hours working on him. And it had been money well spent for one of the top chefs now taking the catering world by storm. Last time she had seen his name in the press he had been accepting an award for a hotel restaurant in Australia. That probably explained the suntan which made those blue eyes sparkle even brighter.

He certainly had filled out. The white shirt stretched out across wide shoulders below a firm neck and a solid jawline defined by expertly clipped short blond hair.

Two things had not changed.

His eyes were still winter-sea-blue. Smiling out at her.

Sharp. Intelligent. Focused.

Tiny white smile lines fanned out from the corners of his tanned face. Well, he certainly had plenty to smile about. He had come a long way from Maria Rossi's tiny trattoria in North London to headline in the Food and Drink Awards 'Top New Chef' list.

And then there were his hands. In this photograph they were splayed out on each hip. Those clever fingers, which had used to move so fast that she'd been afraid to blink in case she missed something crucial. Long narrow fingers. How many hours had she spent dreaming about those hands?

She had fallen for those hands. No doubt about it. The only other man who had come close to having hands like those was Angelo.

Oh, Brett. If you only knew the trouble you have caused me!

She blamed him entirely for giving her a chef addiction virus. That well known form of contagion and pestilence.

At college, Carla had given her the nickname of 'chef magnet'.

Any chef within a hundred-mile radius would somehow sense that Sienna was within range and hit on her.

The chiming of the clock snapped Sienna out of her dreamy thoughts, and she glanced at the photo for one last time before closing the magazine and squeezing her swollen feet back into her shoes.

Drat! She was going to be late!

One more thing to blame on Brett Cameron! Wherever in the world he might be!

She need not have rushed! Sienna had been sitting very impatiently with the rest of the hotel management team for almost ten minutes before Patrick breezed into the dining room with head chef André following a few steps behind.

Patrick was the stylish hotel manager for the company who owned the Manor and a small group of other luxury hotels in the most prestigious locations across Europe—hotels where Sienna had every intention of working as a top restaurant manager. *After* she'd persuaded them to give her the position of restaurant manager here at Greystone Manor, of course.

She wanted this job *so* badly. It was everything she had been working towards since the first time she'd put on a waitress uniform in the Rossi family restaurant back in London.

Little wonder that her heart was racing.

Patrick looked around the room and smiled as he tapped gently on a water glass with a table knife. A sense of anxious anticipation ran around the room as the nervous chatter fell away.

'Thank you all for coming at such short notice. As you know, our brilliant head chef André Michon will be retiring at the end of the month, after thirty-two years of amazing work at the Manor. I'm already looking forward to his retirement party, but in the meantime André's decision has given the management team a real headache. How can we possibly find another chef with the same passion for excellence and quality that has made the Manor so successful?'

Please just get on with it, Sienna thought, bristling with impatience. *Please tell me who I will be working with from next month!*

'I am delighted to tell you that we have interviewed some of the brightest young chefs in the world over these last few months, and after much deliberation there was one clear winner. Ladies and gentlemen, I am very pleased to announce that the new head chef at Greystone Manor will be…TV celebrity chef Angelo Peruzi! I know that you must all be thrilled as I am.'

Sienna clutched hold of the sides of her chair with both hands and sucked in several breaths to keep herself from falling over or running out of the room in horror.

No. No. No. Not Angelo.

No. Fate would not play tricks like that on her. It had to be some sort of mistake. She could not have just heard that name.

Sienna sat frozen, her brain stunned. Exploding in on itself with the implications. And the horror.

Her heart was racing so fast and hard that it frightened her, and she fought not to burst into tears or scream out loud.

Angelo! Of all the chefs in the entire world they had to choose the one man who she wanted nothing to do with again. Her ex-fiancé. The man who had abandoned her a month before their wedding to heartbreak and despair.

This could not be happening. Not now. Not to her. Not here. Not after four years.

No! Hot tears pricked the corners of her eyes, blinding her to what was going on around her.

It took a few seconds for her to acknowledge that Carla was prodding her in the arm and gesturing with her head towards the dais. Patrick was saying something about a new restaurant manager.

'Miss Sienna Rossi has already shown what she can achieve as head waiter. Welcome to the team and many congratulations, Miss Rossi. I know that you will make a terrific restaurant manager. Chef Peruzi simply can't wait to start working with you!'

CHAPTER TWO

Step 2: Add One Handsome Chef in a Kilt

BRETT CAMERON stood with both hands thrust deep inside the pockets of his cargo trousers and stared up at the rubble-strewn building site that was destined to become his first signature restaurant.

Just four days earlier he had been in sunny Adelaide, celebrating at his leaving party, turning steaks on a barbecue and looking forward to working in his own kitchen in central London.

The reality of a wet, grey February afternoon, with deafening London traffic on the other side of this gate, was not quite the warm and glamorous welcome he might have liked, but at that moment he was totally oblivious to the noise and heavy drizzle.

This was it. After years of dreaming and planning it was finally going to happen. And from all of the possible locations in the world he had to choose from there was only one city he wanted to come back to.

It had to be London.

This was the city where he had suffered the worst years of his life as an angry and frustrated teenager, coming to terms with what life had thrown at him.

Back then London had been just one more cold and unfriendly place, where his single mother had dragged him from one cheap rented apartment to another while she found two or sometimes three unskilled jobs in order to pay the rent and keep their heads above water.

Jobs in which you did not need to read or write very well to earn a wage.

The kind of jobs he had come to detest—and yet he had been clever enough to recognise them as the kind of work he would probably find himself doing from the moment he was old enough to leave school.

Who wanted to employ a boy who could barely write his name and address on an application form, even assuming that he could read the questions in the first place?

A boy whom every one of the ten or more schools he had attended had labelled as having 'behavioural difficulties'? No matter how hard he'd worked and worked it had made no difference to the stigma of being classified as slow or lazy. An academic failure.

If he was going to prove to the world just how very far that boy had come, and what he had achieved in the years since he'd last walked these streets, then he had to come back to London.

Brett inhaled the moist air.

No regrets. It wasn't all bad. His life as a chef had begun in this city.

It was hard to believe that Maria Rossi's restaurant and his old catering college were only a few miles down the road! Sometimes it felt like a lifetime ago. A lifetime of exhaustion, hard work and even harder experience.

Maria Rossi hadn't known for sure what she was taking on all those years ago, when she'd given him a chance.

She had taken a huge risk with a stranger, not knowing how he was going to turn out, but had faith enough to make the commitment anyway.

Just as he was doing here.

There might be banks and financiers willing enough to back his new restaurant, but this was still totally personal. His own kitchen.

In a world where even successful restaurants struggled to make a living, it was precisely the kind of crazy, exciting, thrilling project he couldn't wait to get started on.

Energy coursed through his veins. *This was the greatest adventure of his life!*

Even the physical reality of bricks and mortar

was exhilarating. Until now this place had just been an idea. A dream he had talked about with his friend Chris over endless cups of coffee and glasses of wine in the two hectic years they had spent in Paris as students almost a decade ago.

And now he was looking at that dream brought to life.

He had barely slept on the long flight from Australia. His mind had been a buzz of menus and all the bewildering and complex combinations of who and what and where that went into creating a successful restaurant business.

'Where's your kilt today, old chap?' A powerful well-spoken English voice boomed out from the well-spoken, short, stout man who came striding up to Brett between stacks of bricks. 'Left it back in Oz?'

Brett grasped hold of his best friend's hand, then reached back and gave him a slap on the back.

'Don't you start!' Brett replied, in an accent tinged with an Australian twang. 'Brilliant publicity, as always, but you *do* know that I only spent the first two months of my life in Glasgow? I'm never going to live that down in the Cameron clan!'

'I'm sure they'll get over it when this palace of modern cuisine is opened! What do you think of the progress so far?' Chris nodded towards the building site just as a length of waste timber came flying out of a side window and crashed to the tarmac below, to join a mound of broken bricks and wood.

Brett grinned at the fragments of timber and nodded a few times with pursed lips before replying.

'It's good to see people with so much enthusiasm for their work! I'll answer that question after you've shown me the kitchen!' Brett rubbed both his hands together and his mouth lifted into a broad grin of delight. 'I have been looking forward to this for a long time.'

Chris straightened a little, lifted his head, and gritted his teeth together in a sharp hiss.

'Ah. About the kitchen. Slight delay, I'm afraid. Not *quite* ready for inspection yet.' As Brett turned to look at him, Chris gestured with his head towards a huge mound of tarpaulin-covered shapes just inside the main entrance.

Brett swallowed down hard in silence, took a breath, and strode into what would be the main reception area once the walls had been finished. His shoulders were high with tension.

He carefully and gingerly lifted up one of the tarpaulins and stared in silence at the huge packaging crates.

'Tell me that's not what I think it is!' Brett blurted out, his voice a mix of barely concealed horror and amazement.

'Afraid so,' Chris replied with a tilt of his head. 'The ovens were held up in transit. Apparently cargo ships don't like to go out in hurricane-force winds. Winter. Ocean. Big waves. Tricky things. Strange, that, isn't it?'

Brett stared awestruck at the huge pile of boxes and containers and raked his hands through his hair, before turning back to the only person who truly understood the sacrifices he had made to arrive at this point, when his restaurant was so close to becoming a reality.

Chris shrugged back at him. 'Can't do anything until the ovens are fitted and tested. You know that. Your dream kitchen is going to be full of brick dust and filth for at least a couple of days. You wanted the best and you're going to have the best. Only not this week. Maybe longer.'

Chris faltered and raised both hands in the air as Brett groaned in reply and closed his eyes.

'I know,' Chris acknowledged. 'I've already used up all of the slack we planned on the building work. It's going to be tough to make the deadline.'

'Make that *very* tough,' Brett answered with a nod. 'We only have a couple of weeks before the doors open to paying customers, and I still don't have menus or staff. This building needs to be finished as soon as we can, or we could be late on the first payment of the bank loan. And our credibility will suffer.'

His fingers worked through his hair behind each ear. 'Maybe it wasn't such a good idea to invite all the key London food critics and journalists to our opening night when we hadn't started the building work yet?'

'It was great idea!' Chris replied. 'This is why I've set up a meeting with the architects, so we can bring you up to date on the project plan. You're the only one who can decide what compromises you are willing to make to push the project through. They'll be expecting us in about an hour.'

'An hour?' Brett chortled and gave a shake of his head. 'In that case you had better start talking me though the plan. Let's start with the services and—' The sound of an Italian tenor rang out loud from Brett's cellphone. He glanced at the caller ID, and then looked at it more closely before nodding to Chris.

'Sorry, mate. Have to take this one. Be with you in a minute.'

'No problem. Let me get that snag list.'

Brett flicked open the phone as Chris strolled away through the debris, and grinned to himself before answering the call.

'Maria Rossi's galley slave, here. Ready to do your bidding, oh, great one!'

Only instead of Maria Rossi's, a man's voice bellowed down the line.

'Hello? Is that Brett? Brett Cameron?'

'Yes. This is Brett Cameron. Can you I help you?' he replied, holding the phone away from his ear to prevent damage to his hearing.

'Oh, good. This is Henry. You know—Maria Rossi's friend from the ballroom-dancing class. I'm calling from *Spain*. She asked me to call you.'

Henry? Had he ever met a Henry? Maria had so many friends it was hard to keep up.

'Hi, Henry. Is everything okay?'

'No. Sorry, but Maria's in the hospital. Oh, don't worry. She's going to be fine. Are you there? Brett?'

The smile fell from Brett's face and he inhaled sharply before replying.

'Yes—yes, I'm still here. What happened? Has there been an accident? Is she hurt?'

'No, no, nothing like that. Did Maria tell you that she was going on the dance club trip to Benidorm? That's here in Spain, you know.'

'She didn't mention it, but, yes, I understand. What's happened to Maria, Henry?'

'Well. I don't really know. She was on her way back from the banana boat race yesterday afternoon when the pain started. At first we blamed too much paella and sangria in the club last night, but a few hours later she slumped over in the Spanish dancing class. Right in the middle of the Paso Doble. They carted her off to the local hospital.

The instructor carried her to the ambulance. It was very exciting.'

'Exciting? Right. Did they say what's wrong with her?'

'Appendicitis. Caught just in time. Nasty, that. That's why I'm phoning, see. To tell you that she *is* okay. Surgery was fine but she's going to be here for at least— Oh, here she is. I need to pretend to be injured now.'

There was a shuffle, and the sound of fierce whispering on the other end of the line before a familiar and surprisingly cheerful voice sounded in his ear.

'Hello, Chef Cameron. Are you back?'

Brett smiled gently. The irrepressible Maria Rossi! Not even major surgery could hold this lady back for long!

'I am, boss. But never mind about me. What's all this about you being in hospital? Charming the handsome young doctors in Spain?'

A faint female voice laughed in reply. 'I've been kidnapped! One small operation and they want to keep me tied to this bed for two weeks! They even tried to confiscate my cellphone! I've had to crawl out onto the fire escape while Henry distracts them for a few minutes with a paper cut on his thumb.'

'Well, resist the temptation to make your daring escape. You can't fool me, Maria Rossi. There are probably teams of medical staff waiting on your every need. Now for the really important questions: what's the food like, and how are you feeling? And do not try and fob me off. Appendicitis can be serious!'

'The operation went fine, no complications— and I've had worse meals. But I'm knackered. Woman in the next bed snored the whole night. Did not get a wink of sleep.' Maria took a breath before asking, 'Have you got a fast car?'

'I can find one. Want me to drive down to the Costa Brava and pick you up?'

'Don't tempt me with offers like that! Thanks, but I do need a favour. Would you mind heading over to my place to make sure Rossi's is still standing? Sienna won't be able to manage without someone to do the cooking for her.'

'Sienna? Is that the new trainee chef you're terrorising in my place?'

'Sienna Rossi. My *niece*. Frank's sister. You probably don't remember her. Anyway, the poor girl left me a couple of voice messages earlier to tell me she was on her way over to Rossi's to stay with me for a few days. She sounded distressed, but by the time I could call her back her phone was turned off. Sienna doesn't know I'm away. I don't like the idea of her turning up to find me gone and the place closed up.'

Then Maria chuckled to herself. 'I love that

girl dearly, but there is no telling what she could get up to if she is left in charge of Rossi's for two weeks. She'll probably be running herself ragged trying to open up the place on her own.'

Brett snorted in reply. 'I wonder who that reminds me of? Chip off the old block, there. Why don't you just close the place for an extra week or two?'

There was a long pause on the other end of the line.

'Maria? Still there? Or have the nurses dragged you back inside?'

'Oh, still here—but I can't talk for long. Look, Brett. I won't beat around the bush. Things are not going too well at the moment and I need the business. To be honest, I can't afford to close down for another two weeks. Be a good lad and promise me you'll lend a hand?' She paused. 'It would help put my mind at rest if I knew that you could keep the old place going, rake in some cash, and look after Sienna for me.'

'Okay. It's a promise. I'll head over there tonight.'

Maria sighed in relief. 'You're a star. I should warn you that— Oops! I've been spotted. Later.'

And with that she was gone, to the sound of shuffles and muffled voices, before the call clicked off, leaving a stunned Brett in the bustle of electric drills and workmen.

Maria was obviously recovering well, but there had been no mistaking the concern in her voice.

February was always a slow month in the restaurant trade. And many of her regular customers were elderly couples who had been going there for years. Cold winter evenings and tight budgets… Hmm, that could mean trouble for any small restaurant.

Small? Who was he kidding? Maria's dining room was about the same size as the new reception area in the building he was looking at now.

Brett flicked down the cover on his cellphone. He owed Maria Rossi everything. This remarkable woman had taken a chance with a troubled teenager whom the world had labelled an academic failure. Over the years he had made it his business to keep in touch with her. Let her know how he was doing.

It was Maria Rossi who had stood by his side at the Young Chef of the Year Awards.

Maria Rossi who had opened the door to the most prestigious restaurants in Paris, where he'd learnt the true meaning of fine cooking.

And Maria Rossi who had persuaded the catering college to run a test which proved that he was not slow, not stupid, and certainly not lazy.

He had dyslexia.

And now he was back in London for the first time in ten years with something to prove, and Maria wanted him to do her a favour.

Consider it done.

As for Sienna Rossi? Oh, he remembered Sienna Rossi. He remembered Miss Sienna Rossi very well indeed.

'Everything okay? You look very thoughtful!'

Brett looked around to find Chris staring at him in concern, a large bundle of papers scrunched under one arm.

The architects!

'Sorry, mate. Change of plan. I have to help out an old friend for a few days. You're going to have to take the meeting on your own. I know you can handle it. Call me whenever you need me, but I have to go.'

CHAPTER THREE

Step 3: Throw in Two Teaspoons of Shock and Uncertainty

IT WAS almost seven in the evening when Sienna stepped gingerly down from the red London bus and shrugged herself deeper into her raincoat. The drizzle had been replaced by light rain, and the air was moist and heavy with diesel fumes and the city smog of a dark winter evening.

For the first week in February there was still a definite snap of cold in the air, and Sienna regretted her decision to leave Greystone Manor without changing into winter shoes, but it all happened in such a rush!

It had been surprisingly easy to convince Patrick that she needed to take the two weeks' holiday she was owed before the new chef arrived and she started work on their 'exciting new project'!

Pity that she was still as confused and unde-cided as she had been a few hours earlier. The shakes might have eased off, but she knew better. Shock and awe did not even come close! The train journey from Greystone had been a nightmare: sharing a carriage with happy people on their way to enjoy an evening show in London when all she had wanted to do was curl up into a small ball and whimper.

At least her legs were a little steadier. She had almost fainted in the dining room when Patrick had announced Angelo's name. It was lucky for her that everyone had been too busy to hang around and chat about the announcement, and she'd been able to escape to the sanctuary of her bedroom on wobbly legs.

She sucked in a deep breath of cool night air and blinked hard to clear her head as hot burning tears again pricked her eyes and seared her dry throat.

No tears. You are not going to cry, she told herself sternly.

She had done more than enough crying over Angelo Peruzi!

And now he had come back to Britain. To her home. To her safe place.

Sienna sensed her fists clench and unclench, the knuckles white, as she took another deep breath. She was a professional. She was used to handling problems. She could handle this one just like the others.

Focus on the options.

Basically she had two choices. Stay. Or go.

She could stay and be professional and keep her home by agreeing to work with Angelo and take the restaurant to the next level. They would be colleagues. Professionals working together. Nothing more. This could be the chance she had been waiting for to show what she could do on the international scene and persuade the hotel chain to transfer her to another restaurant.

Or—and this second option was so terrible that she mentally braced herself even to think about it—she could leave and start again somewhere else.

She would have to give up the job she loved and…and do what? Ask for a transfer? That was a possibility. She could always find another job as a head waiter, but it would probably set her back a year or two while she rebuilt her team.

Or she could run back to the Rossi clan with her tail between her legs. Her parents might have retired, but her brother, Frankie, was running an Italian delicatessen with his young wife and family—maybe she could ask them for a job?

And throw away four years of very hard work in the process.

No. She couldn't bear to think about that.

One thing was certain. She had to think this through. And fast. Angelo would be at the Manor in less than a week. She needed her parents— except they had chosen the perfect time to take in a cruise. And she wasn't even sure that they could help her.

That left the only person she could rely on for advice. Her aunt Maria Rossi.

Rubbing her arms for warmth, Sienna turned the corner and was immediately struck by the il- luminated signs from not one but two pizza and noodle shops flashing in the dusky gloom. A lot had changed in the six months since her last short visit to this part of London.

Sienna paused on the pavement so that she could look across the narrow street at Rossi's, as it had always been known. This was where her aunt had offered her refuge from the disaster that had been Angelo Peruzi. Ironic that the same man was driving her back here now. She needed a warm hug, a hot meal, and all the advice that Maria could give. *And she needed them desper- ately!*

Under the streetlights there was no escaping the fact that there were a few more things that had certainly changed over the winter months—and not for the better.

Maria had some serious competition here!

Trattoria Rossi stood in what had been a prime

location, set back slightly from the main street with just enough space out front for two or three patio tables. Except this was February, and the rain had a definite touch of sleet in it.

The harsh fluorescent light seemed to highlight the fact that the paint was peeling badly from the hand-painted sign that had once proudly carried the words *TRATTORIA ROSSI*. Several letters had faded to the point where to a passing car the sign might seem to be spelling out *RATT...OS*.

But that was not the worst of it. As Sienna skipped across the road at the crossing, the first thing she saw as she approached the bistro was a large crack in the plate-glass front window. Cracks in one corner spread out like a spider's web, sideways into the glass.

Standing in front of the bistro at that moment, Sienna struggled to recall what it had looked like when she had last visited Maria in daylight—sparkling clean, bright and cheerful. A welcoming and friendly family bistro—an ideal place to spend a lunchtime. What she was looking at now was dismal and dark and the kind of place she would never choose to eat. Even if it was open.

Which it wasn't.

A handwritten sign said—as best as she could read in the dim light and poor handwriting—that the restaurant was closed due to staff holiday and would be open again for lunch next week. Only which week and when it had been written was not made clear.

Her family would have told her if Maria was on holiday. Wouldn't they?

Oh, Maria. Where are you when I need you?

Emotion flooded through Sienna. For a few seconds she allowed the stress of the day to over-whelm her, and she bent over from the waist and clasped hold of her knees with her eyes closed.

Please be here. Please! It was not much to ask! She simply needed someone to be here whom she could trust and take refuge in.

With a loud sniff, Sienna pushed herself back to her full height.

This was what falling for chefs did for you! Dratted Brett Cameron! Or Angelo. Or both!

Perhaps tonight was Maria's night out? The Nifty after Fifty dance club members were some of her best customers and Maria was no slouch when it came to showing her own skills in the ballroom.

Cupping her hands around her eyes and peering through the glass, Sienna was relieved to see that electric lights were on in the kitchen, and she could hear the thump-thump beat of pop music above the noise of the traffic which was whizzing past her.

Someone must be working there. Maria always had at least one trainee chef and a waitress

working for her. Usually one of them lived with
Maria in the cosy house connected to the trattoria. Only, the house was in complete darkness.

Sienna knocked hard on the front door of the
trattoria just as the rain started to fall more heavily.
She had planned to spend the night in Maria's
house, and the keys were inside the bistro. It was
time to either wake somebody up or start ringing
doorbells along the street to find out if anyone else
had a key. Maria was so trusting it would not
surprise her if half the elderly neighbours had
spares.

Except, of course, most of the ladies were
probably with Maria at the their local ballroom-
dancing class, while she stood there and stamped
her feet to avoid being frozen to the spot.

After her third attempt at battering down the
door, and then ringing the doorbell at Maria's
house, Sienna decided that it was time to try plan
B. The rear door to the kitchen.

It was at this point that the rain became a more
intense sleet, which dripped from the tree
branches and cascaded from the rooftops of the
parade of shops onto the pavement below—and
anyone who happened to be walking there, trying
to find the gate behind the bistro. Stiff with rain
and misuse, the old wooden gate stubbornly
refused to open, and Siennà had to abandon her
luggage to the wet yard which was slick with rain

water and unknown slime, and use both hands to push hard and lift at the same time.

The gate gave way in a rush, so that she half fell, half stumbled headfirst into the yard and almost lost her footing. Taking a moment to calm her breathing, Sienna sighed in relief. Her reward was that Maria's kitchen was still brightly lit and definitely the source of the music.

Sliding her luggage forward, Sienna tiptoed as best she could between the rubbish bins, sodden cardboard boxes and discarded plastic trays towards the back door, trying to save her shoes from the puddles of rainwater which had filled the gaps between the broken cement slabs and mystery dark objects which blocked the path. Nothing scurried away, meowed or barked as she dodged the blockade, which was a real plus.

There was a vertical line of light beaming out from the back door—it was open!

Maria must be home!

Her shoulders relaxed in relief. Thank goodness.

There was no sign of anyone through the kitchen windows, but, undaunted, Sienna took a step closer to the gap in the heavy metal back door.

Only at that precise moment the door swung open wider. And in one flash of an eyelid Sienna Maria Rossi took in three startling facts.

Leaning forward in the doorway was a tall dark

figure, whose face was in the shadow of the bright kitchen light.

Attached to one long forearm was a pink plastic bucket, in which something was sloshing loudly from side to side as the arm drew back.

The arm was bent back for a very good reason. The bucket was already moving forward in a graceful arc to be emptied into the backyard. Only she was in the way and there was nothing either of them could do about it.

Half a bucket of warm water hit Sienna straight in the legs, and she only just had enough time to squeeze her eyes shut before the deluge splashed up to her knees, narrowly missing the bottom of her suit skirt as the cascade flooded into the tops of both shoes, filling them with dirty water she did not even want to think about, as well as soaking her luggage.

There was a horrified gasp from the figure standing in the doorway followed by a rasp of deep male laughter.

Sienna squeezed her eyes tighter together. *This person—this man—*was actually laughing about the fact that he had just completely soaked her legs and ruined her best work shoes in the process. Goodness knew what state her luggage would be in.

This was a wretched end to a terrible, terrible day. *It could not possibly get any worse.*

* * *

She slowly, slowly opened her eyes and wiped away the rainwater with one hand, before lifting her head to face the enemy. Only she never got the chance—because before she knew what was happening a strong male arm had wrapped around her wet shoulders and half dragged, half supported her towards the door.

'Hi, Sienna. Sorry about that. It's great to see you again. Want to come inside and dry off?'

Sienna looked up, blinking against the bright kitchen light, and stared, open-mouthed in shock, into the face of the man who was lifting her bag from her sodden fingers. Then the blood rushed to her head so quickly that she felt dizzy and leaned back against the door frame to steady herself before she could trust her voice to say tremulously, *'Brett?'*

A tousle-haired blond with a wide smile touched two fingers to his brow in mock salute.

'Welcome back to Rossi's. It's going to be *just* like old times.'

And at that point the ever cool and in control Sienna Rossi burst into tears.

CHAPTER FOUR

Step 4: Whisk Everything Together in a Tiny Bistro

SILENT TEARS streamed down Sienna's face, blinding her to everything and everybody.

Shoulders heaving, she tried to control her sobs and snatch back some form of self-control in tiny breaths.

This was agony!

There was a lump in her throat the size of an egg, her eyes must be red and puffy, and goodness knows what her hair must look like! What a complete mess!

She had never felt so humiliated in her life!

This, of course, made her feel even more wretched!

There was no way she would ever be able to look Brett Cameron in the face again. Perhaps she could emigrate? To a distant planet?

Or perhaps she had simply imagined the whole thing and the rain and her tears had blurred her vision?

Then he spoke, in a low, caring voice, and her heart twisted.

'Here. Let me take that wet coat for you.'

Before she had time to argue the point Brett had moved behind her and was lifting her raincoat from her shoulders.

His fingertips gently grazed the sides of her throat for a fraction of a second, sending delicious shivers across her shoulders and down her arms. She immediately covered the shiver by rubbing the palms of her hands up and down the arms of the thin cashmere cardigan she had thrown over her silk blouse, as though it was the damp and cold that had made her body quiver rather than the simple touch of those clever fingers.

'You're freezing! Take this. I'm more than warm enough.'

A soft extra-large and very masculine fleece jacket was wrapped around her shoulders, and she sighed in delight and relief before shrugging her arms into the sleeves and pulling the zip high to the neck. She was practically sitting on the hem when she straightened her skirt and snuggled into the wonderful warm comfort. It was like wearing a quilt.

Heaven.

And it was infused with his own personal scent.

'Better?' he asked, looking into her face with concern, then rubbed his hands down the length of her arms, flushing her with glowing warmth—and not just from the soft fabric.

'Much,' she managed to reply with a brief nod, before noticing that he was now wearing only a cotton short-sleeved T-shirt. All the fight and bluff she had planned died on her quivering lips. 'Thank you.'

'How do you like your tea?' He reached behind him to the worktop and picked up a steaming hot drink. 'I take mine white with two sugars. Careful now.'

Brett hunkered down on the wet floor and pressed the hot beaker between her cold shaking fingers, waiting until her sobs subsided before helping her wrap her fingers tightly enough so that she would not spill it.

The look of concern and anxiety in those blue eyes almost started Sienna off again, so she swallowed down a large sip of hot tea, feeling the warmth spread from her throat, and then another sip, until she was holding the beaker on her own.

Only then did Brett push himself effortlessly back on his heels to his full height, his slender strong fingers slipping away from hers, breaking their tenuous connection.

Sienna swallowed down another swig of the

welcome hot tea. Strange that she usually hated sweet tea with milk but at that moment it was the only thing she wanted.

The room seemed to come more into focus. She was sitting on a tiny metal patio chair that not even the local scamps would have stolen from the pavement in front of the bistro—they had *some* standards. She took a breath, squeezed her eyes shut, flicked them open, and did a double-take.

The lights were still on. She had shaken most of the rain from her hair and eyes. And it was definitely Brett Cameron or an identical twin brother she knew nothing about.

There was no mistaking the piercing blue eyes, and they were certainly the same hands which had touched her skin for the very first time only a few minutes earlier.

Too handsome to be true Brett Cameron.

Obsessive, passionate, serious, eyes as blue as the sea Brett Cameron.

The same Brett Cameron who had either totally ignored her or at best acknowledged her presence with a grunt or a nod for six complete weeks when he'd worked as a trainee chef, and then every Saturday evening when she'd worked here as a waitress for her aunt.

The same Brett Cameron who had haunted her schoolgirl dreams and was nowadays being photographed for catering magazines.

That Brett Cameron was at that very moment taking up most of the space in her aunt's kitchen.

And she was wearing his fleece and drinking his tea.

How had that happened?

It was as though the last ten years of her life had been an absurd dream, and she was back to being a gawky, awkward and awestruck sixteen year old.

Then he stretched forward to hoist her bag onto a bar stool and turn down the lively jazz music, and she got the full benefit of the well-worn grey rock-star T-shirt stretched over a broad chest and powerful shoulders.

The over thin, scrawny teenage version of Brett had been replaced by a man who looked as though he had spent his time in Australia on the beach. Or surfing. Those Chefs in Kilts photos had definitely not needed fancy editing!

Shame that those same teenage hormones now flared hot in her veins as a full-colour vision of a topless and tanned Brett in board shorts flashed in panoramic full-colour detail across her mind. Perhaps she had not changed as much as she thought she had?

Oh, no. *Not now.* Not on top of the news about Angelo. Two men. Both chefs. *Doomed.*

Sienna groaned softly to herself. This was starting to feel like a conspiracy.

'Sorry about your nice shoes! I should have paid more attention to the front doorbell.'

Well, that was new! The teenage Brett had used to have trouble saying even a few words over the Rossi dinner table—and then only when her aunt Maria had forced the words out of him. Now he was noticing her shoes!

Who was this man? And at what point in the last few years had he started to notice women's *footwear?*

She stared down at her sodden feet and squelched her cold wet toes inside what had once been designer couture heels. Now the leather felt positively slimy, and destined for the nearest wastebin. And at precisely that moment she realised that she had not packed any spare shoes in her rush to leave Greystone as fast as Carla had been able to drive her to the railway station.

No spare shoes. Not even a pair of slippers.

Her eyes closed and she quivered on the edge of more tears. Self-pity this time.

This was what happened when you dropped everything for chefs!

You left work wearing high heels with soles the thickness of writing paper.

In the rain.

In February.

The sensible and totally in-control version of Sienna Rossi who would have packed a range of suitable footwear to choose from had clearly left the building!

Hearing the name Angelo Peruzi being announced, after seeing gorgeous Brett Cameron in that magazine had clearly puddled her poor brain beyond rational thought. That was the only possible explanation for it. She would have to just sit there in wet shoes for the rest of the evening. Until she could escape to the shops to buy new ones or—gulp—borrow some of Aunt Maria's shoes. She had clear memories of her aunt's more memorable shoes. Bows. Stripes. *Flowers!*

Sienna lifted one foot and then the other out of the standing water on the tiled floor and fixed her heels behind the lowest rung of the back of her patio chair as Brett moved a heavy bucket out of reach and swished an industrial sized absorbent sponge over the tiles below, where she had been standing.

'Thank you.' At this point the sensible part of her brain started to kick in with extra warmth. 'They *were* nice shoes.' She looked at the back of his tanned head and was distracted by the tight-cut dark blond layers above wide shoulders, strong biceps and toned forearm. 'I'm amazed to see you here, Brett! Last time I spoke to Maria you were in Australia! This has come as a bit of a surprise!'

He stopped mopping for a second and turned back towards her, flashing a killer smile she had imagined was the product of airbrushing for those magazine shots.

But this was the real thing. White, white teeth contrasted against tanned blond stubble around a wide mouth which turned up more on the right side than the left as he smiled.

To her absolute horror Sienna's treacherous stomach performed a full somersault and backflip that would have pleased an Olympic swimmer.

Oh, boy.

The Hunk of the Month photo did not come close to Brett Cameron up close and personal— even if he *was* wearing denims which had seen cleaner and dryer days.

How dared he be even more handsome than she remembered from of those years ago?

'You never did like surprises.' He smiled back at her. 'Some things clearly haven't changed.'

He leant back on the workbench and crossed his arms over his wide chest, dominating the space between them as though he owned the place and always had done. His focused gaze made Sienna want to squirm and deny the accusation, but she deflected it by raising her head higher and trying to look uninterested.

'Would you believe me if I told you that your aunt Maria offered me a job mopping up while she was away on holiday in Spain?' Brett continued. 'Hard to turn down an opportunity like that! How could I resist? Jumped on the first plane back to London!'

A muscle twitched in the right corner of his mouth to match the twinkle in his eyes.

He was teasing her.

She was soaked, cold, tired and miserable.

And her aunt Maria was away on holiday.

Suddenly she felt as though the whole world has deserted her. *Double doomed.*

And Brett Cameron was teasing her. Looking for a reaction. Well, she could play the game as well as he could. All she had to was persuade her brain to start working again while she ignored her damp, dirty legs and feet.

At least the kitchen was warm. Even though it was wet. Very wet. *Too* wet.

From her patio chair, the view over the tiny kitchen was of uniformly shiny and wet floor tiles, with deeper standing water in some of the corners.

Brett had not been cleaning the floor. He had been trying to soak up a major flood. At least that explained why he'd been emptying his bucket outside. And why his boots and trousers were dark and soaked through almost as far as the knees.

Strange how knowing that he was also enjoying

the benefit of cold clothing against his legs made her feel a lot better. And now curiosity won the battle between her deciding to be indifferent to his suffering or finding out why one of the allegedly finest young chefs in the world was mopping kitchen floors.

'I can see how you wouldn't want to miss that kind of offer. As for the mopping up… Let me guess. Has there has been a flood? The chest freezer defrosted?'

Brett shifted position and tilted his head to one side. 'Close. According to the girl I found trying to cope, Maria doesn't have a big freezer any more. It sort of caught fire and was never replaced. In fact, you probably had to scramble over it to get to the back door. This—' and he gestured with his head to the far corner of the room where the water looked deeper '—was the dishwasher.'

Sienna looked at him for a second, wide eyed, before blowing out hard. Freezers did not catch fire at Greystone Manor.

'The big freezer caught fire? Right. Any idea what happened to the dishwasher? Was there a power failure?'

'I wish!' Brett replied with a snort. 'Oh, sorry. Actually, it's not funny. Apparently the ancient rust bucket had been leaking for weeks, but Maria never got around to having it fixed before her holiday. Julie came in to open up for you and there was water everywhere.'

'Julie?' Sienna nodded several times before adding in a low voice, 'Oh, yes, of course. That would be Maria's waitress.' Her twice broken heart twanged a little at the thought of Brett chatting up yet another young waitress when he had never wanted to talk to her, then twanged again. He was single. The waitress was probably single. None of her business. So why was it that she could not resist the temptation to tease *him* this time?

She lifted her head and made contact with those remarkable eyes, all thoughts of her wet feet forgotten. 'Well, *some* things seem to have changed! You actually *talk* to waitresses these days! I'm sure Julie was *very* informative!'

There was silence from the man standing only a few feet away from her across the wet cold tiles, and an electric spark of tension crackled through the air.

Then he dropped his head back, uncrossed his arms and let out a deep, rough belly laugh that echoed around the tiny space and vibrated through the floor and worktops. Her chair seemed to tremble with the force of it, and her toes clenched inside her moist shoes so that she would not tumble forward from her stool. Her soul, her heart and her mind filled with the joy of that deep, masculine chuckle.

It was the first time that she had ever heard him laugh, and at that moment she was seriously delighted that she had a worktop to hang onto. She tried to move back, away from him, but in this tiny kitchen there was nowhere for her to go. Her back was already hard against the patio chair.

She revelled in the sensation, her heart soaring, and for a second she was so, so, tempted to join him. She certainly needed a laugh after a day like she had just had.

The day she was still having, Sienna corrected herself. It was not over yet.

Deep smile lines creased the corners of his mouth, bringing his sparking blue eyes into startling contrast. It was intoxicating.

If she had ever thought that Brett could not be more attractive, he was doing his best to prove her wrong—without even realising he was doing it!

He leant forward until he was well and truly inside her personal space, and as he did so his hands came together so he could salute her with a slow clap. Once, then twice, before he moved back and ran his fingers through his short hair.

Then he looked across at her and broke into a wide grin. 'Relax, Sienna. The only girl who has me over a barrel is your aunt. She has me wrapped around her little finger and there is not one thing that I can do about it. I'd promise that woman anything. And she knows it.'

'What do you mean? Did she call you from Spain?'

'Actually, her friend Henry called, but I did have a chance to speak to the lady herself for a few minutes. The lovely Maria is way too busy chatting up the Spanish medics to spend time with me.'

Sienna blinked in surprise before clutching at her knees. 'Medics? What do you mean?' The remains of the tea sloshed onto the floor as she slipped the beaker onto the bench. 'Is Maria ill? Injured? How bad is it?'

Brett reached out and grabbed hold of her flailing hands.

'It was appendicitis. She was whipped into hospital straight away, has had the operation, and is now recovering among her friends from the dance club. She sounds *fine!* If anything she seems more concerned about you staying here alone than the fact that she has just had major surgery.'

'I did leave her several messages, but then the battery on my cellphone went flat. How is she? I mean, how did it happen?' Sienna asked, trying to slow her breathing and bring her heart-rate back to something close to normal.

Brett released her hands and leaned back on the worktop.

'Apparently she was on her way back from a

banana boat race when the pain started. She slumped over in a Spanish dancing class and the instructor carried her to the ambulance. It was "*very* exciting", according to her friend Henry.'

'Banana boats? Exciting? Right. But that still doesn't explain why *you* are mopping her kitchen floor.'

'Ah,' Brett replied, his smile fading. 'Did you see the window?'

Sienna nodded. 'And the sign. How long have you been here?'

'A couple of hours. Long enough to know that Maria is in serious financial trouble and needs Rossi's to stay up and running while she's away—which could be a couple more weeks. She admitted as much just before her phone was confiscated. That's why she made me promise to do something for her.'

'Really? What was that?'

'Well, apparently you have many skills, Miss Rossi, but cooking is not one of them. Until Maria gets back, you're looking at her new chef!'

CHAPTER FIVE

Step 5: Add a Couple of Big Decisions…

SIENNA STARED in open-mouthed horror and astonishment as Brett gave her a jaunty salute and a cheeky wink before recrossing his arms and stretching out his long, long legs, only too aware that this snippet of news was going to take a while to sink in.

He was watching her now. Smiling. Totally confident and comfortable in his superiority. Just because he had announced that they were going to be trapped in this tiny kitchen together.

Trapped with Brett Cameron. Just the two of them. Together. *Alone.*

Her feet took a tighter grip on the chair inside her shoes. Making them squeak slightly.

He heard it and the smile widened.

How more infuriating and arrogant could this man get?

He had known that she was on her way here the whole time!

Known it before she had even got here! He had been expecting her to turn up!

But he still threw that water out of the door without a care about whether she would be standing there or not!

Well, she could change that quite easily. She had no intention of going back to the Manor, so *he* would have to be the one who made the move to…to whatever seriously important opportunity he was working on next as a superstar chef.

The crushing reality of the difference between their options hit her hard. Then hit her again.

Brett was a star. *Destined for great things*. And she was… Well, she was still Sienna Rossi, and she would take control of her situation as best she could.

'Thank you for volunteering to cook,' she blustered, in as calm a voice as she could muster under such extreme provocation, 'but that will not be necessary. I know a few retired cooks who would be happy to step in and help out. I can easily make a call tomorrow morning and have someone here in a few hours. Don't worry, I'll find another chef to take over in the kitchen. I'm sure that Maria would understand how busy you must be.'

Brett merely smiled indulgently at her discomfort and pushed himself to his feet. For one exciting and terrifying moment she thought that he was going to move even closer, but instead he turned back to the worktop, where she could see an assortment of cooking utensils and knives were laid out on a surprisingly clean white tea towel next to cartons of dried goods.

He casually picked up a moist poly chopping board and began drying it carefully with a paper towel before replying, his hands working the towel back and forth as he spoke.

'Sorry, but you don't get rid of me that easily. I'm not going anywhere.'

Those magical hands stilled for a moment as Brett looked intently towards her.

'Maria asked me to help with the cooking and that's what I'm going to do. I made a promise and I have every intention of keeping it. Besides, you're starting to hurt my feelings. If I didn't know better, I would say that you didn't want me here for the next two weeks. I am genuinely pained!'

Sienna clenched her teeth together in frustration. *Why was he not taking her seriously*? What did she have to do to persuade him to pack his bags?

'I'm sure Maria would understand that you have important projects to be working on. Believe me. I can handle this.'

He acknowledged her words with a simple nod.

'I have no doubt that you can handle anything you set your mind to. And you're right. I flew in from Adelaide four days ago, and for the last three months a whole team of craftsmen have been tearing down a shell of a building and creating my first signature restaurant. The building work is behind schedule, and we're opening in six weeks. But from what I've seen, Maria Rossi needs help and she needs it now. I can afford to give Maria a few days out of my life to get this trattoria back on its feet. I owe her that. And I promised her I would do it. End of story.'

He turned sideways to face her and waved a packet of fusilli in front of her. 'Have you eaten this evening? Because I find it hard to think when I'm starving. Do you mind if I make something simple?'

Sienna bit down a quick reply. Lunch was a distant memory and she *was* hungry. And cold. And tired. And drained. At that moment pasta sounded pretty good. But she could *not* let him know how desperately she would love some hot food.

'I don't expect you to cook for me. And are you always so stubborn?'

'Always. And it is my pleasure. Oh, and, Sienna?'

The different tone of his voice was so startling that she flicked her head up towards him.

Too fast. The slight dizziness was back.

He winced at her before gesturing behind him with his head. 'One suggestion—and it is only a suggestion—before you make any decisions about taking on this bistro on your own, you might want to take a look into the dining room while I rummage around for something edible. That way we'll both be facing the horror of the situation.'

Brett swung open the refrigerator door and pretended to be examining the jumbled contents of the small freezer compartment as Sienna gingerly stepped on tiptoe past him into the corridor.

He had to keep his distance.

Not because Sienna scared him—she never had.

Not even when she'd been the family princess in the royal Rossi family and he very much the visiting peasant. Or at least that was how he had seen it at the time—no matter how much the family had gone out of their way to make him feel welcome.

He had been a boy from the wrong side of the tracks and kind-hearted Maria had taken pity on him when the academic world had labelled him a failure and turned its back on him.

Maria would have been horrified to know that he'd felt that way at the time. She had made it clear that the only reason he was in her kitchen—this very kitchen he was standing in now—was because of his talent. A talent she had believed in from the very first meal he had made for her. He might not have been able to express how he was feeling in words or on paper—but he had through his passion for food.

No. When he was around Sienna Rossi, *awestruck* was a better description.

Brett pressed his back against the refrigerator door and looked around the kitchen where he had spent the best six weeks of his life. This was where he had eaten his first real Mediterranean food. Pasta which did not come ready cooked out of a tin. Tomato sauce made from fresh tomatoes and not from red plastic ketchup bottles.

For a teenage boy it had seemed as if a secret door had been opened into another world of endless delights and exciting new opportunities.

In that world he had found the potential to make something of his life without all of the labels he had managed to pick up over the years. Labels like 'difficult', 'sullen' and 'poor communicator'. 'Failure' and 'no future' had sometimes been added for good measure.

Apparently he had talent. All he had to do was prove it to others and convince them that he had potential. Face talking to trained chefs and persuade them to share their skills with him.

Chefs like Frank Rossi and his family, who came from generations of skilled chefs and family cooks.

Frank and his sister, Sienna Rossi, had grown up with wonderful food and high expectations in a very different family from the one he was used to.

He had been so jealous of them back then it had been like a physical pain.

Little wonder that he had kept focused on what he'd had the power to control.

And yet here he was, back at Rossi's.

He turned back to the mini-freezer and his fingers closed over a plastic container with two large, brightly coloured dots stuck on the lid.

The air was sucked out of his lungs.

The red dot meant that this was a tomato pasta sauce, and the green dot told him that it was made using vegetables with herbs and spices. A basic sauce that could be used in a variety of recipes or served on pasta. No meat. No extras.

Unless she had changed her ideas, this was the same colour-code system that Maria has used all of those years ago, to hide the fact that she could not write or read well, and she was still using it now!

Brett carefully closed the freezer door and closed his eyes.

What was he doing here?

Chris needed him! The new business needed him! He should be working on his dream restaurant instead of mopping floors and defrosting pasta sauce!

What was he trying to prove by coming back to this kitchen where it all began? Maria wasn't here in person. And everywhere he looked in this tiny space caught him unawares.

Walking through that door tonight had brought it all back to him.

The uncertainty. The feelings of inadequacy he'd thought he had buried deep inside the outer persona he displayed to the world. It was all still there. Far closer to the surface that he had ever imagined.

And Sienna Rossi was partly responsible for making his world spin out of control.

He'd kept his distance from her tonight because of something he had not expected. Something which had hit him hard and hit him fast the moment he had swung open that back door and looked into her wide brown eyes.

Instant attraction.

Attraction which set his pulse racing and his heart thumping.

He had only ever felt that pull once before—the first time he had seen the most beautiful girl in Paris and been too terrified and stunned to even speak to her.

As usual he had covered up his true feelings with a cheeky smile and lively chatter—the happy go lucky attitude which had become his mask over the years to hide the vulnerable heart that he hid deep inside. Sometimes the mask fitted so well that it took a minor earthquake to make it slip a little.

And Sienna Rossi was certainly a seismic event as far as he was concerned.

The stunning woman in the fitted black skirt suit, designer shoes and tantalising smooth cream silk blouse was as far away from the plump, shy, teenage Sienna as he could have imagined. With her stunning good looks and elegant formality this Sienna was every inch the kind of head waiter that fine-dining restaurants would appreciate.

And that was the problem. He had just spent the last three hours fielding phone calls from Chris during his meeting with the architects, then cleaning up the mess in what had used to be a fine working kitchen—while all the time his brain had been in overdrive, conjuring up a vision of what a twenty-eight-year-old version of Sienna Rossi was going to look like.

Maria had told him that she was working as a head waiter and sommelier, but nothing could have prepared him for the woman who had been standing outside that kitchen door. Which for someone who took pride in their visual skills, he found deeply unsettling.

The suit, the uniform, the shoes. That was all surface gloss—designed to create the professional image fine-dining customers demanded when they were paying for the best. And Sienna certainly did it well.

Her long, straight, dark brown hair had always been tied back from a side parting, but from what he had seen of it tonight, even wet and unbrushed, she probably spent more to create that perfectly smooth, shiny, shoulder-length ponytail than he'd used to spend on clothes in a year at catering school.

She was stunning! Little wonder that his confidence had faltered. Perhaps he did not know who this version of Sienna truly was underneath that surface layer?

Except… It was her eyes that gave the game away.

He would have recognised those amazing deep caramel eyes anywhere—he had spent more than enough time staring at them over the dinner table at Rossi family meals, and then in the kitchen, where he'd never seemed to be able to escape her, no matter how hard he'd tried.

She had the most wonderful, gentle, feminine eyes.

He had certainly known plenty of women over the past ten years he had spent travelling the world—all wonderful, kind, generous and loving

girls he had enjoyed spending time with as he
worked hard to develop his skills.

But not one of them came close to having eyes
like Sienna Rossi.

Eyes he could fall into and drown.

Those same eyes had been wide-open in
shocked surprise when he had opened the back
door—and even wider when he had deposited her
onto the patio chair.

Eyes filled with tears.

Tears which had torn into his heart like sharp
Japanese sushi knives. Shredding his mask of
cheerful bravado into ribbons of need and regret
and loss.

Eyes which could throw him off track in an
instant if he allowed them. Combined with tears
and the fiery mature woman who now lived
beneath the austere black suit.

Dynamite. Absolute explosive dynamite.

Those eyes and those tears had sucked him
back to a place he had not expected. A place
where his heart was still open and he did not have
to protect it from the pain of loss and regret.

She unsettled him.

Perhaps it was time to find out what kind of
woman Sienna had become?

Time to light the blue touch paper and watch
the firework display.

CHAPTER SIX

Step 6: A Valentine Wish…

THERE HAD been something in Brett's voice which had told Sienna that all was not going to be well, but she wasn't prepared for what lay in front of her after she squelched down the hall carpet and flicked on the lights in the dining room of Trattoria Rossi.

Or tried to. Three out of the four lightbulbs in the room were broken, and the one remaining red wall light gave out a positively eerie and pathetic glow, casting the dark, depressing and gloomy room into shadows.

Cold, frigid, damp shadows.

Sienna shivered and huddled deeper into the warmth of Brett's jacket before running her fingers across the old radiator. Icy cold. Terrific!

The central heating had not been turned on, and the cold wet February evening had combined with the wide expanse of glass window to create a distinct chill in the air which no amount of hot soup was going to put right, should a paying customer wander in from the street by accident.

Even the stone walls of the wine cellar in Greystone Manor were warmer than this space.

The only bright thing in the whole room was a handwritten poster, shining white and red in the light beaming out from the kitchen like a beacon in the murk around her.

Rossi's Famous Valentine Day Special Menus.

Oh, Maria! Valentine's Day! Of course! That made it even worse. Rossi's had used to be *the* place to bring your date on Valentine's Day.

Generations of teenagers from the local high schools had brought their first dates to Rossi's over the years. Maria had used to be booked from Christmas! And now look at it!

Valentine's Day? More like Halloween.

If Sienna had needed any more information about how low the restaurant had sunk, this was it. Just when she'd thought this day could not get any worse, she had to see this sad room. It was enough to start her off crying again, but she was not going to let Brett see her so out of control.

She felt humiliated! It was going to be hard enough to face him after that pathetic display without more tears to add to her embarrassment.

But this was heartbreaking!

Maria should try and sell the restaurant and retire while she was still active enough to enjoy herself.

A shiver of cold and dread ran down her neck from a draught.

She was just about to slink back to her relatively warm kitchen chair when the telephone rang at the tiny table which served as reception desk.

Without thinking or hesitating Sienna switched back into head-waiter mode and took the call.

'Good evening, Trattoria Rossi. Sienna speaking. How may I help you?'

Her hand picked up the pen and flicked open the simple supermarket diary that was Maria's reservations book. Her hand stilled as she said, in as calm a manner as she could, 'Valentine's Day? Umm, let me just check for you.'

She took a breath, then another. Not because she wanted to keep the elderly gentleman on the other end of the telephone waiting by pretending that they were fully booked, but because of what she was looking at.

It was so remarkable that she actually held the book up into the light from the kitchen to check. She could hardly believe her eyes. But there was no doubt. Maria had not only taken bookings for Valentine's Day. She had taken *lots* of bookings. Easily enough to occupy three quarters of the tables.

'Oh, yes, I am still here. What's that? You've

been celebrating Valentine's Day here for the last forty years? Well, yes, that is quite remarkable. Oh? You came to Rossi's on your very first date? That *is* lovely.'

Decision time.

Tell this nice gentleman that they were closed and likely to stay that way. *Or…* A totally crazy, outrageous and off-the-wall thought flicked into her mind.

She *could* do something remarkable. *She could stay.*

She could do this.

She could turn this dining room around. This *restaurant* around.

She had the skill, she had some time, and it would give her the boost to her confidence that she so badly needed.

There was a sudden clatter from the kitchen, followed by a smothered groan.

Of course she was going to need more than a little help with the food, and that would mean working with Brett Cameron.

On the one hand, he was obviously a wonderful chef, who was devoted to Maria—the food would be terrific, she had no doubt about that. And on the other he had clearly decided that he was going to be just as stubborn as she was!

She sighed out loud, and her shoulders slumped as the truth hit home.

In theory Brett Cameron and Sienna Rossi *could* be the best team Maria could possibly have hoped for.

They were both professionals with unique skills and talents. Two of a kind.

She owed it to Maria to make an effort and work with Brett. He had his own commitments, but was prepared to sacrifice them for Maria's sake. Surely she could find it in her to meet him halfway?

A smirking smile creased her mouth and she lifted the telephone closer. *Umm*.

Perhaps if she could succeed in working through a refurbishment plan with Brett then maybe, *just maybe*, she could work with Angelo or any other chef.

She would show Brett Cameron that she could put up with any challenge he threw at her.

And help sort out her decision making in the process.

Her head lifted and her voice suddenly sounded full of confidence. As though she was back in control, with a clear plan of what she wanted to do instead of being on the run. 'In that case I could not possibly let you down. Table for two. February fourteenth. Thank you, Mr Scott. I'll see you in…ten days' time. Have a lovely evening.'

Sienna gently replaced the handset and calmly

added the reservation to the long list for February fourteenth.

She very carefully lowered the diary back onto the table, closing her eyes and trying to steady her nerves before going back into *that* kitchen.

Then the doubts started to creep back in. Threatening her resolve.

Things were happening far too fast for her liking.

First, she was on the run from Greystone and the mess that was the new chef, who might not have changed much from the arrogant *old* chef he'd used to be.

Second, the boy who had been her first crush was boiling water and reheating pasta sauce so they could have dinner together. And he was still the best-looking man she had ever met—anywhere.

She was stuck here in the wreck of what had used to be a stunning family bistro only a few short years ago. But it was either that or return to Greystone, while Brett struggled to cook and run her aunt's pride and joy on his own.

Sienna inhaled sharply and curled her toes inside her still moist shoes and stockings.

No way. Not going to happen.

She was here now and she had to make the best of it.

She could work with Brett and run the bistro for a week or two. Of course she could.

Time to get the team in place.

'*Brett?*' she called out as she squelched her way back through into the kitchen. 'What had you planned to do on Valentine's Day?'

'Come next week I'll be working like crazy on my new kitchen. Why do you ask? Looking for a date? You would be welcome in our spot in Notting Hill, only we are not *quite* ready to take guests at the moment.'

Sienna pushed her lips together and blew out hard. Notting Hill? That was where Angelo's had been. Her dream restaurant, in one of the most exclusive parts of London!

Of course Brett had been in Paris when all of that had happened. He couldn't know about that part of her life. Good. Best to leave it like that.

She hid her painful moment by turning it into a wide grin. 'Notting Hill? Congratulations. Maria never said a word, although I haven't spoken to her since Christmas. Work has been mad. Thanks for the invitation, but I plan to spend the day a little closer to Rossi's. In fact, I want to spend it right here. Serving paying customers.'

His half-second delay in responding gave Sienna just enough time to make her bold move.

'It's one of her biggest nights of the year. I'm sure that she wouldn't want to turn away the business. Not on Valentine's Day. I only worked here once on Valentine's Day, to help her out, but it was good fun then and we could make it fun again.'

Brett stopped stirring and slowly turned around to face her. He looked straight into her eyes before he spoke, startling her so much that she fell back to her old nervous habit of twiddling at the antique silver ring she wore on the fourth finger of her right hand.

'You want to open up that freezing cold dining room and serve food to paying customers? On Valentine's Day?' His voice was low. Challenging.

'Yes,' she replied with a smile, suddenly desperate to turn the conversation around. 'Do you remember what it used to be like here? On Valentine's Day?'

'Hard to forget.' Brett pressed both of his palms flat on the worktop and his upper lip curved slightly to one side in a lopsided smile. 'Every one of my classmates was in here with his girlfriend, dressed in smart new clothes their mums had picked out for them. Pretending to be all sophisticated and mature while all of the time they were squirming and itching with their ties and starched collars.'

He returned his spoon to the saucepan and slowly stirred from side to side, releasing the most delicious herby fragrance into the room. 'I was too busy burning my arms on their lasagne dishes and pizzas to catch a lot of the conversation, but Maria was brilliant at making everyone feel at home and taking some of the nervousness out of their big day.'

Sienna watched Brett move between sink, worktop and hob. Fast. Slick. Practised. This was his life.

Pest. But a clever pest she needed to have on her side if she was going to pull this off. She was in control now; she would talk to him as though he was a colleague. That was all. A handsome, talented colleague who had the ability to make her dizzy.

'Exactly. That was what made Rossi's so special. Teenagers could come here for their first date and not feel intimidated. It might have been pasta and pizza, but it was served to them on a table with a tablecloth and napkins, in a real restaurant. I got the feeling that it was almost a rite of passage around here. Like buying your first car. That first date in Rossi's was something you would never forget—even if it did happen forty years ago.'

'Why, Sienna Rossi! I always *knew* there was a romantic streak in you! Where did *you* go for your first Valentine's Day date?'

'Sorry, I don't believe in romance any more,' she replied with a shake of the head and a dismissive sniff. 'And I think you can guess where I went. My dad wanted to keep a close eye on who, where and what was going on. I had no choice in the matter. And stop trying to distract me when I'm explaining why I couldn't say no to Mr Scott. Or any of the other couples who have booked for the evening. It's their special day. The fact that it is also good business is a bonus.'

'A-ha. Thought so. And I don't believe a word of it. Born romantic. Always have been. There is no use you trying to deny it. I do have one question. What will your current date think about you working on Valentine's Day?'

'My date? Oh. I'm between boyfriends at the moment. I always work through Valentines anyway. How about you?' Sienna asked, trying to sound casual. 'Do I need to keep a table for you and your lady friend?'

He smiled to himself. 'Not this year, thanks. Save the tables for gentlemen who want to show their ladies that they are special. *That* is what it is all about.'

'I agree with you. In fact…' Sienna ran her tongue over her lips before going on in a mad rush, desperate to get the words out before she lost her nerve. 'I was hoping that I could persuade you to be the guest chef for the evening. For Aunt Maria's sake. You *did* promise Maria that you would cook for her!' Sienna exclaimed in a louder voice than she'd intended to use.

Brett turned around to look at her, and tilted his head to one side before breaking into a wide smile.

'I did wonder where you were going on your trip down memory lane.'

He nodded once before turning back to the hob. 'Yes, I did make Maria a promise. And I keep my promises. The clock has already started ticking on my new venue. A few weeks from now there will be customers coming through the door. Not to mention top restaurant critics from around the world. I would only have a couple of days spare at most. Plus I have no kitchen, no menu and a massive loan to pay off. And do you know what?'

She held her breath. Waiting for him to come up with some totally credible and amazing reason why he could not possibly cook pasta and pizza for spotty teenagers and retired couples in a tiny bistro when he had a gourmet restaurant of his own to get ready.

He was Brett Cameron. Award-winning international chef. Not some catering student. Of *course* he wouldn't want to do the cooking himself. He probably had a whole brigade of minions at his beck and call.

What had she been thinking? Dreaming, more like.

She braced herself for the bad news. Why not one more thing to add to her disastrous day?

'Maria's sauce has been in the freezer since Christmas. It might have been delicious when it was made, but I've done the best I can to save it. Ready for some hot food? Then I'll tell you exactly how I plan to turn this place around in time for Valentine's.'

CHAPTER SEVEN

Step 7: Two Sparkling Brown Eyes...

BRETT PULLED OUT the ancient patio chair and patted it with one hand.

'Your table is ready, Your Highness. Sorry about the lack of fancy place setting, but I did disinfect the workbench while I was thinking up my master plan. It might not be up to fine-dining standards but it is clean. Providing, of course, you can lower yourself to eat at Maria's kitchen table? Just this once?'

One long, elegant tanned finger tapped the side of his nose, then he carefully folded the white tea towel over the crook of his arm like a silver-service waiter. 'It could be our little secret.'

'Funny. That's very funny,' Sienna replied, and squeezed her eyes together as she slid onto the chair. But he had already turned away to prepare their dinner.

A delicious aroma filled the space, and Sienna lifted her head in curiosity to see what he had managed to conjure up from the meagre contents of Maria's stores. And was stunned by a very nice view of Brett's broad shoulders and snug cargo pants.

He was cooking her hot food.

Maybe she could forgive him, *just a little*, for trying to drown her.

'Tell me more about this master plan for *you* to turn this place around!' she managed to squeak out into the uncomfortable silence, trying to keep her voice light and joking. 'Have I missed something in the time it took me to freeze my feet in the dining room?'

He clearly took no notice whatsoever of the implied sarcasm about his bid for power, and a low rough chuckle echoed back from the plain painted wall he was facing as he cooked.

'I would hardly call it a master plan, but the building work on my kitchen has cut back the little time I have to work on the recipes for my signature menu.'

He pointed his stirring spoon towards his own chest, narrowly missing adding a smear of tomato sauce to his shirt as he did so.

'I have ten key dishes which are going to define what I'm trying to achieve.'

He paused, then turned back to the bubbling

saucepan as he added a colander of drained pasta and gently folded it into the sauce to give it the lightest of coatings.

'Most chefs have three of four. Not me. I want ten perfect recipes for that first night. No arguments. And right now I don't have a kitchen to work in.' He raised the spoon to his lips before hissing, 'And this *still* needs more basil.'

Sienna watched in silence as Brett grabbed a bunch of wilted-looking green leaves from the dehydrated plant barely surviving in a terracotta clay pot on the windowsill, before moving back to the workbench and tearing them into narrow strips with strong deft fingers. Intense focused concentration, energy, excitement. All in those few moments it took to shred some basil which was certainly past its best and stir it into the sauce.

In that instant Sienna recognised the same boy she had known at sixteen. Oh, he might look different on the outside, with all the self-confidence and self-belief that a career as a superstar chef in the top kitchens around the world could bring. But there was no mistaking that flash of passion even in this simple task. He had never lost it. If anything he seemed to have developed it even more!

Brett Cameron in action was mesmerising. And somehow, amazingly, touchingly, a little vulnerable.

She envied him that self confidence.

Confidence enough to be able to create some thing remarkable no matter where he was working, and with ingredients that might not be up to his usual standard.

Suddenly her brain started to defrost like her feet, and she was instantly aware that Brett was still talking. The diverting pest of a man could multitask. *Rats*!

A steaming bowl of soft multi-coloured pasta with the most amazing fragrance wafted past her nose and onto a huge white under-plate on the worktop.

Her tastebuds kicked in the microsecond they savoured the herby tomato tang with a twist of…something she could not quite place. She was used to the best from the best. How could she not recognise that subtle smell? It had to be a special herb or spice. But which one?

She slowly inhaled the aroma of the sauce and closed her eyes in delight. Any thought of holding back on her enthusiasm to make Brett suffer was instantly blown away.

Drat the man for knowing exactly how he could cut through the meagre defences she had built up! Perhaps it was this familiar and homely kitchen? Perhaps that was it? This was home.

'Basil, oregano, fresh rosemary. Garlic and onion with the tomato, and root vegetables and celery. But there is something else. I'm thinking dried chilli and marjoram?'

Brett was watching her with his fork poised to dive in. Waiting for her to try it first.

'I would recommend tasting some,' he said, with a satisfied smile in his low voice, and she took a breath. 'Or are you worried that you might like it too much?'

She opened her eyes, coated a single piece of pasta with the sauce and covered her lips around it.

'Wow,' she breathed, and chewed and swallowed with her eyes closed as pleasure flooded her senses. 'This. Is. Fantastic. Seriously good.'

Brett bowed slightly from his bar stool and dived into his own dinner, chewing through several mouthfuls in silence before gesturing towards her with his fork.

'I'm pleased you like it. Maria made the basic plum tomato paste, but the flavour was too bland for my taste, even with her choice of herbs, after a spell in the freezer. Hence the extras. Chilli flakes with a sprinkle of lemon zest. And fennel. Finely ground fennel seeds. No cheese.'

'Fennel seeds. That's it. That's the subtle richness. And I do like it. I like it a lot. Vegetarian dishes are always popular at the Manor.' Sienna chewed blissfully, aware that Brett was watching her as she ate. 'You could serve this sauce in so many ways. Very clever. And you're right. You don't need parmesan with this dish.'

'Absolutely. Of course it would have been better made with fresh ingredients. Wait until you try my three-mushroom cream sauce on fresh linguini. I'm still working on the best combination of dried and fresh mushrooms, but I'll get there. Or should I say *we'll* get there.'

He lowered his fork into his pasta bowl and leant forward, resting his elbows on his knees so that he could look into her face, his blue, blue eyes working their laser act on hers.

'I am a chef in need of a kitchen. Maria has a kitchen in need of a chef. It seems to me to point one way.'

The air crackled between them, and Sienna licked the sauce from her upper lip as her eyes locked onto his for one long, hot intense moment during which his eyes never left her face.

The heat from that gaze burnt away any lingering doubt she might have had that Brett Cameron had lost his ability to pull her from the real world and into the dizzy magical land where there was even the faintest chance that he might see her as someone he could care about.

'Go on,' she eventually managed to whisper.

'What if I agree to hire the bistro for the next ten days to work on my new recipes? It would mean closing the place to her regular customers, but I'll pay Maria the going rate for a commercial kitchen. Real money. Cash, if you like. What's more, I'll throw in a few extras to sweeten the deal.'

Sienna swallowed down her pasta.

'What kind of extras?'

'I owe Maria. And I can't work in a messy kitchen. Give me ten days and I promise you right here and now that I'll turn this place around. It's a winner. The lovely Maria gets a refurbished restaurant, publicity, and all the new kitchen equipment she wants. And our lovely girl can rest in her hospital bed knowing that her place is in good hands. What do you say? Do you think you can put up with me until Valentine's Day?'

Several hours later, Sienna sat on the edge of Maria Rossi's bed in the same shell-pink, first-floor bedroom which had become her safe refuge four years earlier, and ran the tip of her finger across the silver picture frame she had found on Maria's dressing table.

Laughing back at her from below the glass was a happy couple captured in time on one of the best days of her life. Sienna Rossi and Angelo Peruzi on the day they had opened their own London restaurant.

Angelo was so handsome in his chef's whites,

with his dark curly hair and deep brown eyes. And that smile. That killer smile. How could she *not* have fallen for him?

They'd been young and in love and starting out on the greatest adventure of their lives together. Their own restaurant. Working together to create something amazing.

She had been so happy that day. So much to look forward to.

The Rossis had always loved their family photographs.

Perhaps that was why she hadn't been able to bring herself to destroy all of the other photos like this one, or lock them away out of sight in the special suitcase, along with the wonderful wedding plan and the lovely gilt-edged wedding invitations and the bridesmaid tiaras her future mother-in-law had sent from Los Angeles?

That special place where she had locked away her sensitive and loving heart.

Sienna dropped the photograph onto the bed and closed her eyes as the old familiar pain made her flinch. It was like a paper cut. Sharp. Deep. Only it could not be blinked away.

So what if she had survived the last four years by building tall, thick walls of prickly professionalism to protect her heart from that kind of pain? She needed those solid stone walls to give her some time to rebuild her confidence, so that she was capable and able to do her job without another control-freak chef.

Like Brett Cameron, for example.

Talking through his plans for the refurbishment work, she had come so close to dropping her guard that it scared her.

She was in serious danger of repeating all the mistakes in her life.

How could she fight the attraction to Brett and hope to win? He had all of the weapons he needed. Good looks, charisma, and a level of self-confidence that bordered on arrogance.

She was like a moth drawn to the light and heat of a fire. Destined to be consumed by the flames and fall to the earth and drown.

Only this time she didn't know if she had the strength to find her way back up to the surface for air.

She had to fight this attraction before things spun out of hand.

It had been four years since she had allowed anyone to take control, and look where that had taken her!

Maria had an awful lot to answer for! Even if this project *was* the distraction she needed.

All she had to do was survive the next ten days.

Then she would go back to Greystone Manor and face her past and her future. Alone.

CHAPTER EIGHT

Step 8: And a Pair of Pink Pyjamas

'TIME TO rise and shine!'

'Hmm. Who? What?'

Sienna pushed her nose out from below Aunt Maria's duvet and blinked several times before she focused on the wide shoulders of the tall, fair-haired man who was throwing back her curtains to let in the faint morning sunlight.

It was still raining.

'Oh, you have got to be joking…' she muttered, before pulling the duvet back over her head with a yawn. 'Why are you in my room? Go away!'

'And a very good morning to you too, sleepy-head.'

A long tanned finger hooked over the duvet cover, so that her eyes were just exposed, and she squinted up at the handsome, square-jawed blond who was grinning down at her.

He was shaved, his hair was still moist from the shower, and he smelt like every man should smell first thing in the morning. Fresh, clean, newly laundered, and radiating enough levels of testosterone and pheromones to make any half-drowsy girl want to drag him down under the covers with her.

If they could bottle that smell it would only be available on a medical prescription.

She inhaled another whiff. Free sample.

'I popped in earlier to check what you wanted for breakfast but you were still dreaming of Greystone Towers, so this is your first and only treat of the day. A lie-in.'

He pulled the duvet a little closer to his chest and leant forward, so that he could pretend to peer down under the cover.

'Lovely outfit, by the way. I can see that your fashion sense is still as stylish as ever.'

She instinctively reclaimed the duvet with both hands and pulled it tighter around her chest, to cover up the thick pink-and-white cotton pyjamas that she had found in Maria's wardrobe.

'It was freezing last night. Morning. Whenever I finally managed to get to bed. You might have noticed that the central heating is turned off.'

'Now I *am* offended. I am just across the hall, you know.' He gave her a saucy wink and a quick salute before sitting down uninvited at the bottom of her bed.

'Oh, please. Don't beg. It's embarrassing. And what are you doing, coming in here so early? Or is it very late?'

'Almost nine. I know.' He shook his head from side and side and tutted loudly in faked disgust. 'Hard to believe that anyone can sleep this late. You have special dispensation this morning, but don't think you can get away with this behaviour for the rest of the week. Lots to do, girl!'

'Get away with it? Hang on just a minute.' Sienna shuffled up higher against the headboard, but tugged the covers up over her chest, much to Brett's amusement. 'It was your idea to start working on the master plan straight after dinner! I left you at about one this morning with your head in the oven. Don't you ever sleep?'

'Not much.' He shrugged. 'A couple of hours are quite enough. Besides…' and he patted the bedcover twice for effect before grinning up at her '…I am totally jazzed by our little project. The phones have been buzzing since dawn. There are guys all over London loading vans with tools and catering equipment as we speak.'

'Guys? Equipment? I'm confused. I thought you had only just arrived back in London.'

He nodded in acknowledgement. 'See, I *knew* that you were secretly paying attention while you finished off that second bowl of pasta. My mate Chris is in charge of the building work at my new place. I think he calls himself the project manager, or some other fancy title, but Chris knows who to call when he needs tradesmen, and at this time of year there are usually a few guys who need the extra work or a small job. So I made a few calls. Just to get things moving. This place is going to be jumping with workmen in a few hours, and it might be better for them if you are wearing something less alluring.'

Her chest rose and fell as words failed to form inside her still sleepy head, and she faltered slightly before sitting back.

Sienna closed her eyes, took several deep breaths, and tried to steady her pulse which was racing as anger and frustration surged through her body.

She could feel stiffness building in her shoulders, and tried to clench her toes under the covers.

It has already started.

She should have known and trusted her instincts the night before.

He was already giving orders. Taking control and telling her how things were going to be.

How could she have been so stupid? Why hadn't she stuck to her guns and made him leave?

Stupid, stupid girl. Pulled in by a pair of wonderful blue eyes and Hunk of the Month sex appeal being wafted in front of her over a hot meal!

She should have known that Brett Cameron was too dangerous for her!

For a few hours she had allowed herself to let down her guard.

Well, that was last night. When she'd been cold and exhausted. Not now. Not today. Not any day. Maria was her aunt and she was going to sort out these problems on her own. She didn't need Brett Cameron telling her what to do and how to do it.

Sienna gulped down a huge lump of resentment and disappointment before daring to use her voice. Trying to keep calm. In control without being aggressive. That was the key.

Whatever signal she was giving out, Brett had dropped his grin and now sat in silence on her bed. Watching her with a smiling face designed to weaken her resolve.

'When we talked this through last night,' Sienna managed to say in a low, calm, matter-of-fact voice, 'I thought that we were going to work on this project *together*. Agree the plan of action *together*. You focus on the kitchen and I work the dining room—but we both make sure that the other person is involved in any final decisions. That was what we agreed.'

She paused and licked her dry lips before going on. 'Sorry, Brett, but this is not going to work out after all. There are other kitchens you can rent to test out your recipes, and I can hire another chef to finish the work here on my own. Thanks for your ideas, but I truly don't think we can work together.'

His face twisted into a frown for a few seconds before he replied in a low, intense voice. 'What's the problem? Don't you trust me to call a few contractors to come in and do the work? I might have been out of town for a few years but I trust Chris. His guys won't let us down.'

Sienna shuffled higher up the bed and leant forward, her eyes fixed on his. This infuriating man was still not getting the message! 'No. It's not that at all.'

Brett crossed his arms and tilted his head to one side. 'Then what *is* the problem? You were asleep, we have the clock working against us, and we need to get this ball rolling. Come on—spill. Because I am not leaving this room until I find out what the matter is. And you already know how stubborn I can be when I have a mind to do something. So start talking.'

The problem? The real problem was probably already on his way back from California to take over as head chef at Greystone Manor, but she could not even *think* of Angelo right now!

'It's not you, Brett. It's how you work. I had a problem with another chef a few years ago, who let me down very badly. Since then I don't like being left out when big decisions are being made.'

She paused and gauged his reaction before going on.

'I don't like being sidelined. And I really don't like someone *telling me* how things are going to happen on a project I feel responsible for without asking me first. That is not what we agreed to do. I really cannot work this way. I'm sorry, but it might be better if I hired another chef.'

The muscles in Brett's arms flexed several times, and the thumping in Sienna's chest increased as the silence stretched out between them.

Maria *had* asked Brett to help—she believed him on that point. But the Brett she had asked to help was not the same Brett who had been a willing trainee years ago.

Far from it.

He was an intense, powerful man who was sitting on her bed.

That in itself would unsettle any female with a pulse.

His deep blue eyes were looking at her with intelligence and insight…and something else she could not put her finger on. Disbelief?

Her stomach clenched. Maybe she had overreacted, as he'd said. But it had taken her four years of hard work to build up her cool and controlled exterior. She couldn't allow Brett to knock away her carefully constructed barriers in only a few hours.

He was probably thinking that she was a spoilt brat who was too used to having her own way. And she had just presented him with a get-out clause—on a silver platter.

Brett Cameron perched on the end of Sienna's bed and watched her clutch the bedclothes tighter up around her chest.

She was trying to get rid of him.

Why? All he had done was get the work started while she slept!

What was she so afraid of? Losing her independence?

Or something more fundamental than that?

Why was she so worried that he had leapt ahead? What had this other chef done that was so terrible that she couldn't trust *him?*

He caught her eyes at that moment, and the reality of her fear shone through in a brief moment before she looked away, but too late. She had told him what he needed to know. She had been seriously let down by someone she had trusted—that much was obvious.

This was not the bossy self-centred, always right and very demanding princess talking; this was a frightened woman at the end of her tether.

Well, he could do something about that! If Sienna needed reassurance, that was what he would give her.

'You don't need to hire another chef.' He raised one hand and let it fall to the bedcover.

His next words took her breath away.

'We've all been let down by people at one time or another. You want to be part of the decision process. I can understand that. But I told you yesterday I am not going anywhere! So you're stuck with me…although I *have* been keeping things from you which you are going to find out one way or another.'

The side of his mouth crinkled up to match the creases beside his entrancing eyes, and the tension she had not even realised was between them cracked like a flash of lightning.

She could not help herself. The heated exchange was gone with his smile, and she brought her brows together in mock concern. 'It must be very serious.'

He snatched a breath and shook his head from side to side. 'Oh, it is. Sad case. Thing is…well, I know I can be very impulsive. I desperately need someone around who can point my idiot enthusiasm in the right direction. Think you can cope with that, Miss Rossi? Give me another chance to prove that we can work together?'

His eyes gave the game away, of course. Nobody with those blue, blue twinkling eyes could possibly be taking himself seriously. But Sienna raised her eyebrows slightly when he added, 'Or am I way too much for you to handle?'

'Oh, I think I can handle you quite well, Mr Cameron. Quite well indeed.'

'Good to hear it. Because—again—I am not going anywhere. I made Maria a promise and I keep my promises. Especially to pretty ladies.'

He stretched out his long, denim-clad legs and eased off the bed in a smooth rustle of muscle and suppressed energy.

'I'm going to take my second breakfast in the bistro, so we can start work straight away.' And then he half turned back to smile at her with a cheeky grin. 'If that it is okay with you…boss?'

He dodged out of the way as Sienna's pillow came flying towards him.

CHAPTER NINE

Step 9: Sprinkle with Pink Flamingos

'YOU HAVE A checklist. I like it.'

He also liked her perfume, her flash of a smile and the way their bodies brushed up against one another as they manoeuvred their way around Maria's kitchen like ballet dancers, in some complex, unrehearsed choreography which only the two of them could come up with.

He really, really liked the way she looked in the morning, with her hair loose and messed up on the pillow, one arm flung out on top of the bedcover. Men had striven for years to paint women who looked so naturally beautiful. He had enjoyed a moment of guilty pleasure alone before she'd stirred and he tiptoed out of her room in stock-inged feet to wake Chris up with an early morning telephone call, desperate not to disturb her.

Whatever demons had driven Sienna Rossi out

onto the streets of London late on a wet, cold February evening would not go away after a few hours' sleep, but he wasn't the one who would drag them from her. If Sienna wanted to tell him why she had sought refuge at Rossi's out of the blue like that, that was fine, but he would not press her.

All he knew was that Sienna needed to be here, working, keeping herself busy to escape the inescapable—and he knew about that method. Only too well.

Besides, staying longer in that bedroom would have been seriously bad for his ability to keep his hands off her.

She'd been stunning then and was still stunning now, dressed in simple beige trousers and a light sweater the colour of ripe purple plums, with that lovely chestnut hair smoothed and sleek, pulled back behind her head and gathered inside a wide silver clip.

She looked up at him, her pen poised over the pink pad of writing paper she had found in the drawer in Maria's dressing table. Her pink pen had a jaunty pink flamingo made of bouncy rubber stuck on the end. He would have pulled it off the moment he laid eyes on it, but somehow the paper and pen were so perfectly matched it seemed a shame to spoil the set.

Oh, yes, he also liked the way she savoured and

enjoyed every mouthful of food that passed her lips. Those slim hips must come from the most excellent of genes and a frantically busy life.

Time to think about something else, before he started cooking just to tantalise her with exciting new flavours and foods.

One thing was for sure. He was already looking forward to seeing this woman eat something extra special that he had made just for her. And soon.

'A girl needs a list,' she replied, before biting into a thick, crunchy piece of buttered toast made from a fresh loaf of unsliced granary bread he had bought from the local bakery at some silly hour of the morning. 'Where's *your* list? I need to know what you've been up to when I wasn't around to supervise.'

He tapped the side of his temple several times with his third finger.

'All in here. Shall I start while you eat? Great. Here are my top three priorities.'

He raised his left hand and started with his thumb.

'The cracked window needs to be replaced. My pal Chris is on the case. The glaziers we are using for my building work will be around this afternoon to take the measurements and—you are going to like this—they can etch the glass with anything you like and have it fitted within forty-eight hours.'

His right hand swished through the air. '"Trattoria Rossi."' Then he followed through with a sigh and a grin. 'Problem is that I mentally tuned out the minute the glazier started talking about fonts and layout. We need something classy, but simple. But also fun and easy to read. Big letters.' He gave her a half smile before confessing, 'That's the dyslexia for you. I have no clue.'

There was a sudden intake of breath and a stunned silence from across the kitchen.

'Dyslexia? Are you serious?' Her voice was so full of genuine surprise and concern that he turned to face her.

'Didn't Maria tell you?'

'Not a word. I am so sorry, Brett, I had no idea!'

He shrugged and slipped his toasted cinnamon-and-raisin English muffin onto a plate, before sliding onto the stool on the other side of the table from Sienna, who had stopped eating and was watching him with wide-eyed interest and concern, her toast halfway to her mouth.

He tried to dissipate the tension by taking a bite out of his breakfast and waving the muffin around before answering.

This wasn't the time to tell her the truth about how hard it was living day to day with dyslexia. And he certainly did not want her pity.

So down came the mask as he made light of the whole sorry mess that was pain and frustration, living in a world of words and letters which made little sense to him. Normally he had admin staff and Chris to take care of the paperwork side of the business. Not here. Not at Rossi's.

Here he was, back to being on his own. Without even Maria to help him work through a raft of coping mechanisms.

Unless Sienna helped him over the next few days he would be floundering, just as he had been the first time he came to work here.

And that made him feel even more inadequate than ever.

'It's no secret that I have dyslexia,' he replied in a casual voice. 'The Australian press caught hold of it a while back, and I was invited onto several TV shows. You know the sort of thing.' His hand came up and scribbled a title in the air. '"How I overcame my terrible disability and how it made me a better person."'

He sniffed dismissively and took a sip of coffee. 'I was amazed by how many people have some form of dyslexia and wanted me to talk to them about it. Luckily I had an excellent excuse. Work! So now you know. Making lists and sign painting are not among my special skills and will need to be assigned elsewhere.'

He lifted his head and pretended to look at her list, keen to change the topic. *Now*! His plan worked, as she flapped the paper at him before replying.

'Ah. Now you're trying to be modest. And failing miserably. I am even more staggered by how much you have achieved since the last time we met,' she teased in an amazed voice, before scribbling something on her pink paper, the rubber flamingo jiggling madly as she did so. 'Window-etching in the dining room. Got it. And thank you for your honesty. Now I know, it helps me to see which jobs I have to do.'

He grinned back in reply and seized upon the opportunity to change the subject. 'Teamwork. Right? You handle the window-etching, and in exchange I volunteer to help take out the old dishwasher and fit a replacement. The good news is that the dishwasher from the restaurant we are ripping apart is still on site, and it looks positively new compared to this baby. It should fit, so Maria gets it for free.'

Sienna smiled and waved her toast in his direction. 'Heavy equipment? All yours. Even better when it's a freebie. What's number three?'

He was so dazzled by her unexpected smile that it took a moment for him to reconnect.

'The other good news is that both the oven and hobs work, in their own fashion—they've been replaced some time in the past five years—and the fridge is fine. Except…'

Her last morsel of toast was being crunched noisily. 'Except?'

'Most of the ingredients in the fridge and store-room are either out of date or I wouldn't want to use them. So I need to go food shopping today. More coffee?'

Sienna shook her head. 'I've already had more than I normally drink in a day. The caffeine rush is starting to kick in. Although I needed something to lift my mood after seeing the dining room in daylight.'

She winced and hunched her shoulders before giving an exaggerated shudder.

'Okay, those were my suggestions. Hit me with *your* top three,' he replied, before draining his own espresso.

Sienna tapped on her clipboard, and the flamingo looked as if it was trying to take off.

'Bad news first. The dining-room walls need to be repaired and repainted. They are *so* tired and in need of loving care and attention—but there are special chemicals to help lift the stains. That is my first job.'

She flicked up a glance towards Brett. 'I am going to need help emptying the room. This actually might be a bigger job than I expected. The carpet squidges and squelches when I walk on it. I don't want to even *think* of what has been spilt down there over the years. No more carpet. I would suggest hard flooring, but I'll get back to you with some options as soon as the carpet is gone.'

Her hand paused before the flamingo had time to rest, and her bright, open-eyed face looked up at him.

His heart thumped at how her face and personality beamed back at him for that microsecond, before the serious professional Sienna he had met the previous evening got back to the task.

'Most of the chairs can go out with the carpet! There are only about four I would trust with my weight. The rest are only fit for firewood. Discount warehouses should have what we need. And forget the tablecloths and napkins. Burnt, stained or torn. Darning is not one of Maria's finer skills.' Sienna shuddered before going on. 'I've already thrown them out.'

Brett groaned. 'So basically we don't even have a dining room. Wonderful. Is there any good news? At all?'

She thought for a second before nodding. Once. 'The tables are basically sound. I think Maria inherited them when my parents sold their restaurant a few years ago. I can use them. And I called Frankie at the deli—he says hi, by the way—and apparently there are boxes of old stuff from the restaurant which Dad kept as spares still stashed in my parents' basement. They have been there for ages and he is happy for us to salvage what we can since it is for Aunt Maria. I think that could be a good place to start.'

'Aha. You see? You *do* need me after all.'

She sighed dramatically before replying, instantly taking the wind out of his sails.

'Sorry, but Frankie is busy in the deli and the boxes will need to be lugged up narrow stairs. I need someone who is not frightened by either mutant spiders or heavy boxes, and you're the closest I have to a lugger type. So I'll have to make do.'

'Faint praise, which I accept none the less. So. When do you want to go back to your parents' house?'

CHAPTER TEN

Step 10: Add Hot Pink Psychedelic Flowers

'WELL, THIS is going to be weird. I haven't been back to the Rossi family house in years. Pity your folks are on holiday. I would have liked to say hello!'

'Caribbean cruise. A late Christmas present from the family. According to Frankie they are putting up with fancy cocktails and evening dress in glorious sunshine. Mum is having a wonderful time.'

Brett stared out at the lashing rain between the swish of the car windscreen wipers, and sighed as he turned into the small drive outside the Rossi house. He sat back, drumming his fingers on the steering wheel to the beat of the music playing on the car stereo and the rhythm of the wipers.

'Glorious sunshine! Don't remind me. Adelaide is lovely in February. But, hey, I'm going to be around for the long term. I'll make sure that their names are on the guest list.'

He glanced sideways just as she half turned to him with a distant smile and distractedly replied, 'Mmm. They would love that. Especially if some of the dishes are based on Italian classics. My dad would enjoy telling you how to cook them properly.'

Then she realised what she had just said, and fidgeted even more in the slippery leather passenger seat so that she could sit a little taller.

'Sorry. That came out in completely the wrong way. If the rest of your Italian dishes are anything like that amazing pasta sauce you concocted last night, they will be totally thrilled. Did you know that your name actually came up during Christmas lunch? One of my cousins was in Adelaide and ate in your restaurant. He went so far as to say that the food was excellent. Maria was very proud.'

Brett felt a blush of heat at the base of his neck and shuffled awkwardly. 'She never told me that.'

Sienna faced forward, staring at the house, oblivious to his discomfort as she twiddled her silver ring. 'Well, it would be awful if you developed a swollen head.'

He acknowledged the possibility with a low chuckle, and undid his seat belt so he could focus on the lady by his side, who had remained silent for most of the journey from Maria's.

Between Trattoria Rossi and her old home her get up and go had got up and gone. No sparkle. No fizz. Nothing.

Sienna stayed where she was.

Then, conscious that he was looking at her, she lifted her head and straightened her back, as though she was preparing to go for a job interview instead of visiting the house she had grown up in and called home for most of her life. She glanced up at the front door through the rain and bit her bottom lip. Her bravado faded with her smile.

Some part of Brett reminded him that Sienna's private demons were none of his business. But the girl who had burst into tears when he had soaked her lovely shoes last night was right back in the car with him now. Frozen in her seat.

She was scared! Well, he knew just what that felt like. She needed help and he was right there. As he had told her, he wasn't going anywhere.

'I hate to criticise any lady's footwear, but those are so *not* you.'

Sienna blinked several times at him, and then stared hard at her feet. Maria Rossi's short Wellington boots stared back at her. They were purple, with psychedelic white and hot pink flowers. The only vaguely waterproof item of footwear in Maria's extensive shoe collection. She might fit the same size of shoes as her aunt, but style was another matter completely.

'I would have gone for the yellow daisy sandals I found on top of the refrigerator and put up with wet feet—but, hey, that's who I am,' Brett added, in as casual a voice as he could muster, and shrugged.

She looked up from her boots and stared into his face. Those deep brown eyes that he had admired for so long locked onto his and would not let him go.

Sienna Rossi was holding onto his strength and positive energy every bit as much as if he had been physically holding her in his arms.

And the unsettling feeling swelled into something much bigger.

The only sound in the car was the swish swish of the wipers and the low beat of a Latin dance band for a few long seconds before she gave a weak, fragile smile.

'I did leave some shoes in my old bedroom. And a change of clothes. I should go and get them.'

'Absolutely. Stay right there for a moment, and we'll get ready to make a run for it!'

Sienna watched Brett shrug into his jacket, grab a golf umbrella from the backseat and fling open the car door before dashing out into the lashing rain with a shout. She barely had time to release her seat belt and grab her bag before Brett was opening the door and reaching inside for her to join him.

She let out a long, calming breath and swung her legs out of the car—into the largest puddle she had ever seen in her life. Brett was already beside her, his hand on the small of her back, drawing her closer to his warm body under the shelter of the huge umbrella.

Without thinking or hesitating, she wrapped her right arm around the waist of his jacket and huddled closer, so they could run for the shelter of the wide porch which covered the entrance to the front door.

Yelping and laughing like children, they dodged the puddles and the wet bushes which blew against their legs in the brisk wind. At last they reached the shelter of the stone arch and Sienna immediately started shaking the rain from her hair, grateful to be out of the downpour but reluctant to leave the safe embrace of the man whose hand was still on her back as he closed the brolly one-handed.

His life and passion and energy were exactly what she needed.

Coming back home shouldn't be a big deal, but it was. A *very* big deal. And she was grateful that he was there with her.

'Made it,' Brett joked. 'Maybe those boots were a success after all!'

His warm body was still pressed against her side, and he did not appear to be in any hurry to separate, so she had to twist inside his arms to look at his face, her raincoat sliding smoothly against his padded jacket. His hand drew her closer, so that when the palms of her hands came up to press against the front of his jacket there was nowhere else to look but into his face.

Close up and in daylight it was like seeing a stunning landscape at close range.

The tiny thin white scar that cut his heavy blond left eyebrow.

The slight twist on the bridge of his nose which told her that it had been broken at least once.

And his eyes. The blue was not one solid colour but a mosaic of different shades and variations, from almost white through cobalt, to dark navy and everything in between, each tiny dot subtly different from the others. And they were all looking at her with an intensity and strength and yet a vulnerability that told her far more about the real Brett Cameron than he probably would have liked.

Playing with fire could get you burnt. *And that look was incendiary.*

Her hands pressed a little harder before lifting away. Half of her already missed the warmth and intimacy of being so close to a man like Brett, while the other part shook its head in disgust and reminded her that she had been down this road before with a chef. And look where *that* had got her!

Chef magnet. She hated it when Carla was right.

How many times had the sixteen-year-old version of herself dreamt of being held by Brett Cameron? And here she was, snuggled up with only a few layers of clothing between them. Back home. Back where she'd started. Apparently none the wiser for twelve more years of life.

Time warp.

She was in danger of losing control just when she needed all of the discipline she could muster.

Brett could never know how this house she had once loved with such a passion had become a virtual prison. Her old childhood bedroom a place of nightmares, where she'd spent so many dark and depressed days wallowing in defeat and de-spondency after Angelo had abandoned her, taking her hopes and dreams and confidence with him. If Maria had not offered her an escape route, she would probably still be living here!

'Basement. Do you remember where it is?' she finally managed to ask, in a voice which sounded horribly squeaky against the rattle of the sleety rain.

Brett practically snorted in curt reply. 'Shall we try downstairs?' he said, but slid in beside her as she turned her key in the lock. 'Your dad had me running up and down those stairs for days when I first started. I remember every moment I spent in this house. They were some of the best weeks in my life. Allow me to lead the way.'

CHAPTER ELEVEN

Step 11: And a Box of Warm Memories

'AND WHO is this again?' Brett asked, holding up a very battered black-and-white print of a handsome dark-haired young man in a starched white apron with his arms folded across his chest. 'I'm starting to lose track.'

'Great-Uncle Louis. He was one of the original Rossis who came over from Tuscany to open the very first ice cream parlour in this part of London.'

'Fine moustache. What was the ice cream like?'

'He was horribly proud of that moustache and used to wax it every day.' She shuffled with her bottom along the step, and looked around conspiratorially before leaning in to whisper in Brett's ear. 'The hair wax tasted better than the ice cream. In fact, I think it was the same recipe. But you can't tell a soul.'

'My lips are sealed.' He smiled. His left side was squeezed tight against her from hip to shoulder, but he made no attempt to move to a more comfortable position on the narrow wooden stairs leading down to the Rossis' basement. 'Good old Great-Uncle Louis is still going to look wonderful in the Rossi gallery. Maria is going to love it. Great idea.'

Sienna bit her lip to hide her pleasure, and tried to deflect the attention away from herself. 'The Rossi restaurants have always had family photographs on the walls. I know it seems a bit kitsch now, but as far as Dad was concerned the restaurant was an extension of his own private dining room, and that meant you had your family around you. You know that Frankie has even more boxes of photographs at his place?'

Brett looked around the jumble of boxes and crates in amazement. 'There are more?'

She laughed and waved the folder of photographs they had selected together. 'I think twenty is enough for what we want. Modern picture frames and plain cream walls are going to make these pop. Wait and see.' She smiled up at Brett, only his attention had been taken with a large colour print which he seemed to be examining in great detail. 'Who's that photo of?' And then she caught a glimpse. 'Oh, no. I thought I had destroyed all the remaining copies. Pass it over!'

She made to grab at the offending item, only he swiftly passed the photograph to his other hand and held it at arm's length, high in the air.

'My, my, Miss Rossi. You *do* make a pretty bridesmaid. Is this Frank's wedding?'

She groaned and sat back, with her head in her hands.

'I was shanghaied, kidnapped and sold down the river. Pale green is not my colour. I don't think it is *anyone's* colour, but my future sister-in-law loved it. No choice in the matter.'

'Oh, I don't know…the ruffles are *very* fetching. Perhaps you should wear them more often?' he replied, with a waggle of his eyebrows.

'Oh, please. Like *you* are a fashion guru. I'd like to see your old family photos one of these days. Or do you keep them under lock and key in some bank vault where they can't be used for blackmail?'

His laughter came straight from the gut, and echoed around the long, narrow basement and through the stairs until she could feel the vibration of sound through every bone in her body.

'Sorry to disappoint you, but if there ever were any photos, they are long gone. My mother and I were never much for family gatherings. She was too busy moving from one rented place to another to keep in touch with any relatives we might have had in Scotland, and I certainly can't remember any photos on the walls.'

He glanced sideways at her over his shoulder, with that lop-sided smile he did so well. 'When you are living out of a suitcase, you soon learn to carry only what you need.'

The fluorescent strip lighting overhead in the basement created harsh shadows and dark corners where Sienna knew monster mutant spiders liked to lurk. But looking into Brett's eyes she saw only the type of honesty and frankness that made the breath catch in her throat.

He was telling her the truth and he did not expect her to feel sorry for him. Just the opposite! The way he spoke was so matter-of-fact it was as though he told perfect strangers about his difficult past every day of the week!

It must be wonderful to be so confident and open to the world.

How did Brett do it?

How did he open his life up to such scrutiny?

And how, of all of the people on this planet, was he the only person *she* wanted to open up to? She *wanted* to tell him the truth about Angelo. Not the half-truths that her friends and family had passed around to cover up the whole sordid mess!

Even scarier, she *needed* him to know the truth. The poisonous secrets she kept within her hung like a thick security screen between them, just as they had with every other man she had come close to in the past four years. Except Brett was in another league. The boy who had been her first crush had dropped into her life less than a day earlier, and she already felt as though she had known him as a friend for years. The friend she'd never had.

Maybe that was it? Maybe she wanted to have a second chance to be friends with Brett? She had been too scared and intimidated the first time around to make the move to start a conversation, and he had been so withdrawn and obsessive back then.

Was it possible that she could take a risk and form a real friendship in the few days they would be working together at Maria's? It was probably the only chance she would ever have. One way or another they would soon be heading back to their real lives and jobs, where they would be destined to meet up on rare social events, if at all, when they would be surrounded by other people.

'I don't like it when you go quiet on me. Tell me what you are thinking,' Brett asked.

Not on your life.

'I was just wondering what it felt like to be dropped into the madness of the Rossi household when you took the job here. It must have caused you permanent psychological damage! We do tend to be a little exuberant when a few of us get together!'

He looked at her. Really looked at her. With an

intense focus that made her fight the temptation to squirm away on the hard step and sit on her hands.

'I've carried your family with me every second since the day I left this house and the Rossi restaurant. They taught me everything I needed to know about what a family should be like, and I'll never forget it. They were great! Best six weeks of my life. I lived for that kitchen and those family meals on Sunday afternoons.'

Sienna stared at Brett open mouthed, and collapsed back against the step.

'You *lived* for them? The family meals that turned into yelling matches—or even fights when all my uncles were in town? You actually *liked* all of that? Most of my pals from school ran away, screaming!'

She squeezed her eyes tight shut and took herself back to those huge family Sunday get-togethers, when all the relatives and distant cousins, plus visitors, plus catering crew, would be assembled around one huge extended dining table for several hours.

'The noise! How could you forget the uproar and the arguments? You *cannot* have loved the noise of ten kids and a dozen adults all competing in decibels and speed to get attention! We were all exhausted, deafened and hoarse by Sunday evening. It was manic.'

'You've forgotten to mention the food.'

'Okay, the food was fantastic—but it was still manic!'

'The food wasn't just fantastic. The food was *amazing*. The best. I worked in those kitchens all week, but nothing came close to the wonderful meals your dad made for his family on Sundays. I never expected to be invited to join in, but, *wow,* I was so grateful for the experience. It took me weeks to work out what made it taste so delicious.'

'He always invited the kitchen crew to be part of our Sunday meals. But what do you mean about the food tasting different? Did he try out different recipes on us?'

'No, nothing like that.' He sat back against the wall and hitched one of his legs up, so that he was facing Sienna with his leg down one side of the step and his arm wrapped around his knee.

'It was the love. Every single dish your dad served was made with such love for the people around his table you could almost taste the pleasure he'd had making wonderful meals for his family to enjoy. Didn't you sense that?'

'I suppose it was what I was used to,' Sienna answered, shocked by the emotional depth of what Brett was saying to her. She could hear the passion and fire in his voice, as though he was reconnecting to those Sunday afternoons.

'Exactly. You have to remember that until I started working for Maria my only experience of eating hot meals someone else had cooked were takeaway pizzas and school dinners. And—' he gestured to his chest with one hand '—I am an only child. Put those things together and being dropped into the Rossi family table was like jumping onto a moving roller coaster at a fun fair.'

She tried to imagine how her family must have appeared to someone who had not grown up with them and failed. Miserably.

'It must have been totally bewildering.'

'It was.' He chuckled. 'For the first two minutes sitting at the table. Then Maria pushed a huge plate of antipasti in front of me, and slapped me on the shoulder, Frankie started talking about football, which caused an argument with one of your cousins who supported another team, and suddenly the foccacia was flying everywhere and your parents were laughing their heads off.'

Brett paused and picked up the photo of Frank's wedding, so that Sienna's attention was diverted away from his face when he spoke again in a soft voice tinged with feeling.

'I felt like I had come home. Even though I had never experienced a big family home it was what I had always imagined it would be like. I was completely and absolutely at home.'

Sienna sat in stunned silence. Brett had found

his home within her family. While she hadn't been able to wait to leave it when the going got tough.

How had that happened?

Brett tapped the photo twice with his fingernail. 'Frank invited me to his wedding, you know. But I had just started a new job in Paris and couldn't get away. Shame that I missed it. I would have liked to see you in that dress.'

'Me? Do you even remember me from back then?'

'Of course. I remember you very well indeed.'

'I don't understand. You never said a word to me. Not one word. In the whole six weeks you worked as a catering student. I thought you didn't like me. Couldn't bear to have me around. I was far too shy to talk to you when I worked for Maria, but you could barely manage to say hello and even that was forced out of you. I was so crushed.'

His chest rose and fell, his lips parted, and without warning Brett stretched out his hand and took Sienna's fingers in his, lifted them towards him.

She tried to snatch her hand back. 'Hey! My hands are filthy from working in those boxes.'

'So are mine,' he replied lightly, not giving way. Stubborn.

She stared in silence as he gently turned her hand over, stretching out her fingers in the wide palm of his left hand, stroking the life line with the fingertip of his right.

The feel of that fingertip was instant, and so electric that she gasped out loud. It was probably the silliest thing she could have done.

Hot sensation hit her deep inside. Warmth and welcoming sensations she'd thought she had left behind for good on the day she'd stood at the departure gate and watched Angelo board his flight for California, knowing in her heart of hearts that she had lost him. The kind of heat that was addictive in small doses and killed you in larger ones.

No man had ever done this to her before with one touch of his hand, and she tugged to release herself before he could throw her life and her careful plans even more off balance.

'You see this beautiful hand? It's soft and warm. There are no cuts or burn marks or rough skin from scraping tons of vegetables and fish scales in freezing water.'

His fingertip moved further up her longest finger, stroking the whirls in gentle circles and prolonging the delicious torture she was totally helpless to resist or fight.

'I can see your fingerprint. The skin is so smooth it could be a child's. It is so lovely no man could possibly resist it. Including me.'

He lifted her hand closer to his face, and she sucked in a breath and closed her eyes as he kissed her palm.

'This is the hand...' his mouth moved over the

bump at the base of her wrist with gentle pressure '…of a princess.' Then those lips pressed gently onto her pulse-point, the lightest of pressure. It made her quiver under his mouth, but if he felt it, he did nothing. He was far too busy kissing her wrist.

'I think Maria knew that I felt like an outsider from the wrong side of the tracks, but I was made welcome all the same. I envied you so much. You were born into a wonderful family and you seemed to take it all for granted. Have you any idea how angry that made me feel? How frustrated?'

His eyes locked onto hers.

'That's why I didn't speak to you, Sienna. I was jealous, angry and bitter. And I never once felt good enough.'

Heart racing, she swallowed down the apprehension and found her throat had somehow become completely dry.

So when her cellphone started to ring in her handbag it took only a few milliseconds for her to make the decision not to answer it. Especially when her bag was on the floor of the basement and it would mean breaking her contact with Brett to jog down the few steps and pick it up.

For the first time in a very long time she decided that some things were more important than answering her phone.

Brett shot her a grin, folded her fingers one by one over the spot where he had kissed the palm, and carefully lowered her hand to the floor—as though it was the most fragile, precious object in the world and any breakage would be on his bill.

The wooden planks felt cold and rough compared to the warmth of his fingers, and she shuddered with regret.

'The window guys will be wondering where we've got to.' He smiled at her with eyes that spread the warmth of those fingers all over her body. 'Ready to go?'

Nowhere near. There was music. She was hearing music when she looked at him.

No, she wasn't. It was the ringtone of *his* cellphone.

An operatic tenor was singing in Italian.

'That's probably them now. Excuse me.'

Both legs swung out, and in an instant he had flicked open the cover.

'Hi, Chris. Yeah. Great to speak to you, mate. Yes, we…er…found what we were looking for. It's a *real* treasure trove down here.'

He raised his eyebrows towards Sienna at that moment, and she instantly felt the heat from her blush send fire up the back of her neck.

'Tablecloths, napkins and loads of old family photos. The works. Sienna is really pleased. How are you getting on with that window?'

The smile on Brett's face faltered. 'Tell me you are kidding.'

The tense wire that had bound them together in the silence and intensity of the moment twanged. And snapped.

There was just enough of a pause for Sienna to blink hard, sit up and clasp hold of Brett's arm.

'You're not kidding. Sorry to hear that. Well, here's an idea. We can't let a measly thing like a flood prevent a little girl from having her birthday party, can we? Why don't you have it at Rossi's? I'll trade you one birthday party complete with balloons and entertainment, for one replacement window. Providing you can get the work done in time, of course, otherwise it might be a bit draughty. What do you say?'

The implications of what he was saying slapped Sienna in the last sensible part of her brain, and her fingers bit into his arm as she mouthed the word 'No' and sliced her right hand through the air in a vigorous cutting motion.

He ignored both. 'It's a deal. Thursday. Four o'clock. Looking forward to it. See you in three days. No problem, mate. No problem at all.'

CHAPTER TWELVE

Step 12: Add a Platter of Sweet Dreams

'Is IT safe to come in yet?'

'No. You are still in disgrace.' Sienna fluttered her hands in front of her face to wave him away. 'Go talk to the boys who are loading the skip with rancid carpet and broken furniture while the rain holds off.'

'I did explain on the way back that Jess is Chris's only daughter. How could I let Jess down when her party venue was flooded out? You only have a sixth birthday once in your life. That's special!'

'You are wasting your time looking at me with those pleading eyes,' Sienna said as she pressed tape onto the back of a picture frame.

She raised the scissors and waved the pointy ends at him before he had a chance to reply.

'*How could you do this to me?* How could you

promise a little girl a fabulous birthday party when we don't even have a room to eat in? Three days, Brett. Two for the paint to be dry. There is so much to do it is making my head spin!'

The scissors were put to use on the tape and she added the framed photograph to the stack by her side. 'I am onto your cunning plan now,' she added with a shake of the head. 'You have those male-model good looks and the kind of winning smile that makes girls go dizzy, and then you go and spoil it all by agreeing to things without asking me first.'

Brett grinned at her and leant both of his elbows on the table, so that he could stare into her face with an innocent look. 'Do I make *you* go dizzy?'

Sienna picked up the next photograph and moved the mounting card around until she had the best frame for her Great-Uncle Louis. She fought down the temptation to groan out loud when the memory of the magical ten minutes she had spent with Brett on the basement steps tingled through her body. Dizzy did not come close.

'You did for a few seconds before you went crazy and started making promises without knowing all of the facts,' she replied, when photo and card were lined up. Then her hands stilled. She *was* talking about Brett now, wasn't she? *Not Angelo?*

She shrugged off the idea and carried on.

'Now I can put the dizziness down to low blood sugar and lack of sleep. Could happen to anyone. Lucky for me that Henry's niece is running his fish-and-chip shop while he and my aunt are sunning themselves in Spain. I popped in to say hello and catch up with the gossip on the way back from the flooring shop. Maria is on the mend, Henry is thinking of opening a café on the beach in Benidorm, and I think his niece has succumbed to your dizziness because she offered me free chips if I sent you in… What?'

Brett had started groaning and dropped his head forward to his chest.

'Maria!' He sighed. 'I *knew* there was something I had forgotten to do this morning. Call Maria and let her know how things were going. I know that woman. She will be driving the nurses mad if she is out of the loop and can't control everything, and—'

His head came up, and whatever he was thinking hit Brett so fast and so hard it was like a blow which knocked him backwards and ended up with him slapping the palm of his hand flat on Maria's dining-room table.

'Oh, that is *brilliant*!' he said, shaking his head from side to side.

'An undeniable truth, but what have I just missed?'

His answer was to casually stroll over, take hold

of both her upper arms and physically take her weight while he pressed warm full lips to her cheek.

The intense scent of Brett filled Sienna's senses with delight, and cooking, and Brett.

Blue eyes focused intently on hers and his voice was calm, determined, with only the glint in his eyes giving the game away.

'You are a beautiful, clever woman—and I am sorry that I did not ask you first before I offered Chris the use of the bistro. I am an idiot. Maria Rossi is a genius. You are a princess. I am begging you to give me a *second* second chance. Won't happen again.'

Then he let go of her arms, so that she dropped back a couple of inches onto her low heels in a stunned daze.

'You're doing it again with the dizzy thing. Please explain what strange thoughts are going through that head of yours.'

'I've simply remembered something Maria said to me on the phone the other day. About you being a typical Rossi. Chip off the old block. There is a lot more of Maria in you than you care to admit. Right down to being a bit of a control freak! That's all. Give me another chance. You know that you want to.' And he flashed her the cheekiest wink she had ever seen.

'Do I indeed? Maybe I should have eaten those

free chips after all? Because that makes no sense whatsoever. You have to be the world's best at making my poor brain spin. Take a paper prize. And, yes, okay—one more chance. *One*. Third time and you are out on your ear.'

He laughed. 'Thank you. I love prizes. And here's one for you. I actually came in to tell you that Chris will be here with the gang, bright and early tomorrow morning, to start taking out the big window. Those boys will need some real food in exchange for all of the work I have lined up, and chips are not on the menu. Not in our kitchen.'

Her head came up. '*Our* kitchen? Umm. *Much better*. In that case, Chef Cameron, I should warn you that any minute now two hunky blokes will be laying a new wooden floor, once the horrible smelly carpet has been ripped out.'

'Two-timing me already,' he muttered with much tutting as he planted both hands on his hips. 'No other way you could persuade tradesmen to turn up at such short notice.'

She couldn't help it. She had to press her lips together hard to stop herself grinning.

'Simple. I told them it was for Maria. They were round like a shot, offered me a big discount on a lovely new oak floor and agreed to fit it today. Apparently the boards click together like a jigsaw puzzle. Very clever. Our dining room is going to look superb.'

'*Our* dining room? Like the sound of that. Umm. *Much better*, Miss Rossi.'

And just like that the invisible cord that tied them together was pulled so taut she was frightened it was going to knock her over onto the table and into his arms if she didn't lean backwards slightly.

His eyes softened, the pupils wide and alert. He was feeling it too, and her poor broken heart missed a beat.

This time it was not the sound of music which snapped the cord, but doorbells. And hammering.

'Front door. Flooring,' she said, without breaking eye contact.

'Back door. Dishwasher,' he replied, with the kind of infectious grin that made it impossible for her not to surrender to the smile that had been bursting to come out since he'd planted that kiss on her cheek. 'Later.'

And he turned and was gone.

Sienna stared in silence at the space where he had just been standing. It was impossible to stay annoyed with this man! Drat him for having the most infectious grin! When in the past twelve years had he picked up *that* unique skill? And talk about stubborn!

Strange how much she was coming to like it.

CHAPTER THIRTEEN

Step 13: And Three Wedding Cakes…

'BIRTHDAY cake. Has to be pink, of course. Jess is totally into pink at the moment. Even her pencil case and school bag have to be pink. Apparently it's driving her nanny around the bend.'

'Pink ice cream. Pink jelly. Pink cake. Got it. Do we have pink birthday cake candles?'

'Absolutely. I have already told Chris that pink pizza is out—it's do-able, but you wouldn't want to eat it. Too much food colouring.'

Sienna paused in taking notes long enough to shudder. 'Yuk. Her mother is going to freak. Can you imagine eight little girls high on sugar and artificial colours? Do you have to check the ingredients with her first?'

'Her mother? Ah. Of course. You wouldn't know about Lili,' Brett whispered.

He leant further inside their replacement dishwasher and scrubbed the stainless steel as though there was some form of pestilence living there, and as if he had not already cleaned every surface until it shone, inside and out.

'Lili? Is that Jessica's mum?'

A quick intake of breath.

'Was. Lili died of cancer when Jess was four. Chris has been on his own since then.'

Sienna put down her pen and paper and her shoulders slumped. 'Oh, that's tragic. How terrible. Did you know her well?'

There was just enough of a pause for Sienna to stretch to one side, so that she could see the rear end of Brett as he moved on the dishwasher. Several years of frustrated hormones and deliberate celibacy counted for nothing when she had *that* view to look at. Could those denims *be* any tighter?

He was dirty, scraped with rust and rainwater from manhandling two dishwashers in and out of the kitchen in the dusk of a winter evening, and the hem of his T-shirt was soaked with washing water—but he was still the best-looking man she had seen in a very long time.

And he had been working harder than any head chef she had ever worked with—including her own dad. Angelo had never cleaned and scrubbed in his life. There had always been someone lower down the food chain to do it for him. Not Brett. She admired him for that—and he had stuck to his word. Their new dishwasher was a huge improvement.

Then that fine rear shuffled back, and he stretched up to his full height, rolling his shoulders back to release the tension and restore some flexibility, and giving her the benefit of a flash of exposed skin above his belt as the T-shirt rose higher, stretching taut across his chest.

She swung back in an instant, heat flashing at her throat.

'Sorry—did you ask me a question just then? The rack got stuck.'

I'll say!

'I was just wondering how you came to know Chris and his family,' she replied, trying to keep a casual tone in her voice now that he was within touching distance.

The salty tang of masculine sweat, antiperspirant and cleaning spray filled the space. No expensive perfume could have been so enticing. She lifted her chin and smiled.

'Curiosity. Being nosy. You can tell me to mind my own business if you like.'

Brett wandered over towards her and dried his hands, before collapsing down on a bar stool with a bottle of water.

'Not at all. But I have a question for you first. Do you have a best friend? Someone you can talk to any time, day or night, about anything?'

Sienna tried not to stare at the gleam of sweat on his throat as he swallowed down the cold water, or the wet curls of dark blond hair that extended down inside the shirt.

'As a matter of fact I do,' she gushed. 'Carla is the head receptionist at Greystone. We met on our first day at college. She is a real character! Why do you ask?'

Brett nodded and drained the water. 'Ten years ago I hit Paris, with the address of a restaurant I had never seen in my life on a scrap of paper, about four words of French, and no social skills whatsoever. But I had a fire in my belly and I was prepared to put up with the ribbing from the French guys to make my way.'

He held up one hand. 'There was one other English guy in the whole place. Chris. Oh, I do beg your pardon. The Honourable Christopher Donald Hampton Fraser.'

Brett stood to attention and bowed towards the dishwasher.

'Chris had come straight out of a fancy business school, had several degrees under his belt, and was being fast-tracked to great things with a hotel chain who owned the kitchen. A big one. Some wag at the restaurant decided it would be fun to cram the scruffy, sullen galley slave into the same tiny flat with the elegant smooth guy who spoke perfect French and watch the fireworks.'

Brett grinned and pressed two fingers to his forehead in a silent salute.

'Best two years of our lives. I never worked so hard in my life—or had so much fun.'

Sienna caught his infectious grin and smiled back at him.

'So you didn't kill each other after all?'

'Oh, I wanted to. Especially after he binned all my clothes and then cut my ponytail off when I was asleep.'

Her mouth fell forward with a gasp. 'He did not!'

'A Cameron and a Fraser in the same room! Both born in Scotland! Bound to be trouble—for all of five minutes.'

He leant forward to rest his elbows on his knees, hands cradling the empty water bottle, at just enough of an angle so that Sienna could see further down the front of his moistened T-shirt.

'Chris grabbed me on my first night off, when all I wanted to do was sleep, and forced me to share several bottles of very good wine. Hours later we decided that I was a young, scruffy and ignorant poor mess, he was an older, wiser and richer mess, and together we were going to conquer the world.'

Brett raised his bottle of water in a toast. 'Watch out, world! Here we come!'

They laughed out loud at the same time, Sienna shaking her shoulders in delight at the image.

'So what happened after you pledged world domination. Was there a master scheme?'

'Oh, yes. I was going to become a charismatic celebrity chef who would woo the customers, while good old Chris would run the business side and count the cash. It was brilliant. Except for one tiny, tiny detail.'

She looked up and raised her eyebrows with a little shake of the head, as if to say *carry on.*

'I wasn't charismatic. I was quiet, withdrawn, bitter and angry at the world, and I had zero confidence in myself and my talent. And I had dyslexia. Apart from those small problems we couldn't lose!'

'What changed? How did you do it? I mean, Chef in a Kilt? Excuse me for being so bold, but that is *not* the persona of a galley slave without an ounce of confidence!'

Brett winced and bared his teeth. 'Saw that, did you? Did I mention that Chris is also my manager and publicist? He's the only man alive who could persuade me to don the Cameron tartan!'

'Manager… Publicist…' Sienna nodded sagely. 'Aha. I think my point is proven. Hunk of the Month was a *very* popular feature at Greystone Manor.'

There was a gruff clearing of the throat from the man in the chair. 'Is that really what they called me?'

She nodded slowly, just once, and took delicious pleasure in seeing Brett groan, blink hard, and squirm in embarrassment before she smiled and took the edge off his pain.

'You're a lot braver than I am. Should I be asking Chris to give me some tips on how best to win friends and influence people?'

'Easy. The same way that I persuaded him into investing his hard-earned savings in a joint venture. Namely that special restaurant that we dreamt up in Paris all those years ago, as some kind of crazy wine-fuelled dream. Well, that dream will be opening in a few weeks. One thing was for sure. When I got tired of working as head chef for other people, Chris wasn't the *first* person I called. He was the *only* person I called.'

'Trust. There's a lot of trust there.'

'Both ways,' he admitted with a wink. 'I've sold everything I had in Adelaide to make my investment in the site. He's a single parent who's backing his shirt on this new place. We're both taking a huge risk.'

'But you still haven't answered my question. How did you go from galley slave in Paris—' and she waved her arm towards the darkness outside the kitchen window '—to Hunk of the Month who's about to open his own place?'

Brett leant forward to rest his elbows on his knees and prop his chin up with his hands, and for a moment he had all of the vulnerability of the teenage Brett that she remembered. Her heart leaped.

'I was in Paris. I was single. And I was doing the job I loved to the exclusion of everything else in my life. I didn't go out. I worked twenty-hour shifts. It was mad, but it was all I knew. Chris was the one who introduced me to the wonderful city and a world outside the kitchen that I had no idea existed. He made me talk to people. Talk to *girls!*'

Brett screwed up his face into a look of mock terror and shuddered, which made them both smile.

'I found out who I was in Paris, and eventually I was ready to take the final step and actually ask a specific girl for a date.'

He paused and gave Sienna a poignant smile. Not a full-mouthed grin but something quite different.

Something deeply personal.

He was going to tell her something it would cost him to admit.

Something worth her silence.

He leant back for a moment, to select a perfect strawberry from the bowl on the worktop.

'Lili was a Parisian girl, right down to her manicure and perfect skin. She was clever, polished, elegant, and so beautiful it took your breath way. The kind of girl that every other woman envies and every man wants to have on his arm.'

Sienna's eyes never left his face as Brett held the strawberry by its stalk and took a delicate bite from the juicy fruit. The tang and sweetness of the berry hit her nose with sensory overload.

But she stayed silent.

This was a story that only Brett could tell, and he swallowed down the fruit, his gaze still fixed on the remains of the berry as he spoke.

'I had waited eighteen months to ask her out for a drink on a double date with Chris and his girl-friend. I had hoped and dreamt that she would say yes. But it still came as a shock when she agreed. For a few hours I was the happiest man in Paris. Until the moment Lili laid eyes on my pal Chris. Love at first sight for both of them. Poor fool didn't know what had hit him.'

Brett popped the rest of the strawberry into his mouth and pulled out the stalk and hull in one piece.

'Four months later I stood next to Chris as his best man when he married Lili.'

The blunt statement was made without a hint of hesitation, but Sienna was close enough and focused enough to see the telltale twitch at the side of his mouth. His eyes narrowed and flinched so quickly that anyone else would have missed the signs which shouted out distress before he recovered and forced a light voice and a joky smile.

'I had to make three wedding cakes. *Three*. Five layers of light-as-a-feather sponge with fondant orchids for the British contingent. A tower of fresh profiteroles filled with Chantilly cream served with warm chocolate sauce for her French family and the kids. And of course a low-carb pink champagne jelly with fresh fruit for the fashion models who—'

He never got the final words out, because Sienna couldn't bear to tolerate the deep, deep pain in his voice any longer. and before he could finish the sentence she crossed the few feet that separated them, leant in, and covered his lips with hers.

She tasted the salty tang of his sweat, and the sweet strawberry juice in the heat of his mouth, and he froze for a moment. Then he kissed her back, sweet, welcoming, insistent, blanking out any coherent thought that might have lingered in her brain.

Eyes closed, she felt the soft warmth and taste and scent of his kiss wash over her like a warm blanket, drowning her in the sensation of being held in the circle of his arms, so that when he finally pulled away, her head fell forward onto his chest.

Heat. His unique body fragrance. The background of light jazz music playing on the radio. Her senses reeled with the intensity of the moment.

She was going to capture this in her memory. Savour every second.

Instantly his hand moved to the back of her head, and she became aware of the vague pressure of his lips on the top of her hair as he held her closer.

Her hands pressed hard on his damp chest, the thumping heat of his heartbeat resonated though her fingers, telling her everything she needed to know about the man. Her instincts were right, even if she was not ready to open her eyes and look at him.

No. She wasn't ready for that. Not yet.

His hand caressed the back of her head, and the heat of his forehead pressed against her hair, made her tremble. His voice was low, and so close to her ear that it was more of a whisper. 'What did I do to deserve that?'

'Does there have to be a reason?' she answered, her words muffled into his chest.

His hand slid down her back from her hairline, and she could almost feel the mental and physical barriers coming down between them as he pulled back and lifted her chin so that he could look at her.

The look brought tears to her eyes. Intensity. Confusion. Pain. It was all there.

'No pity. Lili chose the better man.'

Don't say that. Don't ever say that. You deserve better than to feel that way!

She swallowed down the fast response and stroked the line of his jaw with one finger, still not ready to look into those laser blue eyes where she knew she would instantly be lost.

Whatever happened between them going forward, the very *last* thing she wanted was for Brett to think that she had kissed him out of some sense of pity!

Yes, she did feel sorry for him.

Brett had been in love with Lili. Who had married his best friend.

He had lost the woman he had loved not just once, but twice.

First to his best friend and then to disease. But *her* feelings for him were *way* more complicated than that, and they both deserved better.

If Brett believed that he was a lesser man than Chris, then perhaps she could do something creative to redress that balance.

Starting right now.

'Then how about understanding? I *am* sorry for your loss. And,' she replied with a warm smile, 'little Jess is going to have the best birthday party *ever!*'

The tension eased from his shoulders and his chest dropped a few inches under her hands.

'Okay…' Then a second small smile of mutual understanding crept over his face before he repeated, 'Okay…' But this time it was in a stronger voice as he fought to regain control.

His arms moved away from her waist and rubbed up and down her arms for a few seconds as his breathing slowed.

She gave him one long smile, and then slapped the palms of her hands twice against his T-shirt before stepping out of the circle of his arms and casually picking up her clipboard.

'Pink balloons. Let's make that thirty. A girl can never have too many pink balloons, and each of the guests can have one to take home.'

She risked a faint smile in his direction, and was rewarded with a grin and a tip of the head.

'Absolutely! In the meantime I'm heading for the shower. Then how about we pay a visit to the local pizza shop? Check out the competition! Especially when you still have to practise your singing and pizza-making skills.'

'You're on. Except I can't cook and I don't sing. Apart from those two tiny details, I'm starving! Then we need to get seriously busy to make that room ready for a *real* little princess. I'm only a pretend one, after all.'

The scent of strawberry still lingered and wrapped around her senses as he strolled out of the kitchen, so casually it was hard to believe that he had just turned her world upside down.

Time to turn up the heat.

She had meant what she said.

Lili's daughter was going to celebrate her

birthday in a lovely room—even if she had to work all night to finish the paintwork.

Except she had the strange feeling that she would be doing it more for Brett than the little girl whose mother had broken his heart.

Brett was a better man than he knew. And she was the one who was going to show him just how special he truly was. Even if it meant kissing him again to prove it!

CHAPTER FOURTEEN

Step 14: Eight Spinning Designer Rainbow Pizzas...

BRETT STOOD in the middle of the dining room, pushed his hands deep into his trouser pockets and gave a low whistle.

This was his first official viewing of the redecorated room. And it took his breath away.

Sienna had chosen a warm natural oak wood flooring which worked brilliantly against the fresh cream paintwork. The tablecloths, napkins, curtains and lampshades were plain forest green or pastel pink, with a faint check in the same colours as a border.

Even on a cool February afternoon light flooded into the room through the pristine window glass, increasing the sense of space and relaxed comfort.

All in all, the overall impression was modern,

chic, clean—but also comfortable and welcoming.

This was not Maria Rossi's trattoria any more. This was Sienna Rossi's bistro.

Everything about this room screamed Sienna. Her personal style shone through in all the details his trained eye picked up around the room.

The family photos were in plain oak picture frames which perfectly matched the floorboards and the chair backs. But it was the arrangement that was so clever.

Sienna had collected them into groups of four, all hung on one wall—the far wall—so that they would be the first thing the customers saw when they came into the dining room from the street. The eye was immediately drawn to the smiling faces of the Rossi family who had gone before, in order for her to be in this world.

But it was the long, plain dining-room wall which was so amazing that he could only stand and smile at what she had achieved.

The words *Trattoria Rossi* had been painted in forest green in large letters along the whole of the middle section, using the same type of script Sienna had chosen for their new plate-glass window. He would never have thought of using the same stencil that had been used by the glaziers on the outside inside the room. The same name, inside and outside. Fresh green inside, acid etch outside.

It was inspired.

Put that together with sparkling glassware and simple but elegant cutlery, and he was looking at the idealised perfect yet informal dining area he had searched for all of his life.

He had never told Sienna what his dream was, never described it or even mentioned it. Yet this amazing, wonderful, special woman had created the dining room he had been talking to Chris about ever since Paris.

There were already *way* too many formal restaurants, where starchy people in smart uncomfortable clothes were served wonderful, spectacular showpiece dishes made by master craftsmen at the top of their game. Meals were usually eaten in silence, or with classical music played in hushed tones in the background, and children were considered an unnecessary nuisance to be tolerated.

He had worked in hotels and restaurants all over the world that specialised in providing an exclusive experience to the privileged few who could afford the cost of total luxury.

Of course they were brilliant! And he had loved working for those masters of their craft. But that was not what he wanted for his own restaurant. Far from it.

His dream was to serve fantastic food cooked with love in precisely the same type of warm, open, friendly and informal surroundings he had seen in the Rossi family home all those years ago and experienced for himself in family restaurants across Europe.

Whichever country he had visited, for work or holiday, he had made it his business to ask the local people where *they* would recommend for a family meal. Friendly, open and welcoming dining rooms, where whole generations of families could come together to celebrate good food.

He had sought out dining rooms where guests of all ages, all sizes and all shapes were equally welcome. Where they could relax and be comfortable. Free to laugh and argue and sing and dance if they wanted.

All the time searching for his ideal version of a family restaurant, where children would be welcome and the whole family could eat wonderful food at the same table.

That was why Chris had searched all over London to find the perfect location where there would be enough space to accommodate children, laughter and music while he created the food to match.

The irony was that he had found it in the very place where he had started his career all those years ago!

There were footsteps on the hard oak floorboards.

Sienna came to stand next to him, and he could sense her anxiety seeping out of every pore of her skin. A quick glance sideways told him what he needed. She was chewing the corner of her mouth with her top teeth.

The great Sienna Rossi, princess of the Rossi clan, was nervous in case he hated the room she had worked so hard to create, and wanted it turned back to terracotta dark walls and gloomy spider lairs before Jess arrived for her party.

Without thinking or hesitating, he reached out and took her hand in his, meshing their fingers together so that they stood in silence together and looked around the space.

It smelt of fresh paint and wood varnish.

And as far as he was concerned it was magical.

'I only had time for one more coat of paint last night, but it is dry. Jessica and her friends will be fine today, and then I'll clear the walls and finish off over the weekend.'

'You don't need to change a thing. It's perfect.'

'Really?'

'*Really* really. It's everything I could wish for. And more. Maria is going to be delighted.'

He lifted his chin a little and focused on the brass rail holding up the bistro curtain as he squeezed her fingers.

'I love it.' *I love you*.

He was conscious of his breathing speeding up

to match hers, and the gentle pressure of her fingertips as they pressed against his in return.

For a few precious minutes they were not Brett Cameron and Sienna Rossi, with all the baggage those names carried with them, but two people who wanted to be with one another and had worked their whole lives so that they could stand side by side in *this* room at *this* moment in time.

He would not have missed it for the world.

Brett glanced at her from the corner of his eye and his stomach clenched. She was exasperating, stubborn and awkward—and absolutely gorgeous.

Words formed in his mouth, and he was just about to tell her how pretty she looked that morning when there was a bustle of activity and balloons from the hallway and Sienna dropped his hand as though it was burning.

'Did someone place an order for pink balloons?' Chris asked, his fingers clamped around enough balloons for him to be grateful that he carried his own gravity around with him.

Like a guilty teenager caught in a clinch, Brett shuffled as far from Sienna as he could without being insulting, and pretended to be testing that the wall lights worked.

As nonchalantly as he could manage, Brett turned to his friend just in time to see Sienna fling her arms around Chris's neck and kiss him heartily on the cheek.

'Chris. You are a genius. Thank you, thank you, and thank you. You've done an amazing job. The window is fantastic!'

Considering that she had only met Chris once before, when he'd introduced the glaziers, this was a little over the top!

'Hey! I'm right here,' Brett intervened, pointing to his chest. 'And I seem to remember *I* was the one who has fed and watererd six workmen every hour on the hour for most of the day. Don't I get a hug?'

'Chance would be a fine thing.'

She turned back to Chris, who was looking at Brett with thinly veiled superiority and amusement.

'It's so sad when he grovels,' she said. 'Are you bringing Jess later? I can't wait to meet her!'

'My slave driver of a business partner needs me to work on this signature restaurant of his—' he scowled at Brett, who simply shrugged his shoulders '—but I'll be here for the cake bit, and to pick her up.' His eye caught Brett's with a wink. 'Something tells me that my little girl is going to have a whale of a time with you two around.'

'Is there anyone here who likes pizza?'

Every single girl in the room put her hand up. Including three of the nannies and Sienna.

'Excellent. Well, in that case, today we are making...*pizza!*'

Sienna smiled as the room exploded with cheers and waving, and even a pirouette from the twins in identical ballet shoes and pink tutus.

'But not just any old pizza. Oh, no. Today we are making Jessica's special rainbow pizza. *And*...each person gets to choose their very own, special, unique, personal and only for them rainbow, which only they get to eat!'

'Pizza!' Jess called out, and waved her pink sparkly wand in the air while jumping up and down in her very pretty matching outfit, pink from hair to slippers.

'Rainbow pizza. Rainbow pizza!' they all called out, waving their fairy wands so vigorously that Brett had to reach forward and straighten Jess's tiara, which had fallen forward onto her face.

He stretched up onto the toes of his training shoes and put the flat of his hand to the front of his forehead like a cap, eyes screwed up in concentration as he turned from side to side from the waist.

'Where *did* I put those big pizza plates? Has anyone seen the big pizza plates? We can't make pizzas without pizza plates.'

There were giggles from behind the wands as Brett put both hands on his hips in his best sea captain impression and pointed directly at Sienna, who shuffled from side to side, whistling and looking at the ceiling—which was a big mistake, because hiding behind the light shade was a damp patch she had not noticed before—pretending to hide a stack of metal pizza plates behind her back.

'There they are. Aunty Sienna is hiding them! Aren't you, Aunty Sienna? *Naughty* Aunty Sienna.'

Brett wiggled his eyebrows at her and grinned.

He had every right to look victorious. There was no other man in the world who could have persuaded her to wear one of her aunt Maria's girly-pink flouncy dresses, cinched around the waist with a huge pink ribbon tied in a big bow at the side.

Especially when Maria was a good four inches shorter, which made for a lot more exposure of her legs above the knee than she was used to. A *lot* more.

No wonder he was enjoying the view.

'Now, dig your fingers in there. That's it. Stretch it out nice and round. Push into the corners, just like that—see what I'm doing?'

'Katie, sweetie, that's looking a bit square. Stretch it out. Like this—there you go. No, it doesn't matter if your nail varnish goes into it.'

'Wait. What's that music? Can you hear that music? What does the music tell us to do? *Mambo*!'

The kids all bellowed out the tune, since this was the twentieth time they had heard it, swaying and dancing from side to side, and Sienna could not resist joining in with the chorus, which made Brett look up and smile.

'Hey, I knew you had a lovely singing voice inside there! Let's all sing like Aunty Sienna. That's it, Jess, mambo.'

'Now we have to do the dance. Are you all ready? Let's spin that pizza to the music!'

Brett wiggled his bottom from side to side and made his shoulders do a little dance as he turned the dough round and pushed, then turned it again before looking up and dramatically staring around the table.

'Oh, *look* at these fantastic pizzas! One more dance, and then all they need are the magic words!'

Brushing the flour from his hands, he went around the table from child to child, whispering something secret in each ear which made the girls squirm and giggle.

'How does the magic work, Uncle Brett?'

Brett stepped back and looked hard at Jess.

'You mean, you've never seen it?'

She shook her head and looked around at her pals, and they shook their heads and shrugged.

'Well, that is just terrible. Does anyone else want to see the magic?'

Frantic nodding ensued.

'Okay. Here we go. Have to get ready first. Loosen up the old fingers.'

Brett stretched his hands out and wiggled his fingertips up and down on both hands, sprinkling flour everywhere as he did so. Eight little girls did the same, waving their hands in the air, some still clutching the pink plastic wands which Sienna noticed had lost a lot of their glitter. Probably into the pizza dough.

'Oh, that *is* better. You need both hands for this job. Ready everyone? I can feel that magic. Here it comes!'

Before they could answer, Brett flipped up his own piece of pizza dough and twirled it into the air, spinning it into a circle before passing it to his other hand so quickly that it was a blur.

Sienna watched the children stare open mouthed as Brett flicked his wrist and the circle of pizza lifted up into the air again, spun slightly, and fell back into his upraised hands. He slapped it down on the floured board.

'*Wooow*! That was so cool. Do it again, Uncle Brett. Do it again.'

'Yes, do it again, Uncle Brett.' Sienna smiled across at him in between helping the nannies— who were all ogling Brett—with refastening aprons and picking up fairy wings and wands which had lost their charm compared to Uncle

Brett. Not that she blamed them. He was...wonderful.

The love shone through every time he looked at the children. He *adored* them. Being with them, talking to them, sharing their fun. He was one of them.

'For the pretty lady—anything!' He smiled back. 'You see, there are some advantages from starting your catering career in a takeaway pizza parlour on an industrial estate. I could spin sixty a night before I turned sixteen.'

Sienna nodded at the children, who were still entranced by his hands as he draped the dough and then spun it higher and higher, before catching it one-handed and slapping it back to the table.

'Yay! Do it again, Uncle Brett—do it again!'

She nodded more fiercely this time, and he got the message. 'Of course university is much better. But you can always do this for fun at weekends! What do you say? Are you all ready to make magic spinning pizzas?'

'Yes!'

As each of the children lifted and flung their dough shapes around the room, Brett bent down to Jess and lifted her up into his arms, twirling her from side to side to the music, sharing in her childish laughter before she threw her arms around his neck and kissed him on the cheek.

A lightbulb switched on inside Sienna's head.

And her heart broke.

Jess was all Brett had left of the woman he had loved in Paris. She was so pretty, so delicate and dainty and happily unspoilt. Her mother, Lili, must have been a remarkable woman.

All she could do was watch them as they danced and sang together.

The tall, god-handsome blond man, who had always owned her heart from the moment she had seen him as a teenager, and the little girl in a pink tutu.

If ever there was a man who wanted his own family, she was looking at him now.

He had let down his guard, and the loving, caring and oh-so-vulnerable side of the real Brett shone through. And pulled her closer to him than she'd ever thought possible.

He had so many special gifts! She already knew that he could be tender and compassionate. The thought of him going through life alone was so terrible that hot tears pricked the back of her eyes, startling her with their intensity.

Was it possible that Brett could ever open his generous and warm heart to take a chance on love again? With her?

She was falling in love with Brett Cameron all over again, and there was not one thing she could do about it except run away before they broke each other's hearts.

She needed to get back to Greystone Manor. Back to the stone walls and safe places where she would only have to cope with awkward diners— not a handsome and loving blond man who adored children and would make a wonderful father.

CHAPTER FIFTEEN

Step 15: And Two Glasses of Red Wine

THREE HOURS later, the dining room was remarkably quiet and almost calm. The party was over and the clean-up crew had swung into action.

That was to say Brett had worked his magic with their new dishwasher, and Sienna was repairing the damage to her newly painted room. Her frilly dress was gone, replaced with comfy trousers, a waterproof apron and a pair of loafers she'd last worn when she was at college.

Every child had been stuffed to bursting with pizza topped with ingredients they had chosen themselves—she was the only person who had noticed that Brett had discreetly picked off several pieces of banana before dramatically sliding them into the oven with a great flourish.

He was a natural showman. No doubt about it. And he certainly had a way with the girls. But the pizzas had looked and smelled delicious when he'd slowly drawn them out, golden and bubbling, to the accompaniment of 'oohs' and 'aahs' from their designers.

She had rarely seen food enjoyed with so much delight and enthusiasm. The pizzas had gone down even faster than the ice cream, raspberry sauce and gorgeous fruit jelly.

The young ladies and more than a few nannies had then been served pink fizzy lemonade in plastic champagne glasses to wash down the heavenly light pink birthday cake. And Brett had been called into service to hold Jess up while she blew out the birthday candles with her father Chris by her side.

Overall it had been a fabulous party. And well worth all the effort.

Shame that there was always pain associated with gain.

Sienna stretched up on tiptoe to wipe away two tiny pieces of pizza dough which had stuck to the dining-room ceiling after the extra-vigorous tossing practice.

'You wouldn't think that a six year old would have so much strength in her wrist. Watch out, world. Here they come. I'm frightened already. I wonder if I was so precocious at that age.'

Brett replied with a snort, then wiped his hands on the kitchen towel around his waist and carefully pulled the cork on one of the bottles of wine that Chris had deposited in exchange for a carload of squealing young ladies in sparkly pink sandals, clutching goody bags and balloons.

'Jess is a total sweetheart. I can see how she twists all the men in her life around her little finger. Especially her uncle Brett. She's a little diva in the making. No doubt about it.' She stretched higher, but still could not reach the floury patch.

'Here. Let me do that for you.'

Brett stood behind her and pressed his front into her back as he reached up with a wet sponge to wipe away a smear of sticky dough—only then he found another, and another. Any excuse for their bodies to be in contact for as long as possible.

She turned around and gave him a look. 'Thank you, but I think we are done. Time to call it a day.'

Her response was met with a chuckle, but he did concede and sat down at one of the dining-room tables. 'Amen to that. Ready for some supper? I have a very nice platter of antipasti from Frank's Deli, and a vintage Sangiovese from that grower near Pisa that Chris seems to like. And there's always more birthday cake if you need the sugar!'

Sienna groaned and pressed her hand to her stomach as she put away her cleaning materials and untied her apron. 'Thank you, but I'll stick to the antipasti. I was the one who had to share in six table picnics! It's so embarrassing when you can't manage to eat the same amount of pink cake as a six year old.'

Brett very carefully poured a tasting sample of the wine into two large wineglasses.

'Well, I hope this wine goes some way to saying thank you. Chris would like to add it to our wine list in the new restaurant. You're the expert. I would welcome your opinion.'

'Modesty prevents me from bragging, but I do love matching food with wine.'

Brett sat back in the new dining-room chair, legs stretched out under the table, and watched Sienna as she swirled the wine in the glass, her nose deep inside the wide bowl, sighing in appreciation before taking a tiny sip.

Delicate fingers selected a choice sliver of salty Parma ham and popped it into her mouth with pleasure, and a brief moan of delight that had fireworks lighting all over his body.

'That's good with the ham. Actually, I would go so far as to say that it's *very* good.' She lifted the glass towards him for a refill.

'Well, you certainly surprised me today, Miss Rossi.'

'Me, Chef Cameron?'

'You were brilliant! Truly! I always knew that head waiters went beyond the call of duty for their guests, but running a puppet show was a great idea.'

'Oh, it's amazing what you can do with paper napkins and a marker pen! You should try it some time—especially if you intend to run a family restaurant.'

'Which I do! Plus, someone who looked remarkably like you was singing. And for a moment you were actually making pizza with the kids. So tell me what else you don't do.'

'What do you mean?'

'Well, you told me that you don't sing and you can't cook. I was hoping that you would tell me that you never, ever go out with pizza chefs.'

Sienna put down her glass and leant slightly forward before saying, in a clear, low voice, 'I never, ever go out with chefs. Pizza or otherwise.'

There was just enough emotion in her voice for Brett to hold her gaze.

'I take it you have tried it and been burnt?'

'That's right.'

Brett opened his mouth to say something and then shook his head.

'Not André Michon from Greystone Manor? I mean, he's brilliant, and I wouldn't blame you, but…'

Sienna laughed out loud.

'No. I adore him—and so does his lovely wife. No. Definitely not André.'

Brett picked up the extra tension in the room when she was the first to break eye contact and focus instead on the glass of red wine which she was holding onto with both hands.

'I'm surprised that Maria didn't keep you up to date with the gossip on my past love-life.' Her eyes flicked up and saw his confusion. 'Obviously not. The truth is that I was engaged to a chef a few years ago and it ended badly. So that's another reason for me to stay *out* of the kitchen and never, ever go out with pizza chefs.' She raised her glass and toasted Brett with a smile.

'He must have been quite someone. Would I know him?'

She faltered for a few seconds before replying as casually as she could, with a slight nod. 'You might do. It's no secret, and someone is bound to tell you. Does the name Angelo Peruzi ring any bells?'

There was a stunned silence for a few seconds before he replied in a low voice, 'You were engaged to *Angelo Peruzi?*'

'And he was engaged to me. Only he seemed to forget that fact when he moved back to Los Angeles.'

Brett blew out hard and raised his glass towards her. 'Peruzi. I met him at an award ceremony in Milan. Like I say, you are certainly full of surprises. He's a lucky man. I'm sorry it didn't work out.'

She popped a stuffed olive into her mouth and played with some bread for far longer than necessary before answering.

'So am I. And, yes, he *was* a lucky man. Long gone. Or should I say he *was* long gone? The wine is brilliant with the bread but a disaster with the olives. Sorry.'

Brett took a sip of the wine and winced.

'Right again. The wine stays. The olives are out. And you are changing the subject. Do you mean that Peruzi is back in London? I haven't heard anything about that.'

'Then here is a piece of juicy gossip hot off the press. You already know that André Michon is retiring at the end of the month. Well, come March Angelo Peruzi is going to be the new head chef at Greystone Manor. He is definitely back! It was officially announced yesterday, so I think I have a few days' grace before my friends start calling to find out what's going on.'

Brett pursed his lips together. 'How do you feel about working with him again? Isn't that going to be a little awkward? Or do you think you will get back together again?'

'Back with Angelo? No. Never,' Sienna replied in a dark voice, with a firm shake of her head. 'And *awkward* does not come close. But the truth is I don't have many options. I *have* to go back to Greystone.'

She looked around the room before turning back to him with a smile. 'This has been fun, and I want to help Maria as much as I can, but I have responsibilities. People are relying on me. I have worked so hard to be promoted to restaurant manager; I really can't afford to miss the opportunity.'

Brett reached out and wrapped his long fingers around her hand so tenderly that the touch of his fingertips on the back of her hand took her by surprise.

'Congratulations on your promotion. But there are always options. Other jobs.' His head lifted. 'Here is an idea. Why don't you come and work for me? I don't have a head waiter or a sommelier. Actually, I don't have *any* staff at the minute! You can start with a clean slate. The entire Rossi family can visit and party any time they like—there's plenty of space. It would be great!'

He gave her one of those smiles designed to melt the heart of any woman within a hundred paces. And for a moment she was tempted. Very, very tempted. Except of course it would change nothing. She would spend the rest of her life waiting to be let down.

She reluctantly slid her hand away from his grasp as she gave him a thin smile.

'Thanks for the offer. And I really mean that. But it won't work. Why should I run away because my ex boyfriend is back in town? No, Brett. I can do my job. I lost my home and my career to Angelo once before. I'm not losing it again. I know it won't be easy, but I can do it. I won't let any man run my life for me again.'

Sienna turned away from him and gazed out through the new window towards the rooftops, where the light was already fading to dusk in the low winter sun.

Sienna straightened her back, suddenly conscious of the fact that she had said more about her personal life in the last few hours than in the past year. This was the first time she had actually said the words out loud.

But even scarier was the fact that Brett Cameron was sitting across the table from her. Watching her. Studying her.

'Would you mind if we change the subject? That's next week's challenge. Right now I just want to get through Valentine's Day! Here's a question for you. How did the young Brett Cameron come to meet my aunt Maria in the first place? I'm far more interested in hearing *that* story.'

Brett dropped his head back and howled with laughter.

'You mean, she didn't tell you?'

He stretched out his arms on the table as Sienna shook her head.

'I ate all her food! When I was nineteen, Maria came to my catering college to do a demonstration about yeast and pizza dough. Different shapes and sizes and what you can serve with them. That sort of thing. I was in trouble for fighting, and my punishment was to clear up after the cookery class.'

'Hold it there. You were *fighting*?' Her face screwed up in disbelief. 'I find that hard to believe.'

'Oh, believe it,' he replied with a nod. 'I had only been there two months, and every one in my class took it in turns to come up with new insults for the stupid new guy who couldn't even read or write.'

He sighed out loud and grimaced. 'I won't repeat them. Just use your imagination. Believe me, it is no fun when you can't read. I was angry. Angry at my mum for moving—again! Perhaps if we'd stayed in one place someone might have spotted the problem and done something about it, instead of jumping to the easy conclusion that I was stupid, or lazy, and destined to follow my mum as a transient. Most of the time I think they were glad to see the back of me.'

'That must have been so hard. I'm sorry.'

'More frustrating than hard. I was angry at myself because I just couldn't work out what I was missing that the others found so easy! Angry at the teachers who were too stressed to ask why. And then one day a bully pushed me too far and I pushed back.'

She meshed the fingers of one hand between his and was rewarded with a smile.

He leant forward toward her. 'The thing Maria didn't know was that I had been working in the evenings at a pizza shop—my famous pizza spinning lessons—so when everyone had cleared out I picked up the leftover dough and ingredients and started making things with them. After half an hour I had a pretty decent foccacia on the table, and a couple of mini pizzas. My plan was to take them home for dinner, but I was so hungry that I started to eat them. Just as Maria came back.'

'Oh, no. What did she say?'

Brett grinned and shook his head. 'She said a lot. I ate. She asked questions. It didn't take her long to realise that I had memorised the recipes and had some talent. She offered me a job as a kitchen slave six nights a week and every weekend. Right here.'

He paused and looked around.

'Have you ever noticed that there are no cookbooks in your aunt's kitchen? Not one. There are some in the house, but they are for show. Maria recognised that we shared something more than talent and a love of great food. She knew she had dyslexia, and had come up with her own ways of coping. She recognised the symptoms in me, and thought there was a good chance that I had dyslexia too.'

'Wow. My dad told me that she had dyslexia a few years ago, but I didn't really give it any thought. She's my aunt Maria and that's the only thing that matters.'

His fingers moved slowly over the surface of her hand, pressing out her fingers as he spoke with such devastating intensity that speech was not possible.

'She is also an amazingly stubborn lady. It took Maria three months to persuade me to be tested at a special unit. I didn't want to go and have more assessments! More tests and exams that I was bound to get wrong because I couldn't read. I was tired of being pigeonholed as an academic failure who was simply lazy and had to try harder. What a joke that was. As far as I was concerned it was one more way for the system to hang a label around my neck with the word *loser* on it.'

The pressure of his thumb on her knuckles had increased so much that Sienna almost cried out for fear of being bruised, but something stilled in his face as he looked into her eyes, and he released her with a brief smile.

'In the end it was the best thing that ever happened to me. Do you know I had never even heard the word *dyslexia* until the assessor told me what the tests were about? These tests were different. Patterns. Shapes. And logic. Not just words and sentences.'

Brett reached out for his wineglass and took a long sip before going on.

'I remember I was sitting outside the test room with Maria when the assessor came out and said that my scores were some of the highest he had ever seen. I was clever and visually gifted. Artistic and creative. And I had dyslexia. Not a severe case compared to some people, but enough to make a difference in most parts of my life where letters were concerned.'

He glanced up at her. 'Of course the first thing I thought was—oh, great, now the bullies get to call me mentally handicapped. Brilliant! But Maria made me sit and listen to what they could do to help make things easier at college. Like reading the recipes out before class. Using video and tapes. I could even record the lessons. Suddenly I saw I had a chance.' He chuckled. 'It was still tough. Especially at exam time. But Chris helped in Paris. And I have a better memory than most people. The rest, as they say, is history. So now you know. That's how I found out that I have dyslexia.'

He sat back now, and his shoulders seemed to drop a little.

'But, to look on the bright side, my lack of

ability with printed words might have held back my academic studies, but it always felt so natural to cook, to create—I would have missed out on all that with a traditional education.'

Brett lifted his glass and smiled.

'Can I suggest a toast to the lovely Maria? Who taught me that sometimes it pays to be stubborn even when the rest of the world thinks you are worthless.'

'No. I'm going to raise my glass to both of you. You should be proud of what you have achieved. Thank you for being so honest. It means a lot.'

'You're welcome. To Maria!'

'Maria and Brett! Two of the most remarkable people I have ever met.'

She hadn't meant to say that. It had just come out. From the shocked look in Brett's eyes he'd been expecting it even less, and it took him a few seconds to recover.

'Thank you. And you're not so bad yourself. Restaurant Manager Rossi.'

With a sudden burst of energy, Brett stood up from the table and reached across to the worktop for birthday cake.

'Speaking of which, if I am so remarkable, perhaps I can persuade you to change your mind about my earlier offer?'

'Birthday cake?'

'If you like. Or working for me? Take your

pick. Come on.' He bent down to her eye level and wafted the cake in front of her. 'You like Chris and Jess. We seem to get on all right. Come and work with me instead of at stuffy old Greystone Manor. You won't regret it.'

Sienna put down her glass very gently and stood up.

'Thanks, but no. To cake, *and* your job offer.'

Sienna stood in silence and watched one of the few men she had ever come this close to push his hands into his jean pockets, shoulders high to his neck with stress, his disappointment lingering like a bitter taste on the air.

He was so gentle and tender. So understanding.

She wanted to run to him. Hug him. Tell him that she would love to spend time with him in this enchanted place.

But that would mean trusting him with her happiness. Even for a few short days. Until he went one way and she another. And she couldn't do that. To either of them.

Because she could never trust another lover to also be her business partner. She knew now that love demanded absolute truth. In business, that same trust could kill you if the going got tough.

There was no future for her here, or in working with Brett.

Not now. Not ever.

CHAPTER SIXTEEN

Step 16: Smother in Wild Mushroom and Cream Sauce

SIENNA TURNED over and pulled the duvet a little closer around her shoulders as she snuggled down into the pillow and gave a little sigh of contentment.

Mmm. She was almost annoyed that she was being woken from such a sweet dream, in which Brett had carried her in his arms and laid her on a thick, warm bed.

Lovely.

She felt safe. This was such a comfy bed. Ultra-soft feather pillow. She could lie here all day.

Someone was knocking on her door, but she could afford to snuggle just a *little* longer. Birthday parties could be such hard work!

Her eyes creaked open. Just a little. Just to check the time. Strange that her alarm had not gone off.

She stretched out her arm towards the bedside cabinet.

The alarm had not gone off because it was two thirty in the morning.

She pulled her arm back under the warm duvet and closed her eyes. For one complete millisecond. Before snapping them open and sitting up in the bed.

She collapsed back down again onto the pillows with a groan, and pulled the duvet over her head.

This was Maria's house, and something had woken her up in the middle of the night.

And the knocking had not gone away.

'Are you decent in there? I have coffee.'

She glanced down at her clothing before answering Brett. She was wearing her aunt's thick pink pajamas.

Yes, she was decent.

'Coffee would be good,' was her feeble reply, as she pushed herself up the bed and drew the covers up to cover her chest. *Pathetic. This was what happened when you agreed to work with chefs who assumed that you would be available twenty-four hours a day!*

'Have you any idea what time it is? It's the middle of the night! What are you doing knocking on my bedroom door at two in the morning? I should warn you that I have one of Maria's stiletto shoes and my brother's phone number if you try anything.'

Brett stopped pacing her bedroom for a few seconds to stare at her as though the problem was so obvious that she should have been able to work it out for herself.

'The three-mushroom sauce. It's not working. I've made it four times and it is still not working. I am going crazy.' He leant closer, so that their noses were almost touching. 'See these grey hairs? Crazy.'

'Mushroom sauce? Oh, thank goodness. Is that all?' Sienna replied as she collapsed back on the pillows.

'All? Oh, no, no. You don't understand. That is not *all*. Without the mushroom sauce I don't have wild-mushroom pasta, and we don't have anything to finish the braised organic chicken breast. Seriously, that chicken needs this sauce, and I am not going to bed until my recipe is perfect.'

Brett was pacing back and forward so rapidly that Sienna feared for the bedroom carpet. His own coffee was untouched, which was probably a good thing considering how much adrenaline must be rushing around his system.

He was obsessing about a sauce recipe.

Chefs. You either loved them or tolerated them, but either way you had to learn to live with them.

She covered her wide yawn with her hand before nodding between half closed eyes.

'Okay, I understand. Mushroom sauce. Got it. What can I do to help?'

'Thought you'd never ask. I need to borrow those amazing tastebuds of yours, because after four hours of this mine are fried. Tell me what you are about to eat. I want the fragrance of this sauce to tantalise your senses way before it hits, and then…'

'Then the flavour. I know. I can't guarantee that my tastebuds will be very responsive at this time of the morning, but I'll do what I can. Talk to me about the dish. What are the base notes?'

'Not this time. Tonight I want this sauce to do the talking for me. When those lovers taste this baby they will be putty in their partners' hands. So get ready to be blown away.'

'I'll be down in five minutes.'

Sienna sat down opposite Brett in the tiny kitchen and watched him fuss, stepping and reaching from pan to pan, dipping his tasting spoon into one then the other. Then grinding more black pepper and tasting again.

'Oh. Big talk from the big guy. So actually you are doing this for the boys, not the ladies? Is that right? Let me take a look in those pans. I'll soon tell you what I would be prepared to eat. *If* you can take the pressure?'

'Sorry. I want those girls looking at their dates, not the food.'

He reached forward and slid his bandana over Sienna's head, so that it rested on her forehead. 'Perfect. This test we are going to do blindfold.'

She lifted one hand to pull off the bandana, but he wafted her away with his fingertips.

'What? You don't want me to see what the food looks like?'

'It's the only way. I'll bring the pan over and feed you tiny spoonfuls so you can savour it. Then tell me the first thing that comes into your head. Okay?'

'Well, this is certainly going to be a first, but all right. I can tell you what my impressions are.'

'Excellent. But first you need to focus. All your concentration has to be on the dish. Don't mind me as I potter around. Just speak your mind. Ready?'

Sienna watched as Brett drew a tiny saucepan from the heat and left it to cool slightly on one side. She could sense her heart racing as he stepped in front of her. So close that his T-shirt was touching her dressing gown. He smelt of so many savoury odours she could almost have told him the ingredients he had been working with right there and then.

But where would the fun be in that? And, more importantly, what had he left out from the final recipe?

Her breathing sped up to match her heart as

Brett hunkered down a little and flashed her one of his special killer grins as his hands moved either side of her head.

'Ready to be blown away?'

'Promises, promises. Let's go. Some of us need our beauty sleep!'

'I do wish you wouldn't talk about me like that! But you're right. Busy day tomorrow. Here we go.'

The bandana slid over her brow and rested on her nose. The last thing she saw was the burn marks on the underside of his arm as he slid the cloth lower. Her heart went out to him. He truly had suffered to get where he was.

The roof faded into a very dim glow, with only the electric lights as spots she could recognise.

'That works. Can't see a thing.'

'Excellent. I could be cooking topless and you wouldn't know.'

Oh, you are so wrong about that, she thought.

Through the faint sound of the radio in the background she could hear him rubbing the work-rough palms of his hands together as he dried them on the towel tucked into the waistband of his apron. Her whole body seemed to tune out the background noise from the electrical equipment, the hum of the refrigerator and extractor fans, and the gentle patter of the rain as it fell against the glass of the kitchen window.

And the sound of her breath as she waited for Brett to serve her something totally, totally delectable and delicious.

I want this to be the most delicious thing this amazing woman has ever tasted. Anywhere. And it's the worst mushroom sauce I have ever made in my life. What is wrong with me? I have made this in frantic, mad and busy kitchens in Hong Kong, New York and Adelaide and it was fantastic. Then I come to Rossi's and something is completely off.

He turned around just as Sienna shifted her position on what had to be the most uncomfortable chair in the city.

Then I drag this woman out of her bed in the middle of the night. In her pyjamas.

He stepped to one side and took in the view, confident that he was unlikely to be swiped around the head with something solid since she was wearing his bandana over her eyes.

Pink check pyjama bottoms which ended just below her knees. Maria's. Had to be Maria's. That probably meant that she was wearing the matching jacket under Maria's housecoat, which had certainly seen better days.

And probably nothing underneath. The only thing that separated Sienna Rossi from Brett and the outside world were two thin layers of flannelette and a wicked smile.

The metal soup ladle in Brett's hand developed a mind of its own and clattered onto the hard floor, making her jump.

'Sorry. Be with you in a moment. The temperature has to be perfect. Get ready. Three. Two. One'

He leant against the worktop, dipped a new spoon into a small bowl of the best sauce and wiped it on the edge of the saucer before lifting it carefully the few inches towards Sienna and wafting it gently in front of her nose.

Her full, luscious lips opened a little as she inhaled the aroma, and Brett carefully fed her a small spoonful of the sauce between her lips, touching the upper lip so that her tongue came out and licked the thick creamy sauce away.

It was the most erotic thing he had seen in a very, very long time.

Until now he had been totally mesmerised by her eyes. Not now. Not any longer. Her mouth was so enticing it should probably be licensed, or covered up during the daytime to prevent exposure to the unprepared.

She had the power to hold him spellbound, and the warm bowl of sauce was cooling in his hands as he stared, transfixed, at Sienna. Strange how he could not force himself to look away from that amazing mouth.

Her tongue flicked out and wiped across her

lower lip, leaving a moist and succulent impression like dew on a ripe peach.

Intoxicating.

'I'm getting white wine, celery, finely chopped shallots, a touch of garlic and a sweet herb. Tarragon, and I think lemon thyme and parsley with a touch of garlic. Am I right?'

'Uh-huh. Now the mushrooms. Tell me about the mushrooms.'

He speared a few choice segments and raised them towards Sienna, whose lips were slightly apart, displaying perfect teeth, just waiting for the next delicious treat.

He paused for a second and swallowed down too many months of celibacy and many years of loneliness, then brought the spoon close enough for her to savour the aroma with a pleasing *mmm* of pleasure before he popped the mushrooms between her lips.

She chewed slowly, as though savouring every possible experience.

'This is amazing. I'm getting at least three different textures. There is a meaty earthiness in one of the mushrooms—I think it has to be dried porcini or a wild mushroom—but then I find a smooth taste which is so silky with that creamy sauce. The last one is a chestnut. I'd recognise that texture anywhere, but I have never tasted anything like this combination. It's brilliant.'

'One more,' he whispered. 'There is one extra ingredient that's going to make all the difference.'

'More? There's more? I don't know how you're going to top those mushrooms.'

Brett dipped his spoon into the second pan and tasted a mouthful of the strips of caramelised sweet onions and fresh field mushrooms with aged balsamic vinegar he was planning to use as a garnish for the chicken dish.

It was sweet, yet intensely savoury and special. And the perfect temperature.

'This is the final touch. Ready?'

She nodded once and her lips parted.

Brett wet his lips on the spoon.

Leant in. And kissed her.

She kissed him back. Sweet. Soft. Warm. Melting. Tender. Everything he had been expecting, wanting, desiring for so very long since *she* had kissed *him*.

Her hands came up and slid the blindfold away, so that her eyes were totally fixed on his. Unblinking, intense, her mouth still partly open.

'Balsamic vinegar reduction,' she whispered, her mouth only an inch from his as he held his stance with his arms stretched out on the table. 'You're right. It's the perfect final touch. And so much better than from a spoon. Can I have some more?'

This time she was the one who leant forward,

so that he could kiss her more deeply, prolonging the contact between them. They broke off forehead to forehead, her breathing keeping pace with his racing heart rate as he rolled his forehead to the other side so that he could slide his unshaven chin up against her temple and back down to her mouth, the friction acting like wood to the fire.

Her eyes stayed closed as he kissed her again, one hand pressed against the back of her head, drawing her deeper into his kiss. Deeper, and with an intensity that left them both ragged and out of breath when they broke off long enough for Sienna to lift from the chair and slide around the table, so that she could hold Brett's face and then work her sensitive fingers through his hair.

It was driving him mad.

His kisses moved over her chin, down her neck, then across to the other side, and as she tilted her head back with a sigh, she whispered, 'Promise me something?'

'Anything,' he managed to get out, before his mouth got busy on the sensitive skin on her temple.

'You will never make that exact recipe for anyone else.'

'I made it just for you. It's always been just for you.'

'In that case…what were you planning to serve for dessert?'

'Dessert? You want dessert?'

Brett froze in astonishment for a few seconds, before dropping back his head and laughing out loud with warm, joyous laughter that came from deep in his body. Wild, fun, natural and totally happy laughter that was so infectious Sienna could not resist laughing back in return, with a gentle thump on his chest.

'What's so funny?'

'You are.' He wiped away a tear of laughter with the back of a knuckle before shaking his head and lifting away a stray strand of her bed hair.

'Have you always been so demanding of your chefs, Miss Rossi?'

'Oh, this is nothing,' she replied in a mock serious voice. 'I can be much bossier when the occasion demands. Although it will be quite a challenge for you to come up with something to beat that sauce.'

She tilted her head and smiled into his face.

'I am thinking chocolate. Coffee. Cream, of course. The rest I shall leave to you.'

'Well, thank you. I'm sure I can think of something which will hit the spot!' His eyebrows lifted in a cheeky grin and she tutted in response.

'Please. I presume you are planning to serve desserts in this fabulous new restaurant of yours?'

He nodded in agreement and moved back a

little. 'Speaking of which, I told you the other evening that I never break a promise—especially to a pretty lady... Well I have to break one tomorrow. But it is entirely your fault...'

'My fault?' she protested innocently. 'How can this possibly be?'

'I need to see Chris and the architects about some final decisions on the layout. That means heading across to my new kitchen. And I promised that I was all yours for a few days. On the other hand you could always come with me and cast your trained eye over my new building. Are you busy tomorrow morning?'

She closed her eyes and turned her head, so that his stubbly chin would have better access to her throat, trying to remember what day of the week it was and other unimportant things, like her name and what precisely she was doing here.

She had always known deep in her heart that Brett would be an amazing kisser, but nothing had prepared her for the depth of sensation his mouth on her throat would generate.

'Do you mean today tomorrow, or tomorrow tomorrow?'

'Today tomorrow. I'd love to show you where Chris has been spending his time these last few months.'

He moved forward to face her, his hands moving through her long loose hair and lifting it

from her shoulders as it fell through his fingers—
then he smoothed it down her forehead

'You want me to visit your new restaurant?'

'Think of it as a special outing after the
amazing job you did yesterday.'

He moved forward with feather-light kisses
on her forehead, and she closed her eyes as his
lips slid gently down to her temple, heating up
the blood which was already pumping hot and
fast through her body.

'*We* did a good job, Chef Cameron. Are you
looking for an interior designer?'

'No. But I can always use an expert opinion.'

'You make it very hard for a girl to say no.'

'Then don't. I'll make it easy. Just repeat after
me—Yes, Brett, I'd like to see the kitchen where
your dream will come true.'

'Well, when you put it like that… Yes, Brett,
I'd *love* to see the kitchen where your dream will
come true.'

'Then we have a date in about—' and he
glanced over her shoulder at his wristwatch, since
his hand was still busy stroking her hair '—seven
hours from now. Do you think you can be ready
to face the outside world by then, sleepy-head?
Because I do have one suggestion—you might
want to rethink your footwear before we hit the
building site.'

She reluctantly forced her eyes to leave Brett's

long enough to glance at her feet. Then blinked and stared hard. Her left foot was inside a brown loafer. Only the toes of her right foot were poking daintily out from an open toed bright yellow sandal decorated with huge white daisies— Maria's summer specials.

'Oh. You see—this is what happens when I am woken up in the middle of the night by chefs looking for a food-taster.'

'In that case I shall have to do this more often.'

Sienna looked up into those hot bright eyes. There was no doubt whatsoever that he was referring to a lot more than comparing the flavour of sauce recipes.

Electrical energy crackled in the air between them—hot enough to burn paper—and her resolve crisped into white ash in the intense heat of his gaze.

She should be angry with Brett for showing her just how very wrong she had been—about so many things. But as his fingertips stroked her forehead and his lips found pleasure in the place between her jaw and throat it was impossible.

Brett Cameron had shown her that she was a woman a man like Brett could, would, *was able to* find desirable. He had even told her that she was beautiful! Every one of his touches gave her a glimpse of hope that another man *could* come to care about her.

She sucked in a breath as he found a particularly sensitive spot in the hollow behind her ear, and was rewarded with a low sigh.

Was it possible that she could fall in love again? And be loved in return?

Or was she in danger of making precisely the same mistake she had made before?

Chef-magnet.

This was all happening too fast. Too hot. And way, way, too intense for her poor brain to process what had just happened and make sense of it all.

'This has been a long day, Brett. Like I said, a girl needs her beauty sleep. And, no, that wasn't a cue for compliments.'

'You're going?'

She glanced across at the saucepans before smiling up at him. 'Maria made the right choice when she asked you to help with the cooking. I can't wait for that dessert. See you at breakfast.'

His hands moved over her shoulders and down her upper arms before he stepped back.

'Sleep well. Unless, of course, you want me to pop in and wake you up in the morning?'

She swallowed down hard at that prospect!

'Thank you, but I have my alarm clock. Goodnight, Brett. Goodnight.'

CHAPTER SEVENTEEN

Step 17: Mix with Three Heaped Spoonfuls of Tears

'I CAN hear your brain ticking from here! What's the hot topic today? Shoes? Dresses? Or let me guess. Which wine are you going to recommend for the chicken in mushroom sauce?'

Sienna half turned in the passenger seat of the Jaguar and stared at Brett in disbelief.

'I knew that you could multi-task. Nothing about mind-reading! How did you work that one out?'

He flashed a quick smile, which made Sienna grateful that she was already sitting down. 'You couldn't wait to scribble down my crazy ideas for the Valentine's Day menu this morning. Perhaps it was a mistake to talk about my seven-hour braised lamb at breakfast time?'

A puff of dismissal came from the passenger seat. 'I think you selected those dishes just to test me. I mean, ravioli with spinach *and* blue cheese after garlic mushrooms?'

'I prefer to think of it as a challenge to a sommelier of your talents. Guinea fowl with polenta? That has to be straightforward.'

'It would be—if you took out the parmesan and onion crisp garnish. And I really think you ought to reconsider the flavouring on the gnocchi. I'm just not sure the local high school boys are ready for that mushroom sauce.'

'Ah, but it's not for the boys, is it? That sauce is definitely one for the laydees!'

She slapped his knee with a light touch of her notebook.

'A medium red. Black cherry and plum, with some time in oak to offset the earthy mushroom flavours, but not too dry.'

'I can inhale it from here. Fantastic. What about a white?'

'Still thinking about that one,' she hissed. 'Pest.' She tapped the end of her pen against her chin. This pen was in a boring plain colour, and Brett was already missing the pink rubber flamingo.

'You must do this all the time as Head Waiter? Matching food and wine? That's quite a skill.'

'One of my favourite parts of the job. André and I can chat for hours comparing several bottles of the same grape variety from different parts of the world. I love it.'

'I can hear that in your voice. Greystone is lucky to have you. In fact, that gives me an idea. Chris has been interviewing for a sommelier for weeks. I'm going to be working flat out. Is there any chance you could sit in on the interviews and help him get though the shortlist? I need someone I can work with, who knows what they are doing! Unless of course…' He paused for a moment to focus on the road ahead, where there were multiple lanes of traffic.

'Unless?' she asked, when they were safely on a straight road.

'Unless I can steal you away from Angelo Peruzi!' he replied in a jaunty voice, completely unaware of how that simple statement ripped her apart. 'Come to work with me as my restaurant manager. Take a risk for once. Surprise yourself.'

Too late for that! She had spent most of the night after leaving the hot, hot kitchen dreaming about the life she could have with Brett by her side as her lover, if not her business partner. Working through the options. Trying to decide if she could trust this remarkable man to be her friend.

'You really don't know when to give up, do you?' Sienna replied, trying to keep her voice casual and jokey. 'I am deeply flattered, Brett. I truly am. But I know what it is like to open a new restaurant. That sort of pressure can destroy a friendship. I don't want that to happen.'

He quickly squeezed her leg in reply. 'Can't blame me for trying. I agree. Good friends are hard to come by.'

Suddenly distracted by a car horn, Brett turned back to his driving, and Sienna took a breath and looked out across the bustling London traffic to the lovely shops and art galleries they were shuffling past.

They were almost there. The narrow lanes around Notting Hill were just a few streets away.

Sienna shivered inside her coat. There was one thing that she had not told Brett when they set out that morning.

This was the first time she had been back to Notting Hill in four years. Former friends and old colleagues who lived in the area had invited her to their homes many times and she had always refused. The pain and the loss had still been too fresh.

Each street they were driving down linked her back to powerful and emotional memories which only seemed to intensify as they came closer to the site of Angelo's restaurant.

Protective instincts raised their ugly heads, poking fun at her apparent self-control, and the old anxieties rose inside her, low enough for her to master, but nagging away loud enough for her to be aware of them.

Heart racing, she turned for reassurance and

support to the only person she knew would understand. Brett's face was full of all of the excitement and happy anticipation of a child on Christmas morning. It was all there for the world to see.

He started to hum along to an old song on the radio, and her heart listened and slowed a little. Tears pricked Sienna's eyes, threatening, but she blinked them away with logic.

It was only natural that she should feel a little sentimental, coming back to these streets that she'd used to know so well.

But one thing was certain: she was not going to allow her foolish anxiety to spoil Brett's day. This new restaurant was *his* dream, and he had asked her to share with him the special moment when he explored what was going to become his very own kitchen.

He had worked so hard to be driving here today. He deserved this.

Suddenly Sienna found herself joining in with Brett, happy to drink in the enthusiasm and positive energy that emanated from this finger-tapping, song-humming *tour de force*.

Without Brett she would probably never have found the strength to come back here. And with Brett? With Brett by her side she could do anything!

No tears. No trauma. Angelo's was part of her past, not her future!

She grabbed hold of that excuse for putting aside her own lingering doubts about her future role and grinned across at Brett. Friend or lover. She could still share this moment with him.

'Did you know that our restaurant used to be in Notting Hill? You've chosen a great location! And, from what Chris told me, the building work is almost complete. You must be very excited. Tell me about your plans.'

'It's a *fantastic* location! I had mixed feelings about coming back to London, but now the plans are coming together it is starting to feel as though I was meant to be here.'

He turned into a street lined by market shops and gestured from side to side. 'In fact, standing in the kitchen last night, I was thinking about my very first day at Trattoria Rossi.'

Brett laughed and slapped his hands down on the steering wheel as Sienna stared at his face, which had been transformed by such an expression of joy and pleasure it seemed as though every crease in that hard-working face was smiling.

'Maria set me to work paring and chopping vegetables for hours.' He shot her a glance. 'I'll never forget it. I was so nervous about getting it wrong I think I dropped my peeler on the floor a dozen times. I ended up spending more time washing up than actually cooking.'

They both laughed out loud, the sound of their

shared laughter echoing around the confined space, warming her more than the bright sunshine.

'After a few days I progressed to actually frying onions and shallots and garlic, and by the end of my first week I was making minestrone soup.'

'Minestrone! You must have been doing something right!'

'I had a great time. Your aunt Maria gave me a chance, Sienna. Without her I would have spent a lot longer getting started in this crazy world.'

'But you would have got here in the end. Wouldn't you?'

He bowed slightly. 'Maybe, but I know that she made the difference. And of course without Maria I would never have met you!'

Sienna's heart was thumping so loudly she was sure Brett must be able to feel the vibration through the driver's seat. 'Would that have been a loss or a bonus?'

A wry smile creased one corner of his mouth, but he kept his gaze firmly on the road ahead. 'Loss. No doubt. Especially since my satellite navigation system has failed and we are now lost. Do your skills extend to navigating around Notting Hill?'

'I travelled down this road every day for eighteen months,' she replied with a dismissive snort. 'What's the address?'

Brett recited the house number and street that he had dreamt about, researched on the Internet, and planned and schemed about so often that it had become ingrained into his brain. New destination. New start. His dream come true.

'Take the next right turn,' she replied, in a faint voice tinged with anxiety. A few minutes later he pulled into the car park of the building site which was destined to be his new home, screeched to a halt and cut the engine.

He turned to look at Sienna and tried to rub some life back into her cold fingers. Winter sunshine, bright and clear, pierced the clouds and highlighted the pain in her tight-lipped face.

'What is it? Tell me what's going on.'

She seemed to come out of her trance for a moment and looked down at his hands, tracing her fingers along the scars she had never commented on before. White, pink, old and new. The scars of a working chef who had served his time.

'Look at all these cuts. Burn marks.' She lifted her head and faced him on. 'Some of us have our scars on the inside.'

He steadied himself for the hard news that was coming next. She forced herself to smile. That simple twist of her mouth and glistening eyes melted his heart.

'Please ignore me. My own restaurant was down this road. I had no idea that it would be so hard to come back. Too many memories. That's all.'

She shuffled out of her seat to stand next to him, sniffing gently, and stared past him towards the building which, to Brett's eyes, was a lot more like a restaurant than it had been a few days earlier.

'I'm okay. Really. I'm fine now.' She seemed to give herself a mental shake, looped her arm through his and grinned. 'I want to see everything.'

A short, plump, pink-faced, dark-haired man in a warm jacket and yellow safety helmet was striding up to Sienna, and before Brett could intervene Chris thumped Brett hard on the shoulder and nodded towards Sienna with a huge grin.

'Well, I thought you would change her mind eventually. Welcome to the team, Sienna!' He stretched out his hand towards her.

She simply smiled and shook her head. 'Hello, Chris. What team? Have I missed something?'

'Our new restaurant manager, of course. I knew my boy Brett here would use his charm to win you around in the end. You have to admit his interview technique gets results with the ladies!'

Sienna stared at Chris's hand as if it was toxic waste for a second before turning to stare at Brett, who was groaning and glaring at Chris at the same time.

'Interviewing? So *that* is what you have been

doing these last few days. Charming me to come and work with you. Have I understood that correctly?'

'Sienna, please.' Brett stepped in front of her, his face anxious. 'Of course I would love it if you could come and work with us, but I know you already have a great promotion. You don't understand…'

'Oh, on the contrary. I understand very well indeed. Nice meeting you again, Mr Fraser. Good luck finding someone willing to work with this idiot! In the meantime, I'll take the bus back.'

And with that she turned and walked away from them, back towards the road, one hand pressed firmly against her mouth, preventing them from seeing her bitter tears.

Only she never reached it. With a slight stagger, she leant against the wall for support, her legs unsteady and threatening to give way beneath her.

Brett stood there, frozen, watching Sienna retreat inside herself to a place where he could not go. He barely recognised the woman who had leapt into his car with a spring in her step that morning.

Ignoring the fact that Chris and other members of his design team were coming up to greet him, Brett wound his way around the front of his car, looped his arm around Sienna's waist and half carried her as far as the passenger door, where she had some hope of catching her breath, or at least passing out with some dignity.

She faltered on the icy path, and as he held her tighter around the waist, taking her weight, he felt her heart beating under her sweater in the cold air. He knew his fate was sealed as he lowered her into the passenger seat.

She looked up at him in surprise, and then, as though recognising something in him she could trust until her dying day, she stared, white faced, into his concerned eyes.

'Do not say a word. Not one word. Simply get me out of here, Brett.'

'You got it.'

Brett grabbed his padded jacket and wrapped it around her shoulders, but he knew it would take more than a coat to stop this precious woman from shivering.

Doomed.

He was completely in love with Sienna Rossi.

No going back. This was it. He was going to find out who and what had broken this remarkable woman's heart and not stop until he had put those fractured pieces back together again.

Sienna squirmed against the sofa cushions and half opened her eyes, blinking in the glare from a single table light. She was leaning on something soft and pale blue.

She had fallen sideways, and her head was pressed into Brett's shoulder.

Horrified, she slid back to a sitting position and squeezed her eyes shut again as she yawned widely with both hands over her mouth.

When she opened them, Brett was scratching his scalp. It was a gesture she had seen him perform dozens of times before. Right hand, right side of his head, just above the ear. It was a wonder he was not bald in that spot.

'Looking for inspiration?'

He went pink around the neck, but stayed focused on the clever photos of perfect dishes on the pages of a book with a photo of a TV chef on the cover.

'I was hoping that this pastime would make me look more intellectual. On second thoughts, don't answer that. Not many girls fall asleep on me. This could be a bad sign.'

Sienna rubbed the back of her neck, turning her head from side to side.

'Sorry about using you for a pillow. Most embarrassing. Of course I blame you completely, for forcing me to drink hot chocolate on an empty stomach. Always knocks me sideways. How long was I out?'

'Over two hours. And you're welcome to cuddle up to me any time you like.'

He broke the tension then, by raising his eyebrows up and down a few times.

'Oh, slick. Very slick,' Sienna said, and grinned at him as she slid her feet to the carpet and stretched forward to take both of Brett's hands as he helped her stand.

He smiled back before replying in a soft voice, 'That's better. You always did have the cutest smile, Rossi. Even if you *are* dressed as a polar explorer.'

She stuck out the arms of her thick sweater and plucked at the cuffs. 'I work in air-conditioned restaurants and stone buildings all year round, but when I see real weather outside. Brrrr…'

She lifted away one corner of Maria's living-room curtains to demonstrate her point. And stared out. Open mouthed.

'It's snowing,' she eventually managed to pronounce, in a low, intense whisper.

Sienna almost pressed her nose to the glass, ignoring the vibration and engine noise of the cars whizzing past on the busy road on the other side of the pavement.

It *was* snowing. It was truly snowing. She could actually see the flakes against the darkness of the evening sky as they reflected back the light from the headlamps of passing cars and streetlights.

It was one of the most magical things she had ever seen.

'Brett! Look!' Without hesitation or thinking she grabbed his hand and hugged him tight against her so that he could see out of the window.

A wide grin spread out across his face, and she laughed out loud as he grabbed her by the waist and pulled her closer, so that the white flakes appeared to come straight at them through the layers of glass.

At that moment a large truck trundled past, momentarily blocking out the light, and the glass surface was instantly transformed into a mirror. Sienna found herself looking at two happy faces reflected in the glass.

Cameron and Rossi. Best team she had ever worked in.

Her head was pressed into Brett's neck, and he pressed his body along one side of hers so that he could share the first sight of snowflakes.

He was grinning, open-mouthed. So was she.

They were two happy people.

Then his smile faded—as did hers.

The reflection in the mirror window changed as Brett turned a few inches, so that she was close enough to feel his fast breath on her cheeks. She had nowhere to look but into his eyes.

His deep, intense, smiling eyes.

Laser probes burrowed into her skull and turned the sensible girl into mush.

His hand was still at her waist. The other meshed his fingers between hers and squeezed tightly as he spoke, his eyes never leaving hers.

'It's lovely.' *You are lovely.* 'Chris made a mistake this afternoon. I respect your choices.'

'I know. Going back to that street was just all too much for me. I feel quite foolish.'

He took a breath and his eyes scanned her face, as though checking that she was real. It was a millisecond before her neck was burning and her breathing had speeded up to match his.

'Not foolish at all,' he said, and smiled at her. 'But I do think it is time you told me exactly why you can't trust chefs. Stay right there!'

Suddenly he released her and slipped out of the room, leaving her staring ahead at the space he had occupied, while her heart rate struggled to return to normal. And failed.

Something inside her clicked into gear.

He deserved the truth. Even if it meant going back to a place she thought she had left behind.

CHAPTER EIGHTEEN

Step 18: And Two Pink Cupcakes

BRETT BREEZED back into the room, carrying a tray with two steaming beakers and a paper bag with pink glittery stars glued on it, which he opened and presented to her. He collapsed down on the sofa, completely unfazed by the fact that she was still standing at the window, staring out at the snowflakes with childlike fascination.

'Chris came round when you were having your nap. He says sorry for the misunderstanding about the job, and a big hi and thank you from Jess. You are now officially one of the princess gang, and I am commanded to present Your Royal Highness with these fine examples of baked goods as a token of their esteem. Apparently the nanny made them from a packet mix.'

He held up two pink cupcakes, each with a single pink cake candle sticking out from the centre, held in place by a thick blob of white icing.

Sienna and Brett both stared at the candles for a second in silence.

'Jess does have style. Decaf?'

All Sienna could manage was a single nod, and it took her several delicious sips of the hot, bittersweet drink before she was ready to speak.

'Brett?'

'Mmm?' he replied, between mouthfuls.

'Sorry about being so upset earlier. I'm...embarrassed about—well, what I must have looked like, and how my reaction was completely over the top. I had no right to be annoyed with you. Sorry.'

He shook his head and pursed his lips. 'You're not the one who should feel sorry. I should have made it clear to Chris that you had to make your own mind up and that I'd respect your decision either way. My mistake.'

He brushed crumbs into the paper bag, before sliding to the edge of the sofa. 'Now, I am under strict instructions that you have to eat one whole cupcake, or you are not an official princess.'

Sienna looked at the cake and swallowed hard. 'I don't think I can.'

'One whole cake. I promised Jess. And nobody goes hungry in this house.'

He slid the tray closer towards her.

'Slave driver,' she replied, but, since he was staring at her so intently, started peeling off the paper and broke the cake into two.

'That's better,' he said, reaching for his second. 'Hey!'

He brushed more crumbs from his fingers onto the tray. 'Okay. I'm ready to hear the whole story. We have coffee. We have something close to cake. Start talking. You can skip the bit about how his Hollywood charm made you swoon and get straight to the bit where you were working together at Angelo's restaurant. What really happened? What went wrong? And why did Frank not break his nose for you? Because I cannot believe for one minute that Angelo Peruzi dumped you. He's not *that* much of an idiot.'

'Yes, he is.' She found something very fascinating in the paper case. 'It's quite simple, really. Angelo Peruzi fell out of love with me, ran our business into the ground, and ran back home to California. He broke my heart and walked out on me. But in the end I was the one who broke up with him.' She paused.

'About a month before our wedding, I started taking calls from suppliers asking when their bills were going to be paid. Angelo insisted on taking care of all of the financial side of the restaurant, so I mentioned it to him straight away. He said it must be a mistake at the bank and he would sort it out and not to bother him again.' She lowered her head and shrugged. 'He hated to be challenged. About anything. Angelo had worked with his father in their restaurant all his life, and his food was amazing. He had the looks and the talent, and as far as he and his family were concerned he was the golden boy who could do no wrong.'

She smiled apologetically. 'I was not the only one who was dazzled by him. My family adored him. Until…the cracks started to appear. It was hard for him to admit that he couldn't handle the business side of things *and* run the kitchen and do promotional work and the thousand and one things he wanted to achieve. All at once.'

Brett rubbed the back of Sienna's neck—her strain was only too apparent.

'I was organising the wedding. He was in denial and refused to admit that he couldn't cope. Call it pride, arrogance—whatever. The end result was the same. We had a brilliant kitchen brigade and full tables every night. I had no idea that there was a problem with finance.'

Tiny fragments of cupcake icing had found their way onto her jumper, and she slowly picked them off, one by one, as Brett held her in silence.

'I remember the day I had to say goodbye to the staff—the tears, the hugs, the hours I spent sobbing alone that night after I'd closed the door for the last time.'

'Alone? You mean, he didn't even come back to thank his team? He left you here to handle the mess on your own?'

'He claimed that it would be too expensive to fly back for a few days, but I knew it was going to be too painful for him. Too traumatic.'

She shook her head from side to side. 'I still trusted him and believed in him. Even then. Angelo kept telling me that once the London restaurant was sold he would be able to pay off all of his debts and I would be free to move to Los Angeles and make our new home together in California.'

The muscles in Brett's neck clenched at the tension in her voice, and the anger rose in his soul as he suspected what was coming next.

'You know what really hurt?' she continued in a low voice. 'It wasn't the money, or that we had to sell the business. That was nothing compared to the fact that Angelo did not *tell* me there was a problem. I would have understood in a heartbeat. We were supposed to be partners! He knew that I would do anything for him—and that I trusted him without question.'

'He didn't know you,' Brett whispered.

'You're right. And I didn't know him, either. Perhaps that why it was such a surprise when he packed his bags and told me that he needed to go home for a few weeks. On his own. I thought *I* was his home.'

She gave a sarcastic laugh, but the tears still pricked her eyes as Brett asked her the question which had puzzled him from the start.

'I'm still confused about one thing. Why did you tell people that he had dumped you and headed back home? The truth was bound to come out eventually.'

'I didn't tell people anything. The family knew why I had broken off my engagement, but everyone else came to their own conclusions when Angelo did not come back. As for the truth? The Rossi family closed ranks and came to the conclusion that being duped once was humiliating enough for me, but being duped twice? That would make me a laughing stock. So no. The truth never came out. The suppliers were paid. And he got away with it. What a lucky escape. Eh?'

She had wrapped her arms around her body, as though trying to warm herself and block out the bone-penetrating icy wind and the snowflakes on the other side of the window glass.

Brett waited for her to go on, but her voice had grown gradually quieter and more choked as she spoke. Her last words were so full of pain that he felt a shiver of cold run across her shoulders and down her back.

He zipped open his own padded fleece jacket and stepped behind her, pressing his shirtfront against her back, his arms circling her waist, so that she was totally enclosed inside his warm embrace.

Neither of them spoke for a few minutes as Brett followed her gaze out to the snowflakes, his head pressed against her shoulder.

Her head fell forward. 'I should have known. It took him a total of three days after we sold the business to build up the courage to make the telephone call telling me that he thought we should take a break before I flew out to join him. It took me all of ten seconds to realise that he didn't want me. I had ceased to be useful. He was far too cowardly to admit that he did not love me any more, so I did the only thing I could do. I told him it was over. Not the best way for a relationship to end.'

'What did you do?'

A snort and a chuckle. 'I packed up the few possessions I had left and went home to my old bedroom in the Rossi house. I was exhausted, lonely, vulnerable, more than a little depressed, and very, very angry. At everyone! The family persuaded me not to get on a plane to California and confront him face to face, and it was my aunt Maria who gave me sanctuary until I was ready to start work again. I owe her just as much as you do—so thank you for helping me find a way to repay her.'

She glanced up at him over her right shoulder, and the pain in those limpid brown eyes was only too apparent through the faint smile.

Brett looked deep into those eyes and his heart melted.

After all she had been through, she still had the capacity for happiness.

She was remarkable!

He closed his eyes. He was holding Sienna Rossi in his arms, and it felt so right. So very right. How had he doubted that this was what he wanted? What he needed?

There was no way he could allow her to walk away from him.

Slowly, slowly, he dropped his hands to her waist and started to turn her around to face him.

As though awakening from a dream, Sienna realised that she was not alone, and her head twisted towards him inside the huge jacket. As her body turned slowly his hands shifted, so that when her chin was pressed against the front of his shirt his arms were around her back, pressing her forward.

In silence, his eyes closed, and he listened to her breathing, her head buried into the corner of his neck and throat.

Her arms, which had been trapped inside his

fleece, moved to circle around his waist, so that she could hold him closer.

A faint smile cracked Brett's face. She was hugging him back. Taking his warmth and devotion.

He dared not risk taking it any further. Dared not break that taste of trust she was offering him.

But Brett edged closer, hugging her tighter, and dropped his face a little so that his lips were in the vicinity of her forehead.

Sienna responded immediately, and looked up as he moved back just far enough so that their eyes locked.

For that single moment everything that had gone before meant nothing. They were a man and a woman who cared for one another very deeply, holding each other.

It seemed the most natural thing in the world for Brett to run his lips across her upturned forehead, then her closed eyes. He felt her mouth move against his neck. Stunned with the shock of the sensation, he almost jerked away, but then paused and pressed his face closer to hers, his arms tight on her back, willing his love to pass through his open hands, through the clothing to her core of her body.

Warming her. Begging her to trust him. But not daring to say the words that might break the spell.

This was unreal.

A single beam of light streamed out from a passing car on the road and caught on Sienna's face, like a spotlight. The golden light warmed her skin. They were both cold, but there was no way Brett would break this precious moment when the barriers were down and he could express what words would fail to convey.

His hands slid up and down her back. His mouth moved across her cheek and he felt her lift her chin. Waiting for his kiss.

Adrenaline surged through his body, all his senses alive to the stunning woman he was holding in his arms. His heart was racing, and he could feel her breath warm as they looked into each other's eyes, both of them open-mouthed. Nose almost touching nose. His head tilted. Ready.

For the kiss that never came.

It was Sienna who stepped away, sliding out of his arms.

'I felt so worthless. When Angelo left, he took every bit of confidence and self-esteem I ever had with him. It's taken me four years to piece together what was left of my shattered life, one day at a time, and rebuild a future for myself. I promised myself that I was never going to rely on someone else to make my dreams come true ever again. And I've kept that promise. I *have* to make my own way in the world. You understand what that is like better than anyone I have ever met. Don't you?'

He tucked her hair behind her ear and gently smoothed the strands away from her brow before replying in a slow whisper. Intimate and soft, and so loving it hurt to hear it.

'Yes. I do. Which leaves one final question. You may not *need* a man in your life, but is there any room in this plan for a man who cares about you and wants to be with you?'

She swallowed down a breath of understanding and replied with a quivering lower lip. She had seen through him yet again.

'I don't know, Brett. I truly don't know. This job at Greystone has been my only goal for so long I never thought about what came next.'

There was so much confusion and anxiety in her face that Brett took the initiative. He would have to work through the next steps more slowly than he wanted if he had any chance of convincing Sienna to make him part of her life. Biting down frustration and disappointment, he managed a smile before rubbing her arms for one last time this evening.

'I don't know about you, but this has been a very long day and we have the excitement of re-stocking the kitchen cabinets tomorrow. Come prepared to be grilled about this amazing new job of yours. How does that sound?'

A faint smile creased her pale and exhausted-looking face, but she slowly stepped away.

'Well, that *is* something to look forward to. Goodnight, Brett. Sleep well.'

'Goodnight, sweetheart.'

She faltered slightly, stopped in the doorway, and glanced back at him over one shoulder.

Her glance only lasted a few seconds, but something unravelled inside him.

It was as though a door which had been locked tight shut for too many years had been opened up. Rusty. Hesitant. Resisting. A large, heavy door, with a huge lock and chain across it, and a sign saying: 'Worthless. Unworthy of the love of an amazing woman.' Only now the chain had been lifted away and the door had swung open.

This was the same locked door that had made it impossible for him to tell Lili that he loved her. The lock had turned tighter each time he saw how happy she'd been with Chris. The extra chain had come the day his mother had died of a stroke, walking home from her night office cleaning job only a few months before he won his promotion to head chef. She had never had the chance to stand next to him at an awards ceremony, or see his name in the newspapers. He had wanted that more than anything else in his life.

He had created that lock and chain to protect his sensitive and tender emotions from the searing, traumatic pain of loss. To keep them safe and carefully hidden away.

As he looked at Sienna in that fraction of a second each instinct from his broken childhood should have screamed for him to turn the key in the lock and slam that door tight shut again. But instead they were blown away by the force of a hot wind so powerful that he had to physically stand taller to brace himself against the force of it.

He stood in silence, the breath catching in his throat as she tried to smile and failed. The pain in her lovely shining brown eyes shone out and hit him hard.

It was all there in her face. Her lips were parted and her cheeks flushed as if they had just spent the night together.

A warm soft feeling of tenderness and love enveloped Brett and he moved forward to hold her tight against him, but she gasped and shook her head, started to say something, thought better of it, bit her lower lip, turned in his arms and slipped away out of the room.

Leaving him standing there.

His head spinning at the turmoil going on inside his heart.

He had survived childhood by deliberately not making any connections and refusing to love anyone enough to make a difference.

The feelings he had for Sienna were terrifying,

exhilarating—and challenged him more than he wanted to admit.

Only a few days earlier he had imagined that opening his new restaurant was going to be the biggest adventure of his life. Well, he had been wrong. Winning over the whirlwind that was Sienna Rossi meant more.

Telling her how much he loved her was going to be one of the biggest risks he had ever taken—he knew that she cared about him. Now all he had to do was prove that he was worth taking the risk on.

The door was open and passion and determination flooded out creating an echoing empty space where love was meant to dwell.

He had already lost Lili.

No matter how long it took or how creative he was going to have to become, he was going to be the man to show Sienna Rossi that she was loved.

He was not going to lose Sienna. Not now. Not ever.

He had to think, and think fast.

Sienna had made it clear that she did not need or want any man telling her how to run her life. Now he understood why!

Only she thought that she had a few limited options to choose from, where she could be free to make that possible. Perhaps she was mistaken about that? After all, he had seen her transform

Trattoria Rossi into a perfect small local diner. Any family would be happy to eat there....

The perfect family diner...was it possible?

Flicking open his cellphone, Brett quickly found the number for his best friend.

'Chris, mate. How are you doing? Yes, I told Sienna. She was okay. Listen. Is there any chance you could come over here tonight? I would like to talk through a crazy business idea you might be interested in.'

CHAPTER NINETEEN

Step 19: Add One American Chef Without a Kilt

'Hi, Carla. Yes, I'm fine. How are things at the Manor? Yes. I'm sorry that I had to leave so suddenly. What's the best time for me to avoid…? He's what? Any idea when?'

Sienna pinched the brow of her nose tight enough to be painful. 'No. Of course I understand. Patrick is still the boss. Thank you for letting me know. I'll talk to you later.'

She flung the phone down before Carla could answer.

'That interfering—!'

Sienna pressed both hands down firmly onto the hall table to steady herself and closed her eyes to block out the nausea.

'Unbelievable!'

There was a rustle of plastic wrapping from the sitting room, where Brett had been unpacking some of his personal saucepans, and the man himself appeared in the doorway.

She looked up at his smiling face and marvelled at his ability to calm her and reassure her in one single glance.

'Did I hear shouting? Where is the fire?'

Sienna raised one hand and waved it in Brett's direction, before pressing it to the back of her head as she started to pace up and down the hallway in the mid-morning light streaming through the glass panel over Maria's front door.

'Patrick. The general manager at Greystone. He has arranged a planning meeting for the design team for the new restaurant. Apparently Angelo is only in town for a few days, and they want to go through the first ideas before he heads back to California. They didn't even think about calling me until the very last minute! If Carla hadn't reminded Patrick he probably would have completely forgotten to invite me.'

She was gesticulating now, using both hands to strangle imaginary demons in the air, her mind buzzing with excitement and enthusiasm. 'As the new restaurant manager I *need* to be there. I have so many ideas, Brett, but this meeting has come completely out of the blue. I don't even have time to put together a formal presentation to the team!'

Her enthusiasm was infectious, and he smiled

right at her before replying in a calm voice, 'This sounds like the ideal chance for you to make a difference as the new manager. When is the meeting?'

Her voice trembled with frustration. 'That's why I'm jumping.' She glanced at her wristwatch, totally absorbed in the momentum of the news. 'Carla has been told to expect them in about four hours. Four hours—*today*, Brett! I need to be there before they arrive, and then start work straight way on a detailed plan. There are so many things to get sorted out before Angelo takes over that I hardly know where to start.'

Brett took one look at her dancing eyes and knew that her mind certainly wasn't on helping him clean out the kitchen units—or any other excuse he could come up with to be in the same room as her. He had never seen her so animated.

This was how it should be. The scared woman he had soaked with a bucket of water was gone for good. Replaced with a professional manager who was at the top of her game.

The Sienna Rossi he was looking at now sounded confident, self assured and assertive about her new role. Just as he knew she could be.

He wondered how she would react if she knew that he had spent most of the night talking about her to Chris, while they thrashed out an idea for a new business where *she* could be the star. If she wanted it! But it was far too early to tell her about that option. There were still a lot of questions which had to be answered before the deal was final.

Pity that something just did not sound right about her situation at Greystone. He had the most horrible feeling that this amazing woman was about to have her dream trampled to dust under her feet. And that was not fair.

'Are you sure that they actually *want* you to be there for this meeting, Sienna?'

She stopped pacing and looked at him with a slight frown. 'What do you mean? I'm the person who is going to have to make the new dining room work after the paint has dried! Of *course* they want me there. Patrick simply forgot that I was on holiday. That's all.'

'So Patrick and Angelo just have to snap their fingers and you come running? Is that right?'

'Brett! I thought you would be happy for me.' There was such pain and disappointment in her voice that he walked swiftly up to her and took hold of one of her hands in his, meshing his fingers between hers so that she could not escape.

She was so shocked at this that she flashed open her eyes and stared at the offending append-age as though it did not belong to her at all.

'I am happy for you. I simply think you're for-getting something very important. You are an amazing, beautiful and talented woman, and any man would be honoured to have you in his life or on his management team. I have a few concerns.'

'Go on. I'm listening. But make it fast.'

'The way I see it, you have two ways to handle this meeting.' He looked hard into her face, his voice low and serious.

Sienna was about to give her opinion about people who defined *her* choices, when Brett reached out with a not so clean forefinger and pressed it to her lips.

'First choice. Angelo Peruzi pulls up at the hotel with his fancy team of architects and designers. You graciously welcome him in, the two of you make small talk about the weather and the state of the restaurant business and then you start work on the design of your new award-winning dining room. *Together*. As a team. No past history, just focused on the job.'

He moved his hand from left to right. 'He talks, you listen politely, then accept or decline his suggestions in a ladylike dignified and professional fashion and wave at the door as he drives away.' There was a pause. 'Or maybe not so professional, depending on what he has to say. You are totally in charge of the situation and he knows it.'

Sienna started squirming again but Brett continued. 'Stop that. There are pluses to this plan. Best-case scenario: he falls at your feet, begs your forgiveness and tells you that it will be an honour and a privilege to work with you and he has total respect for you in your new role. You both go off into the sunset, or whatever, hand in hand and destined for greatness.'

'Have you been sniffing the icing sugar again?' Sienna replied with a frown.

He ignored her snipe with a brief narrowing of his eyes. 'Worst case: you have to suffer your ex for an hour or so over a conference table. But then the deed is done, the ice is broken, and you can get on with your life and start work on creating something amazing. Worst part over. You've done your duty to Patrick and the team, and maybe Peruzi has an apology for you. It could happen.'

He squeezed her hand once before releasing it. 'But you always have to have a back-up plan. So, onto your second choice… You go back to the Manor, take one look at what this team are proposing, give it up as a lost cause and look for another job somewhere else.'

Sienna gasped and slapped him on the chest.

'Have you not been listening to *anything* I have been telling you these last few days? All I am asking for is the chance to show them what I am capable of achieving. This job will give me that chance, and I am *not* taking no for an answer.'

Her brow furrowed into a deep frown of concern and anxiety.

'You don't know how hard it is has been for me to rebuild my confidence. This is what I want. It's what I've always wanted, and I've worked too long to let this chance slip away from me. I *have* to prove that I can do this work.'

'Prove it to Angelo? Or prove it to yourself?'

Brett's free hand touched her arm, thrilling her with the heat and warmth of his support. 'You're Sienna Rossi. The unconquerable! Have you not just designed, decorated and refurbished one complete dining room on your own? You can *do* this job—but you don't have to. You've already shown what you are capable of. Right here. At Rossi's. You don't need to go back to Greystone Manor and settle for what they have to offer you just because it is comfortable. There are other hotels and restaurants who would love to have you work for them.'

Sienna wriggled and pulled and tugged to free herself—then suddenly she stopped fighting him and sagged down with a resigned sigh.

'Wait a minute. Does that list include Brett Cameron of Notting Hill?'

He sucked in a breath. 'Yes. It does. The job is yours if you want it. But there are others. You have more choices than you know.'

The last few days flashed though her brain. The shared meals, the laughter and the pizza party with the kids. The jokes and glimpses of their pasts. Could she walk away from all that?

Slipping her fingers out from between his, Sienna broke away and stepped back to look at Brett, well aware of the fierce intensity in his eyes.

'You truly don't understand. I could *never* work for you.'

'You can't mean that.'

'It's not you, and I know that the job would be fantastic! I totally admire and respect what you are trying to achieve there. No, Brett. It's me.'

She cupped the palms of both of her hands against his cheeks, her fingers tingling from contact with the blond stubble, and looked deep into his eyes. Pleading for his understanding.

'This is my dream. The dream I created for myself when things were very dark in my life. That means that I am the only person who can see it through to the end. Not Angelo. Not Patrick... And not you. I can only rely on myself.'

'Maybe once. But you must know that I am here for you,' he butted in. 'You don't have to do this on your own.'

She nodded and sniffed. 'I'm sorry if that sounds hard, but it is the truth—and I always tell my close friends the truth. And I hope we *are* friends. I really do. Because people who care about me are in pretty short supply in my life.'

Brett sighed loudly, and before she could go anywhere pulled her towards him, gathered her into his arms and pressed his lips to her forehead.

'You're not coming back to Rossi's. Are you?'
Her answer was a brief shake of the head.

'So that's it? You're just going to walk out on me? On us?'

Her cheek rested flat against his shirt before she found the strength to speak, not trusting her resolve if she saw his face.

'In a few days from now you are going to be working flat out in your new kitchen. Seven days a week. Catching a few hours' sleep when you can.'

'Have you been talking to Chris?' His voice rumbled below the fabric she was leaning on.

'I've been there once before. Remember? Oh, Brett.' She moved back so that her fingers stroked his shirt in gentle circles. 'We're both going to be working harder than we have ever worked in our lives. I don't want either of us to resent the time we steal to be together. That's not fair. On anyone. These last few days have been so unexpected. Thank you for that. But, no. I won't be coming back.'

He ran his fingers through her hair one last time, kissed her gently on the forehead, and then on the lips with the sweetest kiss of her life, and finally he wrapped her tight against him until he was ready to whisper a few words.

'I can't let you go. Not like this. There's so much I haven't told you. So much I want to say—' But his words were silenced.

'Shh. It's okay. It's okay. I am going to leave now, while we still have hope. It's better this way for both of us than facing heartbreak down the line. We both know what that feels like…and I'm not sure I could come back if I had my heart broken again this time.' Her fingers stroked his face as he released his grip. 'You have to let me go. That way we can both hold onto something special. Because you are so very special. Never forget that.'

A deep shudder racked Brett's body, but she felt his heartbeat slow down just a little under her fingers.

The sensation of his hands sliding away from her back was so painful she almost cried out with the loss. He was letting her go. And she was already missing his touch.

'I'm going to miss having someone around to remind me of that. If you have to do this, do it now —before I change my mind. I'll give you a lift to the station.'

Sienna stood, rock-steady now, her back pressed hard against the door.

Brett took hold of both of her arms and looked into her eyes, his love and devotion so open and exposed it was like a whirlwind of confusion and suppressed energy.

'Sienna? You already know how stubborn I can be. This isn't the end. Whatever options you choose, I'll be right here if you need me. *You* never forget *that*.'

He watched as she took a breath, looked him straight in the eyes, gave a sharp nod and then ran up the stairs to get ready to leave, the sound of her footsteps echoing back into the hallway.

'We still have a date here on Valentine's Day—and I'm making your favourite dessert, just the way you like it.'

'You don't know my favourite dessert!' came a distant voice, before the bedroom door closed shut.

Oh, yes, he did. He knew everything he needed to know about the woman he had fallen in love with. Just when he'd thought that his poor guarded heart would never be open to love again.

Brett could feel his throat closing with emotion, and struggled to pull the shattered fragments of his willpower together.

Even the thought of not being with Sienna twisted his heart tight enough to make him gasp. Suddenly the rosy future he had been looking forward to so desperately seemed dark and grey if Sienna was not part of it.

He had two choices. Tell her that he loved her. Or let her go in the full knowledge that the hectic lives they led would make a relationship so difficult it might destroy them with the guilt of all the missed birthdays and special occasions normal couples could hope to enjoy.

She was right about that.

But it would be worth it for every single second of time they spent together.

No. He could not be so selfish. Not with Sienna. Not with the woman he loved.

If he told her how he felt about her…how she had come to dominate his thoughts and his dreams…how he longed to see her, hold her, simply be with her…there was a chance that she might stay for the sake of their relationship—at the cost of her own ambitions at Greystone Manor.

Telling her that he loved her now would only make it worse for both of them. Once said, the words could never be unsaid. And then what? What kind of pressure would that create?

This was Sienna's dream!

He had waited ten long exhausting years to make his own dream come true.

How could he deny this amazing woman the chance to do the same?

He had to let this tender, funny, clever woman walk away and make her own dreams a reality before he could come to her on equal terms and build something where they could both achieve their goals.

He had never thought of himself as noble, but if there was ever a time for sacrifice, this was it.

Even if it did rip his heart out.

CHAPTER TWENTY

Step 20: Beat Vigorously

SIENNA STOOD in front of the full-length mirror in the stone-walled tower room of Greystone Manor, which had been her safe refuge for the last four years, and ran both hands down over her fine cashmere knee-length skirt to smooth away any creases.

She had spent time and money choosing the perfect black skirt suit and glossy designer shoes. It was easy to make the excuse that fine-dining customers expected a certain level of formality in the waiting staff, but the truth was harder to accept.

The last few days had shown her how much she missed working with wine and flavours and colour. Creating something amazing and unique which she knew in her heart that Maria's customers would love.

This suit was part of the armour she wore every

day to convince everyone that she was totally in control and in charge as head waiter.

It was pathetic. *She* was pathetic.

Brett was right.

She was a coward. A brave woman hiding behind a façade she had made for herself.

She had needed these tall, solid walls to give her time to rebuild her confidence that she was capable and able to do her job without a controlling man telling her what to do.

When would she ever get the chance to do that again?

Sienna strolled over to her window that overlooked the stunning grounds of the hotel and let the tears fall in silence down her cheeks, ruining her make-up.

She had looked at this view for four long years, but the hotel had never felt like home. A safe place? Yes. But not home. Closing her eyes, she could still see the view from the spare bedroom in Maria's house, of the busy London street, and longed to be back there.

The vibration of her cellphone broke the spell with a simple text message from Carla.

The design team had arrived. It was time to get this over with once and for all.

Carla was hidden behind a large contingent of men in suits carrying art portfolios and packaging tubes, who were being greeted by senior hotel management from across Europe.

Sienna sucked in a breath and lifted her chin, stretching herself to her full height and fixing a professional smile firmly in place.

In the centre of the laughing, happy group gathered in the reception area of Greystone Manor was the man she had last seen at the departure gate before his flight to Los Angeles.

Angelo Peruzi.

On that fateful day she had watched in silence as he had walked through passport control and out of view. He had not looked back at her. Not once. He had not spared one backward glance at the woman he had asked to be his wife only a few months earlier.

Today Angelo Peruzi was wearing almost the same clothing he had worn that day—a navy blazer, white pressed shirt and designer denims. And dark sunglasses.

In February.

Indoors, in a country house hotel.

She had forgotten how very handsome he was. The years had filled out his face, and there was a certain softness about his body, but life in California had served Angelo well. Every inch of his designer clothing screamed success and wealth.

He looked as though one of the photographer's

stylists had spent a couple of hours working on him with false tan and teeth whitener to impress TV viewers. He probably had no idea how strange and out of place they made him look in this elegant, dignified house.

Sienna locked eyes with Angelo across the room. For a fleeting second she felt as though they were the only people present.

His brow creased slightly in recognition, before he flashed her one of his special smiles and made his way through the group of men in smart suits to stand in front of her. He stretched out his hand.

'Sienna. It's so good to see you again. You look wonderful. Perhaps we can catch up next week?'

'Of course,' she managed to reply through a closed throat, and was saved by Patrick, who had never left Angelo's side.

'Ah, Miss Rossi. Thank you for coming in at such short notice. I apologise for breaking into your holiday, but we only have a tiny window for a meeting with Chef Peruzi, and I know that you want to hear our exciting plans for the new dining room! Please join us. I know that you are going to be totally thrilled with the proposal.'

Thirty minutes later two things had suddenly become very clear.

She was not thrilled with the new proposals. *At all.*

The hotel management had brought in a top team of slick restaurant designers who had taken one look at the lovely antique wooden panels on the walls and the intricate ceiling work in the original hall and tutted. Loudly. This was *not* the space they had planned for the new Peruzi restaurant.

She had twice tried to make a suggestion. And twice been dismissed and talked down. Neither Patrick nor Angelo had spoken up for her, or given her the slightest hint of support and encouragement when she had argued against the obliteration of the very architectural features which made the Manor so unique.

The design team were not interested in anything she had to say—which was hard to believe, considering the outlandish ideas they were proposing.

Californian fusion? *At Greystone?*

Patrick she could understand—his bosses had paid this team of so-called experts to create a 'unique vision' for the new restaurant. He could hardly tell them they were crazy!

The second fact was even harder to accept.

Sienna took a long, hard look at Angelo, who was looking disdainfully around the beautiful oak panelled room, and wondered how they had both come to change so very much in so short a time.

He had walked out of her town, her family and

her life, and now he had just waltzed into the hotel as though he was the cavalry who was going to save them all from disaster.

As though she ought to be grateful that he had taken the time out of his busy schedule to lower himself to say hello. No apology. No explanation. Not even an excuse for what had happened to the restaurant he had abandoned, leaving her to sort out the mess he had left behind.

At least he had not tried to kiss her. Simply shaken her hand.

This was what she wanted. Wasn't it?

For Angelo to treat her as simply one of his colleagues?

She looked across at the slight sneer on Angelo's mouth and in that second the reality of the man hit her hard and fast. This was not the Angelo she remembered!

That Angelo had been some fictitious, imaginary ideal. A mirage. A version she had put together from her own imagination. She had been infatuated with an idealised clone of a man who had never truly existed.

Whatever relationship they might have had once was long gone. That part of her life was finished.

There was a very good chance that he would destroy everything André Michon had built up. And she wanted no part of it. In fact, the more she thought about it, the more she realised that it would have been a horrible mistake for her to come back and try and work with Angelo under *any* circumstances.

Brett Cameron had shown her what it could be like to work with someone she trusted and who respected her opinion. Valued her. Cared for her. Maybe more than just cared for her.

Which made her the biggest fool in the world.

A wave of nausea and dizziness hit Sienna, forcing her to lean against the table for support. The coffee. She should have eaten breakfast. Now just the thought of food made her dizzier than ever, and she fought to get air into her lungs.

Sienna tried to control her breathing, and lifted her chin just as Patrick caught her eye and waved his empty coffee cup from side to side, gesturing towards the door.

Yes. It *was* time to leave the room. Only it wouldn't be to make more coffee. It would be to start packing.

CHAPTER TWENTY-ONE

Step 21: Finish with One Portion of Chocolate Tiramisu

SIENNA BENT down from the waist onto the pristine white dining-room tablecloth with her arms flopped down each side of her body, and bobbed her head down twice onto the hard surface before resting her forehead on the cloth.

'I think Patrick got the message in the end,' Carla said as she gathered together the glassware in the now empty dining room at the end of evening service. 'Apparently he has never had anyone resign from a management job before. It's a new experience for him.'

Sienna did not even attempt to raise her head to reply, so the words that did emerge were muffled by a lot of blubbering and a tang of self-pity.

'Perhaps you shouldn't have asked him for a

reference? That might have been a bit cheeky? Anyway—stay right there. I'll be back in a moment with dessert, and you can tell me all the lovely details.'

A loud groan followed by a whimper coincided with the sound of her forehead thunking down again on the table.

Her eyes might have been tight shut, but Sienna could still hear the sound of a chair being drawn out and a china bowl sliding across the tabletop. The most delicious smell of cocoa, coffee, sweet liqueur and rich mascarpone wafted into her nostrils, making them twitch, and her mouth watered in anticipation of the smooth lusciousness of her favourite dessert.

'That was fast! Oh, Carla. I've really done it now, haven't I? Career over. Finished. Kaput. Perhaps I can ask my brother for a job?'

'Well, you could do that, but I have a better idea.'

Sienna flung herself backwards in the chair with shock at the sound of her favourite male voice, and almost toppled the chair over.

'Brett?'

He was wearing a superbly tailored dark suit with a beautiful pale pink check shirt and a tie the exact same shade of blue as his eyes. Her heart soared and screamed a halleluiah in joy.

She had missed him so much that just the sight

of him sitting there, with his elbows on the table-cloth, smiling across at her, made her world suddenly bright.

This was why she had been so miserable for the few hours since they had been parted.

'Hello,' she whispered, trying to be brave and not embarrass herself by leaping into his arms with joy and kissing the life out of the man.

'Hello, yourself. Medals for courage under fire are in short supply at the moment, so I rescued some of my special tiramisu. I thought you might need the encouragement. It seems I need not have worried after all. Congratulations.'

'I don't deserve a medal,' she replied, lifting her head slightly to look at the bowl, heaped with delicious creamy dessert, a gold spoon leaning on the rim.

Her head lifted a little higher.

Enticing curls of dark and milk chocolate were scattered across the top of the creamy stuff in the bowl.

'Resigning from this job was a totally reckless thing to do,' she added with a sniff.

His finger slipped under her chin and lifted it higher, so that when he bent down to her level he could make direct eye contact.

'Not reckless. Right. How did you feel when you told them that you didn't want the restaurant manager's job after all?

'It felt so good!' She managed a thin smile and pushed out her lower lip before lifting her head a little more. 'Actually, it felt wonderful!' She sat bolt upright and nodded at Brett. 'You're right! It was the right thing to do! I deserve better!'

Then she remembered the flipside of that statement and groaned. 'I have been a total idiot!' She almost slumped down again, except Brett had seen it coming and propped her up by lifting up the dessert bowl and wafting it higher and higher.

'Not another word until you have given me your expert opinion on the dessert. I'm still not sure about the chocolate curls, and you know that it has to be perfect before Valentine's Day or I won't be happy.'

She reached forward and took a heaped spoonful of smooth, creamy-chocolate flavoured mascarpone and soft, soaked sponge, and the wonderful aroma hit her senses only a few seconds before she tasted the amazing dessert. Her eyes flickered in delight and sensual pleasure as each of the ingredients was savoured in turn.

'Wonderful. Absolutely wonderful. Just don't tell Chef André. He would be terribly upset.'

She replaced the spoon, before she embarrassed herself even more by scoffing the entire bowl, and felt her shoulders drop down by at least four inches.

Brett was sitting opposite her, elbows on the

table and both hands under his chin. Watching her. Simply watching her. And delighting in doing so.

'Feel better?'

'Much. Thank you.' She reached out and took the hand that he was holding out to her.

'Oh, Brett. I am so disgusted with myself. I've wasted four years of my life grieving over some idealised version of a man who probably never existed in the first place. I thought all chefs were the same—you've shown me how wrong I was. When I think of all of that pain…'

She shook her head in disbelief and gave in to the tears which had formed in the corners of her eyes, swallowing down her fears and regrets.

The long, sensitive fingers tenderly smoothed the hair back from her forehead, his blue eyes flicking longingly over her face.

She sniffed before smiling back at him in thanks. 'I missed you.'

'I missed you too. You've only been gone a few hours and Rossi's is simply not the same without you.'

She took a few calming breaths, eyes closed, before daring to look at Brett. One look. And her anger crisped, burnt, and was blown away in one sweep under the heat of that smile.

'Oh, Brett! I've made such a mess of things!'

He pretended to ignore her flushed face and puffy eyes, released her hair and took both of her hands in his before saying in a quiet and controlled voice, 'Not necessarily. Last night we talked about making choices. Well, now I have one more to offer you. What if you were in charge of *your own* business? Would that make a difference to your options?'

'What do you mean?' Sienna replied, intrigued.

'After you went to bed last night I started talking with Chris about a new idea which goes way beyond my signature restaurant. A long way!'

Brett squeezed her fingers in excitement as his eyes locked onto hers. Shining eyes, brimmed full of energy and enthusiasm.

'We want to open a chain of family restaurants. Imagine an informal but clean and well-run bistro a teenager could bring his high-school sweetheart to on their first big date. We'll run them as a franchise, based on the recipes that I come up with in my own kitchen, and with the same basic design of dining room you created this last week for Maria.'

He grinned at her with such love and fire and passion that the breath caught in her throat.

'Young couples all over Britain will have the chance to create their own version of Trattoria Rossi in their town. Good food. Informal and friendly. And not just for Valentine's Night but every other night as their family grows up. I think it would work. How about you?'

Her mouth formed a perfect oval for all of two seconds before she flung her head back and bellowed in laughter, slapping her fingers against Brett's in delight.

'It is a wonderful idea! I love it! I can't tell you how totally brilliant, brilliant and brilliant it is.'

She leant forward and kissed him, hard and quick on the lips.

'You clever man. No wonder you are excited!'

'I am. Except Chris and I have a major problem which could seriously hold the project back.'

She shrugged and pulled one hand away from his clutches to wave it in front of her face.

'Nothing that you can't handle. You're Brett Cameron! Superstar! Superhero! Tiramisu maker extraordinaire!'

'Thank you for that, but even superstars can't be in two places at the same time. I have worked all my life to open a dream restaurant in Notting Hill—and you know how that feels. It needs my total focus and dedication.'

He paused and gave her one of his special smiles before blurting out, 'I need a business partner to run our chain of family trattoria. Chris will be able to raise funding for the first year, and your aunt Maria has agreed to let me lease Rossi's from her at a special rate so that we can develop our first trattoria there, to be used as a model for the franchise—but we don't have a manager.'

Brett let that sink in for a few seconds before rushing on with his pitch. 'The ideal person would have to be used to dealing with very discerning customers, capable of running the whole business, and it would be a big help if they liked my food. And I have to be able to trust them. Completely. Know any likely candidates who might fit that description?'

Sienna froze. The smile faded on her lips.

'Are you serious? You're offering me the job?'

'No. I'm offering you a partnership in the business. You would be running *your very own* chain of family trattoria. *With* me. Not *for* me. This would be your project, using the amazing talent I've seen over these last few days. You can do this. I have no doubt about that whatsoever. You are the only person I could trust.'

'You trust me that much? You are willing to relinquish absolute control and let me make decisions without trying to interfere all the time?'

'With all my heart.'

'Wow, you know how to take the wind out of a girl's sails. I don't understand. This is *so* exciting. Why didn't you mention it before now?'

'Ah. I only came up with the idea after you had gone to bed last night, and I had to be absolutely certain of something very important before I even mentioned it. And there's the fact that you seem to like my food, of course.'

'Of course. Now talk to me. What could be that important?'

'I had to find out if you were willing to sacrifice everything to make your new job here at Greystone a success. Or not.'

Sienna sucked in a breath and stared hard at the wonderful man who had just offered her the chance to realise her dream, and something clicked into place which she had never even thought of before—and yet suddenly it made so much sense.

'Before I answer that, I do have one question for you. And it is equally important. I trust you to tell me the truth.'

She picked up the bowl of tiramisu and licked the chocolate from the spoon.

'This tiramisu wasn't just a lucky guess. Was it?'

He gave a brief shake of the head and a closed-mouth smile.

'You remembered. It was twelve years ago. But you remembered that tiramisu is my favourite dessert.'

His answer was to lift up the hand he was holding and kiss the back of her knuckles.

'Oh, Brett.'

'I was the poor boy from the wrong side of the tracks who was never going to be good enough to ask the Rossi princess out on a date. So I locked up my heart and hid the key so that it would be safe.'

His fingertip traced the curve of her eyebrow
So tenderly and lovingly it almost brought Sienna
to the brink of tears again.

'So beautiful. Clever. Destined for great things.
I might not have been good enough, but I paid at
tention.' He smiled as Sienna shook her head in
disbelief. 'Your aunt Maria noticed, but kept quiet.
Your dad just thought I was clumsy. I was so en
vious of the wonderful start in life you and Frank
had. You had the family. The restaurant. You were
living the kind of family life I had only dreamt
about.'

Sienna groaned and pressed two fingertips to
his lips.

'This might not be the best time to tell you that
there was a very good reason why I stalked you
every working day. Crush. I had a total girly crush
on you. Only I was too shy to tell you.'

Silence.

'Not possible. If you saying that to make me
feel better, I appreciate the sentiment but…'

She shrugged. 'Nope. You have the honour of
having been my first crush, Brett Cameron.'

Then she grinned. 'Do you remember the other
day, when I asked you to stay in the basement at
the Rossi house when I went up to my old bedroom
to hunt for shoes? I was *terrified* that you would
come across my diary. Which includes the daily
detailed itinerary of when I saw you, what you

were wearing, what you said, what I did… Need I go on?'

'You…had a crush on me?'

She nodded several times, biting her lower lip, then gave up completely and started giggling, then stopped, then giggled again, then carried on giggling until he was forced to give in and roar with laughter.

'Could we have been more pathetic? You were in the kitchen, frightened to speak to me when I came in the room, while I was miserable when I wasn't in the same room as you. Both of us too shy or too scared to talk to each other. How ironic is that?'

'Crazy. I wish I'd known.'

'Me too. I do have one more question. And it's totally personal.'

'After that little bombshell I'm almost frightened to hear it, but fire away. I can handle it.'

'In that case I need to know if you are still in love with Lili. Or not.'

He stopped laughing and turned his attention to her jawline, his fingertips moving in gentle circles, then curving so that her face was being held in his hands.

'I'll never forget her, but I'm only capable of loving one woman at a time, and I'm looking at the woman I'm in love with today, and will go on loving for the rest of my life.'

Sienna looked into the depths of those amazing

eyes, and what she saw there made her heart sing. Her words gushed out in joy. 'Then you will be pleased to hear that my answer is...not. A great big definite *not.*'

Brett never broke eye contact with her as he reached into his jacket pocket and pulled out a small velvet box.

Her heart was thumping so loudly in her chest that breathing and thinking and listening at the same time suddenly became a major challenge.

With the ease that suggested someone who had been practising, Brett flicked open the lid and pressed the open box into the palm of her hand.

Sienna looked down on a pink, heart-shaped solitaire diamond on an elegant platinum band, and pressed her free hand to her chest.

It was the most beautiful thing she had ever seen in her life, and she told him so.

'You're an amazing woman, Sienna Rossi. I never thought you could surprise me any more, but you have done. Any man would want to have you in his life. Want you in his bed. Make you the last thing he sees at night. The woman he wakes up with every morning.'

She knew he was smiling by the creases at the corners of his mouth.

'I was a boy who thought that he would never be good enough for someone as beautiful and clever as you. Will you give me a chance to prove that I have become a better man, who is finally worthy of you?'

'I like the man he became quite a lot. I trust him with my life—and my heart. And my dreams.'

The smile faded, his eyes darkening.

'I'm also the man who wants to hold you in his arms and have you by his side every day. I want to spend the rest of my life showing you how much I need you. How much you mean to me.'

He swept both hands down from her forehead, smoothing her hair down, over and over, building the strength to say the words. His eyes focused on hers, and his voice was broken and ragged with intensity.

'I love you, Sienna. I walked into that kitchen a lonely young man in a frightening place, terrified that he would make a mistake and mess things up, and be back on the streets. Then you turned to me and gave me a tiny shy smile.'

Her eyes glistened as he stroked her face.

'And I knew that everything was going to be okay.'

His voice broke and he could only draw her up to her full height, so that his hands could wrap around her back, pressing his body closer to hers, his head into her neck. She could sense his heaving chest as they both fought back years of suppressed desires and hopes.

She could feel the pressure of his lips on her

skin, but everything was suddenly a blur. If only the fireworks would stop going off in her head. Rockets seemed to be exploding in huge ribbons of light and colour.

Brett loved her. Brett Cameron. *Loved.* Her.

With all the strength she'd thought she had lost, Sienna slid her hands from his waist up the front of his chest, resisting the temptation to rip his shirt off, and felt this man's heart thumping wildly under the cloth. His shirt was sweaty, and she could feel the moist hair under her fingers as his pulse rang out under her touch.

She forced her head back from his body, inches away from this remarkable, precious man who had exposed his deepest dreams to her.

'It broke my heart when you left for Paris. Since then I've looked everywhere for the missing part, but nobody was able to mend it. How could they, when you were simply holding it safe for me? I was just so scared that you would break it all over again. So scared.'

Her hand came up to stroke Brett's face as he looked at her in silence, his chest heaving as he forced air into his lungs. She could still hear the pounding of his heart as he spoke.

His voice was full of excitement and energy, the desire burning in every word.

'Come and work with me. Run your own business. Sleep in my arms every night.'

His eyes scanned across her face, trying to gauge her reaction.

'Will you come and live with me? Will you be my partner, my lover, and the mother of my children? Can you do that? Can you take a chance at happiness with me?'

She gasped in a breath as the tears streamed down her face, knowing that he was saying the words she had waited a lifetime to hear.

'Yes.'

He looked back at her and his mouth dropped open in shock. 'Yes?'

'Yes!' She laughed, 'Yes, yes, yes. Oh, Brett. I love you so much.'

She had barely got the words out of her mouth before she was silenced by the pressure of a pair of hot lips, which would have knocked her backwards if not for the strong arms that pressed her body to his. Eyes closed, she revelled in the glorious sensation of his mouth, lips, skin and firm body. Lights were going on in parts of her where she had not known switches existed. She felt as if she was floating on air.

Her eyes flicked open to find that she *was* floating in air. Brett had hoisted her up by the waist, was twirling her around and around, two grown up people hooting with joy, oblivious to the tableware. A kaleidoscope of happiness, colour and light.

Sienna slid back down his body, her extended arms caressed lovingly by strong hands, looked into Brett's smiling face, stunned by the joy she had brought to this precious man, and grinned.

'Take me home, Brett. Take me home.'

CHAPTER TWENTY-TWO

Step 22: Keep Mixture Warm until Valentine's Day; Top with a Red Rose Before Serving with a Kiss

PINK FAIRY lights still twinkled and sparkled in the branches of the ornamental bay trees inside the refurbished dining room of Trattoria Rossi.

The last few days since Sienna had left Greystone Manor had passed in a blur of excitement, joy, and a lot of very hard work—but the Trattoria had finally been ready to welcome their guests on a very special Valentine's Day.

It had not only been her first Valentine's Day as the new owner of Trattoria Rossi—but the perfect engagement party, with everyone she loved around her. Even Carla had managed to escape Greystone that evening!

The last of the paying customers had gone home, after what many had told her was the best meal of their lives. There had been Valentine kisses, holding hands under the table, and a lot of laughter and chatter. But best of all, Maria Rossi had been there in person, to help Sienna say goodbye to one part of her life and prepare to start a new one.

Sienna smiled and shook her head. The irrepressible Maria had escaped her hospital bed by promising to take it easy and recover slowly, but there was no way that lady had been going to miss her final Valentine's Day before handing the place over to Sienna and Brett.

The tables were now pushed together to create one long central eating area, with enough space around the chairs for Frankie's children to run around, laughing and playing with Jess and her new very best friends—Henry's granddaughters, who both lived in the area.

For now the room belonged to the family. *Her family.* Old and new.

It was as though every precious, warm feeling she had ever associated with her Rossi family meals had come together in one place. Now she understood how Brett had felt all those years ago.

Carla had already found a seat next to Chris, and was chatting away about the chain of Italian trattoria style bistros he was going to run for the future Mr and Mrs Cameron, while Maria took centre stage with the Rossi horde, talking of her plans to run a beach café with Henry under the Spanish sunshine.

Trattoria Rossi was still Trattoria Rossi. Only now it was Sienna's very own place. Not in competition with Brett's Notting Hill restaurant, but her own space, where she could serve wonderful food in a warm and welcoming cosy room.

This was the family restaurant she had known as a child, only better—because Brett was here. The man she loved was sitting next to her brother, Frankie, the two men flicking through one of the photo albums her mother had kept all her life, laughing as they pointed to one image then another.

Albums in which photos of her own children would be given a place once day.

Her heart expanded to take in her joy and happiness.

Palms sweaty, she gawped at the best-looking man in the room. He was wearing a chef's apron over a crisp white shirt, open at the neck, designed to highlight his deep tan and the brightness of his smile and eyes. Absolutely gorgeous.

Brett glanced over his shoulder at that moment, and her breath caught in her throat as he returned her smile and reached out for her with a grin that made her melt and her heart soar with happiness.

Sienna bent over and kissed Brett, before leaning back and smiling at the man who had brought such joy into her life.

A single perfect red rose lay across a crystal tulip dish filled with his special recipe chocolate tiramisu.

'Happy Valentine's Day,' he whispered, his voice so full of love it took her breath away.

Today marked the end of one part of her life and the start of a lifetime of perfect Valentine's Days. With a man who knew the perfect recipe for her happiness.

ROMANCE 2-in-1

Coming next month

AUSTRALIA'S MOST ELIGIBLE BACHELOR
by Margaret Way

Corin Rylance is super-handsome, super-rich, and way out of farm girl Miranda Thornton's league. Until Corin's sister takes Miranda under her wing and puts her within touching distance of Corin...

THE BRIDESMAID'S SECRET
by Fiona Harper

When glam editor Jackie arrives back in Italy for a big **Bella Rosa** wedding and sees her old boyfriend Romano, her groomed façade disappears. She has a long-kept secret to tell him...

CINDERELLA: HIRED BY THE PRINCE
by Marion Lennox

Struggling cook Jenny gets hot under the collar when she accepts a job on gorgeous stranger Ramón's luxury yacht, and discovers Ramón's not a humble yachtsman – he's a secret prince!

THE SHEIKH'S DESTINY
by Melissa James

Without a kingdom to rule over and a public to serve, Sheikh Alim El-Kanar believes he has no future. Can nurse Hana give him a glimmer of hope?

On sale 2nd July 2010

Available at WHSmith, Tesco, ASDA, Eason and all good bookshops.
For full Mills & Boon range including eBooks visit
www.millsandboon.co.uk

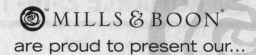

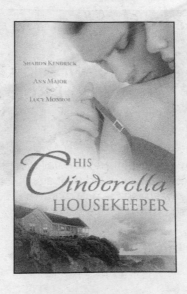

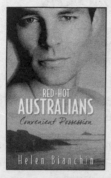

2 FREE BOOKS
AND A SURPRISE GIFT

We would like to take this opportunity to thank you for reading this Mills & Boon® book by offering you the chance to take TWO more specially selected books from the Romance series absolutely FREE! We're also making this offer to introduce you to the benefits of the Mills & Boon® Book Club™—

- **FREE home delivery**
- **FREE gifts and competitions**
- **FREE monthly Newsletter**
- **Exclusive Mills & Boon Book Club offers**
- **Books available before they're in the shops**

Accepting these FREE books and gift places you under no obligation to buy, you may cancel at any time, even after receiving your free shipment. Simply complete your details below and return the entire page to the address below. You don't even need a stamp!

YES Please send me 2 free Romance books and a surprise gift. I understand that unless you hear from me, I will receive 5 superb new stories every month including two 2-in-1 books priced at £4.99 each and a single book priced at £3.19, postage and packing free. I am under no obligation to purchase any books and may cancel my subscription at any time. The free books and gift will be mine to keep in any case.

Ms/Mrs/Miss/Mr _____ Initials _____

Surname _____

Address _____

_____

_____ Postcode _____

E-mail _____

Send this whole page to: Mills & Boon Book Club, Free Book Offer, FREEPOST NAT 10298, Richmond, TW9 1BR